BENT COIN

To: Billie McDermott
with best wishes
Steve Boys
10/24/00

BENT COIN

A story of
grief and greed
love and disillusionment
vehemence and revenge

Stephen P. Byers

BENT COIN

This is a work of fiction. Names, characters, places and incidents either are the product of the author's imagination or are used fictitiously. Any resemblance to any actual person living or dead, events or locales is entirely coincidental.

ISBN: 1-929663-01-3

Library of Congress Catalog Card Number: 99-96420

Published by:

BOOKS BY BYERS
PO BOX 3095
BELLA VISTA, ARKANSAS
72715 - 3095
1 - 501 - 855 - 6493
http://www.booksbybyers.com

Printed in the United States by
Morris Publishing
3212 East Highway 30
Kearney, NE 68847
1-800-650-7888

TO

SISTER ANNE & BROTHER PAUL

By the same author

The Naked Jaybird

Available from:

BOOKS by BYERS
PO BOX 3095
BELLA VISTA, ARKANSAS
72715-3095

(501) 855 6493
http:/www.booksbybyers.com

Chapter 1 - Death Walks In

1.

On Sunday afternoon, July 4, 1898, Albert Beauchamp hurried into his modest home off Roosevelt near the western limits of Chicago. Sarah, his wife, worked in the kitchen preparing supper. She looked at him and gasped.

"What's the matter? What's happened?"

"Mrs. Haldimann done drowned."

"Drowned? Where? How?"

"On the lake. That wind come up and … well, I don't know no details."

Sarah could see the tears welling in her husband's eyes. She fought to control her own emotions, collapsing into a chair and wiping her face with her apron.

"What about the child?"

"Joe done saved her. But … Oh! Sarah. … What we going do about Joe?"

Practical and resourceful, Sarah pondered the question. She jumped to her feet.

"Albert, you go see Mr. Syd right now. He's probably with Mr. Joe but that don't matter. Wherever he is, you find him. You tell him to tell Mr. Joe to bring that little girl to me."

"But, Sarah—"

"Now, Albert, you do as I say. You know I've tended rich folks' children for years. You tell Mr. Syd. Now go on."

Everybody loved Joe Haldimann. He told stories that encouraged people to improve their lot; tales with morals like Æsop. Seemed like he could turn anything into a good yarn. Some folks judged him the damnedest liar they ever heard but he claimed he never lied. He used stories to teach his employees. They responded with respect and hard work but none worked harder than Joe himself. For a time after his wife drowned, he stopped storytelling; didn't talk much. Some gossips guessed he blamed himself for the accident; others whispered he worried about his daughter. The sudden silence when he entered a room unnerved him; the inability to discuss his grief made it worse. Still, he couldn't bring himself to do anything about it.

Albert obeyed Sarah and the next day the little girl came to live with them. Joe considered his alternatives for a few months. One evening, sitting on the porch with Sarah and Albert, he made his decision.

"I've decided to sell the house in Evanston," he said.

"Where you going to live?"

"I'm going to buy that lot around the corner. I'm going to build a house and live right here."

When the last tradesman walked out of the new house, a nanny named Roberta walked in. With Sarah around the corner, the little girl adjusted to Roberta. She forgot her mother, dividing her affection between two doting caretakers. Joe buried himself in his work, said he'd never marry again and pledged devotion to his daughter. The pain and grief melted away. He resumed his old work habits but never forgot his pledge. A bond developed between father and daughter.

Throughout Suzanne's growing-up years, Sunday was their day. Games and picnics, snowmen and sleigh rides, treats and happy birthdays filled those special days. At Beauchamp's, every seventh day concluded with a memorial to happiness on Daddy's knee by the fireplace with stories, cookies and milk. In the new house, she ate breakfast with him and waited for him in the evening; and those wonderful Sundays never changed. Her life unfolded from childhood to womanhood with Nanny Roberta struggling to substitute mother-love while Daddy steered her towards the business world away from fantasies of love and family dreams. At convent school, on to college and into business, father and daughter shared enchanted Sundays and their everlasting bond of love. Through the years, he told her stories about coming to Chicago, about her mother, about everything in his life. She loved the story of old man Tolliver, especially the part with the naughty word.

2.

Near midnight on Sunday, October 8 in 1871, I heard the animals fussing. Maybe a weasel or fox, I thought. On my way down the porch steps, I saw a glow in the sky. I looked back towards the city. Another Chicago fire; there'd been three or four that week and I didn't think much about it. The next morning billowing smoke and flames licking the sky made me realize it was no ordinary fire. On Wednesday—let's see, that'd be October 11—I came to Chicago. Rain the night before made the city a steaming, smoldering mess. I sloshed along LaSalle Street through the burned-out ruins. I was fifteen years old, not a penny to my name. Excited? Sure I was, like you on Christmas Day, Suzanne. But there was nothing to be excited about. Stinking water-soaked wood; rotten putrid smell of dead animals; misery and despair everywhere; there wasn't anything to be happy about and yet I was. Horses stuck in the mud tugging at overturned drays; whiffletrees split, traces broke and men cursing and yelling everywhere. I helped one big fellow right his wagon, wired the tree and attached the traces. He slipped a coin into my hand. I could tell without looking it was a dollar—a silver dollar; enough for five nights and breakfasts in a rooming house. I helped where I could, accepting nickels and dimes, piling up dollars, each one good for another five nights. But I tell you, Suzanne, the thousands of black people huddled in makeshift shelters broke my heart; their homes gone and near all their possessions, too. They moaned about the coming winter as if the Lord owed them a miracle. When was He going to deliver? I'm not much on religion but somehow I felt that He was calling me. What could I do? The little money I had wasn't enough for me to live on, let alone help. That's when I called on Mr. Tolliver.

"Sir, I want to borrow some money."

Miserable cuss he was; miserly old skinflint with heart of stone. They used to say he'd put orphans and widows out of their homes for a penny. I stood by his desk in mud-splattered overalls and dirty, scuffed boots with him staring at me as if he couldn't believe his eyes. He twisted his scrawny figure into a chair like a coiling snake, his mouth drawn down at the corners.

"Who cuts your hair and does your boots, huh, kid?" Sneering at his own sarcasm, he waved me out. "Get out of here 'fore I call the police."

"Sir, I own this here farm." I held the deed out to him. "I want a mortgage for ten dollars an acre."

Tolliver pushed it back without a glance. He shuffled papers, preparing his work for the day. "Don't make me laugh, Sonny, it's too early in the morning."

"Mr. Tolliver, it's good land. Down to Tupper's Corner west of the city. Worth a sight more 'n that."

His lip curled under a scowl that would terrify a bank robber. "How'd you get it?"

"My daddy give it to me." I pushed the deed across the desk. He picked it up.

"You forge this?"

"No, sir. Uncle Jim and me work the farm since my daddy went to war. He's crippled; can't work hardly at all no more so he give it to me."

Tolliver stood, leaned across his desk and shouted.

"So it's fallow, gone to weeds. T'ain't worth a coon's ass that way."

Every time Daddy said coon's ass, Suzanne gasped, covered her mouth and hunched her shoulders.

"You said something naughty."

Joe laughed and look shocked then whispered in her ear.

"We don't talk that way in public. But just between us two, that's what he said." Then the laugh came again and he looked bewildered. "Where was I?"

"As insulted as the Sunday preacher."

"Oh! Did I ever tell you the story of the Sunday preacher accused of stealing from the collection plate?"

"Daddy! I don't want the story of the preacher. I want to hear about Mister Tolliver."

Well, I was just like the Sunday preacher, I didn't give up 'cause I knew I was right. I put both hands on the desk same as Tolliver, my face inches from his.

"My daddy brought me up to be honest. I ain't telling no fibs. Uncle Jim and his boys is cultivating it; tending the animals and such. They pay rent."

Tolliver sat. His eyes roamed over me from head to foot. He cocked his head to the right, then to the left never removing his stare. He slapped the desktop and took a bottle of ink from a shelf behind him. His eyes burned into me while he removed a quill from his desk.

"How much rent?"

I stared right back at him.

"They feed the herd and tend the layers. We split the selling money 'cording to our needs and they pay a hundred dollars to boot. I make more 'n two hundred dollars a year."

"Huh! Quite a little businessman, ain't you?"

"I know what I'm doing, sir. How about the mortgage?"

Tolliver shuffled papers, his mouth turned down. In black hat and black coat, with black goatee, he looked miserly enough to bite gold coins. He argued with himself as if I wasn't in the room. "Ain't no young whippersnapper gonna fool me." His sputum hit the brass cuspidor in the corner with a ping and a splat. He smacked his lips with the pride of a man who never missed, then wiped his mouth with a soiled handkerchief pulled from his sleeve. He looked at me for a long moment, as if peering into my mind to see if I lied. "Naw. You ain't." He raised his voice.

"Tell you what you do. You get your Uncle Jim to sign a lease what says what he's willing to do. You get your Daddy to sign too and I'll think about it." He turned away as if done with the interview. "Now get out of here."

It wasn't over for me and I wasn't going to let the old codger push me around.

"What do you want the old man to sign for?" Tolliver's head came up with a jerk but I didn't back down. "He's already signed the deed."

"Sassy kid. How do I know you even got a daddy? Maybe you killed him and forged this here deed. You want your money; you get your pa's signature. Understand?"

"Yes, sir."

"And Uncle Jim's too." Tolliver glared across the desk. "And get George Tupper's signature," he snarled. "Get him to sign a piece of paper what says your daddy's alive. Understand?"

"Yes, sir." I agreed before he thought of more people to sign. "How much you going to lend me?"

Tolliver's mouth curled into an ugly display of yellow broken teeth that I suppose passed for a smile.

"You brazen brat! I'll give you two dollars an acre at seven percent."

I reached out. He took my hand. Not meaning to, I crushed hard when we shook. He bellowed in pain and pulled back quickly.

"Thank you, sir. I'll be back."

That was Joe's first deal. Sometimes he asked Suzanne what she thought his life might have been had Tolliver said no. She supposed he'd have found the money somewhere else. He allowed as probably that was right. Joe delivered the signatures and got his money. Soon he was back in old skinflint's office; and there sat Tolliver as grumpy as ever.

"I need another loan," I said. "I got six properties I want to borrow against. I'm building houses on them and I need money for lumber."

"Come back in a couple of days," Tolliver said. "I want to see for myself."

The next day Tolliver visited the houses I was building. A man came with him and I could hear Tolliver boasting about his boy Haldimann. "You ever seen anything like this? Them families building new homes; look at them. Haldimann here trades land for material and labor for rent. Few more weeks them families gonna move into them new homes what's built on land they used to own. Now Haldimann owns the land and the houses, too, and they think he's the second Son of God."

I stood at the door of Tolliver's office the next day waiting for an answer. He didn't say he would and he didn't say he wouldn't. He growled at me in his usual manner.

"If I lend you more money, what you gonna do with it?"

"Build houses like I said."

"How many?"

"Many as I can to help folks."

"Humph!"

Tolliver's snort meant agreement. He lent me the money and kept on lending me more. It wasn't long before I expanded into commercial building. I found lots of work for black folks. They worked hard for me; harder than for anyone else. When the city spread west as far as our farm, I was ready to develop my own property. Tolliver lent me even more money while fretting about the deeds and papers overflowing his filing cabinet.

"Joe, you need a business partner. You're a great negotiator and the best builder I know but I've never seen a man so bad at paperwork. Why you don't know what you own."

"Oh yes I do. I know every one of them. I look after my properties and I care for my tenants."

It was true. I didn't cheat my tenants with sleight of hand and crafty maneuvers. The folks I helped were destitute after the fire. I provided a way for them to recover and gain self-respect, treating them fairly. They respected me in return, specially when I provided jobs for them.

"You're something else, Joe," Tolliver mused. "Near twenty years ago you was a muddy, scruffy beggar boy. Look at you today, more money 'n you know what to do with. You're good, Joe, but no matter how good you are, I say you have to get yourself a partner. You can't do it alone. Your ancestors must have been Scots. I never seen a miser like you."

I heard the echo of his words—*you can't do it alone*. I had to find somebody. Not just any paper-shuffler to write numbers in a book; it had to be right, the perfect fit. And find him I did.

"Mr. Tolliver, I want you to meet Sydney Sidorowitz. He's my new office man who is going to organize the paperwork. He'll set up proper bookkeeping and set everything in order. He's a lawyer, Mr. Tolliver."

The next year Tolliver died. Syd and I sent flowers and went to the funeral.

3.

Syd's first job was to organize the paper trail. It took him a year to clear the mess that Tolliver understood and Joe didn't. He created small companies and assembled them under the blanket of Haldimann Enterprises. In 1893, the companies came together under one roof in a new building on Roosevelt Street. Joe and Syd bought and sold, bargained and swapped, built and renovated in the manner of addicted gamblers. Syd's penurious Jewish distrust combined with Joe's openhanded Christian geniality as if fate made them for each other to blend their lives in entrepreneurial compatibility. Alike in agnostic ignorance, they were, in fact, a perfect pair of opposites. They worked together for thirty-six years amassing wealth in the form of Chicago real estate.

Syd closed the door, spread his files on Joe's desk and prepared to begin the monthly review. Joe rubbed his chest and mumbled about a pain. Syd paid no attention until Joe's hand swept across the desktop pushing everything to the floor. Syd bent to gather the papers, stifling the curse on his lips when he saw Joe's left eye twitch, flutter and roll upward. Joe's mouth distorted as if an invisible demon clutched the side of his face. Syd stared at the disfigured horror. Joe grunted and struggled to his feet while his head twisted to the left. His right hand clutched the edge of the desk; the other quivered at his throat.

"Water," he rasped, staggering two short paces with terror-filled eyes. Syd moved too slowly. Joe crumpled headlong to the floor and squirmed sideways. His chest heaved. His left hand swept aimlessly and caught the lapel of Syd's coat. The feeble grasp pulled Syd until his ear came within an inch of Joe's mouth that emitted a raspy croak. A strained whisper delivered his last words.

"Look . . . after . . . Suzanne."

The hand fell away, the head rolled sideways and the eyes closed. Joe's pain ended. Syd sat back on his haunches, gaping open-eyed across the chasm of heartfelt grief. He wanted to pray. The corpse of his friend, the man he honored more than any deity warranted a farewell. The Orthodox churches performed extreme unction; the Catholics called it last rites. He didn't know any rituals but he thought raising his eyes to the Lord, to the Caretaker of Souls, would be fitting. He'd ask a blessing but he wasn't sure how.

"Have a good trip," he said aloud, pulling himself to his feet, denying guilt at his inability to pray. He sank into Joe's chair, staring down at the body as the final behest registered.

Look after Suzanne!

I'll do that, Joe.

Look after Suzanne!

She hates me, Joe.

Look after Suzanne!

Whatever you say, Joe.

Syd stood to examine his pocket watch; twenty past three in the afternoon of November 24, 1920. He shrugged and accepted the death of Joe Haldimann as an irreversible fact. Immune to emotional crises, he opened the door.

"Suzanne! Where's Suzanne?"

He failed to camouflage the urgency, which reverberated off the walls. She ran through the hall, stopped abruptly and clutched the door jamb.

"Oh! God. No! No!"

Blinded with tears and mewling uncontrollably, she staggered sideways, lost her balance, screamed and collapsed. Her head struck the desk and banged on the floor. Her body convulsed. The whimpering stopped. She lay motionless across her father. Syd perspired in the doorway, hiding a dispassionate reaction to the tragedy while exuding sympathy for the girl. He stumbled forward as the office staff crushed behind him, jabbered questions and elbowed into the room.

"Look! Her head's bleeding," a voice said.

"She's passed out," chimed another.

"Better get her to the hospital."

"Take her in my car," Syd ordered. "Have you got a blanket or something? Keep her warm. She's in shock."

After the police went and the undertaker removed the body, Syd left the office at five fifteen. He visited the hospital and talked with the doctor outside Suzanne's room.

"Only an abrasion on her forehead," the doctor reported. "I doubt if she suffered a concussion."

"May I see her now?"

"She's asleep. I've given her a sedative. She needs rest. We'll keep her here tonight for observation. There's nothing to worry about."

The next morning Sid announced his position.

"I want you to understand, Doctor, on his deathbed Mr. Haldimann assigned me the task of protecting her interests. She's over twenty-one and doesn't need a legal guardian. She needs the Wisdom of Solomon to avoid disaster manipulating her father's assets."

Who knows what thoughts passed through the doctor's mind as he looked askance and nodded his head. They entered Suzanne's room together. Syd listened by her bedside as the doctor encouraged her to talk about her father, reveal her feelings. She looked at him through her tears.

"Who to?"

"It doesn't matter. Let yourself go, open up, expose your grief and the delusions will vanish."

She tried.

The doctor held her hand and judged it a good beginning.

"You don't need me. There's nothing wrong with you that love won't heal." As he turned to go, he spoke softly to Syd. "What she needs, Mr. Sidorowitz, is Eros, not Solomon."

Love? Without Daddy, it wouldn't exist in Suzanne's life beyond the measure Roberta contributed. Dear, sweet Roberta managing the household; cooking, cleaning and shopping, meeting every demand and responding to every need while spouting motherly platitudes about care and caution. Barely able to read and write, she could offer nothing except hard work and loyal devotion. Suzanne's love did not extend to baring her soul to Roberta as one might to a parent or an intimate friend. Parents and intimate friends had vanished from Suzanne's life. Still, Roberta struggled to share her grief becoming the sounding board for Suzanne's meditations. She offered a reflecting voice neither enhancing nor diminishing but echoing, allowing Suzanne to pour out her bereavement unashamed of her tears. To speak of the tragedy helped Suzanne bridge the loneliness of a childhood grown into the barrenness of her adult existence.

Syd drove Suzanne home from the hospital. She sat in the front seat afraid to look at him. She knew if she did, she would see the face of Death. Syd talked as he drove.

"Your father directed me to look after you. I want you to understand I'm here to help you. Business-wise, there's nothing for you to worry about; I'll look after everything."

He left her in Roberta's care. She took a pill after supper and tried to greet him pleasantly when he came back in the evening.

"Hello," she said.

"You feeling all right?"

"Yes, I think so."

"I've looked after everything. I've talked with the undertaker. Everything's looked after; funeral next Wednesday. I don't want you to worry."

"Thank you." She closed her eyes and tried to smile.

"You know your father was my best friend. It's difficult for me to repay, he did so much for me. I'll look after the estate, the probate, everything. There'll be no charge."

"Syd, do what you have to do, but please . . .." He could see the tears welling in her eyes.

"I'm sorry. I should have— "

"Please, Syd."

Roberta heard the door close and hurried in with a blanket. Before she could speak, Suzanne was on her feet.

"I don't know how Daddy put up with that man for so many years."

4.

On the second morning after Joe died, Roberta wheeled a service cart into the living room with coffee and scones for breakfast. Suzanne sat curled in her favorite chair.

"Morning, honey. You sleep better last night?"

"I'd be lying if I told you I did."

"Tell me what you was thinking."

Roberta's sympathy mingled with worry but she said nothing as she served. Suzanne tasted the scone, sipped her coffee and spoke at last.

"Death."

"What?"

"I was thinking about Death."

"Honey, please. You got to talk about it; about your Daddy. It's the only way."

"It wasn't about Daddy. It was about Death. I think Death will follow me all my life."

"Suzanne! Don't think like that."

Suzanne smiled, shrugged and sipped her coffee.

"I'm wrong, ain't I." Suzanne's eyebrows raised as Roberta's throaty snicker brought a smile. "One breath I'm saying you got to talk and the next I'm saying don't." She rose and passed the scones, freshened the coffee cups. "Honey, you tell me. You tell me all about it."

"I was trying to remember how I felt when Mummy drowned. Daddy told me the story so many times, I'm not sure I can distinguish between what I remember and what he told me. I think it's like this."

Daddy said a squall whipped Lake Michigan into a fury but I don't remember the storm. But I'll never forget the bubbles whooshing past my face. They made a gargle noise like blowing through a straw into a glass of water and I couldn't breathe. Daddy said he held me on top of the upside-down boat with the water swishing everywhere. He said I spluttered and coughed and would have fallen into the water again if he left me. I don't think I remember that either. I'm not sure but I think he had his clothes on in the water.

He carried me upstairs and ran a hot bath while I took off my damp clothes leaving them in a pile on the hall floor. I brought toys and threw them in the tub. Before clambering in, I went to find him. The image that lingers in my mind is Daddy in the hall kicking my clothes downstairs.

"What are you doing, Daddy?"

"Get in the bath," he said. I ran to the tub, tested with one foot and felt the tingle of the warm water. I smiled at him standing in the doorway. Suddenly, he started to cry like the boy next door when I hit him with a stick.

"What are you doing, Daddy?"

He buried his head in a towel and left. I heard him flop on his bed and Mummy didn't answer. It was the first time I was afraid of Death.

In the morning, I ran to Mummy's bed. It was empty. I found Daddy downstairs on the sofa.

"Where's Mummy?"

The July heat permeated the house. He took me in his arms, his singlet damp and smelly. I clutched his neck and rubbed my cheek against his. It scratched and I whined.

"Where's Mummy?"

"Are you hungry?"

"No."

"Do you want breakfast?"

"No. I want Mummy."

He carried me through the swinging door to the kitchen.

"What do you eat for breakfast?"

I crossed my arms and put my head down, my body throbbing between gulps of air.

"Your mother's not here. Stop crying and tell me what you eat for breakfast."

"I don't want breakfast. I want Mummy."

He found cereal in the pantry, poured milk on it, searched for a spoon and set it in front of me. I swung my arm without raising my head. The bowl shattered on the floor.

"Suzanne!" With both hands on the table, he leaned over me, yelling. "Now you listen, young lady—"

Without warning, the door from the dining room swung open. I thought it was Death bringing Mummy to me. I was scared. I covered my face and could hardly breath. I peeked through my fingers; it was Mr. Sidorowitz.

"What are you doing, Joe?" He found a dishcloth somewhere and dropped to his knees to wipe the floor.

Daddy yelled at him.

"Get out of here, Sidorowitz."

Syd kept wiping the floor. "Go upstairs," he said to Daddy, "and get whatever she needs for a week. If you don't know what she needs, take more not less."

"Listen, Sidorowitz—"

"Go, Joe. Don't argue. Go."

Daddy went.

I raised my head and watched Syd clean the floor. Even as a little girl, I didn't like him. His dark Semitic features scared me; long hair dangling below the bald spot covered his ears making him look like an ogre. He always wore messy clothes with string ties and dirty shoes. When I was old enough to understand, Daddy told me Syd had a brilliant mind. Later, I discovered he was a creative genius. He wrote for legal journals and courts with many of his articles widely quoted. But he never worked for anybody except

Daddy. Anyway, I stopped crying and watched Syd clean the floor.

"Where's Mummy?"

"Your mother's not coming back, Suzanne. You remember yesterday your Mummy didn't come out of the water."

"When is Mummy coming home?"

He lifted me into his arms.

"Not for a long time, dear child." He sighed. "Not for a long time."

I remember how scared I was. I wanted to scream for Mummy but I was too scared. I closed my eyes and hoped Death would put me down. He pushed the swinging door with his back, carried me through the dining room into the hall.

"How you doing up there, Joe?"

Daddy's head came over the railing. I wanted him to come, to take me away from this horrible man. But he didn't do anything except yell back.

"What am I supposed to be doing?"

Syd trudged up the stairs with me in his arms, my face turned away from him.

"Tell Daddy what you need to visit Mrs. Beauchamp for a few days."

He put me down. I ran to Daddy but he didn't pay any attention. He pushed Syd backward through the doorway and into the hall. They yelled at each other but I don't know what they said. I threw myself on the bed and screamed for Mummy. They ran back. Daddy picked me up, kissed me and helped me pack a little bag with clothes and another with toys. He carried me downstairs and put me in the carriage where I sat between the two of them. He handed me the reins; I remember that ever so clearly.

"Show me again, Daddy."

"Just raise up your hands and drop them so the horse feels the reins across his back."

"Like this, Daddy?"

"That's it. Now say giddy-up."

Albert Beauchamp was supervisor of the cleaning and maintenance crew at the janitorial service, one of many companies belonging to Haldimann Enterprises. Sarah, led Suzanne through her new home while the men talked in the parlor.

"Sarah's going to take good care of her," Syd said, "but you have to take time every day to visit. She'll be asking for her mother for weeks, maybe months. It's going to be tough, Joe and there's no sense in getting mad. If you want to lose your temper, go beat your head against a stone wall somewhere but don't take it out on the little one. She needs love not anger."

Suzanne was lonely at Beauchamp's but Sarah was up to the task.

"Y'all got to eat supper somewhere," she told Joe, "so you may as well eat here with your little girl and read her stories."

Suzanne stopped questioning the absence of her mother but Death lingered in her mind. Sometimes Death came in her dreams and he always looked like Syd. Gradually, she learned to direct her affection to Sarah, Joe and Albert. A month passed before Joe began arriving late for supper. A few more weeks and he missed supper altogether. Sarah scolded him but he told her his work was important.

"You men are all the same," Sarah said. "You ain't never got no time to tend to the young ones."

Joe took the problem to Syd.

"I can't keep running out there for supper every night. My God, they eat at five."

"Maybe so but Sarah's right. You have to devote time to that little girl."

"I'm planning on spending every Sunday with her. I'll have breakfast with her, stay the day and put her to bed at night."

Syd looked into Joe's eyes.

"You're a man of your word, Joe, everybody knows that. Are you prepared to commit yourself and live with it?"

"Damn you, Sidorowitz. You want me to swear to it on a stack of bibles."

"Yes, I do."

Joe never regretted the commitment. He played the full parental role; taking her to church, attending school functions and helping with homework. He developed an immense affection for his daughter and encouraged her work ethic in every way.

5.

Suzanne worked part time and summers in Daddy's business while attending university. A mathematical whiz, she specialized in finance and economics, with a natural talent for words and writing that came from her mother's side of the family. Soon after graduation, Joe urged her to start a business in her own name. Sidorowitz stood in the way. Joe ignored Syd's advice and engaged Phillip Silverstein to set up her company. A middle-aged lawyer, short, fat and rich, Silverstein bustled about in perfumed elegance, constantly examining his pocket watch. He reminded Suzanne of the White Rabbit. When her name appeared on the office entrance door, her joy equaled that of childhood Sundays. Like Daddy, like daughter, she regarded work as play. With Haldimann Enterprises as her first client, she assembled a competent staff. Joe urged her on to bigger responsibilities and greater risks. She responded with enthusiasm sowing the seeds for a renowned career.

She could not escape the grief of her father's death. As time passed, her distrust of Syd aggravated the agony. The first day she returned to the office, two weeks after the funeral, she sat at her father's desk in the private office, listening to Syd who slumped in a visitor's chair on the opposite side.

"Your father was a fine man, Suzanne; so unpretentious in his overalls and old fedora. When we moved into this building, he placed planks across a couple of sawhorses for a desk." He chuckled. "I insisted such antediluvian austerity wasn't acceptable for a man worth millions. He told me to look after it. That's when I bought this walnut furniture. He said it was a damn waste of money." Syd laughed at the memory.

She smiled, avoiding a display of her feelings.

"What about the estate?"

"My dear Suzanne, you are the sole owner of Haldimann Enterprises, a holding company valued at eighteen-million dollars for tax purposes. It's an overwhelming responsibility for a twenty-six-year-old woman."

She cringed and almost leaped from her chair. His statement showed how little he understood. Her father's voice came to her, his *joie de vivre* loud and clear, encouraging her to be herself, to accept the challenge of new adventures unafraid of the unknown. *"Because you're female doesn't mean you can't play in the marketplace."* Her self-confidence was not a fluke. It developed because he energized her to act, assigned her responsibilities and guided her into ventures she might never otherwise have tried. He persuaded her to find happiness in business. Love and marriage, children and housekeeping were not for her. She accepted his assertion without challenging his motivation. His death sapped her confidence, leaving her to a lonely vigil she wasn't sure she could handle. She needed a crutch and half-hoped Syd might provide it. For all her knowledge of the companies and the dealings between Syd and Joe, she never understood why there were no other shareholders. At last, she could demand an explanation. She moved to the window and stood with her back to him.

"Years ago when your father hired me, we reached an understanding," he said.

A lame answer, indeed. Would she always have to put up with evasive talk?

"What was the understanding?"

He spoke softly, his words hesitant as if he held a secret, debating whether he should reveal it. Not wanting to look into his eyes, she listened without turning. She could barely hear.

"Only that I, well, I mean, I've never been an employee or a shareholder either. I mean, your father, he contended I had to be independent without, you know, conflict of interest and well, he just didn't think I should be part of the company." She had never heard him talk this way, so out of character. Was he shielding history from her? She hoped he would reveal his secret but he continued his stumbling speech. "I bill monthly for services."

"Syd . . .." She was about to say his answer was unacceptable when she realized if he was neither an employee nor a shareholder, she could discontinue his services whenever she wanted.

"And the other employees?"

"Your father was a generous man and rewarded them according to their merits without involving them in ownership."

"Oh," she said, her back still turned to him. Daddy always said to keep matters separate and he meant it. Now she understood what Syd meant when he offered to do the estate settlement at no charge. She resolved to ask Phillip to keep his eye on progress. She resisted kicking Syd out that minute thinking she should cross all the bridges first. She swung around to face him.

"What do I do next?"

"You move into this office, sit at his desk and wait for the employees to recognize you. It'll take time. Your father was their master, the genius they loved who could do no wrong. You have to earn their respect or sell out."

The following weeks became a futile exercise in exerting her authority. Nobody paid attention to her. They said good morning, mentioned the weather, listened to whatever she might say and continued to perform as they had always done. To make matters worse, Syd persisted with never-ending innuendoes about selling. In her father's absence, she called the one person in whom she had confidence, Phillip Silverstein.

"It's terrible around here, Phillip. Nobody pays the least attention to me despite the fact they're all working for me."

"The answer to that is to do something dramatic, exercise some authority."

"All right. I want to sell the operating companies. Will you set it up for me?"

Two months later they invited Albert Beauchamp, who was now in full charge of the janitorial company, to a meeting.

"Albert, I want to sell you the cleaning business."

"Miss Suzanne, I don't know what to say." He hung his head. "I ain't got no money as amounts to anything. I couldn't pay you nothing."

"That's not important," Silverstein declared. "What's important is, do you want the company?"

"Well, I don't know, I mean, yes, I guess so."

They agreed that Albert would pay for it out of profits over a five-year period. Six months after Joe's death, they completed similar negotiations with the principal employees of Haldimann Construction Company. Thus, Suzanne disposed of the two main subsidiary companies leaving her with a substantial income while retaining full ownership of her father's real estate assets.

"Thank you, Phillip, my position is much better. All that's left is for the courts to wrap up probation."

6.

Fifty-two weeks ago Daddy died in this room. She thought she'd never make it through the worst time of her life but here she sat wishing the lawyers would finish their work and go away. David, the office manager, stepped into her office.

"Have you looked outside?"

"What's going on?"

"First big storm of the season. Maybe Syd won't get back in this snow. I'm closing up and sending everybody home. You better go, too, before it gets worse."

"Thank you, David, I'll wait awhile."

She watched the spiraling snowflakes seeking refuge in the littered alley. A mournful smile crossed her face; her eyes closed. She felt as though she had lived this moment before. *Daddy, why don't you put blinds or curtains or something on this window to shut out that ugly brick wall crumbling to pieces?* He probably never noticed it; not at his pace. He never looked out any window, not even the window of life. An entire year and still the shock of his passing remained. At unexpected moments, directing the office staff perhaps, or a serious business meeting, or maybe dining in a restaurant, he appeared without warning, demanding her attention. Suzanne's unblinking, motionless eyes signaled his illusionary presence. Sympathetic glances supplanted the stalled conversation, interrupted by clearing throats and simulated coughs, until a visible shiver ran through her body and she returned to normal.

She does not hear Syd hurry into her office without removing his topcoat, eager to deliver the news. He stops when he catches sight of her at the window and he knows she stares like a statue with unseeing eyes. It saddens him to see the tall, graceful woman so stricken; the girl he loves as if she were his own daughter. He remembers the slim figure, barely a hundred pounds, in her last year of high school, marching across the gymnasium floor, spine ramrod straight, hooked elbows securing a broomstick across her back with a book balanced on her head. "Look at her," Joe says, "isn't she a darling? What a beautiful figure; a real woman, like her mother." Christmas Eve: Syd comes in to wish Suzanne and Roberta a Merry Christmas. The mature college student curled by the fire brushes her lustrous shoulder-length black hair. "Thank you, Syd, and same to you." The day after graduation: "Now you pay attention to her," Joe says, "she's got a master's degree from Northwestern." The full-figured executive with hair longer than most women, wears a monstrous hat at a jaunty angle secured by two pearl hatpins. How beautiful; looks more like thirty-three than twenty-three. Joe scolds her preparation for going out in the cold winter blasts: "Daddy, I refuse to wear those detestable cloche head sheaths that look like medieval helmets." Syd smiles at the laughter resounding in the office as the staff join in. "Put on your woolen toque and scarf," Joe orders, his smile belying the severity of the command.

> Joe is always spellbound in her presence and the fussiness that yields such beauty: "It's ridiculous, Syd. She buys that dark-red custom-made lipstick because it blends with her black eyes." Syd studies her beauty; her normal complexion is a creamy paleness that her powder cannot disguise. He blinks a couple of times and clears his throat.

"Sorry." Her eyes fluttered and a slight tremor seized her body. The sense that Syd took advantage of her, making his offer as he did at the moment of her greatest distress, had not left her. Even as she regretted her submission, she could not bring herself to revoke it. Silverstein protected her interests and represented the estate in court. "Did you say something?"

"Just got back from court. Silverstein did a great job. It's settled and we can decide how you want to proceed from here."

She knew what would be next. The recommendations never varied. *"You'll be better off to sell the properties. That's what your father would tell you."* Real estate experts, bankers, mortgage brokers and investment counselors analyzed the estate, echoing Syd's gospel. She suspected he coached them. After every meeting, he delivered the same report in a hundred different guises. *"You don't have the experience to run these companies yourself. Good time to get out while the market is high. Best advice we can give you, Suzanne."* The message did not escape her: How could a twenty-seven-year-old woman, or any woman for that matter, manage assets of this extent?

"Syd, I haven't told you this before because, well, it's all so overwhelming. I vowed at father's funeral that my life's work would be preserving and perpetuating my inheritance as a memorial to Joe Haldimann."

He looked at her quizzically. "I'm delighted, but how does that affect what I'm telling you?"

"Because I won't sell."

"Why, for heaven's sakes?" He gazed in wonder as the color rose in her cheeks beneath the thin cosmetic mask.

"Stop it, Syd, I can't stand any more. Your inference that I'm some sort of female bookkeeper who can't do anything beyond arranging a hairdressing appointment is insulting and degrading. You think we live in a male world and only a man can run this organization."

"Suzanne, please— "

"Don't patronize me." She glanced out at the winter storm. Of course, he wanted to sell everything; how else could he earn a fee? She turned to face him. "I've made up my mind. I will not allow the sale of a single one of father's properties."

"Oh, God," he mumbled, "it's at moments like this I'm glad I never married."

"What did you say?"

"Nothing. It doesn't matter."

"Yes, it does matter," she barked. "It matters because you're wrong; undeniably and utterly wrong. Father would not endorse your advice. I will manage this company as I am sure he would want and expect of me."

A grimace creased his face, the distress evident as he shrugged his shoulders and shook his head from side to side.

"As you wish. Get your coat. We better go before the storm gets worse."

"I'll walk. I need the air."

"Suzanne! There's a winter storm out there. Be mad if you like, but don't be obtuse."

"I'll do what I like. Besides I've a couple of letters to write before I leave."

"If you want to catch cold, it's no concern of mine." He turned and left.

"God, you sound like Roberta," she yelled at his departing back. She subsided into her desk chair, put her head down on her crossed arms and giggled. She felt better than at any instant in the last twelve months. The President of Haldimann Enterprises, owner of sixty-two Chicago properties, raised her head prepared to challenge the world in the name of women's rights.

Chapter 2 - Hello Love

1.

When Suzanne heard Syd stomp out of the office slamming the door behind him, she raised her head, pushed around in the swivel chair and saw the dismal brick wall. Yes! She would order new curtains, have the office redecorated and buy new furniture. Memories of her father flooded her mind with warm compassion. She took pride in Joe Haldimann's bountiful charity that extended to more people than she realized.

At the wake, hundreds had filed past his casket, overflowing the chapel, crowding the foyer and spilling down the steps into the street. A constant stream of unfamiliar faces mumbled condolences, some embracing her, others grasping her hand. Syd and Albert, Roberta and Sarah hovered in the background providing moral support. At last, the procession ended and Suzanne sank into a chair.

"Now, honey, you just rest awhile," Albert said.

"I want to leave here, Albert. I want to go, I mean, from this neighborhood. I want to escape; the house is empty." She wiped her eyes and reached for his hand. "Oh, Albert, I miss him so."

He drew up a chair and put her hand in both of his.

"We all do, honey, we all do. But y'all got no special place to go. Now is not the time to go. It's better to stay. We needs you here, honey, and we wants you to stay. This is your home. Y'all been here since you was a little girl."

She could never recall Albert saying a harsh word; his way was gentle understanding. In truth, she didn't have a reason to run away. Leaving these kind, considerate souls for loneliness somewhere else made no sense. They went to Beauchamp's after the burial. That same night she yielded to Albert's persuasion and promised she'd remain in Daddy's house with Roberta. His response floated back, so sincere and tender.

"Y'all remember how afraid you was to go out in the dark. I used to walk with you so's you wouldn't be afraid." His deep chuckle brought memories of that fear. "You was afraid of what you didn't know and that's what you're afraid of now. It'll go, just like your fear of the dark went."

Such a homespun philosopher, he was right again. She often walked the four and a half blocks from office to home in the dark—one block west on Roosevelt, three north then west again. Still, with all their loving kindness it had been a difficult year.

In some inexplicable way, voicing her determination to manage the real estate elated her. She imagined a bird escaping from a cage, singing a joyful song of release. Her captivity ended. She laughed, unbound from the fetters of mourning by a selfish spat with Syd. Marching through the snow cloaked in exhilaration, her woolen toque pulled down over her ears, she made the turn off Roosevelt humming a lilting tune with the snow cascading around her. The streetlights created flickering cones of fantasy fanning out like showers of white confetti. A little rhyme popped into her head.

I see the snow in the sparkling light.
It glistens and shines in the moon at night.

The illumination through the big window at Danny's Place created an island of light on the sidewalk. She knocked on the glass, waved to Mabel and the few customers seated at the counter. Turning from the bright glow and taking a few steps into the darkness, she heard someone sloshing behind her. Looking over her right shoulder, she felt a stab of pain in her left arm. A man wrenched her wrist.

"Stop! My purse!"

She whirled to follow the fleeing thief. He lay face down in the slush. A hefty man huddled over him, one knee planted in the snatcher's back.

"You black bastard," the man growled, "give it back." He hoisted an emaciated, lanky teenager to his feet, forcing the boy's right arm behind his shoulder blades making him squirm in agony.

"Give it to her," he snarled. When the boy made no movement, the man repeated the command like an army sergeant.

Suzanne, paralyzed by her discomfort, struggled for composure and clutched her injured shoulder. More sloshing feet and three black faces appeared in the dim light.

"What's going on?" The shrill voice aroused Suzanne from her paralysis.

"It's all right, Mrs. Baker," Suzanne said, "the boy tried to steal my purse."

"Steal your purse!" Mrs. Baker screeched a half octave higher. "Where you come from, boy?" She sneered with the prestige of a magistrate. "You don't belong in this neighborhood. We don't have stuff like that 'round here—"

"It's all right, Mama," Suzanne said, putting her hand on Mrs. Baker's shoulder. "The man got it back and the boy's going home now." She turned to the thief.

"Look at me," she ordered. Waiting until their eyes met, she took her purse from the outstretched arm.

"Thank you." She smiled. Mrs. Baker's tongue stopped, the dumbfounded captor stared and the boy looked as if he expected another night in the precinct station.

"Son," Suzanne said, "you won't get anywhere stealing and robbing except in jail. I expect I'm not the first to tell you that and I guess I won't be the last. To help you remember, I'm going to give you ten dollars."

Mrs. Baker let out a hideous wail. "You gonna what?"

Without a glance at the neighborhood busybody, Suzanne continued.

"You take this ten dollars to your mother or father or whoever it is looks after you and you tell them where you got it. Next time you want to steal, you ask yourself if there isn't a better way. Now let him go, please, sir. And you Mama, and you others, all of you hurry on home too, your families are waiting for you."

The boy careened past Danny's Place clutching the money. Mrs. Baker shuffled off with, "Well, I never . . . " and the muttering gawkers scattered. The captor remained with his hands in his jacket pockets, a smile lighting his unshaven face.

"You are one crazy woman if you think that'll teach him."

"I don't suppose we'll ever know, will we?" Her provocation coupled with the chilling cold sent tremors through her body. She turned to go. "Thank you," she said.

"Wait a minute, lady, why'd you do that?"

"You make me feel so good about the way I behave, but I didn't do anything. You caught him. I tried to make it a different experience for him."

"You're a lunatic."

The finality of his judgment caused her to study him for the first time. He dressed like her father in high leather boots half-laced, dingy overalls, leather jacket and an old fedora pushed back on his head revealing unkempt brown hair.

"I suppose I am but who are you to judge? Why don't you see if you can't clean up a little; your tongue as well as your clothes?"

They parted in opposite directions.

2.

Suzanne never liked the view from the window in her father's office. After it became her office, she liked it even less. She wanted something cheery and feminine to brighten the room. The decision to install drapes involved no emotional expense until after lunch the following Tuesday while waiting for the contractor to bring samples and take measurements. Shifting her eyes in fear of somebody watching her, she looked into the alley overcome with a sense of impiety as if installing curtains blasphemed her father's memory. Her mind leaped back to Tolliver who was sometimes a rich banker at the top of a high building and sometimes a miserly old curmudgeon in a deep dungeon. With so many disguises, did Tolliver ever exist? She would never know, but no matter who he was or where he worked, Tolliver always said, *"T'ain't worth a coon's ass that way."* She gasped involuntarily, hunched her shoulders and clasped her hands to her mouth. A truck driver stared up from the alley below. She turned away.

A little man with heavy glasses, carrying a stepladder twice his size, hurried into her office. She stood by the window examining the samples one by one while he measured. The truck driver started his engine, looked up and smiled. The peeping Tom leering at her as if she stood naked in the window annoyed her. He tipped his hat and drove off. She almost called the warehouse to find out his name.

"How soon will you have the curtains ready?" She did not hear the answer as the little man scurried off, closing the door behind him.

3.

On the same Tuesday, Harry Matheu made a delivery to Haldimann's warehouse.

"We'll unload after lunch. Come back in a half hour," the warehouse man said.

Harry parked his truck in the alley and sauntered over to Danny's Place where the pleasure of eating lay not in the food but in the fun of teasing the owner's wife, Mabel. A buxom, red-haired, Jewish matron smeared with rouge and garish lipstick, she resented his insults about the woeful establishment and told him so. Harry barked his greeting to the entire patronage of the tawdry hole-in-the-wall.

"Hey there, Mabel, what poisonous mix has the old man dreamed up today?" The blowsy woman swung around, a smirk on her face, arms akimbo.

"Hey what's with you?" Harry toned it down to the innocence of the child who put the tack on the teacher's chair. "What'd I do?"

"Some guy, you are, dearie. Here all this time I thought you was in love with me. You, carrying on with them high society dames."

He strutted to an empty stool in the rear and stubbed out his cigarette. "What the hell you talking about?"

Mabel shadowed him down the service aisle, past the ice-cream cooler and the glass enclosed pie rack with the cockroach crawling up the side. She leaned over the sandwich board, one hand on the counter and the other tugging at her loose blouse offering a clear view of her hefty bosom and deep cleavage.

"You know," she said, wiggling a little.

"Hell, I do." He gazed into the abyss.

She turned away, put a hand on her hip, tilted her head back and looked down her nose in a coquettish pose. "Carrying on with Miss Haldimann behind my back."

"Miss Haldimann! You crazy or something? I don't even know Miss Haldimann."

"Oh yes you do."

"Come on! Hey Danny, what's for lunch? Your wife's gone crazy. Better ship her to the nut house before she gets dangerous."

Mabel ignored the interruption, swaying her shoulders back and forth, her breasts undulating like gelatinous balloons and her head cocked back looking at Harry over her shoulder.

"'Member that lady," her right hand went to her hip and the left patted her coiffure, "what give the black kid ten bucks?"

Harry nodded.

Mabel swung around, hands on hips, glaring into his face.

"That, smart ass, was Miss Suzanne Haldimann."

Harry's eyes opened wide.

"Holy shit! It was!"

A roar of laughter escaped the patrons.

"Don't you use words like that 'round here," Mabel chided, "or that's what you'll get for lunch."

Harry said not a word as he ate. His mind devoured his good fortune. The pot of gold no longer lay hidden at the end of the rainbow; it was in the office across the street. How could such a stroke of luck happen? He didn't plan, he didn't contrive, he didn't scheme; he didn't even know it when it happened. More than opportunity knocking, clearly Lady Luck stood beside the door waiting to usher him in. If he knew anything, he knew enough to grab the Lady's hand when she offered it. Silently, he praised the Lord God Almighty, a practice he never engaged in except in the most needy circumstances. Apologizing for the irreverent use of His Name from time to time, Harry asked what to do next. The first suggestion seemed inappropriate. Maybe place something on the horses down at Hialeah? Hell, no. Lady Luck beckoned with a bigger prize than a mere horse race could offer. How about the opportunity of seizing the filly herself? He pushed his plate away, shook a cigarette loose, tapped it violently against the packet and struck a match with his thumbnail. He drew in a deep drag and exhaled noisily.

"Not a bad lunch," he said.

The unloading began as he walked into the alley. Climbing into the cab, he settled down to finish his smoke when his eye caught sight of the office window. Maybe she's in there working her pretty little ass off. Maybe she'd like a visitor. Maybe she'd like to go out to dinner some night. Now how the hell does a guy pull that off? As if answering his plea, she appeared in the window looking this way and that. She put both hands to her face, covered her eyes and hunched her shoulders like a little girl hearing a vulgar remark. He couldn't take his eyes from her; how beautiful in daylight without the stupid woolen hat on her head. Removing her hands, she saw him, looked horrified and disappeared. He blinked. Did he see her or was it a vision? A small man with a yardstick clambered about measuring for something, maybe new window blinds or curtains.

"Six hundred twenty," somebody yelled. Harry fished around for the delivery slip and slithered out from under his daydream.

"That's right," he said, "sign here."

He climbed into the cab, took one last look and there she was at the window. Harry smiled, tipped his hat and drove off confident Lady Luck would remind her who he was.

4.

Humanitarian reformers and street-corner gospel singers were no deterrent against the boldness of Chicago criminals. Areas of the city flourished as if prohibition didn't exist. The Sicilian district south of Grand, the district called Bloody Maxwell centered around Maxwell and Sangamon Streets and the Old Levee district on twenty-second south and east of State flourished in prostitution, gambling and liquor. Organized gangsters, abetted by corrupt politicians, fought territorial wars massacring one another in reckless contempt of respectable society. Neither a mobster nor a bootlegger, Harry got his kicks in these areas, playing on the fringes in the belief that riches awaited the bold spirit. He associated with an obnoxious character named Rocco Rossetti, a tough enforcer who used brass knuckles and switchblades to subdue his rivals. He and Harry usually met in a speakeasy on west Taylor Street near Wentworth.

Harry spent the afternoon considering how he might share Miss Haldimann's good fortune. He took the problem to the speakeasy to develop a strategy. Rocco's idea of romance was walking in and taking off his pants. When Harry raised the subject, the problem eluded Rocco.

"What you talking about? You got a dame then take her upstairs and screw her. Jesus! You dumb or something?"

"Not this dame, I don't."

Harry thought of nothing else the next day and into the night. He checked his billing records. Lady Luck stood beside him. In his hand, he held an unpaid invoice due from Haldimann Construction. Normally, he didn't press clients like Haldimann for payment but this time he'd make an exception; say he was short and could he speak to Miss Haldimann while waiting for the check? Lady Luck agreed. He looked skyward. God? Yes, the Lord agreed, too.

Leaving his truck in the garage, Harry drove downtown in his car. He wore new overalls over a clean white shirt with a conservative blue tie. His boots glowed; he shined them twice. Hair trim, shampoo and barbershop shave, with the latest eau de cologne transformed him to a sensuous dandy. He admired himself in the barbershop mirror; felt great and looked better.

"Miss Haldimann. My name's Harry Matheu."

He stood in the doorway to her office, surprised at the violence of his heartbeat. In a spasm of panic, he realized he'd walked on stage without rehearsing his lines. His knees quivered and his vision blurred; he saw a halo around her head. Looking up from her work, their eyes met with no sign of recognition. He blinked and the halo disappeared.

"I caught the boy who stole your purse last Friday. Perhaps you remember."

"Yes, I remember."

"I'm sorry I didn't recognize you; one of my best clients."

"Really! I have your account card here and it's not too impressive."

"Well, you know it's just—"

"I understand you came in for a check. Please wait in the front hall. Good day, Mr. Matheu."

He left, dismissed even before the search for the pot of gold began, perhaps never to have another chance. A fortune spent on new clothes and tonsorial treatment, not to mention his glistening boots, and she dismissed him. He searched within himself for courage. The image of his loony mother appeared. Her father, a majordomo in a wealthy home in Vienna, taught his daughters the cultures and manners of the rich. Harry's mother, Olga, religiously imported what she believed to be traditional European customs and manners into the Cincinnati home where Harry grew up. She adjusted for the lack of servants by casting herself in myriad roles; cook, housekeeper, nanny, laundress, back to cook and a return to nanny. Day after day in her dream world, she played each part in a different cap or apron presumably so she could remember who she was at any particular moment. Despite Harry's distaste for her fantasies, Olga force-fed him good manners. Until this moment, acceptable social conduct served no purpose in his life. Boldly, he returned to Miss Haldimann's office, walked to her desk, not in an act of despair but in the role of *Aristide Bruant dans son cabaret.* He recalled Toulouse-Lautrec's portrait in the Cincinnati Art Gallery; red scarf wound carelessly around his neck and flung over his shoulder, and the rakish broad-brimmed hat tilted back with the left edge turned up.

"I would like to apologize, Miss Haldimann, for my unfortunate choice of words and lack of courtesy on the occasion of our previous meeting."

"What?" She looked at him in wild-eyed bewilderment.

"For my cursing and derogatory statements. I'm sorry. Sometimes—"

"Thank you. Now if you'll excuse me."

He did not flinch, but accepted the challenge as he imagined *Aristide* might have done.

"I wondered if you would care to join me for dinner on Saturday evening, allowing me the pleasure of your company and the privilege of apologizing for my regrettable conduct."

"Dinner?"

"Yes. Perhaps I could pick you up at home. I know an elegant dining establishment."

Fearing rejection and praying for acceptance, he imagined he stood for two or three hours immobilized before her desk. Later, when he told his friends at the speakeasy about the agonizing wait, the imagery confounded them. "Why didn't you sit down, ferchrisake?"

After an eternity, Miss Haldimann's eyes twinkled. Those penetrating black eyes mesmerized him. His fears and prayers evaporated; Harry felt at peace. More than at peace, he became an agent of manifest destiny inoculated with supreme confidence as he stood in the presence of the owner of the pot of gold while he clutched the hand of Lady Luck.

"Yes."

She offered her hand.

"Yes, I would like that very much on the condition that you continue with the extraordinary improvement in your vocabulary and costume."

"I promise. Saturday at eight, then."

Harry did not offer his concluding remark as a question, but rather as confirming an agreement. He considered kissing her hand, but with the contract sealed thought better of it. Grasping her hand for an instant, he bowed from the waist and left.

5.

Suzanne sat alone at the supper table, her head in her hands. Roberta hovered about until she could not bear the silence a moment longer.

"What's the trouble, honey?"

"Sit down." Suzanne did not raise her head. "I'm ashamed to tell you what I've done."

Roberta poured coffee.

"Don't be that way. You just got to forget about your daddy, poor child."

"That's not it," Suzanne said letting her eyes meet Roberta's gaze. "On Saturday—"

"Y'all have a date. You don't need to tell me, I can see it your eyes. Who's your man? What dress you gonna wear? Oh! Honey, that's wonderful."

Roberta's excitement did nothing to relieve Suzanne's remorse.

"You won't think it's so wonderful when I tell you I accepted an invitation from a truck driver. A truck driver! I can't imagine why I ever accepted. Roberta, my date is a guttersnipe with a frightful vocabulary who switches to stage acting with a glib tongue and phony manners." She ignored Roberta's audible, romantic sigh. "What's the proper dress for dinner at eight with a truck driver?" She finally decided when a gorgeous corsage of orchids arrived at five o'clock on the fateful day.

Roberta, clad in full-length black skirt and white blouse, peeked through the front window eagerly awaiting the arrival of the guttersnipe, a term she translated as knight-in-shining-armor. As Harry stepped from his car and approached the house, she flung open the door and tried a graceless curtsy. The astonished visitor reached out to restore her equilibrium by taking her hand in an artistic bow, immediately winning Roberta's heart forever. She welcomed him, clutching his hand and dragging him into the house in the spirit of a matrimonial agent.

"Thank you, Mister Matheu," she cooed, her face flushed and smiling at her own ineptitude. "Come on in, sir, and sit down. Miss Suzanne be ready in just a minute."

Harry retrieved his hand from her grasp and stepped into a tiled vestibule with white paneled walls. In the central hall, his feet sank into a carpet so plush he looked down to see if his ankles were visible. Elegant furniture, delicate antiques and exquisite artwork filled the parlor. Two classic paintings hung on the wall in ornate frames bordering the fireplace with individual lights above them. The other walls displayed various paintings, a small oriental tapestry and several brass *objets d'art* that he imagined commanded a significant price. Suzanne watched him taking in his surroundings.

"Good evening, Mr. Matheu." Harry jumped. "I didn't mean to scare you," she laughed, "but I guess that makes us even."

"I'm overwhelmed by the magnificence of your home, Miss Haldimann. It's not what one expects in this neighborhood."

Harry's concern that he might be overdressed evaporated. She looked gorgeous in an elegant, sleeveless, royal blue gown of seductive simplicity with a diamond hair brooch and matching earrings. A long string of pearls circled her neck and elbow-length white-kid gloves adorned her arms. He placed her mink stole around her shoulders and caught the scent of the orchids; or was it her perfume that intoxicated him?

"Good-night, Roberta," she called. "Don't wait up."

Harry exuded confidence, holding the door for her and helping her into the car with the same courteous manner she noticed in the office. He took Roosevelt, swung on to State and worked his way to the lakeshore heading north. The downtown hustle, the noisy streetcars and hooting engines faded away in the exchange of polite conversation. Her anxiety yielded to excitement as she considered the handsome man in elegant tuxedo with red cummerbund, gray tie displaying a diamond stickpin and his patent leather shoes that looked new. Absorbed in conversation, she lost track of their whereabouts, thinking, perhaps, they passed the city limits when he turned into an empty, unlit area and stopped near a RESERVED - NO PARKING sign. He opened the door and took her hand. She did not move.

"Where are we?" She spoke with a tremor in her voice.

"It's a private club. Please do not be alarmed."

"Why is nobody here?"

"Miss Haldimann, I assure you everything is under control. The law of the land—"

"You mean this is speakeasy?"

"No. Please trust me. It's a fine club that takes certain precautions. There's nothing to worry about." Still holding her hand, he urged her gently.

"No! Let's go somewhere else."

Pulling her hand free, she slammed the door. The cozy euphoria of the drive evaporated. She shivered and cast about for alternatives. What could she do? The extent of her error dating the truck driver traumatized her. Never again would she agree to a date with an unspecified destination. Her escape was the automobile itself. The ignition key caught her eye. She had merely to step on the starter and drive off. Impossible. She had never driven in her life, didn't know where she was and did not possess a driving permit. Unable to escape, she watched Mr. Matheu walk up three steps to a darkened door. He knocked. The door opened. She could see a man's silhouette in the doorway and a sign in the reflected light: CLOSED UNTIL FURTHER NOTICE. She watched the hand-waving conversation but she could not hear with the windows closed. In a moment the two men came down the steps to the car and opened the car door.

"Miss Haldimann, this is Carlos, the maitre d'."

Carlos bowed and spoke in a heavy Italian accent.

"Good a evening, Madame. I invite a you into our club. It is a fine a club with the finest a food in Chicago. Would you enter, please?"

He turned and left, his silhouette disappearing as Harry reached for her hand. Resigning herself to the outcome, she stepped out of the car into the night.

6.

"Ah! Good a evening Mr. Matheu." The maître d' in tailcoat and white tie, sporting a hairline mustache, reached out to greet Harry as if it were their first meeting of the evening. Suzanne caught a glimpse of folding money changing hands that produced a practiced smile on the host's face. With head cocked slightly to the right, he recognized her presence.

"Madame." He drew the word out as if he were spelling instead of saying it. "This a way, please."

He led the way through a foyer where he pulled aside a curtain allowing them to pass ahead into a dimly lit hall. "Third a door on the left," he announced. In a mysterious move, he somehow glided past and stood at the open door before Suzanne could reach it. A red bulb in a single wall sconce lit the room. To her right, she saw a table draped in white linen with place settings for two and a silver candelabrum set between them. The maître d' lit the five candles, crossed the room, switched on a floor lamp and unlocked a corner cabinet. Two large chairs upholstered in black imitation leather faced a huge, off-white settee stretching along the opposite side. The light-colored fabric created a startling contrast to the chairs. Two mahogany end tables, one beside each chair, matched a large glass-covered coffee table in front of the settee. The entire mish-mash sat on an oriental carpet that stretched across the room from end to end. The hideous conglomeration reminded Suzanne of something she read about houses of ill repute in some place she couldn't recall. Odious dark-red flock paper covered the walls and the black ceiling created the aura of a dungeon. Three large prints of Italian works—Michelangelo she thought but wasn't sure—were of such size and so inappropriate and out of place, she couldn't escape them. The maître d' bowed to Suzanne offering an ersatz smile on his unctuous face as another exchange took place. The door closed behind him. They were alone. Had she not exacted a promise from Harry about his language, she might well have used some rather tactless words. She refrained and asked, "Where are we, Mr. Matheu?"

"We are in an exclusive establishment operated by some friends of mine who find it expedient to exercise caution because of the current laws prevailing in this country."

Her eyebrows arched and she drew back but elected to let his ridiculous, long-winded response pass.

He mixed and stirred a shaker and set it on the coffee table with two long stemmed glasses. She imagined a troop of Keystone Cops from a Charlie Chaplin movie hurling themselves into the room with flailing nightsticks.

"Are we the only ones here?"

"Heavens, no. The place is full, I'm sure. Many of the patrons are law officers, which lends a certain degree of security. They're always here but it's not good to be inquisitive about such matters so I never ask."

"I'm sorry. I'm flabbergasted, that's all. I thought places like this only existed in books and foreign lands."

"There aren't many as fancy as this, nor as safe either."

"It may be safe, and I hope it is, but it doesn't qualify as fancy. What happens in a police raid?"

"The red light over the panel goes out, we grab our coats and leave. That's the alarm signal. We walk out the panel-door, get in our car, which is now parked just outside the door behind you, and drive off. It's as simple as that, but I wouldn't worry; I think the mayor owns the place."

At last, Suzanne perched on the edge of a chair that was big enough to swallow her if she leaned back. Harry plunked down on the settee and drank in the vision of the most beautiful woman he ever escorted in his life. Her blue dress against the black leather, her ivory face accented by the red background, her hair, her eyes, the glittering diamond jewelry and the beautiful orchids hypnotized him. She was rich too; her beauty almost made him forget her wealth. Suzanne leaned forward to pick up her drink when a waiter wheeled in a huge food service cart. Harry paid once more.

Trying to dispel her obvious nervousness, Harry smiled and served the hors d'oeuvres with a flourish. She watched, fascinated with his display of expertise. His manner puzzled her. Such a delicate touch and this guy is a truck driver. She watched the graceful motion of two plates gliding on to the table. He picked up his glass.

"Here's to you, Miss Haldimann."

She did not touch hers. He paused with his drink in the air.

"Let's get a few things straight. First, my name is not Miss Haldimann; it's Suzanne. Second, your name is not Mr. Matheu; it's Harry. Last, you invited me to dinner in what you alleged to be a nice place. Instead, you drag me out here to the sticks and lock me in a dungeon I may never escape from unless I know the password. Even worse, where I expect to be arrested and spend the rest of my life in jail. Now let's have some definition of the rules of this game." She paused for breath.

His face contorted into a comic mask.

"And furthermore, don't laugh at me!"

His expression changed to a quizzical look and she realized he was trying to decide how to respond. Did she offend him or did he not understand her teasing? Without explanation, he stepped from the room, closing the door behind him. Alone and terrified, she expected sirens and gunfire convinced that she would never date another truck driver. What explanation could she offer for her presence in such an establishment? Syd would surely exploit the incident as evidence of poor judgment. A loud pounding sounded on the door. Sure the police stood on the other side, her right hand involuntarily covered her mouth stifling her scream. The door opened. A deep, resonant voice sang out of the darkness.

"Miss Suzanne, may I present Mr. Harry." He appeared in the doorway with a courtly gesture, marched across the room and offered his right arm.

"Good God! You scared me."

"May I have the pleasure of your company, Miss Suzanne?" His face showed no sign of amusement except his twinkling eyes.

Despite her trembling limbs, she struggled to her feet and did a full curtsy.

"Delighted, Mr. Harry."

She looped her arm through his and they paraded once around the salon, picked up their drinks, and faced each other.

"How do you do, Miss Suzanne?"

"Quite well, thank you, Mr. Harry."

"Here's to you," they said simultaneously, touched glasses and sipped their drinks.

Suzanne collapsed on the settee wondering if her violent heartbeat came from her fright or her amazement.

"Don't you ever do anything like that to me again. You scared me half to death."

"I thought it was a magnificent performance," he replied as he refilled the glasses.

He served dinner from the cart and poured the wine. His manners and table talk were faultless. He avoided improprieties, overdoing the good behavior with sanitized tongue and circumspect conduct. The waiter cleared the table and removed everything except the candelabrum. Side by side on the settee, drinking coffee and stingers in the soft candlelight, they shared stories of their families, their backgrounds and their childhood memories while the red sconce light offered assurance of uninterrupted security. Suzanne found the conversation exhilarating defying her pessimistic anticipation of an unbearable experience. Late in the evening, their eyes met. He stared at her, goggle-eyed in dumb stupefaction. A surge of passion flowed through Suzanne; a prurient desire that swept her breath away and she wanted to cry out. Oh! Harry. I love you. I love you. I love you. She smiled at him. Their eyes held, hesitated and she looked away, fearful he might read her emotion. She stammered with the words on the tip of her tongue.

"Oh! Harry. I . . . I think it's time to go home."

Chapter 3 – Facts or Fancy

1.

A*ristide Bruant* rose in the morning and swaggered into the bathroom. He posed with his head turned so he could see his profile in the mirror. Such grace and charm. He faced the mirror, took a deep bow, the audience rising as one with a standing ovation. Bravo! Magnificent! He brushed his teeth and rinsed with gin mixed with orange juice. He stood on the two-rung stepladder in the kitchen accepting the cheers, his head swollen with the pride of self-restraint having not tried to bang her. He surmised the upper reaches of American society judged banging on the first date abnormal. Above all else, he wished Miss Haldimann to regard him as normal, regardless of his own particular views on normalcy.

As Harry pondered the events of the evening, he resolved to turn a new leaf. His usual dalliances granted his sexual favors on those who lay on their back at the first opportunity or those who did so for cash compensation. Although he preferred the former, love as a reason for fornication exceeded the boundaries of his experience—and maybe hers, too. When he asked about her social life, she replied that it did not exist. He surmised that no man shared the pleasure of her company now and, incredible as it seemed for a twenty-seven-year-old, none ever had. Could it be in all those years no one laid her? Perhaps she wished not to remember. She would never tell him anyway and he didn't care. She mentioned love for

Daddy but he died. The Jewish guy could be her grandfather. Regardless of his angle of view, Harry could reach only one conclusion; he stood alone without competition like Captain Kidd on the quarterdeck lusting for the buried treasure. He pictured a vault heaped high with gold. Her body, while shapely, well proportioned and elegantly adorned, came as an inconsequential bonus. If she looked like a witch, it would make no difference. He intended to entice her until her sexual desire demanded satisfaction that he would gladly satisfy in exchange for the key to the vault.

He had never imagined his three-year army experience would serve him well in later life. His mind overflowed with military-speak about careful definition of objective and clear evaluation of hazards. How true; he must exercise care in scaling the walls of elite society and infiltrating Chicago aristocracy. He saw the goal with clear and unobstructed vision; to share the wealth and blessings so deeply cherished by those who lived on high and to hell with the hazards. In the tradition of the military, he labeled the exercise with a code name; he called it "Operation Golden Fleece".

2.

At the Haldimann home, tradition dictated Sunday brunch with Daddy at ten after Mass, sometimes with Syd or other guests, but always father and daughter sharing that happy day. With his passing, Suzanne's life lay in shattered ruins and Mass took on a new dimension. For long periods during the service, she knelt in prayer. Afterwards she often sat alone grieving in silent mourning or went for solitary walks, arriving home in tears, her face pale and haggard. Nevertheless, Roberta maintained the routine, prepared to cater to Suzanne's wishes whatever they might be. The unpredictable behavior persisted and indeed, on the morning following Suzanne's late night with Harry, continued.

"Any coffee this morning?" Suzanne asked.

"Land's sakes, honey, it's just twenty to eight." Roberta didn't comment on the bright colors of the Sunday frock, nor did she overlook the rosy-pink cheeks. "Y'all enjoy yourself last night?"

“My head aches. I drank too many stingers.” She twirled around, gave Roberta a hug and kissed the old woman’s cheek. “It was wonderful.”

“That’s nice. Coffee’s not ready yet.”

“That’s all right.” She danced her way out of the kitchen and returned with her coat over her arm. “I’m going to Mass at eight thirty.” She hugged Roberta again and started for the door.

“Brunch be ready when you get back. Anyone else coming?”

“No. Why do you ask?”

After Mass, she went to the Parish Hall for coffee. Father Lalonde, a rotund prelate usually found near the food tray, greeted her.

“Why, Suzanne,” he said, “we missed you. So nice to see you attending coffee in the hall again.”

In a gay mood, she almost invited him for brunch but judged an apologetic expression more suitable in the circumstances.

“It’s been difficult, Father, but I feel a little better now.”

“I’m glad. I must say you look charming.”

He left to continue his campaign for a luncheon invitation. Suzanne walked home at a brisk pace, invigorated by the cool morning air and bright sunshine.

“I’m home.”

“Everything’s all ready,” Roberta replied.

After breakfast during which she deflected Roberta’s references to romance, Suzanne curled up in her favorite chair with a novel she set aside months before. She fluctuated between reading and dozing until Roberta carried in the silver tea service at four.

“Mr. Syd coming for tea today?”

“Probably not. He’s been sulking since our row last week.”

Roberta poured and settled down in the opposite chair, a pleasure she enjoyed when Suzanne was alone. She continued her promotion of a romantic adventure, memorializing the previous night, hinting at future possibilities and jabbering on in her ceaseless effort to resurrect Suzanne’s spirit from the grave of Joe Haldimann.

“Why don’t you ask him for dinner some evening?”

3.

"No chicken liver for this boy," Roberta said. "He's a he-man and he's going to have a he-man meal and that's all there is to it."

Harry arrived at seven on Wednesday with a box of chocolates. Although Suzanne kept a small cache of illegal whiskey, she did not serve it. Instead, they sipped a fruit cordial that brought a strange expression to Harry's face as he looked in the glass with dismay. He refused a second but she poured one anyway. They carried their drinks through to the dining room to indulge in Roberta's idea of a he-man meal. Clad in the long black skirt and white blouse with a frilly cap that drew a stifled snicker from Suzanne, she wheeled in a teacart with a large, savory roast of beef and potatoes with mixed peas and carrots. First, she served side salads. Then she set a delicate portion of the main course in front of Suzanne. Returning to her cart, she prepared Harry's dish. With a flourish, she wheeled around and placed a monstrous plateful of food before their guest.

He gasped, then sighed, choking off a profane bellow. Disbelief etched his brow. He put his elbow on the table and lowered his head so the bridge of his nose lay between his thumb and forefinger; a pose reminiscent of a man in prayer. Suzanne closed her eyes and turned away. Embarrassment was too mild a word to describe her distress. Roberta, with a single blow, destroyed every semblance of decorum. The remnants of Haldimann propriety lay bare before the truck driver with the loony mother. The choices were few.

"Excuse me."

Suzanne removed Harry's plate and marched into the kitchen. Without a word, she found a clean plate, arranged a reasonable portion, returned to the dining room and put the plate in front of him.

"I'm sorry."

She sat but did not look at him.

In moments of panic, the human mind responds instinctively. Such was the spontaneity of Harry's reaction, which unwittingly produced admiration in her mind for his aplomb and savoir-faire. By ignoring Roberta's faux pas, he relieved Suzanne's chagrin. He opened a new subject to break the awkward pause as if nothing happened.

"Let me tell you about my father," he said.

4.

"My old man was the youngest of seven, all big, strong kids that their father loved because they were free labor to work the farm."

Harry cut his meat with the right hand and ate with his fork in his left hand. Suzanne nibbled at her salad.

"Dad was a shrimp, maybe premature, I don't know. His mother named him Stefan after Saint Stephen condemned to martyrdom. She figured this kid was in the same boat and would be lucky if his father didn't feed him to the hogs."

Harry sipped the cordial, grimaced slightly and took a large drink of water.

"He was sick half the time, an emaciated little runt. He played with dolls and liked sewing and knitting. On his twelfth birthday, his drunken father sat the kid on his knee and made him drink beer. No sooner did the beer go down than oops, up came everything the kid had eaten in the last two days, all over his father. That did it. They sent him off to Vienna to apprentice under a clothier. He never returned home."

Harry continued to eat with elegant European manners as he did on their first date. Where she expected truck drivers wolfed their food, this one ate with aplomb.

"It can't be the end," she said, "he still has to come to America."

Harry looked up from his dinner. His eyes froze for a second staring at her breasts, then moved to her shoulders and upwards until their eyes met. He examined her as though evaluating a gallery portrait. With a transient blink, he escaped the trance and continued eating, picking up the story.

"It was the end of his life at home. In Vienna, he spent every free minute prowling the museums and art galleries. He loved that junk and despised his father who didn't have one ounce of culture in his soul. He loved the theater, the actors' costumes and the way the lords and ladies dressed. In his last year of apprenticeship, he bought a ticket to the Vienna Boys' Choir. A girl named Olga Oberlein took the seat next to him. It turned out they're a pair. Everything he liked, she liked and vice versa. Three months later, he proposed to her and that was the turning point of their lives. They married and planned to live in America. Before they left I was born."

Suzanne let out a whoop of triumph. In her mind's eye, a little, wizened boy won his independence from a bearded giant who wallowed in a vat of suds; David and Goliath cast in a new play.

"Hurrah," she yelled. "Three cheers for Quirinus; a triumph of moral rectitude."

Harry paused, his fork halfway to his mouth.

"What are you talking about?"

"Your father was armed with pins and needles. The Roman patron of the armed community in time of peace was Quirinus. Just some trivia I learned in college. Did your grandfather go to the wedding?"

"I have no idea. Probably not."

"Go on with your story."

He set his knife and fork together on the edge of his plate.

"I'm sorry, I'm having difficulty keeping my mind on the story."

Suzanne sensed the color rising in her checks. She turned away, sprinkling a salt on her salad. Lifting her eyes to his, she spoke in a voice that didn't quite sound like her own.

"Why?"

"You're a very attractive woman. I—"

"Please, Mr. Matheu, go on with your story."

"Yes. Well, umm, oh yes! Olga's younger sister, Magda, came with them because she wanted to get away from their father who made the girls live a pretend life that she thought was crazy."

As he talked he looked at the end of the table as if there were a third person present.

"Months later, we sailed past the Statue of Liberty. What they thought was happiness was really misery. Stefan couldn't understand the directions spouted by the guard who spoke a different language from the English they studied. The guard said, 'Mac, you go sit over there,' but what they heard was one single word coming through the guy's nose. It sounded like matheugosovatha."

Suzanne's laughter drew his eyes and he smiled at her.

"They followed the pointed finger and sat. After a long wait, the guard blew another instruction out his nose that sounded like matheugouptha."

She laughed again.

"They followed the pointed finger. Finally, they passed through the door to America and into an even worse pickle where nobody cared what they did or knew what they said."

"I can't imagine what that's like. It's one thing to be on your own in a strange city, but when you can't talk the language, really it must be a terrifying experience."

"That's right. New York was not like Vienna. They were lost in the noise and bustle. One way and another Stefan steered his family west until they ran out of money in Cincinnati. They ate in bread lines and lived in Salvation Army hostels. Olga wanted to go home. Magda couldn't stand the bellyaching so she took off on her own. But Stefan's a determined little bugger—I mean, excuse me—fellow and he was lucky because they were in the heart of the American clothing industry. It wasn't good planning, just good luck."

Harry reached across the table and touched Suzanne's hand.

"It sort of runs in the family," he smiled, "being in the right place at the right time."

He squeezed gently. She smiled resisting the urge to squeeze back.

"Two or three weeks and they had more luck. Stefan got a job cutting patterns for men's suits. The guy who tested him said he'd never seen anybody cut a pattern so fast. Well, why not; the old man had been doing it since he was twelve. They paid him eighty cents an hour, almost fifty bucks a week."

She heard the pride in his voice. He had told her on Saturday he didn't care for his parents. He said he never wrote or went to see them. But when he said eighty cents an hour the words rang with admiration.

"Goodness! Eighty cents an hour in 1898 was huge."

"He's never worked another job in his life."

"I'm speechless. Let's take our coffee in the parlor."

Roberta wheeled in her teacart with clean cups and fresh coffee. In silence, she poured the coffee, lifted the cover from a silver dish and left the room. The gift of chocolates lay neatly arranged on a little plate.

"Thank you for the candy. Help yourself and keep going with your story. What happened next?"

"They Americanized their Austrian English and decided to change their name—Matuszewski was too cumbersome. Stefan remembered Ellis Island and the man who spoke through his nose. He searched the telephone book and finally came up with Matheu. They wanted their son to have an American name, too. They selected Harry and we got our American citizenship six years later."

"Is that the end?"

"Yep. That's it. They still live in the same place doing the same thing."

"Is he good at it?"

"Good at it? He's the best. From what I heard when I worked there for a summer, the company thinks he can walk on water. There's nobody like him. He's far past the cutting stage. He's the chief designer, gets good money and, hard as it is to believe, manages a staff of six or seven designers and pattern makers."

They sat silently munching chocolates and sipping coffee. Suzanne lay back on the pillows and gazed at the ceiling.

"Gee, what a story. Wouldn't it be wonderful if he owned his own shop instead of working for somebody else."

5.

After Harry's departure, Suzanne lay on the settee in the parlor rehashing the events of the evening. A warm feeling enfolded her that she didn't understand. What purpose would it serve to scold Roberta? Besides, the incident could be Suzanne's fault for abdicating her supervisory duties, which she would not fail to exercise in the future. In retrospect, the experience narrowed the cultural gap with Harry. The story of his parents resulted in the same conclusion. If the romance bloomed, the day might come when she would tell him about the problem of her heritage. The slight difference between them lay in educational background and financial matters. His etiquette and social manners needed Americanizing but she could handle that. Her concern was the gap in his life he never mentioned. She knew he left home after high school, came to Chicago, joined the army and got his discharge early in 1919. In November 1921, he made her acquaintance as a cartage contractor. Whatever his faults, she wanted to know about those hidden three years. Her intuition led her to believe that a difference in moral values lay between them. She called Phillip Silverstein.

"Phillip, I haven't thanked you for settling that terrible probate business."

"I think you should give Syd the thanks. He did all the work. I just did the talking."

"You belittle yourself."

"I won't argue the point. What can I do for you?"

"I'm interested in finding out about a local cartage contractor."

"Call the Better Business Bureau."

"No, you don't understand. I mean personal information. It may be, well I'm not sure what."

"Checkered?"

"Yes it might be."

"See Sergio Cellini. He's an exceptionally well-informed source of information with a wide network, but he doesn't make house calls. You will have to go to his place in Cicero. Take a taxi and have the driver escort you into his office. Do the same in reverse coming home. That it?"

"Yes. Thanks."

He was gone. His terse conversations always yielded immediate decisions or directives for action. That was why she consulted him but in this case, he might have taken a moment more and wasted a few words.

The nerve-racking taxi ride to Cicero almost convinced her to return home. Hundreds, perhaps thousands, of foreigners crowded the unfamiliar neighborhood. Her anxiety reached a fever pitch as she alighted outside a hovel, so different form the expensive downtown property that Silverstein enjoyed. One look at the place horrified her. She continued only because of Silverstein's referral. What seemed like a horde of people sat in the waiting room, all of them clad in rags, smoking and jabbering in a foreign tongue. A peroxide receptionist, masked in ill-suited cosmetics, typed at a furious rate oblivious to the hubbub surrounding her. Without interrupting her work, she greeted Suzanne with a what-do-you-want grunt.

"I have an appointment with Mr. Cellini."

The woman continued typing without a pause. Suzanne had never seen anyone type so fast. She ripped the pages from the machine, arranged carbon paper between several new pages, inserted them and continued typing. In a voice barely audible above the noise and clatter, she said, "You the woman that called yesterday?"

"Yes."

The receptionist, who could type and carry on a conversation at the same time, did not look up from her work.

"Sit down," she ordered.

Suzanne looked around. The choice of seats did not appeal to her. The discomfort of boring eyes increased her uneasiness. She did not intend to wait while each of these disreputable animals disgorged their problems one after another; it could take hours.

"Mr. Cellini told me to be here at ten thirty. It is now ten thirty."

The click-clack stopped.

"I know the goddamn time, honey. You don't need to tell me."

"I'm not telling you. I'm asking when I may expect to see him?"

"How do I know?"

The typing resumed.

"You're the . . .. "

To continue was pointless. She walked to the corner farthest from the waiting clients and lit a cigarette to squelch the odor of unwashed bodies. If he did not receive her when she finished her smoke, she intended to leave. Two minutes later, a door opened and a dandy appeared. He wore a light gray homburg and a belted trench coat. Beneath the hem she saw royal blue trousers with a heavy pin stripe and pointed suede shoes. He ignored Suzanne, muttered something indistinguishable and everybody in the waiting room rose and left.

"You're next, honey," the tough blonde announced without a pause in her work.

Suzanne stubbed her cigarette and entered the open door. A huge man sat behind a desk at the far end of the room. His head was big and his shoulders broad. His neck tapered out from his ears and disappeared into a forest of black hair protruding from his open-neck, white shirt with embroidered monogram. His high-quality clothes, tailored in foreign style, were obviously custom-made. She guessed his age at mid-forties.

"You'll excuse me if I don't rise, Miss Haldimann, but I can't."

His arms propelled his wheelchair from behind the desk and she saw that he did not have legs.

"Please sit down. Would you care for coffee?"

His melodious, pleasant tone suggested a singing voice. It projected warmth that attracted her and she instantly liked the man, grotesque as he was.

"No, thank you, Mr. Cellini."

"Very well then," he said while his eyes roved from her face, down her body to her shoes and rose again. He made no pretense to hide his study, yet his appraisal did not project indelicacy nor did it cause her embarrassment. He could have been estimating her weight in the manner of a circus sideshow performer. Perhaps she would win a doll if he guessed wrong. He spoke at last.

"Silverstein said you have a problem. What may I do to help you?"

"It's about a truck driver."

"Name?"

"Harry Matheu."

"Ah! Yes."

An air of amusement crossed his face and vanished.

"What would you like to know about him?"

"I would like to know his occupation in the years since his army discharge."

"Ah! Yes."

The abbreviated smile touched his lips again.

"Before I proceed I need to know your purpose. What will this information be used for?"

His question startled her. She did not intend to reveal her romantic interest.

"It's confidential."

He shrugged, reached for the wheels and began to propel himself in a circle.

"Then I can do nothing for you."

"Why? Phillip said—"

"Miss Haldimann." He turned back to face her and spoke as if to a child. "My business involves the discovery of facts and figures about people that live in this state. Unless I know why I am doing it, I cannot conduct a suitable investigation. It is necessary for me, because of my handicap, to rely on others, some of whom you may have seen in the waiting room. They do not need to know why they do what they do, but I must. A simple matter of giving them the right instructions. Now, please, tell me why you wish this information."

He gazed into her eyes with intensity that compelled a response.

"Well, you—"

"Oh come, Miss Haldimann. I'll make it easy for you. Is he a lover who has jilted you or a lover you are considering?"

She sighed, defeated by his forthright perception. Later, when she thought about the interview, she wondered why she succumbed so meekly. The thought of this strange man prying into her personal life, so unabashedly dissecting her both physically and mentally should have provoked her. But it didn't. Nor was she mortified. It amazed her that he could so expertly analyze her motive leaving no choice but to confess the objective.

"The latter. I want to know—"

"Ah! Yes."

He paused. The brief look of amusement passed as before while he propelled himself into a position opposite her.

"Very well, I will tell you."

"You know him?"

"Not personally, no, but I have information about him."

"But how?"

He frowned and sighed.

"Miss Haldimann. I would not consider it proper for me to ask how you intend to manage your father's affairs." His voice did not reveal any irritation, rather it sounded like the tone a teacher might employ. "Likewise, I do not consider it proper for you to ask me how I manage mine."

"I'm sorry."

His words humiliated her. She looked away, opened her purse and withdrew a pack of cigarettes and a lighter. More words from her would serve no purpose. She waited for him to continue.

"No offense taken." His smile projected such warmth, she immediately felt better. He watched her extract a cigarette.

"I would prefer you didn't. I'm cooped up all day with little fresh air and smoke does me no good. Would you care to change your mind about the coffee?"

"No thank you."

Again, he deflated her, yet, as before, it did not upset her and she wondered what strange power this man exercised.

"Ah! Yes." The curious, brief smile appeared again. "Let us begin. Here is the short version of what you want to know. At the beginning of prohibition, Harry enjoyed a mild flirtation with the underworld. The Mafia hired him to organize and maintain a fleet of trucks and keep them in tip-top shape because he's a good mechanic. He was a transport master sergeant in the army. Perfect credentials for the job they wanted done. They made the mistake of paying him too much money as those fellows often do. He may have been a little over-ambitious but anyway, they kicked him out. They didn't squeeze him too badly, which I attribute to his close association with a fellow named Rocco. Harry got out with enough money to buy a truck. He continues a social connection with Rocco. They kick around together, drink a lot, do the usual boy stuff, you know, whistling at girls. Harry likes to play the big shot but he's not an underworld type. He has a loose tongue and I suspect the Don removed him on that account, although that is supposition on my part. He banks at a small institution that started up after the war called The Blankenship Bank. He drives his own truck and works independently of the Teamsters, which may lead him into problems if he tries to expand. Do you want me to go into this further or is that enough?"

"What was the nature of the problem that caused him to lose his job?"

"Ah! Yes." He smiled and wheeled himself behind his desk. "Your phraseology displays your inexperience. In the underworld, you do not lose your job. They kick you out with the choice of keeping your mouth shut or they dump you overboard with your feet in a bucket of concrete depending on how much you know."

She felt as if she were an open book to this clairvoyant man. No matter what she said, there was nothing about her he couldn't guess accurately.

"You're right," she admitted, "I am inexperienced in their world."

"It's as well. They paid him two hundred fifty a week—"

Suzanne gasped.

"How much?"

"You heard me correctly."

She leaned forward on the edge of her chair.

"For heaven's sakes, why so much? Is he that good?"

"Yes, he's good. They hired him to teach others how to manage the fleet. For reasons I do not know, however, they also gave him a five-thousand-dollar gift." Suzanne's eyebrows arched and she gasped again. "With almost no personal expenses, his money piled up fast. While doing his teaching job, he got a swelled head and opened a second-hand car dealership. He did very well; too well in fact, so they pushed him out of that, too. Who knows, maybe they planned to push him out anyway as soon as he successfully trained their people to take his place. He escaped with several thousand dollars, perhaps more, but in any event plenty to establish a reasonable line of credit with Blankenship who financed his truck."

"Do you know anything about him besides that? I mean his personality, for instance?"

"I know he's smart. He's ambitious. He's loyal but, I regret to tell you, I doubt if he is always truthful."

"Is he in any danger from the . . .."

"Mafia? No, as long as he keeps his mouth shut. If he doesn't, then they always find out and when they know, well . . .." With his hands spread wide, his voice trailed off.

"I have no more questions. Is there anything else you would care to tell me?"

He laughed. This time genuine warmth accompanied his melodious chuckle.

"I do not give advice to the lovelorn, it is too dangerous a field. I prefer to deal with the underworld, it is safer. However, I am constantly reminding many of my clients to pay their taxes and it would be my guess through his close association with those gentlemen that he, too, failed to pay taxes on his earnings. Otherwise I have nothing to add."

Suzanne rose and shook his hand.

"I trust you will excuse me, Mr. Cellini, but I would like to say that you have a remarkable voice. Do you sing?"

His eyes fell to the desk and his face colored.

"No longer. It's a sad story but I thank you for asking."

She hoped he would elaborate but the sadness in his eyes signaled otherwise.

"You have been most helpful. Please send your account to Mr. Silverstein."

6.

Suzanne pondered her reaction during the taxi ride home. Did Cellini's revelations kill her romance? Why should they? Harry filled her heart with happiness. Only two weeks since their first date yet the truth was plain; in that time, she scarcely thought of Joe Haldimann at all. It used to be drudgery to drag her body from bed in the morning but now she looked forward to the day, to meeting Harry, delighting in the joy that came to her each time they met. Unquestionably, Harry's company made her happy. Logically it followed that she should not accept hearsay evidence; he should have a fair and reasonable chance to present his side of the story. She would put the question to him on their next date.

She asked to go to a quiet restaurant, a legitimate place without liquor. After dinner, she suggested they go home.

"Would you like to come in?"

He jumped at the invitation. She offered coffee. He accepted and commented on the pleasure of her company without alcoholic indulgence.

"Kind of a new experience for you?"

Her conversation appeared casual and simple but, in fact, she baited the trap. She laid her plans thoughtfully, direct and to the point. In school, sometimes her well-formulated questions and astuteness had startled her teachers. The same occurred when she entered the business world; men came to meetings prepared to deal with her quick mind and aggressive tactics. She did not cultivate the technique but rather it was her natural style, the way her brain worked. While it faded into dormancy after her father's death, Harry stimulated her intellect like spring reawakening the flowers. Her direct approach with no preliminary introduction stumped him.

"I know nothing about bootlegging, prostitution and the other rackets but I know enough to know I don't want any association with gangsters or friends of gangsters. What do you think about that, Harry?"

"Well—"

"I mean, you wouldn't be involved in anything like that, would you?"

"No . . . of course not."

Her acuity perceived his apprehension. She did not seek to embarrass him but rather to create a position where he could not lie.

"You worked for the Mafia fixing their trucks, didn't you?"

His face blanched to a mask of terror. She suspected he felt an overwhelming need for whiskey.

"Yes," he admitted.

"Tell me about it."

An awkward silence followed. He sipped from his empty coffee cup. Suzanne kept her hands folded in her lap. He lit a cigarette with his regular ritual and thumbnail light but forgot to offer her one. She remained immobile. He exhaled noisily, crushed out his cigarette and raised the empty coffee cup to his lips again.

The plan advanced marvelously; no further gain would come from making it any more painful. She had prepared him for confession that she knew would be difficult. Confession was difficult for most people who practiced regularly. For him it could well result in a barrage of lies.

"Curious how I know?"

"Yes."

The act of speaking relieved the pressure. He sighed and shrugged. His expression suggested his tacit submission. Perhaps he already conjured up something to tell her.

"I went to see Sergio Cellini."

His face paled to an ashen gray and a hint of fear clouded his eyes. Then he laughed; not his comic laugh that melted his face but a sardonic, mirthless chuckle of resignation. She was confident her contact with the Italian community surprised him. Did he know Mr. Cellini or was he searching for an excuse to escape so he could ask Rocco about this guy?

In a squeaky voice, he asked, "Who's he?"

Suzanne did not anticipate the dramatic effect of her disclosure. She changed her plan.

"A friend of mine," she said casually, "who specializes in tracking people and knowing where they are and what they do, both past and present. He has a beautiful voice."

Harry's agitation increased. She worried that she created too much pressure, that he might be so afraid he would abandon her. Little did she know his choice of action was no choice at all. Since he would not sacrifice Operation Golden Fleece, the truth was the only alternative.

"I suppose there's a first for everything. Anyone but you and I'd deny it into my grave. But you, well, you're different." Her heart jumped when she heard those words.

He told the story. It started with Rocco offering two fifty a week to prepare a fleet of trucks and teach people to maintain them. They moved into the numbers game. Then came the used car business that involved loan-sharking to suckers who wanted to buy a car on credit. Finally, Rocco booted him out and waved a gun under his nose telling him the consequences of squealing. The story finished with Blankenship, a legitimate banker who financed his truck. He told her everything except his drinking and whoring expeditions late at night with Rocco. He smiled at her.

"That's it." And after a slight pause, he added, "You know, I feel better."

"I knew you would."

She walked across the room and kissed his cheek. He looked surprised but did not respond. She filled their coffee cups and returned to her chair.

"And now, Harry, I'm going to teach you about lawful business."

Chapter 4 - Matheu's Men's Furnishings

1.

On the Saturday following New Year celebrations of 1922, Suzanne and Harry went to her office after lunch. He recalled *Aristide Bruant's* bold intrusion into her life, a moment that would live in his memory for years. They stopped before the closed door to her office where *Aristide* stepped across the threshold of destiny into her world of wealth. Holding hands, they admired the new paneled walnut door with gold leaf letters.

Suzanne Haldimann, President.

"Beautiful, isn't it?"

"Gorgeous," he replied, curious about the cost.

She unlocked the door and the fragrance of a florist's shop assailed his nose. The closed drapes admitted no light. She flicked a switch and four wall sconces, two on each side, produced a subdued, tranquil atmosphere reminiscent of a museum. Her father's walnut desk and chair stood in the center. In one corner, three upholstered chairs surrounded a circular conference table. A matching settee stretched along the opposite wall. Two visitor's chairs sat in front of the desk, two filing cabinets behind it and a typewriter on a small table to the right. A light-brown carpet complemented the dark walnut furniture. The drapes blended brown lines with bold patches of green and white in a pattern that suggested springtime foliage and gave the room a cheery atmosphere. In the corner, a three-foot high brown urn contained cut flowers and ferns that filled the room with majesty.

"Do you like it?"

Harry eyes roamed the elegant office that looked like the drawing room in a millionaire's mansion.

"Yeah, looks neat. That your father's desk and chair?"

"Yes, but everything else is new." She closed the door. "I haven't picked the artwork yet. Would you help me select it?"

The sole purpose of their meeting could not be to admire the office décor. He feared a trap unable to imagine the snare she set for him this time. In their short acquaintance, he had learned the sudden introduction of unexpected subjects signaled a new offensive.

"Sure. Yeah . . . er, yes, of course."

"Sit down over there." She pointed to the round conference table and switched on an overhead light. "I want to show you something."

Harry sat like an obedient child while she unlocked a filing cabinet, selected a heavy ledger and laid it on the table. One by one, she showed him the details of her inheritance. Each revelation tantalized his dream of riches never before attainable. In his hypnotic state, he could not speak. She laughed and closed the books.

"That's it Harry. I'll have to sell a few properties or borrow funds to pay the rest of the taxes but there'll be twelve or thirteen million left when it's over. Meanwhile I have a large monthly income."

She spoke of twelve or thirteen million in the off-hand manner he thought of twelve or thirteen dollars. His mesmerized mind conjured visions of opulent splendor as he gazed in wide-eyed wonder, knowing he should say something. Staggering across the room searching for words, he emitted a long slow whistle. He found his voice but when he tried to speak, he felt a constriction in his throat. His breath came in gasps when at last a word emerged.

"Wow!"

He gulped and tried again.

"For the first time I understand that expression of yours."

"What."

"I'm speechless."

He paused to catch his breath.

"And your father did all this?"

Another breath.

"All those tenants paying rent every month. Holy smoke! And the janitor and construction guys paying off their debt. Wow! Is this real?"

"Yes," she said, "I realize how blessed I am."

She switched off the bright light and took both his hands in hers. They faced each other.

"So many blessings, so many opportunities." She gazed into his eyes. "Harry," she said, "I want to try something new and different."

He tensed in the realization the display of wealth was diversionary. She had assembled her forces to assault the true target of this foray.

"What exactly do you have in mind?"

"Would you like to join me?"

Join her? His eyes locked on hers. Never had he heard that expression before. What did it mean? Could it possibly be? Is that what they called it in high society? In his circles, they called it banging.

"Delighted," he said, careful not to reveal his surprise. "Where?"

"Right here in Chicago."

What's the matter with right here in the office? She talked in riddles while he fretted about his inability to interpret her meaning. Was she serious? He cast aside his doubts. Obviously, she planned a mysterious excitement here, in the office, hidden from Roberta.

"What do you have in mind?" He whispered tenderly.

"Men's clothing."

What could she possibly mean? Her reference to men's clothing might be a hint; what about her clothing? Their bodies pressed together, her pelvis touching his. He could feel her warmth and he experienced a throb of passion.

"You're kidding."

"No, I'm not. I know the perfect man to do it."

His eyes blinked. An anticipatory glow flowed through his body. He thrust towards her, enfolded her in his arms and murmured fervently into her ear. "Who?"

She smiled and hugged him back.

"Your father."

"My father!" He gulped for air and managed to squelch the involuntary, violent curse before it erupted. She must be joking. He slipped his hands to her buttocks and pulled her tight so she could feel his desire. "I'm willing to do it." He eyed the settee along the wall.

She pulled away. "It's unchristian."

God Almighty! Here was this religious crap again. What does that have to do with it? Bewildered and confused, he let out a wail.

"Not where I come from it isn't."

She circled her desk, sat in the swivel chair and looked at him with a self-satisfied smirk while he stood in the middle of the room leering at her.

"Do you remember the fourth commandment. Honor thy father and thy mother that thy days may be long in the land the Lord thy God gave thee."

He didn't know the fourth commandment from the twenty-fourth commandment. This cockamamie baloney arose at the damnedest times. His lecherous rapture became a cloud of incomprehension.

"What are you talking about?"

"Your parents. If misfortune intervened or some tragic event forced your separation, it would be understandable; but deliberately exiling yourself is unforgivable."

Her scolding sailed over his head. The mere thought of his parents subverted his passion. He tried to recover by moving to the settee and inviting her to join him.

"Come on, Susie."

She remained seated at her desk.

"It's time for you to visit your parents."

Her words held the same degree of finality his mother used when he was young enough to be under her control. At this point in his life, he would not visit his mother. It was an irrevocable decision. If she wanted to see his parents, she could go alone.

"I won't do that."

"Sure you will. It's only proper that you should. How could you abandon them without caring what might happens to them?"

The argument rang the death knell to his ardor. He sat alone on the settee gawking at her. She broke the silence.

"I dare you."

"You dare me?"

With his lust collapsed, his mind reverted to Operation Golden Fleece and the subject of money. The colossal dollar sign in his head marred his perception of her game. If she wanted to meet his parents, perhaps he could finagle it to gain access to her mountainous wealth. Still, her proposal bordered on insanity.

"Look! They're happier without me and I'm happier without them. You think they live in a sleazy accommodation in the slums and he works in a sweatshop. It's not like that, Susie. He's got a good job and they live in a swell neighborhood so what do you gain by picking up the spilled apples now?"

"I think it's an opportunity."

"What?"

"Your parents."

"What the hell are you talking about?" He stood in front of her with both hands on her Daddy's damn desk, resolved to drive this stupid notion from her mind. "So they left their families and came to America; what's so wonderful about that? Millions of people did it. I did it when I was one year old for God's sake. So what are you talking about?" He left the desk and paced back and forth across the room.

"I imagine a threefold opportunity," she replied calmly. "First, I see an opportunity to thank you for the purse-snatching incident by reuniting you with your parents."

"Ridiculous. You've lost your marbles."

"I have not lost my marbles and please hear me out without further rude interruptions. Are you listening?"

"Yes."

"Where was I?"

"At number two, I think."

"Oh, yes. Second is the opportunity of extracting Mr. and Mrs. Matheu from their servile existence and giving them a piece of the American dream. For Heaven's sakes, will you sit down? Third is the opportunity of leasing my vacant store downtown."

She smiled, plainly without a care in the world, following his pacing. He suspected a trap when he came to the office and by God, she'd done it. Just like the night she made him confess his shady deals with Rocco, now she conned him into visiting his parents and he didn't know why. She sat at the desk with folded arms, incorrigible and confident. Again, he lost the battle and he couldn't do a goddamn thing about it. He resigned himself to her whims as a prisoner of war faces captivity. He plopped down at the conference table, reached deep inside himself and recalled the purpose of his mission. He smiled back.

"Well?"

"Is your father really good at making clothes?"

"Sure he is. The best."

"Then we'll set him up in business in an ideal downtown location."

"Whoa!"

Harry jumped to his feet. Mission or no mission, this lunacy demanded that he withdraw his capitulation and fight a rearguard action to protect his parents.

"Maybe you can do magic with your big bucks but you can't turn my old man into an executive. He's a dreamer and an artist. Set him up in business and he'll fail for sure. No, I couldn't let you do that to him no matter how I feel."

"How can he lose?" She swiveled her chair back and forth, following his movements as before. "You said yourself he's the best. If he's good, he can't lose as long as he has enough financial backing."

Damn her. He plunked on to the settee for an instant; then rose and continued pacing while she continued.

"We can find him good helpers and apprentices to train; sales people, a suitable manager, whatever it takes." With every word, her voice rose and the phrases spilled out faster. "We'll set him up in downtown Chicago where he can sell high quality suits for a good price. We'll get him living quarters nearby so he doesn't have to travel. Your mother will love Chicago. Come on Harry, let's do it."

This qualified as the dumbest proposal he ever heard. Obviously, money diseased her, affected her mind. Maybe it's contagious, contaminating all rich people who believe they can inflict their will whenever they want.

"I don't know, Susie. Do you really want to invest your money in a clothing business run by an old man?"

"Yeah!" She sang it out like a college cheerleader. "What do you say?"

He perched on the edge of the desk looking down at her. His decision lay not in what she wanted, but in what he wanted. If she wanted to hire his old man, she had the dough to pay and it didn't matter a damn to him. He chastised himself for his agitation. The decision was easy; nothing could stand in the way of Operation Golden Fleece.

"Okay, you win. I'll talk to my father about it but only if you come with me, which means we have to go to Cincinnati because he'll never come here."

"I knew you'd see it my way. You're a dear. Of course, you can't go alone. It would be impossible for you to sell the idea after alienating your parents for so many years."

She dialed the telephone and he wondered what in God's Name came next. He listened in amazement as she asked for reserved space on the train to Cincinnati for Monday night. “Just one moment, please.” She took the receiver from her ear and covered the mouthpiece. “There are no berths or single bedrooms available; only a double bedroom. Will that be all right, Harry? Can I trust you?”

At last, Harry got the message. She raised the subject first, he didn’t. There could only be one interpretation. Her intent was obvious but he failed to understand the purpose of joining on a train; some foolish, female romantic notion, he supposed. Not caring in the least where they did it, he nodded and waved his hands in affable agreement.

“That’ll be fine,” she said into the telephone, “I’ll pick up the tickets at the station. Thank you. Oh! Haldimann.” She spelled it for the clerk.

2.

Harry had a haircut and a barbershop shave with the best aftershave lotion in the house. He bought slick under-shorts and fancy pajamas, not that he intended to wear pajamas but he thought he might need them for show. He dressed in his finest, bought a half dozen roses and went to the station. Suzanne prepared herself for the trip too. She looked gorgeous and her perfume got him so excited he couldn’t wait to get to the bedroom. She brought her own protection; a bottle of whiskey. He poured their second drink when she stood to put her cigarette in the ashtray. She couldn’t reach. The train lurched. As she tumbled over, she put her hand out to stop her fall. It struck his stomach and slide down between his parted legs. Harry construed her action as the signal that joining time arrived. He helped her scramble to her feet and yanked at his tie. Somebody knocked on the door.

“Why don’t you folks go on down to the dining car while I makes up your room. Everything be ready when y’all get back.”

After dinner, she poured doubles for Harry while she sipped thimblefuls. In the morning, Harry awoke sitting in the chair fully clothed.

"Cincinnati next," the porter yelled.

Harry staggered off the train in a foul mood. His head throbbed and the thought of confronting his parents made it worse. His normal cure consisted of a hefty belt of gin or a few beers. He lacked the courage to suggest they search for a speakeasy. He tried the available cures—coffee and bicarbonate of soda—without success. He ate a large breakfast in the hope food would soak up the alcohol but it made him feel sick instead. Finally, Suzanne dragged him into a taxi to face his parents.

The Matheu apartment, as different from Suzanne's expectations as black is from white, amazed her. They lived on the second floor of a three-story brick building in a comfortable middle-class district. The noise and bustle on the busy street did not detract from the interior. The décor suggested a dollhouse with delicate furnishings. The most startling feature, however, was Mrs. Matheu herself who projected the image of a miniature Dresden maiden. Her brown hair was short and curly. Her face glowed with self-content and her eyes reflected a buoyant enjoyment of life. She was beautiful in simple, plain clothes that provided an ideal complement to her pleasant disposition.

Harry greeted his mother by picking her up but she made no secret of her displeasure at his failure to keep in touch. Suzanne watched them in each other's arms wondering how such a tiny woman managed to produce such a bulky man. Mrs. Matheu ushered Suzanne, bag and baggage, into the main bedroom. Harry would occupy the spare room while Mr. and Mrs. Matheu slept in the living room. Olga swept aside Suzanne's protests and suggestion of a hotel room.

The day passed with lunch, four o'clock tea and conversation. Harry spent the afternoon sleeping and felt better by suppertime. Mr. Matheu arrived at six-thirty. The moment Suzanne set eyes on him, she recalled Harry's description of his parents as a pair; whatever he liked, she liked and conversely. He was small and dainty with thin brown hair and delicate features, meticulous in his dress with perfect manners. His speech was intellectual but his capacity to listen made it matchless. He heard the conversation and responded in careful, well-chosen words. Above all else neither he nor Olga could veil their respect for each other. It flowed out of them as they behaved like doves in a cage. Suzanne never before witnessed such mutual adoration and politeness between two people, let alone husband and wife. Her heart warmed to these two souls and she wanted to take them into her arms to insulate and protect them as one wants to protect innocents from a world of brutality. As she lay in bed, it occurred to her that maybe she even wanted to protect them from herself.

The next morning Suzanne introduced her proposal. She put it simply and frankly; she intended to start a clothing business in Chicago and she wanted Mr. Matheu to be part owner and share in the benefits. She explained the downtown store location, the apartment on Michigan Avenue and the financing, presenting pro forma statements that were meaningless to them as well as Harry.

"Your golden years would be so much happier in Chicago with the family united again," she suggested.

"In downtown Chicago!" Harry muttered.

Suzanne glared at Harry, restrained her wish to hit him and continued her sales pitch.

"The way you are now, you never come to Chicago and Harry never visits Cincinnati. You don't see one another from the beginning of one year to the end of the next. In Chicago, you'll be together again. And you, Olga, will be close to your sister. I have such a beautiful little store with a lovely park in the rear. And the apartment is close to Lincoln Park. You'll adore it."

The overture created turmoil for Stefan and Olga. Cuddled together, they whispered in the privacy of the living room after the others retired.

"Stefan, we are happy here, in Cincinnati"

"That is true."

"I remember what it was like the day we arrived. I was so afraid. Now we are familiar with the city."

"Yes, Olga. And I do have a good job."

"My artwork! I have sold a little of my artwork. I am getting better."

"You do not want to go, Olga?"

"No. I never want to leave here."

"What about Magda?"

"It is not a good enough reason. She never cared much for me anyway. And you, do you want to go, Stefan?"

"No, not if you do not want to. No . . . no . . . but . . . "

"What are you thinking?"

"Well, my own store, my own place. It would be so exciting, Olga."

Three days later they arrived in Chicago with Olga feeling like a tornado had picked her up. Four days before, she was a dreamy homemaker in her own world three hundred miles away looking after the needs and care of her husband. This city bewildered her; the constant noise, the elevated trains and the street traffic shattered her serenity. In her confusion, she stammered and stuttered incoherently. Gradually, she recognized the futility of her objections. Stefan's excitement about his own business after so many years provided the justification.

Suzanne felt guilty. Relief would come from the discovery of an exciting occupation for Mrs. Matheu to exorcise her dream world and bring her to reality. She quizzed Harry about his mother's interests.

"I only lived with them when I was a kid. I don't know what she likes to do. Keep house maybe, or cook or stuff like that."

"Ridiculous," scoffed Suzanne, "she can't play housemaid all day and queen of the castle all night. She must like something besides dolls and painting. Art? Sewing? Books? There's so much more available in Chicago, surely we can find a hobby that will interest her. Maybe she'd like a job that earns a little money so she could travel; buy her own clothes; have some freedom to go to the theater and the art gallery; musical concerts maybe."

"I don't think so. She's never worked in her life except at home."

Suzanne wasn't listening.

"Maybe a half shift at Northwestern? No, too far away. What about the Art Institute, just a few blocks away?"

In a casual conversation Mrs. Matheu lamented how she would miss the Redlegs.

Suzanne looked puzzled. "Miss what?"

"The baseball team. After Harry left and I was alone in the house all day, I listened to the baseball games in the afternoon while I painted."

"You can do that here. There are two teams in Chicago, the Cubs and the White Sox. Have you ever attended a baseball game?"

"No, never. It probably looks different than I imagine. It might be fun to go sometimes."

A season ticket to the Cubs games at Wrigley Field solved the problem. Olga could go whenever she felt like it, she could watch all the game, part of it or throw the ticket away. Suzanne taught her how to use the public transportation. The second summer Olga became more confident. She took her knitting and often attended.

"Gee," Harry marveled, "I wouldn't have believed it."

3.

In the months that followed the trip to Cincinnati, Suzanne created an organizational plan. She led Harry through the development phase while his father and mother moved into the apartment. Side by side at the conference table in Suzanne's office with the organizational papers spread out, she explained her proposal.

"The first step is to create a holding company," she began. "I thought we might call it Mathard. Do you like that name, Harry?"

"Sure." He spread his hands and shrugged. "That's okay."

"Now we have to deal with the financing. I think twenty-five thousand is enough capitalization to start. Do you think that'll do?"

Harry exercised a little more caution this time. Was she looking to him to put up money?

"Well, that's probably okay for a start."

"We'll split sixty-forty in my favor. I'll invest fifteen thousand and lend you ten thousand at five-percent interest for your share. Okay?"

"Yeah."

Her offer blew him away into a galaxy of exploding stars. He had never imagined a time would come when he would actually be speechless but his mouth hung open as he struggled for words. For weeks, he tormented himself with schemes to open the vault, all of them futile. As if by magic, the door opened of its own accord and ten thousand dollars popped into his hand. There stood Lady Luck showing him in to yet another inner sanctum. A tingling sensation ran through his body, which was not the same as making love but a close second. Her suggestion sounded ideal. He almost whooped to think she didn't expect him to put his own cash in the pot. He reached for her hand.

"You're sweet."

"Then we'll form another corporation in the name of the store. What name would you suggest, Harry?"

He expected to be a bystander and had not prepare himself for an active role in this venture. He spouted the first notion that entered his mind.

"Matheu's Men's Furnishings."

She accepted without hesitation and suggested Mr. Matheu hold twenty-five percent share in the store that he could pay for from future profits. Week after week, she guided him through leasehold improvements and arrangements with suppliers. Bunches of applications arrived in response to the advertisement for a sales manager. Harry threw them in the air, closed his eyes and asked Lady Luck to pick. She selected the one that landed nearest his right foot. A dark-haired, handsome matron named Carole presented herself in a conservative business suit. Suzanne suggested he engage her at once and negotiate a suitable salary, which to Harry meant pay her whatever she asked. They advertised for tailors with experience in men's suits and hired two middle-aged men.

Aware that financial matters, especially when conducted by the female partner, could wreck a romance, Suzanne laid out the details with great care. The rent money for both the store and the apartment came to her real estate company and her professional management firm would do all the paper work, payrolls and bookkeeping for a fee. Harry admired her organizational skill.

"It's a pretty slick deal," he told Rocco. "She's provides the dough. I get forty percent of seventy five percent and the old man gets twenty-five. If it fails, what the hell, it's a free ride for both me and the old man."

The organization impressed Rocco, too. He understood and admired that kind of deal—no downside risk, only potential for gain. He thought it reasonable she should receive benefits because of her investment. Harry appreciated the advice, concurred with Suzanne's proposals and considered it a good start for a successful partnership.

In Harry's eagerness to help his father, as well as his need to impress Suzanne, he told everybody about the new store. Rocco, of course, headed his list.

"Now here's the deal," Harry explained. "You tell all your guys about it. When five of them order suits, yours is free, no charge. Then you strut around town telling everybody where you bought it."

Rocco liked the idea but if he strutted Harry's suits then the first should be free, regardless of how many guys he brought in.

"You know, Harry, like I told you before, no downside risk."

They struck a deal. Then Harry visited his trucking customers, city hall and everybody else he could think of, except he didn't offer any more free suits.

The store opened on June 22, 1922 offering everything for the complete men's haberdashery. The number of men in Chicago who needed new suits astonished Mr. Matheu who, at the age of forty-nine, became petrified at the thought of selling to the public. He hid in the basement and appeared when directed by Carole to take measurements.

Suzanne had made Harry a believer, it all seemed so easy.

Chapter 5 – Up the Ladder and Down

1.

Harry rhapsodized, draining his glass. "She's beautiful and she's rich. I mean rich like Croesus."

Rocco gulped his beer, hunched his shoulders, put both elbows on the bar rail and ordered another round.

"Who's he?"

Harry gave him a good-humor slap on the back.

"Never mind."

Rocco glared out of the corner of his eye with his one-more-time-and-your-dead expression.

"Did you lay her?"

"Hell, no. She's not that kind."

"Bullshit." Rocco snarled as if asked to believe that water flowed uphill. "There ain't no other kind."

Harry's association with the opposite sex dwindled after Suzanne entered his life. Distorted visions of opulence warped his thinking into a dazzling fantasy of urbanity—chic clothes, classy cars and Cuban cigars; every indulgence in male satisfaction would soon be his. He considered he had risen above wanton women and prostitutes.

"Gorgeous paramours clamor for my affection."

"Aw, shut up!"

"Listen to them, Rocco. They plead for my love." Harry staggered to his feet in the licentious persona of *Aristide Bruant*. "I caress the Grand Duchess of Something, embrace the Princess of Someplace and kneel at the feet of the Lady of Somewhere." He acted each phrase opposite a visionary beauty, then roared with laughter.

"You're drunk, fercrisake. Sit down."

Suzanne's segregation from the silver screen of his drunken escapades did not bother Harry. He excluded her entrance, real or imaginary, from the taverns of his debauchery. In her presence, he meticulously avoided overindulgence. Gradually, his carousals decreased as the momentum of his amorous affair increased. Passionate evenings at home or dignified nights on the town supplanted all other interests. Even his cartage business suffered, but he never lost sight of the objective. At last, the moment arrived. He proposed. She accepted.

"Meet my family," Suzanne laughed. "You already met fifty percent of them when you met Roberta. The only blood relative I have is my maternal grandmother, Martha, who is in her seventies and I know you'll be sorry to meet her."

"Why?"

"Because we cannot marry in this city without Granny making a big splash on the society page. She has bags of money and there is no other way she would rather spend it. The alternative would be to elope. I could never do that to her."

This revelation resounded in his mind like the notes of a beautiful aria heard for the first time. The shrill tones of the trumpet rang in his ears summoning him to set sail for this new source of treasure a heartbeat away. His resolve to scale the heights multiplied tenfold. Overflowing with eagerness, he recognized the need to be cautious. How sickly and feeble was this possessor of good fortune? Would other relations share this unexpected bounty? He held Suzanne's right hand in both of his and began his exploration in a soft and tender voice.

"Tell me about your mother," he ventured.

"I don't remember her. She—"

"You don't remember her?"

He failed to bring tears to his eyes but he tried hard, wondering how actors cried on cue.

"She drowned in a boating accident when I was four."

"I'm sorry." He enfolded her in his arms, kissed her cheek lovingly and exuded sympathy as if the death occurred the day before yesterday. "What happened?"

"We were boating on the fourth of July. The wind came up and we capsized. Daddy was never sure exactly what happened."

"How terrible! I suppose you stayed with your grandmother."

"No. Martha opposed my parent's marriage from the beginning. She felt Daddy was beneath the family station. She claimed a premonition the marriage would end in disaster and when it did, she blamed him."

"How dreadful!" His uncharacteristic exclamation escaped involuntarily as he cringed at the thought of a family feud complicating the inheritance. "Where did you live?"

"At Albert's."

"Who's he?"

His anxiety-tinged voice could have been mistaken for genuine concern.

"Daddy's supervisor in the janitorial business." Her gaze centered on the fireplace kindling her memories. "After a while, Daddy sold our big house . . .." She shook her head as if coming out of a dream. "But I've told you that before. Surely you don't want to hear it again." Without waiting for an answer, she floated back to her dreamy mood as if hypnotized by the dancing flames. "We lived right here in a black community. He never gave it a second thought. Granny couldn't understand. She doesn't know what it means to be colorblind." A shiver ran through her body and she turned to smile at Harry. "Of course, the result is I'm colorblind too. I've walked the streets in this neighborhood since childhood without the least apprehension. Funny, isn't it, how familiarity dispels fear. I'm never afraid, even at night."

Harry sat quietly waiting for her to continue, not wanting to interrupt her reverie hoping somehow it would lead back to Granny.

"He sent me to the local Catholic school. The kindness of the Sisters strengthened me in the Catholic faith. Under their guidance, I had a good education and a happy childhood." A chuckle escaped her lips. "They made me self-sufficient and idealistic. I have no memory of sadness or depression because my mother wasn't with us. I didn't know I had a granny at that time."

A self-sufficient, granny-less, idealistic woman walking the streets with colorblind eyes missed the point.

"What about Martha while all this was going on?"

"I don't know. I was in my teens when I learned about my mother's side of the family. It devastated me. I couldn't believe Daddy and my grandparents lived in the same city and didn't communicate. It was beyond my understanding, utterly unchristian. He was, well, I don't know. I hate to say malicious but he was certainly bitter. He said she erected the barriers and it was up to her to knock them down."

"And did she?" Harry asked with a quaver in his voice.

"No. I did."

He let out a victory cheer one might expect at a sporting event.

"Hurray! Good for you."

"When Grandfather died, we met at the funeral. She hadn't seen me since early childhood. It was like meeting for the first time. She regretted the years of separation. I remember what she said. 'You are not the reincarnation of your mother. Your black eyes and black hair are not the least like her. But every movement you make, every step you take is exactly like her.' Now, I'm her only living relative. We're very close and I visit often."

Harry heaved a sigh of relief. He imagined a second mountain of gold ingots guarded by a dignified figure busily inscribing Suzanne's name on each one. In his imagination, he kissed the blanched face of the feeble matron, closed the coffin lid and laid her to rest. A smile lit his face.

"No," he said, "we wouldn't want to elope."

2.

Two hurdles remained to spoil the splendor of his conquest; children and religion. Try as he might to leap them, his nerve failed. Several times, he tried to voice his concerns but his courage evaporated at the last minute. Discussion of marital expectations was urgent but the wrong answers would be disastrous. With wedding plans under discussion and dates set, resolution of his apprehensions was critical. In subdued lighting, coiled in each other's arms, he paused, then leaped.

"Do you want to have children?"

"No," she replied without hesitation.

Harry's heart soared over the hurdle. Lady Luck cheered and rang the bell.

"I don't want a family either," he whispered, scarcely believing his good fortune. To him, children were a troublesome interference that would screw-up his impending life of luxury. With a mountain of money to dispose of, who could possibly want children. He never imagined a complication existed in her family pedigree. He mistook her blush as embarrassment when, to his surprise, she quickly shifted to religion.

"Harry, I want you to re-affirm your religious beliefs. Your parents brought you up in the Catholic Church but you haven't attended in years."

No suitable response came to mind. In his desire for admission to the four-hundred, he groomed his cultural enlightenment and intellectual gentility. He attended classic opera, danced at charity balls and visited cloistered museums, but he drew the line at religion. Her exclamations of uncivilized this and barbaric that hammered at him. Religion stood as the remaining barrier to eternal bliss. He brooded in silence. She waited.

"Why is it," he asked at last, "that Galileo was the first person to figure out the world was round?"

"What's that got to do with anything?"

"Well, why didn't Jesus tell everybody the world was round?"

"That's ridiculous, Harry. I don't understand."

"Every kid knows what his father does for a living. Maybe not orphans or abandoned kids, but everybody else knows. Go out on the street, ask anybody, 'What does your old man do for a living?' You'll always get an answer. Jesus was the Son of God. How is it nobody ever asked him what his Daddy did for a living? He must have known his Daddy made round worlds and set them spinning in space. Why didn't he tell anybody? How come somebody else had to discover it by accident fifteen hundred years later?"

She jumped up, her voice raised in anger ignited by his gross irreverence.

"I couldn't live with an attitude like that."

He wavered under her attack, his insecurity missing the ambiguity of her statement. He interpreted it to mean she couldn't live with somebody who expressed such an attitude. This violent counterattack resulted not in retreat, but in capitulation. He accepted. If he wasn't going to have children, he supposed he could put up with religion.

"Of course, I'll re-join the church," he said, waving a carefree hand like a white flag of surrender and smiling as if it had been his intent from the beginning. She threw her arms around his neck, obviously delighted with his response. She held the embrace and whispered into his ear.

"There's something else to discuss, Harry."

His nerves tensed. He quivered at the thought of yet another barrier reef. Navigating these continual shoals was a nerve-racking task. He longed to sail into the deep water away from threats of disaster. His voice strained with emotion.

"What is it?"

"I'm a member of the Lucy Stone League."

He guessed a religious connection and feared the worst.

"What's that?"

"Women's suffrage."

"Oh!"

Clinging to him, her arms tightened around his neck, her body tensed as if she expected he would hit her. Then she blurted out her fear.

"It means when we marry I will keep my birth surname."

He turned his head and saw her eyes tightly closed. He had no idea why.

"Okay," he said.

3.

Before the official announcement of their engagement, Suzanne presented Harry to Granny Martha. He eagerly accepted the challenge. Blessing his mother for the years of formal dinners and etiquette instruction, he happily took part in a postgraduate refresher course offered by his fiancée. Suzanne sought to moderate the swings from emotional overacting to disheveled sloppiness. She pleaded with him to strike a happy balance, which indeed he did in fear that his failure to do so would sour the engagement. As their intimacy expanded, his knowledge of art, opera and the classics led her to believe beneath the surface of this rough diamond there was a genuine treasure.

His first sight of Mrs. Charles Arlene staggered him. She was anything but old and feeble. In fact, she looked as if she had just finished a rousing game of tennis and expected another as soon as the party was over. Without prior knowledge, he would have guessed her age to be late fifties. She was radiantly attractive, with a robust, athletic figure and a face that exuded beauty and eyes that laughed at life. She wore conservative jewels and exquisite finery, inspiring Harry to heights of eloquence he didn't know he possessed.

Harry wore striped gray-black trousers, black morning coat with white beading on the vest, gray spats and a gray ascot tie with a diamond stickpin. No one at the gathering compared with him in elegant costume and he relished center stage. He made a formal bow and kissed Mrs. Arlene's hand. His manners were faultless; rising when women entered, giving the men a hearty handshake, placing his serviette daintily across his knee and drinking his tea with his pinky delicately extended. He declined to smoke, admitting that he often enjoyed a cigarette, but it was inappropriate in such a beautiful home. He gave Suzanne a surreptitious wink and a broad grin as she, too, declined to indulge. Throughout the proceedings, he discussed what he could recall about opera and music. What he couldn't remember he blandly disguised by confessing it had been sometime since he had attended a performance of the particular subject and perhaps Mrs. Arlene could refresh his memory.

Suzanne and Harry married in a Catholic ceremony in Evanston, Illinois on November 18, 1922, under the aegis of Mrs. Charles Arlene.

4.

The sensuality Suzanne experienced in bed with Harry overcame the last throes of despondency about Joe's death. Her dreamy recollection of enchanted childhood Sunday afternoons grew dim.

"It's a voyage of discovery, Harry; of joys I've never known."

His hands were everywhere. He kissed her neck, caressed her breasts and roamed her body until her desire reached a longing she could barely endure. He gently placed his body on top of hers. She thrilled in the slow, deep penetration and the prolonged pause as he pressed into her. Then he began the gentle rhythmic motion, quickening the tempo leading to the final thrust of the brutal, almost violent, exhilarating climax.

It became their habit after sex to light a cigarette. Occasionally, they had a drink and sometimes a repeat performance. The emotional adventure of love raised Suzanne to a new level but the physical side of marriage thrust her on to a platform of airy beatitude.

They lay in bed, naked, tenderly caressing.

"Merchandising is like making love, Harry."

"The hell it is."

"I mean it's new, it's different, something I never experienced before."

"I guess that's true."

"You've changed my life, Harry."

Her hand messed his hair. She kissed his neck.

"Oh, Harry," she whispered into his ear, "the euphoric exploration of your world has opened a life of excitement. The insidious distortions have imperceptibly transposed my daily ritual."

"Jesus, Susie, you're using words I don't even know what they mean."

"That's the way I feel, Harry, darling. Poetic."

"It doesn't sound like poetry to me. What are you talking about?"

The talk ended.

In the languorous bedroom atmosphere, she meditated on the wonderful changes Harry introduced. Before they met, she seldom drank. As their courtship progressed, so did the frequency of her imbibing. After they married, the few drinks on a date became cocktails every night.

Her hands drifted across his chest.

She enjoyed getting a little tipsy before dinner when their voices grew loud and the arguments vociferous. The debates never dealt with income, but rather with spending and acquisition.

Her right hand swirled around his stomach and a finger explored his navel.

Harry suggested a new car. They argued about what make. He won. She paid for it. He joked about his wardrobe, saying he had a friend who owned a clothing business. They discussed suits and style, jackets and casuals and the proper accessories for each. She paid for them, too.

She caressed his thighs and her fingers moved ever so gently up and down.

He said two hundred a week spending money would be satisfactory. She gave it to him. The intimate dinners in quiet surroundings turned into whoop-de-do carousals. She loved being on the town, slumming and dancing at the Trianon Ballroom. She did not think about her sporadic attendance at church.

She straddled him and forgot to remind him of his commitment to religion.

5.

At the soirées given by Mrs. Arlene, their circle of friends expanded and they moved into a wider social arena. Harry's concentration during courting precluded his recognition of name-dropping as an important artifice among the nouveau riche. Their new friends mentioned prominent names in every conversation forcing him to dream up responses to their mundane palaver.

Over cigar and port after dinner: "I lunched with Mr. Big Wheel yesterday. Do you know him, Harry?"

"Yes, that is I'll probably be discussing our investment portfolio with him."

At tea on Sunday afternoon: "I shan't tell you what I'll be wearing at the Snobbish Ball, darling. Do you have your costume selected, Harry?"

"I'll be talking to my father. He's marvelous at that sort of thing."

At the Charity Ball: "We'll sit in the Governor's box. Will we see you at the opera, Harry, dear?"

"Unfortunately not, Mrs. Highhat, I'm expecting a visitor from out of town."

Since he found the cocktail talk absurd and did not want to expose his uncomfortable feeling to Suzanne, he sought to cultivate somebody who could guide him through the door of acceptability. He chose Jim Blankenship, the young banker several rungs above him gaining prominence in the same social circles. Of course, asking directly would display his insecurity; hence, he beat around the bush searching for whatever hints might light his way and keep him out of trouble.

"I tell you, Jim, Suzanne has done a great job in the store. Some important people are buying. Do you know the mayor, Jim?"

Of course, the mayor didn't come into the store personally, but somebody who knew him once did.

"It's been a success since the day I hired Carole."

Not wanting to miss a chance for realism, Jim asked, "You still driving that truck?"

"Not much. Don't have time. I could hire a driver but then I'd have the payroll problem. Must be some better way."

"Mr. Carthauler's always buying trucks."

"Think you could arrange a meeting, Jim?"

Mr. Carthauler bought the truck and introduced his wife in the process.

With Mrs. Arlene's help, Harry and Suzanne followed Jim up the ladder. They met Mr. and Mrs. High Society, Mr. and Mrs. Big League, the Reverend and Mrs. Rich Church and many others who circulated in the strata that considered name-dropping gauche. Harry became popular among this crowd. They classified him as an old-world court jester who normally would use the servant's entrance except that his darling wife deserved better.

With the truck sold and his wife at work all day, Harry found plenty of time to discuss the clothing business.

"You know, Jim," he remarked one day at lunch, "that clothing business is an eye-opener for a guy like me, brought up to believe that earning money means toiling with your hands. The entire venture has fallen into place with no physical labor on my part. A little planning and organizing, that's it."

"That's the way you get rich."

"It sure is a change when you're not involved in the daily routine. I keep my finger on the pulse but the truth is I'm making money and not doing much of anything to make it happen. Hell of a lot better than selling cars and driving trucks. By the way, why don't you drop by and pick up a new suit?"

Harry struggled to explain Suzanne's doctrine as if it were his own strategy.

"It's simple. Hire the least number of mechanics—that's a term I adopted from the trucking business—to perform the necessary tasks and keep the professionals out." Harry found it a strange coincidence when he realized that Rocco managed precisely the same way but he knew better than to mention it. Jim lost interest in Harry's obsequious bootlicking.

"Do you think your wife would move her account over to my bank?"

Harry didn't hear the question.

"The other day Suzanne told me when she worked for her father after college she watched business organizations hiring more and more people creating higher and higher overhead. This didn't make sense to her. She thinks when you hire an engineer, an accountant, a lawyer, or any professional you automatically commit yourself to care for him and his family forever. She says they eat into the organization and bury themselves like wood beetles in a tree. They lose their incentive to produce. What do you think, Jim?"

"Huh?"

"I don't know," Harry continued as if Jim were in total agreement. "Suppose you pay a guy ten thousand a year. Based on a fifty-week year and fifty-hour week that's four dollars an hour. You could hire permanent people for less than that."

Jim dragged himself back into the conversation.

"I don't think that's what she meant," he said. "She was talking about part time employees."

Harry played the conversation back to Suzanne at cocktails that evening.

"Jim's right," Suzanne said. "You don't hire them full time; you hire when you need them. Just look in the telephone book. Any service you want is available. If you don't like the mechanic you get, you kick him out and get another and another until you find the good one. Believe me, Harry, he's out there somewhere. You leave all that to me. I'm telling you, it is much better for a small organization to buy services from outside the firm."

Leave it to her he did without mentioning that he saw her theory as self-serving. The rapid expansion of the business demanded more and more services resulting in ever increasing bills from her professional agency. He assumed her bull-headed reason was that she made money from the store whereas he only gained from the net profits. Still, he kept his mouth shut. His polite nod of the head yielded an astonishing surprise.

"Harry, I have a suggestion. I want you to be a success, like your friend Jim. At one time, you were in the car business and you're a good mechanic. Maybe you could find something in the automotive line. I know you're proud of your Dad and the store and . . .. Well, I guess what I'm saying is you need something of your own. I'm willing to lend you another ten thousand. It'll give you some working capital or you can use it as collateral with Jim, if you like."

The next day she called his bank.

"This is Miss Haldimann speaking, Mr. Blankenship." She went through the details of her offer. "And I want you to send me a copy of the monthly account statement."

In his first direct conversation with Miss Haldimann, Jim gladly adopted any arrangement she wanted. "Of course, it'll be confidential," he offered.

Meanwhile Harry construed her offer as evidence the spending spree continued unabated. He did not realize the ecstasy of the marriage bed had worn off. As Suzanne settled to earth and totaled up the bills, she stopped the unrestricted spending. In her view, it was a good party; she paid for it but the frolic was over. Harry had not yet learned Suzanne was more cautious than any banker ever thought of being. He assumed the inexhaustible distribution would be his for the asking.

Harry's enterprise, whatever it was, produced a startling return on investment. He refused to reveal the exact nature of his business.

"The funds are for my use," he reminded her. "It's going to be my secret until I'm well established."

The second monthly report revealed an increase that amazed Suzanne.

"I don't want to pry into your business, darling," she said, "but how is it going?"

"Well."

"What exactly are you doing?"

"Trading."

He refused to tell her anything more and she chose to await further developments. Her questions might suggest a degree of distrust that could adversely affect their marriage. Each month she launched the same conversation and each time he sidestepped. She considered he might be gambling but discarded the notion. The degree of success was too phenomenal. She had several choices to attack the issue. She chose a discussion with Sergio Cellini and made her way to the filthy Cicero office.

"It's foolish, Miss Haldimann. Your husband is playing a dangerous game, financing an activity that's against the law. But the danger is not the law, which can be easily subverted, it is with his associates who have neither morals nor scruples. It would be wise if he gave it up."

"What is he doing, Mr. Cellini?"

"Loan-sharking."

Suzanne gasped. "With Rocco, I suppose."

"Exactly."

"Can you tell me anything else?"

"They're in a fifty-fifty split. They each put twenty-five in the pot. If anything goes wrong, Rocco attends to the dirty work."

"Twenty-five . . . hundred?"

Cellini laughed. "You've a lot to learn, Miss Haldimann—twenty-five thousand."

At the first opportunity, she tried to make it as painless as possible for Harry.

"There are two rules of business you must never violate," she told him pleasantly. "First, don't ever do anything illegal. Second, declare all your income and pay all your taxes."

Harry worried about how much she knew. Could she possibly be in contact with Rocco in some mysterious way? Or was it that other guy she knew? He didn't dare ask but the inference was clear. He violated her rules and his excessive fear of upsetting her dictated an end to the friendship with Rocco, who cursed and swore violently when Harry announced his withdrawal. After Rocco tempered his fury, he refused to give Harry the last five thousand.

"After all I done for you and now you fink out on me," Rocco said.

Harry could do nothing but accept the terms of separation.

"Some day I'll—"

Rocco laughed.

"Any time, sonny boy, any time at all."

Harry vowed the day would come when he would even the score. He figured Rocco had screwed him for more than fifteen thousand dollars over the years. If it took a lifetime, he'd get it back. In his ruminations, Harry remained unaware how close he came to the bottom of the lake.

6.

Harry had about fifty thousand dollars in the bank although he owed Suzanne twenty and Jim fifteen. Still, that was enough to elicit a comfortable feeling of affluence. He bought clothes made by his dad, traded for a new car made by Henry Ford and smoked expensive cigars made by Cubans. After his break-up with Rocco, he had nothing to do. He discussed his problems with Jim.

"I can't get the clothing business out of my mind. We don't make the clothes, my father does. We don't sell the clothes, Carole does. Suzanne's got her empire. I have nothing. What I need, Jim, is a bunch of mechanics to perform their daily chores for the benefit of Harry Matheu."

"Have you every thought about the stock market?"

"No."

"I'm going to put you in touch with a friend of mine named Moat. He's very conservative. Talk with him. Explore the possibilities. That'll give you something to study to fill the time on your hands."

Harry worked hard at understanding the market and bellyached whenever the opportunity arose.

"Damnedest game I ever saw. Legal gambling, that's all it is. And slow; hell I made more money in a week in the lending business that I make in six months in the market."

The unexpected benefit was the respect it produced. Being an investor in legitimate stocks and bonds fostered esteem; a plateau from which one could dish out any amount of lies and nonsense.

"Bought two hundred Brazilian Traction today at twenty-two. Moat expects it'll go to twenty-five next year." Big deal; ten to twelve months to earn six hundred dollars. Rocco made that much in the morning on a bad day. He stuck with it because Suzanne admired his ameliorated conservatism.

His impatience with conservatism and yearning for wealth led him to another broker; an astute risk-taker named Abie Fishbein who preached "buy in the morning, sell in the afternoon." With plenty of time on his hands, Harry learned to read the ticker tape, to recognize what moved, and which way. He arrived at Abie's office before eight each morning and didn't leave until he reviewed the closing averages. He ventured into commodities, puts and calls, short and long sales.

"This is more like it," he said, "the kind of action I enjoy."

"Just keep reinvesting," Fishbein replied, "and watch your money grow."

"That's great advice," Harry laughed. "Your fees grow pretty good too."

"Don't you worry about my fees. You sit right there and worry about your money. Let me tell you this. What you're doing only works if you're sitting here everyday. It's a full time job, making money. You turn your back and the market will wipe you out in a day. If you aren't sitting here, then sell out and buy Ma Bell."

Harry bought heavily on margin and borrowed extensively from Blankenship. His manipulations yielded profits far above the interest charges and more than covered the losses.

"Suzanne, my dear, I am paying my taxes, I'm living within the law and that son-of-a-bitch Rocco is out of my life."

He had a full time occupation making money with nothing to worry about. The marriage dividend he craved came to fruition. He wondered if she noticed his manicured nails.

The excitement soon paled. In six months, he did well enough to clear his margin account and pay off Suzanne leaving about thirty thousand in cash and securities, debt free.

"Susie, I'm going to get out of this rat race. I'm going to buy the safe stuff and look for something else to do."

"I'm delighted, Harry. I think you're wise. You've had a good, exciting run, but you can't keep it going forever." Harry's dissociation from the underworld, investment in conservative securities and interest in a lawful business lent a degree of assurance to their marriage that was comforting.

"What do you have in mind?"

Despite his fear of Rocco, he admired how the guy operated. He admired how Suzanne did her business too. He ached to achieve the exalted status of Rocco and Suzanne.

"I don't know. I'll look around."

7.

Harry entered a candy shop to buy Suzanne a treat. He lingered a while questioning the young woman behind the counter. He found what he wanted.

"I'm going into the candy business," he told Suzanne. "But I'm going to make it an ice cream business in the summer and candy in the winter. Set up an operator same as the old man in the clothing business."

He found a manufacturer who agreed to supply ice cream at Harry's stipulated price and chocolate syrup that, when put in contact with the cold ice cream, hardened almost instantly. He offered a complete package, guaranteed the store lease, underwrote the supply contracts and waited for the money to roll in. The girl invested nothing. Her name may or may not have been Mabel, Suzanne never knew, but Mabel-Cones became the name of the store.

"In honor of Danny's wife," he explained to Suzanne, "who first told me about you."

Harry was ecstatic. Suzanne's daring created the clothing business. This would even the score. It would be his accomplishment equal to hers. This time they would split sixty-forty in his favor.

"If you're interested. If not," he shrugged, "I'll finance it myself."

Suzanne was skeptical and declined to participate. She warned him it was his money at risk, not hers. He judged this remark as one of envy.

"Harry, I don't think you should be so willing to finance everything. The girl has no investment, no incentive to stay."

He ignored her advice.

"Rented office space today," he reported. "Hired a manager," soon followed. Then came, "New bookkeeper on board to-day. Wages are reasonable. Much less than I'd pay for outside professionals." He'd show her he could get along without her goddamn professional interference. He carried on like the sorcerer's apprentice, completely out of control.

He searched for a second operator and opened another outlet. In the following summer, he offered the same package to a third and a fourth. He put his own twist on the deal. Each one of them must call herself Mabel and must personally work in the store.

Throughout Chicago, Mabel-Cones became a recognized trade name. "Mabel-Cones Inc.," raised Harry to an executive position and he ordered business cards with the title "President" beneath his name. He longed for an office with a walnut door and gold leaf letters but his landlord refused to allow it. At every opportunity, he boasted; from army sergeant to entrepreneurial magnate in four years and the first in his family to achieve the American dream. A limit did not exist on the horizon of the future, nor could he see any storm clouds in the sky.

"Harry, I hope your business is not too seasonal. Your prices are low and ice cream has a short season, " Suzanne said.

"Don't worry. Chocolate in the winter is as popular as ice cream in the summer."

"I hope so."

Harry was wrong but his pride precluded the admission that small summer profits did not cover losses experienced in the winter. What he lost on individual stores he thought he could make up in volume. He opened more stores.

8.

The behavioral exceptions to their high life were the numberless visits to Mrs. Arlene, nearly always promoted by Harry. On each occasion, he dressed magnificently and performed flawlessly.

"I've got a great idea," he said one night on the way home from the big mansion. "Let's have a dinner party and take everybody to the opera. I noticed the other day they'll be presenting The Girl of the Golden West by Puccini."

"That's a wonderful idea. I'll do the guest list; you arrange the box."

Harry came home at noon on the day of the party. He poured a drink.

"Everything organized, Roberta?"

"Miss Suzanne told me exactly what she wants and you stay out of this, Mr. Harry."

He poured another drink and went to the kitchen to harass Roberta.

"What's the menu, tonight?"

"Mr. Harry, I told you to get on out of here. Miss Suzanne looked after everything. Now go on. Get out of here."

It was a test of his will against hers but clawing at Roberta would gain no points from Suzanne. He conceded victory and flopped down in the drawing room to finish yet another drink.

"Roberta, I'm going out," he yelled through the kitchen door. "I'll be back about five."

"The guests is coming at six. Don't be late."

Goddamn it. He hated that black bitch. He wandered over to West Taylor Street. The place was empty. He sat alone and drowned his anger in beer.

He returned home a little after five. Suzanne flitted about directing a house full of imported servants.

"Harry, we won't be serving any drinks tonight. Granny's coming and you know how she feels about liquor."

"Now you mind," Roberta added.

He swung around with his hand raised about to strike her.

"Harry! Stop it!" Suzanne stepped in front of him. He lowered his arm. "Go dress!"

In a seething rage, he stopped at the bar, mixed a jug of martinis and carried it to the bedroom. When the guests arrived, he was foolishly drunk. He overplayed his graciousness with inappropriate jokes and monopolized the conversation in a vociferous tone. The final insult occurred at the opera when he fell asleep and snored like a slumbering hog. Mrs. Arlene was indignant. Suzanne was furious.

"You better damn well apologize and do it quick," Suzanne warned the next morning. "I will not accept insulting Granny Martha. I'm going to see her this afternoon to apologize and I'm going alone. So I suggest you do something about seeking her forgiveness, if that's possible."

"I know the men drink," Martha moaned. "It's deplorable and I hate it. I heartily endorse prohibition. But in public! Really, that was disgraceful, Suzanne."

"I'm afraid it's worse than you might guess."

"Why? What on earth do you mean, dear?"

The ill wind from Harry's debacle had indeed blown some good. Suzanne divulged the distortions in her life; the late nights, the heavy drinking and the frequent carousals. She spoke from embarrassment and shame.

"Harry and I have been living a fast life," she confessed. "We've cast Church by the wayside, I'm ashamed to say. And he's become vindictive with this ridiculous ice cream business."

Suzanne's confession aroused Martha's sympathy but she hesitated while the maid brought in the tea service. Suzanne moved to the settee and watched Martha pour.

"Cream and sugar?"

"Thank you."

Suzanne passed the scones, helped herself and gently stirred her tea.

At last, Martha broke the silence.

"My dear child, I, too, have a confession to make," she whispered. "When I first met your husband he so impressed me I actually wished your mother had found such a man. How mistaken I was! I hope you will understand."

Suzanne smiled weakly.

"Yes, Granny, I understand." They sipped their tea.

Again, Martha broke the silence.

"May I ask you a personal question?"

"Granny, you may ask me anything."

Martha hesitated.

"Do you plan to raise a family?"

"No," Suzanne responded, almost defiantly. "Harry and I have agreed we will not have any children."

"It's for the best."

"You know why, don't you?"

"Yes, I do. Your father told me. While I think your forbearance is a terrible burden, I do believe it's for the best. More tea, dear?"

Confession welded the union between grandmother and granddaughter with mutual support and comfort. Harry shrugged. He lied to himself that he didn't give a damn about the sponsorship by Mrs. Arlene. If she chose to be as narrow-minded about her granddaughter's husband as she was about her daughter's husband, then he would behave as Joe Haldimann did. He would remember the date, February 1925, and see how long it took her to regret her snub.

Chapter 6 – Stefan Arlene Matheu

1.

Suzanne experienced a foreboding of disaster after Harry's fall from grace. Some comfort emerged from her disclosure to Martha but relating her transgressions over tea did nothing to ease her turmoil as she entered the confessional.

"Yes, Father, I am truly contrite."

Father Lalonde administered penance and forgiveness. The next week she invited him to dine, being careful to select a night when Harry would not be home.

"Your youth was extraordinarily difficult," Father rhapsodized as he liberally sprinkled sympathy and understanding. "I remember your father, so devoted to you and such a great supporter of the church." On his departure, she gave him a check for five thousand dollars and suggested a Mass for Joe Haldimann.

Absolution failed to relieve her discomfort, however. Perhaps the weather brought on her depression, the melting snow creating an appalling morass of ugliness. Impossible! After living through thirty years of Chicago springs, surely she was immune to dirty slush. The morning nausea created thoughts of incurable ailments acerbating her tendency towards hypochondria.

Married life reached a plateau of mutual tolerance as Suzanne and Harry virtually ignored each other. She rose late, stayed home and went to bed early. He left early, stayed out and went to bed late.

When they talked, he inquired about her health and suggested she call the doctor. After repeated denials, he stopped asking. She didn't care that her sullen irascibility provoked his anger. Her appetite disappeared and she gave up smoking and alcohol, which did nothing to improve her disposition shuffling about the house wrapped in a blanket. They followed their separate paths; she to read, write or sleep and he, well, she knew not where and chose not to ask. Every evening she huddled in her cocoon in the living room. He seldom joined her.

In the third week of March, imagining herself with every disease known to humanity, she consulted her doctor. That evening, she waited for Harry in the living room. At half past ten, he sauntered in wearing a silly grin with a pompous air.

"Hey! Still up?" He flung his hat towards the closet door and left it lying on the floor. "Feeling better?"

"Yes, thank you."

"I think I'll have a beer. How about you?"

"No thanks."

He uncapped a bottle and filled a schooner.

"Cigarette?"

The empty bottle banged on the bar.

"No thank you," she said.

He flopped in a chair and opened the newspaper. She watched.

"Harry . . .."

Perhaps he didn't hear her lonely cry. Although he sat in the room, she felt alone. Loneliness never bothered her before. She thought of solitude as a heady wine that intoxicated her with freedom. She loved the quickening beat of early spring alone in a forest glade. High on a hilltop, she heard the silence of a majestic mountain. When the world fell silent, nature made noises everywhere as the creatures communed with each other. This evening, solitude filled her with bitterness and a burden she could not bear alone. She wanted love and tenderness. Harry lit a cigarette; sipped his drink From behind the newspaper, a smoke ring soared up to the ceiling. Suzanne sat with her head bowed, hands in her lap; not drinking, not smoking, not moving.

"Something bothering you?"

She sighed deeply.

"Yes."

"What?"

"I saw a doctor today."

"Oh, yeah." His head did not appear from behind the newspaper. "Sick?"

She tensed at his indifference. She wanted to rip the newspaper from his hands and demand his attention; she wanted to scream that she was dying; at least she wished she would die, which was the same thing.

"No," she answered.

"Then what's the matter?"

Her classmates watch, cajoling her to dive mindless of the terror in her heart. Their screams reverberate from the roof, the walls, the water below, endlessly jeering. Her palpitating heart wants air her lungs will not provide. She stands immobile, a statue in space on the high board. A shiver creeps through her body, her limbs begin to tremble. Two laughing girls clamber up the ladder. They will force her to . . . she gulps for air and dives. Down and down, she plunges into the water. The bubbles make a gargle noise like blowing air through a straw into a glass of water. She cannot breathe. She runs to the dressing room, buries her head in a towel and cries and cries. Even Sister Marguerite cannot console her.

She knew she had no choice then and she didn't have one now. She must dive again. She closed her eyes and leaped into the abyss of sordid hopelessness.

"I'm pregnant."

She held her breath and waited.

"Did you say something?"

"Yes. I said I'm pregnant."

A chuckle emerged from behind the newspaper. Did he hear or was he reading the comics? She had worried from the moment the doctor confirmed her condition, unsure what reaction to expect, but she never, in her wildest imaginings, thought he would laugh.

"Harry! For God's sake, it's not funny."

He sat, unmoving, as nonchalant as if she said his parents were coming to dinner.

"I think it's funny as hell. When's the abortion?"

She sat upright, hands clutching the edge of the pillow seat suppressing a scream. She closed her eyes to stop the flood, hoping the ringing in her ears would cease.

"I'll think about it."

"What the hell is there to think about?" He laughed again. "We made a pact, no children. You agreed to an abortion so get on with it."

She pushed forward to the edge of her chair, white knuckles squeezing the pillow.

"I agreed to no such thing. I said I didn't want a child but I never said I would have an abortion."

"Christ Almighty! It's the same goddamn thing. You'll fucking well get an abortion and that's all there is to it."

She jumped to her feet.

"Don't you ever use that word in my presence. Never! Never! Never! Do you hear me? Never!"

She stormed out of the room, up the stairs to the bedroom, locked the door and flung herself on the bed. She needed succor and cuddling; he gave her disdain and vulgarity. So easy to pledge when a life wasn't at stake. The embryo within her body changed everything. Perhaps somebody else's fetus, somebody else's body—no, even then she knew she could not destroy life. The doctor had listened to her story. She did not want to hear his answer but she knew she must ask.

"Can you do anything?" She looked at the floor struggling to mouth the word she did not want to say. "An abortion, perhaps?"

His peremptory dismissal of her suggestion strengthened her conviction.

"I will not entertain any thoughts of an abortion. It's contrary to my Hippocratic oath and it is contrary to your religion."

She lay still craving help, pleading for consolation. An hour passed, perhaps two. She ached to talk with Daddy. He would help. Youthful disobedience, teenage rebellion and mature impetuosity—he soothed them all with love, understanding and comfort. She was alone on the threshold of the greatest emotional crisis of her life. She recalled Daddy's words.

> I never knew my mother, Suzanne, I never saw her in my life. My father wasn't sure; he was drunk at the time. He thought she may have been a mulatto, but maybe she was an Indian. I can't take back what the old man did but I can warn you there's danger in being a mother. Look at yourself, Suzanne. Black hair; all the family has brown or tan hair. Black eyes; my father, Aunt Jane and all her children have blue eyes. I know nothing of biology or genetics but it looks like you carry the traits of that unknown woman. At your conception, I wanted your mother to abort but she wouldn't hear of it. Now you know why I've directed you to other pursuits, to fill your life with interests that will provide you with fullness instead of childbearing.

With the facts before him, the doctor's spoke softly.

"I think there's a possibility your father may have been right. There is a chance the traits will be evident in the next generation. It is impossible to predict."

She fell asleep thinking of her mother, the beautiful woman in the pictures who faced the same situation and did not yield.

2.

Roberta and Suzanne sat in the sun porch overlooking the garden of the Evanston home purchased shortly after the wedding. Beside the garage, the first tulips pushed through the melting snow. Ecstatic about the pregnancy, Roberta likened the miracle of childbearing to the reawakening of nature.

"Why honey, when you was sick, I was so worried and here all the time wasn't nothing to worry about."

"I worried, too. I was so sure I'd never have a baby I didn't consider it. But there's nothing to worry about now."

The noticeable tremor in Roberta's hand was more important. Suzanne didn't miss the occasional grimace of pain on the old woman's face. Roberta would suddenly sit unable to continue. When Suzanne asked, the answers were denials. The thinning hair, the gnarled fingers and the stooped shoulders told their story.

"I'm all right but I'm worried about you."

Roberta sighed.

"The chars and day-maids never does the work right. I chases them all the time; may as well do it myself. I is so tired at night when the cooking's done I can't hardly stand up. It be too much for me, Suzanne, my dear. There just ain't nothing I can do."

Suzanne laughed.

"I don't suppose there's ever been a day in your life when you could let somebody else do the work. Do you remember when you first came to our house?"

"I remember well." She wiped at her face with her apron. "I remember your years growing up and that memory fills my heart with joy. Everything's worked out so nice. My! My! How happy your daddy would be to know you's gonna have a child."

"I wish that was true," Suzanne mumbled. Deep in her reminiscence, Roberta ignored the remark.

"Honey, I got to tell you my job's done. All I wants is to sit quietly until it's my time to go."

Roberta's pain was obvious on her face and her plea did not alarm Suzanne who provided an apartment and a full-time nurse.

When, at last, she died, Suzanne did not find the experience as devastating as her previous meeting with Death. She had time to visit, time to devote to Roberta's needs and time to prepare for the inevitable. Suzanne accepted the situation with composure, arranged a gracious funeral and proper burial.

The replacements were never satisfactory. Suzanne routinely hired and fired servants—youthful women, middle-aged women, women with children, married couples—nobody pleased. One day Olga Matheu told Suzanne her sister's eldest daughter and her husband sought household employment. Nadia and Josef moved in. It astounded Harry to learn Nadia was his cousin.

3.

Almost five years had passed since the death of Joe Haldimann; five emotional years that carried Suzanne from reclusive virginity to troubled motherhood. One of the ramifications of child bearing that worried her was the real estate. She reflected on her obstinacy in refusing Syd's counsel and, as usual, asked Phillip Silverstein.

"I think my insistence on keeping father's real estate holdings may have been a mistake."

"Why?"

"Two reasons; my pregnancy mainly and, while I hate to admit it, the real estate has no personal meaning for me. Listening to renters bellyache is not a mother's job. The properties are a millstone around my neck, albeit a golden one."

"That's a long-winded way of saying you want to get out."

"You always come right to the point don't you."

"That's what you pay me for. Talk to Sidorowitz."

"Sidorowitz! Phillip I thought you would have something better to suggest. I'm embarrassed to call him. Once I told him—"

"We all make mistakes. There is nobody better to suggest. Swallow your pride, call him and apologize."

Syd's voice reflected his surprise.

"Of course I'll look after it for you."

He continued the conversation asking questions about her welfare, pleased to learn about her pregnancy.

"It'll take time to sell." he cautioned. "Your properties have never been on the market. I'll have to make it known they're available."

She wondered if Silverstein had made a mistake. She casts her doubts aside for never once had he misguided her.

Three months later Phillip called to say he had a proposal from a New York firm.

"It's more favorable than we expected but it involves long-term financial participation on your part. It'll take eight years, closing in December 1933. Good company; I think you should accept it."

Not only was she out of the real estate business and into the mortgage business but she had made her peace with Syd Sidorowitz.

4.

With abortion eliminated, Suzanne hallucinated in bed at night. Nightmares tormented her sleep—a disfigured child shunned in school, haunted by cruel playmates and ostracized by a heartless world. The worst that always woke her was a hideous girl in a sideshow reaching out endlessly repeating the single word, "Mummy". Awake, tossing and turning, she fought to protect her child from the stranger asleep beside her. How would Harry behave? Would he abuse the child? Was her marriage finished? Alone in the dark kitchen sipping warm milk, she struggled to put a positive face on her fears. She had money to employ nursemaids, provide tutors and select the best school. Back in bed, the images came again—freakish images, scrawny, skeletal, deformed creatures—depriving her of sleep. In the second trimester, a psychiatrist analyzed her anxiety. She faced Harry with the truth.

"Regardless of your belief that I am breaking my vow, regardless of my promise to love, honor and obey, regardless of my business interests, I have irreversibly charted my course. I will not abandon my child. I dedicate myself to overcoming whatever handicaps she may encounter through no fault of her own. My daughter will have a truly devoted mother." Harry could do nothing in the face of her determination.

On November 11, 1925, she bore a son. Harry tried to play the glad-handing father, passing out cigars but the birth mortified him. He was aghast when he laid eyes on the child.

"He looks like a goddamn nigger. I told you to have an abortion, but no, you wouldn't listen to me. Well it's your damn problem, not mine."

"No," the doctor said, "the child is not Negro. He is definitely Caucasian but he does have dark skin. He appears to have high cheekbones that will mold his face somewhat as he matures, perhaps slant his eyes a little. I would guess an Oriental cast rather than Indian or Negroid. Your husband is wrong and unjust in his accusation."

5.

Suzanne sought Harry's help in selecting a name, hoping for companionship. He disclaimed any interest. With no contribution from him, she turned to her mother-in-law.

"I'm thinking about the baby's grandfathers, Olga. I want to use the name Joseph but I'm intrigued by Mr. Matheu's name."

Olga, who sometimes spoke without thinking, said, "Your father's name was Joe, not Joseph." Reluctantly, Suzanne agreed.

They did not debate the selection of the middle name. It would be Arlene in memory of Suzanne's mother and to honor her grandmother.

She and Olga considered every possible combination. Having narrowed it down to the choice between Joseph and Stefan, they chose the latter because the initials SAM seemed better than JAM. They laughed, thinking it a silly basis for deciding. Harry surprised them, opting for Sam the moment they told him. Suzanne made an effort to use the Christian name but soon gave up. Forever after, she called him Sam.

The baby fascinated Suzanne.

"Look at him, Olga, beautiful dark complexion. I don't think of his color as black or red. It's oriental mandarin blended with polished ivory."

"He'll be a distinctive man with his black hair and deep, mystical eyes."

"Look how those little crests beneath his eyes accentuate his square face; and the cleft below his mouth and the broad chin."

The two of them fussed over the child convincing themselves whatever chromosomes the unknown ancestor contributed, Stefan was an adorable, beautiful baby.

Suzanne knew when she arrived home from the hospital, she would need permanent help. In the interim, Olga was at hand.

"I am free," she told Suzanne, moving into one of the spare rooms, forsaking her husband. "I can devote the entire winter to little Stefan."

Neither the euphoric atmosphere nor the convivial domesticity lasted long. The pressure was too much; from the puling child, from the anxious mother, from the forlorn mother-in-law, from the forsaken father-in-law and from the uncomfortable father. The friction heated the household into aggravated petulance; tempers flared with raised voices and slammed doors.

Nadia and Josef, both of whom came from Old World families, were aghast at the performance. Child bearing was a commonplace event expected to bring joy, happiness and sharing. They made suggestions to each other as to how they might help. Nadia deplored the situation with tears in her eyes proposing they seek employment elsewhere.

"No! No! Out of the question. We never find another job as good as this one," Josef admonished.

So they remained silent and closed their minds to the turmoil swirling around them. Nadia dared not say a word about her thoughts to Miss Haldimann. Much to her surprise and delight, she didn't have to. Suzanne brought the problem to Nadia.

"When we engaged you, Nadia, I remember you telling me you were the oldest in a large family. Have you had experience with children?"

"Oh yes, Miss Haldimann. I did everything for my youngest brothers. Twins they were and mother was sick for a few months after they were born. We couldn't afford help so I was the nursemaid."

The savior had been there from the beginning.

"Would it be unreasonable to ask you to help me with Stefan?"

Thus, Nadia embarked on her second career as a surrogate parent while attempting to teach Suzanne how to be a mother; a formidable task since she had never had one. Tranquillity returned. Voices calmed. Laughter melted the icy atmosphere. The new family member entered a confusing environment with a distinct lack of paternal affection and a bewildering assortment of females, any one of which may have been his mother.

From the day the baby came into the world, Harry became a non-entity in the household. He took no interest and did not participate in discussions or decisions. Suzanne brushed aside his requests for money and shunted his conjugal desires to a sidetrack. With no knowledge of when women resumed sexual activity after childbirth, he became exasperated. Her reports of meetings with her doctor always endorsed her position and denied his. At the height of his despair, he walked out, called his adversary Rocco for the first time in two years and got drunk.

He woke up the next morning in a whorehouse.

Chapter 7 - The Walls Come Tumbling Down

1.

Nadia held the baby by the feet, cleaned his bottom and removed the soiled linen. She stepped aside, handing Suzanne a clean diaper and safety pins.

"Now, Miss Haldimann," she said, wondering if the baby would experience another puncture or two. Nadia hated Miss Haldimann's dismal efforts inflicting wounds until the child looked like a pincushion. She winced as the point disappeared into the cloth.

"Damn it!" Suzanne pulled back and examined the blood oozing from her fingertip. "Here, Nadia, you do it."

"Yes, Miss Haldimann." She did not have the courage to suggest Miss Haldimann leave.

"Good gracious. I've stained my dress. You feed him, Nadia, please, while I clean up."

"Yes, Miss Haldimann."

Nadia had a baby to care for and to love. Every night she prayed that Miss Haldimann would soon lose interest and confine herself to displaying the child at her many social functions. And indeed, in the subsequent months the Lord responded directing Miss Haldimann's attention to her business leaving Nadia alone to look after Sam. Her enthusiasm for the job contributed towards saving the Haldimann/Matheu marriage, at least for a while. Had someone mentioned her impact on the union, it would have surprised her for she believed she simply did what Miss Haldimann asked. Olga kept Magda apprised of the situation.

"Really Magda, your timid little Nadia has become a dispenser of happiness. She spreads it around as if it were a medicine."

"Of course," Magda responded. "I would be disappointed if she did less."

Olga and Magda, existing on the fringes of the family circle, shared their observations privately without Suzanne's knowledge. Martha Arlene, in unexpected circumstances, brought the change to Harry's attention.

2.

Not only did Harry's head hurt the morning he discovered himself in bed with a prostitute but for the first time in his life, he felt mortified. He had not previously violated his marriage vow. The immediate thought that he might be absorbing some of the religious crap terrified him. He dismissed the notion without a second consideration and left to join Rocco for breakfast at eleven in their usual eating establishment.

Harry had ceased to talk to the boys about his family. How was he to explain he had a chink for a son? When he did mention it, they laughed, harassing him with corny jokes—better stay home at night, Harry, your wife's taking in laundry. Trudging down the street to the café, he mused how Suzanne had played a nasty, stinking, rotten trick. The closer he came to the restaurant, the greater his infuriation. Despite his moment of chagrin, he deemed the end of his marriage as a fact.

Harry barked his order to the cook, slumped into a booth while Rocco, no less hung-over than Harry, collapsed opposite him snorting a painful greeting. The waitress brought coffee. They hugged their cups and stared at each other. Rocco grunted an unintelligible phrase.

"Huh," Harry muttered.

"Good time last night?"

"She doublecrossed me," he moaned. "I'm getting out; let her have her damn baby."

"What are you talking about?"

"My wife."

Rocco grunted and glanced sideways with a puzzled expression.

"That wasn't your wife, Harry."

A few chuckles came from the eavesdroppers. Rocco could not miss an opportunity to joke at Harry's expense.

"Hey, boys, Harry thinks he laid his wife last night."

The establishment rocked with laughter amid a chorus of lousy one-liners. Harry looked pained.

"Shut up, Rocco. I know what I did last night."

"Hell, you do." Rocco feigned a punch that would have knocked Harry out of the booth if he connected. "You're an asshole if you gonna leave your wife. Crazy! Leave the money! On account of she had a kid? You dumb bugger, Harry that's what women are for, fercrisake."

"Go to hell."

Leaving half his breakfast, Harry tried a cigarette. It tasted awful. He stomped out, walked all the way to the waterfront, plunked down on a bench and stared across the water. He needed a drink to stop the pounding in his head and took a cab to Wentworth where he ordered a beer that tasted terrible. Slumped in a booth, nursing his drink, the pain in his head eased a little and the beer began to taste better. He downed two more before he left to find his car.

He parked in the driveway at home and sat in the car looking at the house. Damn! Rocco was right. Conceding defeat and turning your back on the enemy would be cowardly. No recourse came to his mind but to hold the ground he had all ready conquered. He would have to apologize—the thought raised his ire once more. He emerged from the car and kicked some stones.

"Why?" His shout, loud and brazen, bounced off the garage wall. "It's not my fault."

The backdoor burst open. Josef hurried down the steps.

"Did you call, Mr. Matheu?"

"Oh! Hello, Josef, where is everybody?"

"Is something wrong, sir?"

"No. No. Mind your own business. Where the hell is everybody?" He strode across the porch towards the kitchen door, Josef in pursuit.

"Miss Haldimann went to lunch with Mrs. Arlene. I believe she had a meeting later. I'm to get her at four downtown. Nadia is walking the baby."

"Oh!" Harry stopped abruptly forcing Josef to leap sideways to avoid hitting him. "Did you say Mrs. Arlene?"

"Yes, sir. Would you like lunch, sir?"

"Mrs. Arlene." A smirk crept slowly across Harry's face. "Mrs. Arlene."

Harry stood as a graven image, softly whispering, "Did he say Mrs. Arlene?"

Josef watched the eyes enlarging as if seeing a vision. The smirk changed to a sly smile. Then a sudden alertness and batting of the eyes as if Mr. Matheu awakened from a trance.

"Ah … huh! Oh! Lunch? No. I'm going out."

He turned abruptly and pounded through the kitchen. Half an hour later, Josef observed him freshly shaved in a conservative suit, new shirt with bright tie and shining shoes going out through the front door. Peeking through a window, Josef watched him stride across the lawn to his car, whistling as he went.

Harry stood on the threshold of the big mansion and rang the doorbell. The butler answered.

"James, so good to see you again. Is Mrs. Arlene at home?"

"Yes, Mr. Matheu."

"Would you be so good as to announce me. And I do apologize for not calling in advance. It's a matter of some importance."

"Certainly, sir. Would you step in, please?"

Harry waited in the drawing room. James returned to a announce that Mrs. Arlene would join him for tea in about twenty minutes and would Mr. Matheu like a magazine to read.

"Thank you, James. Kind of you but I think I'll just sit quietly and rest. I had a frightful evening yesterday and a trying day today."

Alone in the room, Harry evaluated his performance. He'd done quite well putting on the dog for James as a kind of warm-up for the interview. He remembered *Aristide Bruant's* encounter with Miss Haldimann but he discarded him; this was not a romantic encounter. He searched for another role model. Unsure of *Lord Byron*, he thought *Alfred Lord Tennyson* would serve better. He heard Mrs. Arlene coming down the stairs. *Tennyson* it would be.

"My dear, Mrs. Arlene, do forgive me for this unannounced intrusion." She smiled and extended her hand. He held it gently in both of his.

"I shall come straight to the point. I wish to apologize. I am aware that I behaved abominably at the opera. Frankly, I was too embarrassed to call on you. Last evening—and again this morning—I met with my spiritual advisor who insisted my neglect was a gross mistake. I really am so terribly sorry."

He released her hand continuing to pour out the drivel until she had to stop him in self-defense.

"I accept, Mr. Matheu. Shall we have tea in the sunroom?"

The conversation revolved around the baby; what a dear sweet child he was. Harry, carried away by his own performance, braved a question.

"Do you think his, ah … coloring will be a problem in later life."

"Not at all. Not with that wonderful girl to tend to his needs."

Harry looked puzzled.

"Excuse me," he mumbled, "you mean …"

"Nadia, of course."

Harry forgot his manners for a moment and mopped his brow with the serviette. Whew! A close call.

"Yes, isn't she doing a marvelous job. So competent."

Harry could hardly wait to get home. He raced into the house to find Suzanne in her office, talking with Martha. She hung up and smiled at Harry.

"It took a long time," she said. "Thank you, Harry."

"Yeah! What the hell is Nadia doing to Sam?"

3.

Harry's apology filled Suzanne with resolve to set the marriage problems behind them. She called Silverstein to explain Harry's distress over her violation of the understanding about a family.

"The fact is," Phillip interjected, "you did conceal the atavism from him, didn't you?"

"Yes, I did. I suppose to some degree he's justified, but . . . well, he's still the boy's father."

"What's his financial status?"

"Since the beginning of my pregnancy he has not confided in me. I really don't know but I would guess he's still relying on my guarantee. I'm sure the ice cream losses are mounting up and he's gone back to the stock market to generate cash."

"In that case, we should withdraw your guarantee before it's too late."

The conversation took a turn she had not intended but she decided to play along. Perhaps Phillip would encourage Harry in his business endeavors.

A few days later Blankenship received a letter requesting his attendance at a meeting in Mr. Silverstein's office. Phillip was brief and to the point as usual.

"I want to assure all present that it is Miss Haldimann's continuing desire to encourage her husband. I congratulate you Mr. Matheu, on the astute manner in which you have managed your investments and have accumulated such an impressive account. I understand the ice cream business is expanding rapidly and will, no doubt, yield considerable profits when the current expansion program is complete."

Silverstein's performance sucked Blankenship into the vortex of spellbinding words and so enthralled him that he waxed eloquently on his confidence in Mr. Matheu's abilities.

"Then it is understood," Phillip concluded, "that Miss Haldimann's guarantee is now superfluous."

The color draining from Blankenship's face belied his mask of enthusiasm. He looked dejected and quickly turned to Harry.

"Under the circumstances, Mr. Matheu, you might consider pledging your interest in Mathard Inc., as collateral in case an unexpected need for funds should arise."

"That is a matter between you privately," Silverstein countered, "and not relevant to the present discussion."

The meeting ended.

Mr. Blankenship experienced a complete reversal in his confident attitude with the realization that Miss Haldimann no longer stood foursquare behind her husband.

"I'll expect to see you in the morning," he said to Harry as they parted. "And bring the Mathard certificates."

Harry left the meeting in an expansive mood. Silverstein's words confirming his wife's desire to encourage him played like a Tchaikovsky symphony. Endorsements by Phil Silverstein, seconded by Jim Blankenship, would undoubtedly open doors never before accessible. Exclusive clubs and private golf courses needed investigation. Without so much as a backward glance, he vaulted over the milestone on his imaginary road to high society. The next day he bounced into Blankenship's office and plunked down the Mathard certificate. Nothing had changed; instead of Suzanne's guarantee, he had Mathard's, which to him was exactly the same.

While Harry bounced around Chicago in a jovial mood, Suzanne talked quietly with Silverstein about Harry pledging the Mathard stock as collateral.

"We can do nothing about it," he told her. "The stock is his and he has repaid you for the loan to purchase it. Your only recourse would be to offer to buy it from him."

"I don't want to do that," she said quickly without explanation. Silverstein didn't need to know that facing Harry with such a proposition might reverse the restructuring of the marriage.

"I have one more question. In your opening remarks, you indicated my willingness to encourage Harry. Did you mean financial encouragement?"

"No," he replied, "I didn't mean that and I plead with you, please, do not give him any more money. Or guarantees, either."

4.

Suzanne escaped the burden of her consulting business without difficulty. Her employees accepted her offer to sell but pleaded that she continue as an associate partner since she alone developed the contacts that brought in new business. She retained fifteen percent allowing the right to her name. Then she entered the world of motherhood by creating an office at home, obtaining a private post office box and resolving to blazon her management theories through authorship of articles and books. Her office hours, previously ten in the morning until four with a two-hour lunch followed by shopping or visits to Matheu Men's Furnishings, shifted to sunrise until late at night. Consultation, research and speaking engagements demanded frequent travel. The whirlwind left Nadia dumbfounded in her devotion to the baby. Occasionally, Suzanne inquired about her son as she hurried out the door or rushed to her work.

"Are you getting along all right, Nadia?"

"Yes Miss Haldimann."

Harry did not delude himself as to the object of his endeavors—to spend all he could extract from Suzanne's fortune. In public, he played the role of the devoted husband escorting his wife in high society. His assaults failed to yield success. Perhaps, he employed the wrong tactics. The purse-snatcher got ten dollars. Why? It must have been a gift from her heart in the belief she did something to help him. Several times, not counting the spending spree during their first six months of marriage, she gave him large sums of money when he least expected it. The attack plan became obvious and he implemented it unmercifully going so far on one occasion as to refuse a five-thousand-dollar gift. Three days later, he reluctantly accepted ten thousand instead, an act that filled Suzanne's heart with love. It was beyond anything he could understand but it worked. Deceived by what she believed to be a contented marriage and absorbed in her business, she paid little attention to where he went and what he did. He reinforced his deception by providing toys galore, most of them unsuitable, while he reconstructed his association with Rocco, who was to him what Father Lalonde was to Suzanne.

5.

Clarence Burroughs picked up the telephone, an essential instrument he detested.

"Burroughs."

"Clarence, this is Suzanne Haldimann."

"Who?"

No wonder his wife left him. How could anyone tolerate this terse genius?

"Clarence, you know very well who. We were at Northwestern together."

"Oh! That Suzanne Haldimann. Did we date?"

"I must say you haven't changed. Yes we dated."

"Why didn't we marry?"

"Stop it, Clarence, for heaven's sake. I want to talk business."

Clarence Burroughs preserved his select and wealthy clientele with the primary aid of only two employees; Mildred Jackson, client liaison and general manager, and William Shomacher, stockbroker and analyst, bonded, discreet and competent. The other two staff members performed clerical duties. He managed about two hundred million of other people's money earning about a quarter of a million dollars a year. With Shomacher's support, he constantly reviewed portfolios, watched market trends and searched for new opportunities. His clients praised his genius. He held a master's degree in economics and finance from Northwestern University.

Harry wheeled into the driveway almost hitting the Cadillac. He stormed into the house.

"Josef! Josef!"

"Here, Mr. Matheu."

"Who the hell parked that goddamn car across the driveway."

"It's Mr. Burroughs' car, sir."

Who ever the hell Mr. Burroughs might be, Harry instantly disliked him.

"Where is he?"

"In Miss Haldimann's office."

Harry stomped down the hall, pushed the office door open without knocking and confronted Mr. Burroughs sitting opposite his wife with the desk between them.

"Is that your Cadillac out there?"

Suzanne gasped.

"Harry!"

Clarence rose, smiled and extended his hand.

"Clarence Burroughs. And who, may I ask, are you?"

"I damn near hit it."

Tall, handsome, wavy black hair and laughing eyes, Clarence looked a poster boy for Wheaties. Suzanne stepped between them. With her hand concealed, she pinched Harry.

"Ow!"

"This is my husband, Harry Matheu."

"A pleasure." Clarence smiled. "I seemed to have upset you with my inept driving skills."

"Jesus,"—another pinch—"Ow! I don't know how you drive. It's your parking I'm bitching about."

Clarence turned his back.

"Shall we get back to business, Miss Haldimann?"

Harry opened his mouth. Before he could say anything, Suzanne pushed him out the door. She hoped Clarence didn't hear his parting remark.

"The son-of-a-bitch turned his back."

Harry worried about Clarence taking control of Suzanne's finances. He contemplated offering his own services as gatekeeper at the vault but her recitation of Burroughs' qualifications discouraged him. He apologized for his unwarranted behavior but denied Burroughs the same courtesy. With increasing frequency, Harry noticed the Cadillac parked in the driveway, although always well to the side. For a while, he wondered if some kind of hanky-panky occurred but then realized he didn't care. If she was getting hers, it was okay with him. If she wasn't, well, too bad. He became a patron of a house on Twenty-fourth east of Michigan. Sex was not a topic Suzanne and Harry discussed.

6.

Sam's infant years were uneventful. In accordance with prevailing medical theories, the doctor removed his adenoids and tonsils. Coughs, colds, temperatures, earaches, croup and chicken pox passed normally with doctor visits, mustard plasters and Nadia's affection. Sand piles, swings, tag, snowmen, sledding and wading pools accompanied by a multitude of over-paid nursemaids protecting youngsters from the perils of Chicago filled the pre-school years. At home, he existed in an incomprehensible and horrifying world.

Suzanne recalled Sundays with Daddy, picnics in the park and cuddling on his lap for bedtime stories with cookies and milk. Harry refused to provide the same for Sam never forgetting the deceit she perpetrated. Sam contended with a disgruntled father, who, given the choice, would have exerted the family dominance of his paternal grandfather and fed his unwanted son to the hogs. Often, particularly if Harry was drunk, turmoil reigned in the house. Sam, terrified of his father, could never guess what to expect. Like a haunted animal, he retreated to the safety of his bedroom, an enclave never frequented by his father. Nadia read to him, played games and shared cookies and milk in his room with the door closed. If she left the door open, he howled and yelled unmercifully.

In the meantime, Harry and Suzanne grew farther apart while publicly projecting the appearance of a happy couple. With Clarence barring the door to the vault, Suzanne's handouts came to an end. Harry tumbled into debt to Abie Fishbein and Jim Blankenship spreading confusion and deceit like a street-corner con man. His stock market skills kept him afloat and consumed most of his time. Each Friday he visited the stores, collected the cash and paid the bills; otherwise he spent his working hours in Fishbein's office. Jim Blankenship recovered his confidence mesmerized by Harry's sleight of hand and increasing assets. He admired Harry in as much as Mabel-Cones was not so dumb after all; it provided a convenient tax loss against stock market profits. Like sex, Harry's activities were not a matter for discussion at home.

The divergence in their marriage continued until a month before Sam's fourth birthday when an unexpected turn of events surprised Suzanne and altered the family relationship.

7.

The 1929 stock market lured Harry into accelerated buying on margin. He would have preferred to liquidate Mabel-Cones Inc. but explaining such a move might stain his reputation. Hence, he deposited with Fishbein the maximum available from Blankenship, a small mortgage he managed to negotiate on Mabel-Cones and all his personal assets save pocket money. In September, he read about an intriguing initial stock offer. He bought modestly, watched carefully and held on. The market moved up and down erratically. His audacity drowned in a sea of foreboding. On Monday, October 3, after a weekend of worry, he elected to abandon ship.

"Sell," he told Fishbein.

"Everything?"

"Yes, everything."

"Well, I mean, Harry, that's a little drastic. The market's not that volatile."

"Don't argue, Abie, sell and get some more fat commissions."

Harry was ecstatic the next day watching the market tumble to lows nobody considered possible. Not only did he call the shot, he called it to the very day. He enjoyed an intoxicated evening with Rocco, gloating over his accomplishment and spent the night in the whorehouse. The next day he scrutinized the wreckage and devoured the advice of the experts; a modest correction, a fundamentally sound market and a good time to buy was the near universal advice. He wasn't convinced but he was willing to look. Two days later Fishbein showed him an article extolling Canadian mining stocks. The minerals were in the ground waiting for extraction by sound Canadian companies; no question of speculation with confirmed assays. In these times of market volatility no safer investment could be found as evidenced by the tumble of October four when the good mining stocks moved hardly at all. Fishbein recommended nickel on the Montreal market. Harry's first purchase was at forty-two on Monday, October 19. The stock inched up. Harry talked it over with Abie.

"Gained a half to-day. What do you think?"

"Buy!"

The jitters repeated daily.

"Market's moving up. A little edgy but it's moving."

"Buy!"

The stock followed the market up and down, but always a little more up than down. Harry bought in the valleys.

"I think its good, Harry. Like the article said, the stuff's in the ground, no question. And they're pulling it out. Even in the worst possible circumstance, like another October fourth, it's not going to move much. You saw yourself what happened. In fact, I think a significant market drop would be good for nickel. Everybody will be looking for a place to hide and that's sure to be a popular spot. But Harry you're in pretty deep. You'll have to clear some of the margin before the end of the month. I can only give you until Monday, the last day of the month. That's it, then you'll have to come up with cash or sell some stuff."

Harry sold everything except nickel.

"Buy!"

His last purchase was at 47 on October 28. He held 10,000 shares at an average price of 45 and the stock was already inching past 47. He planned to sell at 55 for a profit of one hundred thousand dollars, a staggering figure for a single transaction.

"No problem," he assured Fishbein on Thursday night as he left the office. "Don't worry. I'll look after it with Jim. We'll settle up on Monday."

The truth was that the absolute maximum cash available from all sources left him fifty thousand short. His solution was to avoid the broker until Monday. Then he'd put down what he had and talk his way into a few more weeks.

With his decision made Harry relaxed. His ice cream people were in turmoil shifting to candy and he hadn't given them a thought all through October. Early on Friday, October 29, he lay low by doing the tour of the Mabel-Cones Shops, compensating his operators for his delinquency and easing his conscience through various commitments to make expenditures of one sort and another. He moved from shop to shop, chatting with the girls and spreading goodwill, deliberately keeping his whereabouts secret. After a leisurely lunch, he strolled back to look in on Fishbein and check the closing price of nickel. Pandemonium reigned. Worming his way into the office he learned Fishbein had entered a sell order for all of Harry's stock. It had already sunk past the price where he could recover the margin principal, let alone the interest. The associate broker in Montreal reported bedlam and chaos on the floor of the Canadian Exchange. Slightly after three o'clock in the morning Harry, tired and dejected, learned everything was gone and he was eighty-five thousand dollars short. He struggled into a taxi and, with no place else to go, he went home to Suzanne.

7.

It was not the first time Harry came home in the wee hours of the morning. When he did, he was generally drunk but long ago they moved into separate bedrooms so she didn't always know. On this occasion, he seriously considered waking her but with only a few hours to sunrise, why bother. She found him asleep on the living room couch at seven o'clock the next morning. She roused him intending to chastise him for his irresponsible conduct but as soon as he opened his eyes, she knew something was seriously wrong.

"Are you sick?"

He sat up rubbing his eyes. "No."

She watched him closely. He avoided her gaze.

"Something's happened, hasn't it?"

She waited.

"Are you going to tell me?"

He did not answer nor did he look at her.

"You better have some coffee."

She took his hand and drew him into the dining room.

"Well, Harry," she said, "please start from the beginning."

He stammered an incoherent tale of woe. She asked dozens of questions before grasping the sequence of events. Neither scolding nor accusing, she assimilated the facts, then suggested he go to bed and get some sleep.

"I'll see what I can do," she said and left him alone to do as he saw fit.

In the privacy of her office, she spoke first to Blankenship then to Silverstein. Silverstein called Blankenship then called her back. Blankenship called and then he called Silverstein. The negotiations went on into the afternoon. At half past three, she informed both men of her final decision. Blankenship was delighted; Silverstein was aghast.

She woke Harry and suggested he bathe.

"As soon as you're dressed please come to my office."

At last, he plodded down the stairs and, as she expected, headed for the bar. She stood at the living room archway watching him mix a jug of martinis. The moment he finished she strode across the room and poured the entire contents down the sink.

"Please come to the office," she said as she left him glaring after her. His profane reaction died on his lips and he meekly followed.

"First things first," she told him. "I won't accept any outsiders in Mathard. I am going to pay off Blankenship and re-acquire those shares." Then to Harry's stupefaction and against the vehement advice of her legal advisor, she offered to give him a guarantee of fifty thousand dollars for collateral to maintain Mabel-Cones business.

"I may have to provide additional working capital but that can come later." She rose from her chair, walked around the desk and sat beside him. Looking into her eyes, he knew the worst was yet to come.

"You're not in a very good bargaining position, Harry. You have treated your son and me abominably in the last four years but you are still my husband and the father of my child. In exchange for my support, I want your respect. That is my first condition. Nothing more. I don't ask for a conjugal relationship, for you to love me or to sleep in the same bed with me. But you must treat your son with courtesy. You don't have to love him but you have to be fair. He did not create any of this and he should not suffer for it. And absolutely you must stop calling him Chink, both publicly and privately. It is degrading, belittling, insulting. Stop it, Harry, and stop it now. If you don't want to give your son and me your respect then refuse my conditions and I will file for divorce."

Harry made an effort to respond but she held up her hand to stop him.

"Hear me out, Harry, then you can give me your answer. The second condition is that you must devote your time and energy to operating the Mabel-Cones business to the exclusion of all other endeavors including the stock market and Rocco's foolishness. You must adjust your costs and your prices in any way you see fit so that the operation is profitable. Finally, you must recognize that I am giving you the collateral for the sole purpose of operating your business and I expect you to keep me fully informed regarding your progress. You must make whatever long-term arrangements are required to pay your personal debts that you have concealed from me but declaring bankruptcy is not one of them. I will not have my name or the memory of my father tarnished in public through court proceedings. I told you in the beginning, and I am repeating it now, under no circumstances will I invest in the ice cream business. I was opposed to it from the start, I said so then, and I am telling you again. My position is absolutely unequivocal; I am investing in you, my husband, not in your business."

In her heart, she truly wanted him to have a second opportunity not only in the hope it might save her marriage but also that he could make a success of business and fulfill his obligation as a parent. Once more, that fateful day when a boy on the street received ten dollars for another chance crossed his mind. It remained an act beyond his comprehension.

"I'll let you know," he said and left her office.

His departure did not distress Suzanne. She thought she perceived humility and knew it would take time to recover.

Two hours later, Harry returned.

"Thank you," he said, standing in the archway looking askance.

Suzanne set her cocktail glass aside and greeted him with a kiss.

"Could I mix you a martini?"

"No."

He slouched into a chair, head down, his penitence startling to behold. She returned to her chair.

"Where have you been?"

"Walking."

His silence begged the question she could not resist.

"Do you have an answer for me?"

"Yes."

Again she waited, surprised at the tenseness she felt.

"Well?"

"We'll play it your way."

Blankenship paid off the broker, accepted a demand note of fifty thousand dollars from Miss Haldimann as collateral for Harry and returned the Mathard shares to Miss Haldimann in consideration of a payment of sixty-two thousand five hundred dollars.

Harry's seven-year romance with Lady Luck ended.

Chapter 8 – The Growing Boy

1.

On arrival in Cincinnati in 1899, Stefan's fretting and Olga's whimpering annoyed Magda. "I am leaving," she announced. "I cannot stand your endless waffling. Each time I make a suggestion, it takes the two of you three or four days to decide anything."

"Leaving?' Olga shrieked. "Oh no, Magda, you cannot leave us."

"Stop sniffling, Olga, for heaven's sakes." She turned to Stefan. "Give me my share of the remaining money. One-fourth of whatever we have left. That's all. You may keep the rest."

For three days, Olga and Stefan argued.

"Perhaps we should return home."

"No, Stefan, I am not going back."

"What about Canada?"

Magda stood firm.

"Olga, I am going west. There are trains leaving everyday. I'm going tomorrow even if Stefan gives me only enough money for train fare. That is final."

The next day, with no idea of her destination, she boarded a train heading west. A day later, at five o'clock in the morning, she got off in Calumet City thinking she was in Chicago. A fortuitous error; six months later she seized on the alliterative title of Madame Magda Magdelaine and married Pierre Magdelaine to make it legal.

With large bosom and broad hips, she presented a robust, sturdy figure in the image of her mother, in contrast to her sister Olga who was slight in the image of their father. She radiated confidence that demanded respect as an authority and love as a mother. Pierre and Magda devoted themselves to their children with the Roman Catholic Church the instrument of education, discipline and devotion.

"Magda's going to have a baby."

"Good Lord! How many is that?"

Every two or three years, the neighbors marveled at the peasant woman from Austria who brought another child into the world. Alas, the sixth birth brought twins and a difficult delivery that ended her childbearing.

"Don't be silly," she said to Pierre, "you can't quit work. How will we eat? Nadia will tend to the babies. The doctor said I'll be on my feet again in a few months."

Nadia did not inherit her mother's large figure, being more slender like Olga, but she inherited the confident, happy disposition. She adored looking after the babies. After she married Josef, her heart broke when informed she would never bear children of her own.

"Josef, I am so sorry. It is my fault. Do you want me to leave. We could annul the marriage. I'm sure the priest would understand."

To Josef, she wasn't the same carefree, happy person he married but he loved her, always consoling and seeking ways to help her bridge her disappointment. Then suddenly, the problem evaporated. Nadia had Sam to love. The restoration led her to unofficial director of children's entertainment headquartered in the Haldimann house.

"Nadia, will you never rest?"

"Josef, I'm so happy. Isn't Stefan wonderful. I do wish his parents didn't call him Sam."

She organized countless events in the parks or on the lakeshore, then subdued the exhausted children with stories before sending them home with their nursemaids. In the long summer evenings, she played ball with Sam behind the house. Always aware of his father's whereabouts, he would unexpectedly slink off behind the garage or the garden shed. A few seconds later Mr. Matheu appeared. No sooner did his father leave than Sam reappeared.

All too quickly in Nadia's view, Sam reached the age that no longer required chaperoning. Baseball became his favorite pastime. He and his friends imagined tense games before huge stadium crowds. Throwing a tennis ball against a wall, they played out their fantasies. If one of them missed, they chalked an error on the pavement and replayed the scene. The boy with the least errors won. Sometimes, after Nadia served Miss Haldimann's tea at four o'clock, she went to the park where she could watch them play before dragging Sam home for supper.

"Is my father home?"

"Sam, it doesn't matter."

"Yes it does matter. Is he home?"

If she answered, "Yes," Sam sneaked in the back door going straight to his room; if "No," he went to his mother's office to talk.

Olga Matheu's interest in attending baseball games had died shortly after Suzanne bought the season ticket in 1922. She attended a few games but soon returned to her dream world. The second year, she told her husband she found the stadium a lonely place.

"Why do you go?"

"Because she gave me the tickets. She thinks I should go."

After supper two days later, Stefan raised the subject again.

"I spoke to Miss Haldimann about the baseball."

"Stefan! You didn't."

"There's nothing to be concerned about. She did it for you. She's never seen a baseball game in her life and doesn't care if you go or not."

So Olga returned to her world of fantasy, visiting her sister in Calumet City and going as often as possible to visit her grandson in Evanston. She never became accustomed to the noise of Chicago as opposed to the quiet of Cincinnati but it was a small price to pay to see her husband so happy in his work.

In 1933, Nadia told Olga about Sam's interest in baseball. Olga went straight to Suzanne.

"I'd love to take Sam to Wrigley Field; to mid-week games during summer vacation."

"Of course. That would be wonderful, Olga. Josef will drive you and wait to bring you home."

Each time they went, Olga brought a gift related to baseball, most often a book. Sam's baseball library grew large. He always carried a clean unfolded program home from the stadium. He read the stories four or five times, devoured the technical books and studied every word in the programs, including the advertisements. He'd ask Nadia for help with difficult words or concepts he couldn't grasp.

"Olga, it's wonderful," Nadia said. "His reading skills are so much better and improving all the time."

Towards the end of the summer when Sam was eight, Nadia wanted to take him to visit her mother's home in Calumet City.

"Miss Haldimann, may we take Sam to see my parents sometime? On a Sunday afternoon perhaps or on Thursday when we're off?"

The words spilled out so quickly they took Suzanne by surprise. The two women stared at each other for an instant.

"Well, yes, I suppose so. I've never considered it. We'll have to discuss the when and how."

On the first visit, Sam was shy and retiring. When they returned, he didn't say much except he liked Nadia's mother but wasn't sure what her name was.

"Yes," he said, "I had a good time. I liked the train ride. May I go again sometime."

School started. Suzanne told Nadia it would be better not to consider a second visit that year.

"We'll talk about in the spring, when the weather warms."

The next summer, Nadia and Josef took Sam to Magdelaine's at every opportunity. The twins were a year and a half older than Sam. They tussled and fought in the manner of boys although Sam usually came out on the losing end. With new friends and playmates, he was a normal, boisterous, game-loving, misbehaving, obstreperous boy. At home, he was a sprite always alert for the marauding troll.

Suzanne fretted about the effect of the recurring visits and tried to involve Harry.

"Do you think we should allow this dual existence? Sam says he loves going with Nadia."

"Sure. Why not?"

"He raves about the baseball with Olga."

"Okay."

"I suppose. It can't hurt to be with Christian souls like Olga and Magda. Nadia is walking proof; well-mannered, polite and decorous."

"Look, I don't care. I'm happy the kid's out of here. If that's what he wants, let him do it."

2.

In January 1936, Sam was ten years old in grade four. On one of his papers, he wrote his name as Matthews.

"Sam Matheu! That is not your name. Please write it correctly."

"No. I've changed my name."

After the fifth incident, the teacher lost patience.

"This is ridiculous. Go to the principal's office."

He stood stoically through the chastisement; returned to his class where, at the first opportunity, he did it again.

"I'm reporting this to your parents."

"Is it about your father?" Suzanne asked in the privacy of his room. He kept his head bowed. Gently, with her hand on his chin, she raised his eyes to hers.

"Sam?" He tried to turn away.

"Yes or no, Sam. Is it about your father?"

Sam nodded affirmatively. The tears welled in his eyes. Biting his lip, she could see the struggle to hold them back, unwilling or unable to speak. She released his chin.

"Sam, what is it about your father that troubles you?"

His lip pouted. He lowered his head. At last, he spoke.

"Your name's not the same as his. Why do I have to have his name?"

"You can make a name change. Is that what you want, dear? When you're older, you can change your name through the courts. You could change your name to Haldimann if you wanted."

He did not reply.

She waited.

"There's something else, isn't there, Sam? Don't be afraid to tell me."

He raised his eyes to meet hers; then his words gushed like a geyser disgorging heated spume.

"I don't look like you. Or him. I don't look like anybody. He calls me Chink. They all call me Chink. Everybody laughs at me. I hate him. I hate everybody. I look different from everybody. Nobody looks like me."

Her irritation over Harry's indifference towards Sam erupted into a flame of vengeance. For ten years, she demanded that he respect their son. For ten years, he denied her petition. She held Sam close not trusting her voice. The doors to the cloisters of her mind that she kept firmly shut, began to open. She had never admitted her marriage was a mistake. She provided money and all that goes with it; Harry's only response was to ask for more. She struggled to calm her emotions, closing the doors and searching her mind for the words to comfort Sam. As her anger ebbed, she talked about her own school experience.

"Although my hair is black, my classmates called me Whitey because my skin wasn't black like theirs. They called me Whitey all through school but it didn't change me one bit."

He put his arms around her neck.

"I guess I understand."

"Try, Sam. Name-calling is not important."

"I'll try."

"If it continues, will you be sure to tell me, please?"

"Yes."

3.

Suzanne hugged Sam and put out the light. She sank into the circular armchair she bought a year ago Christmas to make his room more comfortable. The arms curved around the sides creating a well large enough to tuck her feet in beside her. She kicked off her shoes and cuddled up. The upholstery was a soft maroon velour; a remarkably comfortable chair. Sam's breathing assumed a regular rhythm and her mind shifted back to his admission. A bitter sigh escaped her lips. She remembered the exact date she told Harry her conditions—October 30, 1929 in the afternoon in her office. *"Stop it, Harry and stop it now,"* or something like that. *"Accept my conditions or I'll sue for divorce."* He accepted all right and immediately forgot. He masked his name-calling. Until this evening—January 14, 1936—she never imagined that he continued to call Sam Chink. A sense of guilt pervaded her, creeping up from her stomach, up through her body, up into her brain until she wanted to scream. She should have asked; she should have known; she should have protected Sam. Instead, her preoccupation with business and writing left the care of her child to Nadia. She had sacrificed her son on the altar of egoism. Burying her head in her hands, she let the tears flow.

Two hours passed before she left Sam's room, grateful Harry hadn't come home; afraid if she talked to him, she might lose control. Had her marriage come to the end of the road? November would be fourteen years. What should she do?

The next morning she began her day by reviewing her affairs; the extent of unfinished commitments embarrassed her. She had fiddled with her book manuscript for months, never satisfied. Articles she promised to write were in various states of preparation, some past their deadlines. She had neglected her associate's request for a meeting that came before Christmas. Her greeting cards lay on the desk, half-finished. The only business she attended to in the last month was the store, the one area that didn't need her; Carole and Mr. Matheu were doing a fine job. She prepared a schedule determined to discipline herself in her work. Everyday she would set aside time to be with Sam. But what about Harry? She looked at the empty chair, the chair he sat in seven years ago. She spoke aloud, unemotionally stating the facts as if he sat opposite her at that moment.

"I give up, Harry. You defied me and there is nothing left in our marriage. I know you have ten thousand reasons why it's my fault. I know you'll want money. I won't give you that satisfaction, Harry. I will ignore you and wait till you leave."

She marched into the kitchen.

"Nadia, Josef, listen to me."

"Yes, Miss Haldimann."

"From now on, dinner will be served at six o'clock. You will set a place for Mr. Matheu whether he is here or not. Is that clear?

"Yes, Miss Haldimann."

4.

At six o'clock the next evening, Suzanne and Sam waited as Nadia served their dinner.

"Nadia, please serve Mr. Matheu's dinner."

"But Miss Haldimann, he's not home."

"I'm aware of that."

"Shall I put it in the warming oven?"

"No."

Sam and his mother chatted pleasantly throughout the meal. As they moved away from the table, Nadia looked puzzled.

"Shall I remove Mr. Matheu's dinner, Miss Haldimann."

"No. Leave it, even it sits there all night."

At seven forty-five, Harry stared in disbelief. He could have cursed the servants, fought with his wife or trundled off to visit Rocco, none of which provided any satisfaction. He had had enough. Free cost of living or not, he could stand no more. Fed to the teeth with everything in his life, he sauntered into the living room, mixed a jug of martinis and contemplated a dismal future without money. In an inebriated state halfway through his second jug of martinis that he drank too fast, he determined the time had arrived for another military operation. He mixed another batch of martinis to celebrate.

In the morning, the only recollection he had was a resolve to skin her for a hundred thousand. Then he'd walk out. The problem was the means of strategic retreat. He remembered a word he read in the newspaper a month or two before. He had looked it up in the dictionary. With his head throbbing, he tried to remember the word—apoco something—but only the definition came to mind. *"The concept of a cosmic cataclysm"*. The words had a ring to them, like words in a song, and he liked them. The explanation went on, something about God destroying the powers of evil but since he wasn't on speaking terms with God, he fell back on his military experience. He regarded his army career as the only education he ever received in cataclysmic planning, whatever that might be.

"If you have to get out, careful planning is the answer," the captain said. "Don't panic and don't forget the walls have ears. Every time you share your plans with anybody, you run the risk they'll leak it."

Harry marveled that he could remember those words he heard nineteen years before. He liked the code names used by the military. He loved 'Golden Fleece', an endeavor that yielded seven years of glorious spending and seven years of misery. Now the time had come to engage the enemy in another conflict. He brooded without success. Schemes of torture popped into his mind with regularity but nothing practical. One day walking along the street, the enlightenment shone like a beacon in the sky; Suzanne was not the embodiment of the powers of evil. No sooner did Rocco become the target than a hoax flowered in his mind like a morning glory in the sun. He snickered like Simon Legree concealing his devilish subterfuge. Indeed, he named it "Operation Morning Glory" and went quietly about his business, a smile creasing his face.

5.

In April, Miss Haldimann received a handwritten letter from Madame Madga Magdelaine inviting her son to spend the summer in Calumet City. She wrote about a planned baseball league with teams coached by the parish men. She thought it a wonderful opportunity for Stefan who enjoyed baseball so much.

"Please, mother, can I go?"

"May I go not can I."

"May I. Please. Can I?"

Suzanne sighed.

"I thought we agreed you were going to camp in Wisconsin."

"Gee. I want to play baseball at Granny Madga's."

"I think camp in Wisconsin is better than Calumet City."

Sam begged with an endless stream of cajolery that left no doubt he didn't want to go to camp. He loved baseball. Better happy where he wanted to be than unhappy in Wisconsin. She came down on the side of baseball, a decision she never regretted. In late June, Sam Matheu joined Tom Gordon's team, the Giants.

Neither Suzanne nor Sam objected to Magda's condition that Sam must accompany her to morning Mass and receive instruction from Father Henderson or one of the Sisters afterwards. As soon as his lesson finished, Sam pedaled furiously to the ballpark where he was the spark plug that organized the boys into teams. Some resented the rich kid from Chicago but Sam judged the talents well and created balanced teams resulting in competitive games. Stories spread through the community. Parents questioned their children about the ten-year-old kid they accepted as a leader. The general explanation assumed the Lord cut the odd-looking boy from a different pattern and gave him unusual talents to make up for his strange face.

Sam listened, absorbed and rationalized the instructions from his baseball coach. Long on enthusiasm, short on talent, his skills did not improve to any noticeable degree but he exuded contagious eagerness. His hunger to learn set him apart from his teammates. In recognition of his poor ability and inferior play, they hung the moniker Sadsack on him.

Of the four teams in the church league, the Dodgers dominated. The White Sox and Cubs moved back and forth between second and third place. The Giants were a dismal last.

On the evening of Tuesday, August 6, the Giants' opponents were the invincible Dodgers. Tom wanted his best players on the field to face the superior team. He could not bring himself to let young Sadsack play while better players sat on the bench. He made up his mind to explain the problem when Sam pulled at his sleeve.

"Can I coach at third base today?"

Tom admired the boy's determination, his willingness to keep trying, never yielding to discouragement.

"Yeah! That's a great idea Sadsack. Yeah! You go ahead and coach at third base."

The Giants were the home team for this game. In the top of the first, the Dodgers got two runs. The Giants went down one, two, three.

"Look here you guys I told you to pay attention to Sadsack. What happens? You miss the first signal."

Tom ranted for some time until the umpire yelled at him.

"Hey Tom! You going to play ball or you conceding?"

Tom hustled the boys on to the field. Sam sat beside him on the bench and said nothing. The Dodgers first two batters reached base safely. Sam was up and yelling at the shortstop.

"Move over to second. Move. Move closer. A little more." Then he ordered the third baseman to move to the shortstop position. This confused the boys. They looked at Tom who told them to do what Sadsack said. On the third pitch, the batter hit a liner to the third baseman who stepped on second for a double play. Tom made a note to ask Sadsack about the play after the game.

Sam took his position in the third base coaching box and Tom brought a folding chair and sat near him. Sam and Tom were a team, the manager giving the orders, the third base coach signaling the play. Sam tugged at his sleeve, pulled the bill of his cap, touched his elbows, rubbed his thighs and crossed his arms. Excitement ran high among the parents. This was good. This was like the pros. The Sox and the Cubs played this way. This was real major league stuff.

"Hey! Did you see that there Matheu kid?"

"Tom's really teaching these kids ain't he?"

"How'd Tom get 'em to do this? Huh?"

They shouted themselves hoarse. One slapped his neighbor on the back knocking his Coca-Cola to the ground.

"I'll betcha some of these kids is gonna make it to the big leagues."

"Look! There he goes again. Hey Matheu! Atta boy, Matheu!"

A roar of laughter cheered Sam on. Not only that, but the entire crowd shifted their support to the Giants. They wanted to see the underdog come through. The Dodgers went on to score three more runs. The Giants came off the field, dejected, expecting another thrashing.

"Come on Giants! Let's go! Let's get some runs here!"

The shouting and laughter encouraged Sam, a baseball coach who knew what he was doing and proud of it. The ludicrous performance captivated Tom. Normally, the parents never paid much attention to the games. They came to chide their neighbors, make penny bets that "my kid's team is better 'n yours", eat popcorn, consume soft drinks and drop a nickel or a dime as the box passed in support of Father's baseball program. Tom listened and watched as he sat in his chair, working with Sam and reminding the boys to pay attention to Sadsack. He didn't expect to win and no harm came from letting Matheu put on his show. He smiled. The kid was good. He must have stood before a mirror practicing for hours. He had the act down pat. Incredible for a ten-year-old! The Giants went down one two three in their half of the second. The score was five zip.

The Dodgers loaded the bases in the third but failed to score when one of their guys watched the crowd and the umpire called him out when two Dodgers stood on the same base. In the bottom of the third, the Giants got a base runner. Sam's aggressive shenanigans had them running, stealing bases, taking advantage of every break. Score: Five-four Dodgers. The Giants were jubilant. Tom had never heard so much noise from the parents. People hurried to the field to investigate the racket. The crowd swelled and the hullabaloo increased. Tom had to calm his players and hustle them on to the field.

"There are four more innings to this game. Get on out there and let's see you play to win. Come on, now. Let's go."

Sam sat on the bench beside Tom.

"Great job, Sadsack, great job," Tom said, patting him on the back.

The Giants managed to stay in the game through the sixth inning. The Dodgers picked up a run in the top of the seventh. The score stood at nine seven with the Giants coming to bat for the last time. It was dismal. They got a walk, another strike out, the tenth of the game, and a hit batter. Sam thought surprise had the best chance. He checked with Tom who agreed. Sam displayed his signal routine one more time. In the middle, he reached up pulling on the bill of his cap. He was alert and watching. As soon as the pitcher moved toward the plate, Sam waved his arms yelling "RUN! RUN! RUN!" Urging the runners on, he moved down the third base line halfway to the plate with no intention of holding the second runner at third. The bunted ball bounced in front of the catcher who recovered quickly but threw low to first. The right fielder picked it up, ran in a few steps and threw. Sam kept waving the runner on. "SAFE" bellowed the umpire. The score was tied. The Giants were in wild celebration. Wait! The Dodgers coach appealed to the umpire, saying the runner took a four-foot shortcut passed third base. A discussion followed. The umpire consulted the crowd and ruled in favor of the Dodgers.

"That's right," Tom agreed.

The last out was a pop-up. Final score: Dodgers nine - Giants eight.

The parents stood, cheered and clapped.

"Great game! Wonderful! Best game of the year! That Matheu kid, ain't he sumpthin'!"

Sam had coached his first baseball game and he almost won. After the crowd dispersed and the players started home, Tom took Sam aside.

"Tell me, Sadsack, in the second inning how did you know to move the shortstop over to second and put Jack beside him?"

"We play scrub all the time. I knew their guy always hits toward second base or between second and first." Sam tried to talk as he imagined his heroes did in the baseball books he devoured. "I figured he'd hit a liner and we might get a double play. We did, too."

"One more question. Where did you learn about signals?"

"In one of my books. There's a chapter on how to do them. It's neat. My granny Olga took me to Wrigley Field lots of times. I've seen them do it."

"Nice going, Sadsack. You did a great job"

Sam became the regular third base coach. Tom taught him strategy and tactics, encouraging him to experiment and learn through his mistakes. His teammates boasted about their secret signals and were proud of being the only team using them. Spirit increased and they won three games in a row but lost the consolation round on Labor Day. Sam returned home having won the hearts of the community and the blessing of Father.

He never forgot that glorious summer with the first game he coached etched in his memory forever.

Chapter 9 – The Swindle

1.

The Mabel-Cones shops in the suburbs closed one after another. During the winter of 1932, only three downtown stores remained open. In the summer, ice cream sales justified reopening some on a seasonal basis. With diminishing results and decreasing interest, Harry toiled on, trapped like an animal on a tether. He dreamed of the rollicking twenties and the carefree life, unable to envision surrendering his free cost of living.

Those at the top of the economic strata complained about the reduction of investment returns but their life of luxury continued unabated for the most part. In keeping with her affluence, Suzanne bought new cars, maintained quality wardrobes for herself and Harry, kept two servants in her home, employed gardeners, laundry women, furnace men and assorted day labor. Harry upheld the image of the perfect marriage escorting her wherever she chose to go. In the confines of the home, they rarely talked to each other.

Harry nourished his discontent through frequent trysts in the lower echelon of society. Accepting his lot, he lived in two worlds nurturing his thoughts of revenge. He perceived Sam as the object of his disgust. If the little Chinese bugger got in the way, Harry belted him. More than once, Suzanne had to defend Sam against unwarranted beatings. A row would ensue and they didn't talk until they masqueraded in the whirl of the next social function.

By the spring of 1936, Harry, having conceived a plot to even the score with Rocco, wrapped himself in research and planning. He learned the legalities from a friendly lawyer for a small fee. The forms were simple enough and, after a little research, he found a notary to accredit the documentation. Seemed like there wasn't much to it; fill in the forms; get the signatures and drop them in the mail.

Next came the more difficult task of displaying the profitability of Mabel-Cones. Each operator kept a separate bank account for her daily deposits. Harry visited on Fridays to verify sales. The girls wrote checks for his share. He cashed them as he made his rounds ending the day with a substantial bankroll. Carrying a wad of bills always exhilarated him. As a boy, he stole from his parents and kept the money in his pocket. He spent a little now and then but flashing a big roll in front of his pals was the real thrill.

When he made his deposit at the Blankenship Bank, he kept a modest roll to show the boys for he never admitted the truth of his circumstances in the speakeasy. When they met on Friday nights, he flashed his wad. This always drew Rocco's attention; amazing how Rocco could smell money.

In the warm weather of July and August, the best sales months of the year, the cash swelled to three or four times the average. To prepare his imminent departure, he withheld about half of each deposit creating a cache in a safety deposit box. Each time he met Rocco, he flashed the bankroll. Rocco took the bait the first week of August. Without turning his head, he squinted out of the corner of his eye.

"How's it going, Harry?"

"Getting better. I think the country's coming out of this damn depression."

"Yeah! How can you tell?"

"People are buying. That means they got extra money to spend on luxuries."

Rocco swung around on his barstool, putting his mouth close to Harry's ear.

"How much you make a week?"

Harry shrugged and whispered in an equally confidential voice.

"After expenses, four, five grand."

Rocco turned back to his drink.

"No shit."

The seeds of greed lay planted in the mobster's brain. It only remained to cultivate them.

In his preparation for departure, Harry considered the angles. He destroyed personal documents that might incriminate him. His tools, stored in the cellar of the Evanston house, were valuable and expensive to replace. On a Thursday, when the servants were out and Suzanne was downtown, he loaded the tools into his car and drove to Gary, Indiana looking for a storage warehouse.

"I'll be away for some time," he told the manager. "I'll pay a year in advance."

"Okay. But if them tools is here one extra day without no payment out they go. Ain't no credit here. And you got to put your name on them."

Harry obliged by writing out tags that bore only his name and stuck one on each toolbox.

2.

"How about lunch, Harry?" Blankenship asked.

"Sure, Jim. Next Tuesday?

"Swell."

At lunch, Blankenship probed delicately for information.

"Sales not quite as good this year?"

Harry hadn't wanted to go to lunch with Jim. In fact, he hoped he'd never see him again. He looked around the room as he delivered his reply.

"Not bad."

"Your deposits are down compared to previous years. I think you should reduce your loan, Harry. You're paying me a lot of interest."

So that's what it was about.

"Thanks for bringing it to my attention. I'm so busy I don't have time to check those details. How much do you suggest?"

"What do you say to reducing your loan to twenty thousand."

"Something the matter with Suzanne's note?"

"No. Nothing like that. I'm worried about your cash flow."

Harry resisted the urge to say Jim would do more than worry about cash flow by the time he got through with him.

"Well, all right but I think twenty's too low. Keep the line open at fifty—you got Suzanne's guarantee—and I'll undertake to reduce the balance. If it gets tight, I'll let you know before I go above twenty."

"Well, all right. But you keep me informed," Jim said.

Harry had two telephone calls back at the office, both from suppliers looking for payment.

"You bet," he told them jovially. "Just came from my bank. Writing the checks right now." He wrote checks for twenty-five percent of the amount owed, carefully put the checks in the wrong envelopes and held them over the weekend before mailing.

On Friday in the second week of August, he made his regular deposit in his account and the secret cache. On his way out of the bank he wrote a deposit slip showing $32,632 cash deposited that day, kept the carbon copy and threw the original in the trash.

"You forgot to stamp my copy of the deposit slip," he said to the teller, sliding it towards her with his hand over the amount.

"Sorry, Mr. Matheu."

She quickly stamped the acknowledgment copy as her face turned scarlet.

"Thank you. Don't worry about it."

He scribbled a note across the face: Expenses $16,589; net $16,043.

On his way home, he joined Rocco for a drink. Downing his second martini, he pulled out his wad of bills. A paper slipped from the bundle and dropped to the bar. He paid his tab and stopped on his way out to adjust his tie in the mirror on the opposite wall. Rocco's eyebrows arched when he spotted the paper lying on the bar. His hand reached out and flicked it into his pocket. Harry smiled and hailed a cab.

"Garden's looking good," he said to the driver. "A little bloom of avarice on the vine."

The next week his principal supplier threatened to stop deliveries. Harry made a partial payment that emptied his account to a few thousand dollars, keeping his loan under fifteen thousand. He avoided Blankenship while he waited for Rocco's craving to mature into compulsive envy. He made his weekly deposit, and guaranteed his suppliers he'd be current after Labor Day. By the third week of August, he worried that Rocco might pass up the opportunity for yet another exploitation of Harry's moronic stupidity. He went around to the bar.

"Hi ya, Rocco, how you doing?"

He bellowed as if he didn't have a care in the world.

"Where you been, Harry?"

"Busy. Never seen it so good."

Rocco took a long pull on his drink.

"That so."

"Yep."

Harry ordered a second round. Rocco interrupted.

"Tell the waiter to bring it to the booth," he said to the bartender. He dragged Harry across the room. They sat opposite each other.

"Listen, you lying son-of-a-bitch," Rocco blurted, putting the fake deposit slip on the table. "You told me you was making four or five a week. How the hell do you explain this?"

Harry leaped from his seat in anger.

"Where did you get that?"

"Sit down and shut up."

Harry sat.

"You listen to me," Rocco sneered. "I want the truth. How much you banking? And don't give me no shit."

"I ain't telling you nothing." Harry managed a real edge of anger in his voice. "You ain't muscling in on me."

Suddenly Rocco's tone was conciliatory.

"Now listen, Harry, you and me been friends for a long time. All I'm asking is how you're doing. Any guy draws sixteen in a week, you got to ask what kind of business he's doing."

"If you're asking me to tell, ask again, Buddy, cause I ain't talking."

Rocco shrugged and ordered more drinks. Harry knew the tactic well—get your boy drunk, then ask. He played along, sipped his drink, smacked his lips and downed the rest in one gulp. It was his second drink of the night but he made as if it was his twelfth. He rolled back in his seat and blinked his eyes.

"Gimme a cigarette." He slurred, tried two or three times to light a match with his thumbnail, lost his temper and threw the cigarette on the floor. "Don't make them matches like they used to."

Rocco ordered another round. Harry took a couple of sips, fumbled through his pockets for another cigarette and managed to knock his drink over.

"Hey bartender, get me 'nother drink."

He sipped again, then pushed the glass aside, looked both ways to see if anybody was listening, leaned across the table, grabbed Rocco's coat collar and pulled him close.

"It'll cost you twenty-five if you want to get in on this deal."

"You crazy, Harry. Think I'm going to pay you twenty-five. For what?"

"Like we was before, old pal," Harry whispered. "Fifty-fifty partners."

Rocco didn't try to pull back.

"You put that in writing, Harry?"

"Sure. Gimme a piece of paper."

He took Rocco's pen and scribbled a promise that Rocco was a partner in Mabel-Cones. He signed his name.

"Now gimme my dough."

"Not so fast, Harry, I want proof.

"I'll bring you a bank statement."

"You get the goddamn president to sign it, too, like it ain't no horseshit. I don't want none of your crap."

"Bank's closed. I'll meet cha here Monnay night; show you what I got in the bank. You bring twenty-five and I'll let ya see a statement signed by Mr. James Hotshot Blankenship hisself. Lesh have another drink to celebrate."

He took his drink, staggered to the Men's Room and poured it down the drain. When he came back, Rocco sat in his usual spot at the bar.

"Feeling better, Harry."

"Yeah. A whole lot better."

3.

The streetwise bohunks of Chicago classified Harry as dumb. Rocco placed him in that category, often declaring him an asshole, both to his face and behind his back. Suzanne's opinion worsened over the years until she concluded shortsightedness was his problem. Mr. Matheu couldn't evaluate his son and relied on Olga who believed Harry was too smart for his own good. Jim Blankenship wavered, allowing Miss Haldimann's fortune and goodwill to distort his judgment. He was never sure what her unpredictable husband would do next and was continuously afraid of offending him risking the security of her wealth. Abie Fishbein never formed an opinion of anybody in his selfish pursuit of wealth. Sergio Cellini evaluated Harry as an astute liar who suffered from the misfortune of being a self-serving psychopathic fortune hunter. Silverstein considered him a crook. Harry didn't care what any of them thought.

4.

Saturday morning following his evening with Rocco, Harry entered his office at the usual time. He closed the door and withdrew a file from the cabinet. He smiled as he examined his bank statement that was barely three weeks old. It bore the signature of James Blankenship, President, authenticating the balance of $216,735.86 held in the account of Mr. Harry Matheu with no outstanding loans.

The superb penmanship altering the dates and figures of his 1929 statement elated him. The only remaining task was to enter the date beneath Blankenship's signature. The forgery cost five hundred dollars with one hundred more for entering Monday's date.

Harry displayed his authenticated bank statement with a flourish. Rocco's eyes glistened as he devoured the numbers. Harry's exhilaration was that of the soldier charging into the face of enemy fire, all sense of caution gone, an unconquerable spirit urging him on, heedless of the dangers. He drew out the bundle of documents.

"Rocco, I want you to understand Mabel-Cones is a legit business, registered with the Secretary of State and all that. Pays taxes and everything."

"So what?"

"So I got to register you as a new partner."

"Why?"

"Because that's what the law says and that's the way my wife set it up."

Rocco stared at him.

"Naw, I ain't signing nothing. Papers with my signature ain't going to some government secretary some place, no matter who the hell he is. It don't fit my way of doing business."

"Okay," Harry shrugged, "the deal's off. I don't care."

He gathered the documents while his imagination saw a hail of gunfire and his heart raced. He did not lose his composure nor let his voice betray his excitement. He looked up, shrugged and said, "It's your loss, not mine." He was about to push the papers into his pocket when a big hand stopped him.

"Show me what I gotta sign."

"This. All this fine print don't mean a thing." Harry folded and shuffled the papers quickly, disclosing only what he wanted him to see. "Look, right here on this line. It says you're in the business that's all. This other one here, that's a share certificate that proves it. See. I signed it and it says you own 100 shares." Rocco signed. Harry slipped another piece of paper in front of him. "This one, too, Rocco, both places." He signed twice more without any further explanation. Harry gratefully accepted the envelope and verified the twenty-five thousand in cash.

"You're a new owner," Harry said as he handed Rocco his certificate for 100 shares of Mabel-Cones Inc. "First time for everything, Rocco. You ain't never owned a legitimate business before." Harry laughed loudly but Rocco looked bewildered. "We're even Rocco. Feels pretty good, don't it." They shook hands and ordered a drink.

"By the way, just initial my copy of the receipt," Harry said as he slide a paper across the bar. Rocco scrawled his initials with the comment that all this signing was a lot of horseshit.

5.

Suzanne shared Harry's conviction the depression would never end. Year after year through the thirties, the news grew worse. Suzanne did not suffer financially. Liquidating her real estate turned buildings into cash thanks to Syd Sidorowitz. Everything he told her came true exactly as he described. Unknown to her, he remembered Joe's last words and regularly checked on her welfare.

The clothing business was her pride and joy. It slowed, like everything else, but well-to-do executives continued to buy expensive wardrobes. Carole succeeded in persuading Rocco and his Mafia pals to go elsewhere. She wanted nothing to interfere with delivering the best quality to the distinguished men of Chicago. Mr. Matheu's tailoring ingenuity and creative teaching developed a brand of unsurpassed quality. The branch stores offered the same exclusive, high-priced goods as the downtown store. Throughout Chicago, they clothed the wealthy from head to foot with one-stop shopping. Nobody working for Matheu's Men's Furnishings lost their job because of the depression.

Suzanne missed Sam during the summer of '36 when he was away in Calumet City. She accepted his passion for baseball and elected to let him enjoy it without her interference. She wrote weekly and received pleasant rewarding answers that contained no hint of homesickness. According to Nadia, he was the essence of happiness in Calumet City. Suzanne imagined Nadia exaggerated when she related how Sam coached the team but she choose not to challenge the report. Nadia might not have the facts straight but she clearly delivered the message that Sam was having a great summer and his letters confirmed it.

On Tuesday morning in the fourth week of August, Harry left the house early. Suzanne noticed a change in his deportment in the last few weeks; an unaccustomed swagger in his step and hidden excitement in his speech that she had not witnessed since their early marriage. It mystified her but she opted to maintain her indifference. Her mind was on Sam. She sat on his bed examining the paraphernalia in his room, idly turning the pages of his large loose-leaf book where he recorded his own statistics of Cubs and White Sox games. He had individual records for several big-name players. What an odd child he was. His homecoming was less than a week away. Would it be the end of his happiness for another school year, living in this house with a beast he hated? Unexpectedly her day dreaming transformed itself to irritation because Harry had never taken Sam to a baseball game. Despite the expressed willingness after the 1929 debacle to respect her and tolerate their son, the malicious treatment of Sam continued and he left it to Olga to take his son to Wrigley Field. Her irritation subsided as she realized Harry wasn't going to change. Maybe she could take Sam to a baseball game. She resolved to do that before this season ended.

5.

While Suzanne sat at home musing about Sam, Harry hurried to wrap up "Operation Morning Glory". He appeared at the bank the minute it opened at nine.

"Has Mr. Blankenship come in yet?"

"I'm afraid not, Mr. Matheu. He normally doesn't arrive until ten or a little after."

"That's too bad." Harry feigned disappointment about a fact he knew. "I need a cashier's check for thirty-five thousand. Damn. Oh, excuse me. I'm sorry. I'm so upset. My supplier insists on a payment this morning. I guess I'll just have to tell the girls to shut down. A shame with the weather so hot." He grimaced, expressing the hope that Mr. Blankenship wouldn't be late. Then he said he had an important meeting at nine thirty. If he missed it, he would be in serious trouble. "I've got a deal to take in a partner and I need the cash." Swinging between despair and anxiety, he effectively befuddled the employees to the point where none could clearly understand his purpose. The nature of the emergency, whatever it may be, and his long association with Mr. Blankenship, with whom he often lunched, urged them toward a solution. Indeed, confusion was his trademark. After more than fifteen years of experience with Mr. Matheu, they knew his normal conduct subjected his account to wild swings.

"Your loan is way down, Mr. Matheu," the assistant manager said after verifying with Blankenship by telephone at home that the collateral was sound. "We can go ahead and issue the check."

While he waited, Harry cleaned the cash out of his safety deposit box into his briefcase. The check was ready when he returned from the vault.

"Thank you," he said in his most gracious voice, "you've saved my life."

He hurried to Abie Fishbein's office.

"It's been a long time, Harry," Abie said.

"Yeah." Harry had no time for generalities. "I want you to open an account for me, Abie. Here's a cashier's check for thirty-five thousand. I want the entire amount invested in Bell Telephone, nothing else. When you get the certificates, send them by certified mail to me care of General Delivery, Peoria and mark them hold for pick-up."

"I think—"

"Don't think, Abie, just do what I say. The less you know the better off you're going to be."

Harry didn't wait for an answer. Abie, burnt once by Harry, verified the check at the bank then followed the instructions, glad to get the commission.

Next, Harry went to the notary's office. Two hundred fifty dollars bought signature and seal certifying he and Rocco personally appeared before him and signed the documents in his presence. At a quiet corner in the public library, Harry reviewed the paperwork. By eleven o'clock, everything was in order; documentation to the Secretary of State, certification to Blankenship Bank, letter to Silverstein, announcement to his suppliers and the press. He mailed them and headed for home. The only remaining item was to touch Suzanne. He'd ask her for something. If she fell for it he'd take whatever he could get, then he'd kiss her good-bye and get the hell out.

7.

Suzanne's irritation turned to humor as she thought about Harry's ridiculous exploits; perhaps she could write a book about him. It would have to be a comedy. Foolhardy commitments, unwarranted support of franchisees on the edge of failure and long-term guarantees to leaseholders devastated his funds. To incorporate these terms in the first franchise agreements was a questionable inducement in the euphoric state of the economy during the twenties. In the thirties, taking over second hand, failed ice cream parlors was an insane proposition. With her imagination running wild, she made her way to the dining room for lunch.

Harry bounded into the room and sat opposite her. Excitement illuminated his eyes bringing to mind the early days of their association. She could not recall seeing him so elated, bursting with pleasant chatter that aroused her suspicions. The topic switched casually to money.

"Listen, Susie, I'm in a bit of jam. The ice cream guy wants to be paid today or else. Would you consider fifteen thousand on account?"

"On account of what?"

"On account of I need it." He laughed uproariously and slapped the table.

"No."

"I don't have time to pledge shares and all that crap." He maintained his best pleading smile remembering how'd he'd won her heart with it. "I need cash."

"Harry! You don't have any shares to pledge. You lost them in 1929. Remember, I bought them back from the bank."

"I wasn't talking about Mathard. I need cash, Susie, that's all. I'll sell some stock and pay you back next week. How about a check for ten thousand?"

"That's impossible."

"Come on, Susie, it's not my fault. Everything would have worked out—"

"Harry! Stop it. Listen to me. It's—"

He didn't like her tone. She sounded angry.

"Wait now Susie. You listen to me." He stood and moved towards her, his hands reaching out like a beseeching beggar "Everything would have worked out fine with the fifty thousand except for the damn depression. I mean, who would have ever guessed it'd go on so long?"

Suzanne rose to face him.

"You wouldn't listen to me, would you? Two or three years ago I could have done something if you'd had the courtesy to consider my advice. I tried in 1929. But no, you blunder on making the same foolish mistakes over and over."

"Aw, come on, don't get excited, I only asked for a little help for God's sake. You said you invested in your husband. I asking you to do just that one more time. What the hell! Have you changed your mind?"

Her hand trembled visibly and she felt her face reddening. Her heart thumped. Further conversation would lead to trouble. She wanted to escape and pushed past him toward the door. He grabbed her right arm above the elbow.

"For Christ sake, Suzanne, I need money and I need it now."

The veins in his neck throbbed and his face was red. The good humor gone, he looked as if a heart attack was coming on.

"Let go. You're hurting me."

"I'll more than hurt you."

She swung as hard as she could with her left hand, striking his cheek a glancing blow. His mouth opened and he let go of her arm. She raced up the stairs and into the bedroom. Before she could close the door, he pushed in behind her, throwing her backward across the bed. Her temper exploded as the smoldering fuse of anger detonated the bomb of rage. She gasped for breath and blurted out her grievance.

"Harry, you've never once taken Sam to a baseball game."

"Baseball!" Harry's mouth dropped open. "Baseball! What the hell has baseball got to do with me? I need money." He spelled it, one letter at a time. "M O N E Y. Do you understand? Money."

"You're not going to get it." She clambered from the bed to face him. "Not from me. I refuse to give you anything."

"Jesus! Damn kid could go to every bloody Cubs' game this summer." He struck her hard on the chest with the back of his hand driving her backward on to the bed. "Why didn't you take him if it's so damn important?" She struggled to rise and he knocked her down again. "Instead, you send him away to that wacky aunt of mine down in Calumet. How come that's my fault?"

Harry blamed somebody other than himself for everything. Nothing was ever his fault. She rolled across the bed, rose on the far side and walked around to face him again.

"You think he's going to tell you anything? You don't even say good morning to him."

"What are you talking about? Just as soon as the little bugger comes home, he hides somewhere. He doesn't want me. Why should I bother with him? Stick to the subject—money!"

Putting money on a plateau above Sam raised her anger to a new high. Her frustration was uncontrollable. She swung at him and he retaliated with another blow to her chest sending her sprawling across the bed face down. She screamed.

"Go away, Harry. For God's sake, go away. Get out of here! You and your stupid goddamn ice cream shops."

She rolled over and flung one of her shoes at him.

His eyebrows arched as she cussed but he easily caught the shoe. He threw it back full force. It struck her face. With bleeding nose and flailing fists, she came at him, bellowing. "Go, Harry, go go go, for God's sake get out of here."

"I don't know what's got into you and I don't care."

He struck her across the face with his open hand, a vicious blow knocking her to the bed once more, then stomped to the doorway slamming the door behind him. She lay motionless face down. The door opened.

"If you won't help me Rocco will."

"Rocco! Are you out of your mind?"

She jumped from the bed and ran at him. He nimbly stepped aside and pulled the door shut. Her head hit with a horrific impact. She collapsed on the floor. She did not hear Harry yelling through the closed door as she lay semi-conscious on the floor.

Slowly Suzanne dragged herself to the bathroom. Her cut lip bled inside her mouth. She rinsed with mouthwash. It stung. She rinsed again finding it a little less painful. She held her lip back and examined the wound. It was deep. She padded it with a cotton swab and held it tight to stop the bleeding. She spat out more blood and examined her nose. She washed gently, treated her mouth again and sat on the bed, too distraught to care about Harry. She heard a gentle knock on the door.

"Come in."

It was Nadia in tears.

"You must go to bed, Miss Haldimann. Should we call the doctor?"

"No, I think not."

"Please. Josef and I can look after everything. Please, Miss Haldimann, lie down and rest."

Suzanne complied. Her head pounded where she hit the door. She felt an egg-size swelling.

"Could I get you anything else, Miss Haldimann?" Nadia wiped her eyes.

"Yes, my nightgown. Is he gone?"

"Yes, Miss Haldimann. It was terrible."

"What did he do?"

"He ran down the hall, shouting and cursing. He said Rocco was his—he used that awful word—then he said, I remember because I was so surprised. He said, 'Wait till you find out what you're stupid—another awful word—husband has done.' Then he pushed us out of the way and swore at us. I thought he was going to punch Josef."

"Good Lord! Did he hurt him?"

"No. Oh!" Nadia shrieked. "Look, Miss Haldimann, look! You have bruises on your chest."

"It's all right, thank you, Nadia. If you would just close the curtains please, I'll rest awhile."

Reluctant as she was to take pills she had to do something about her throbbing head. Nadia brought headache tablets from the bathroom with a glass of water. Her last thought before falling asleep was her gratitude that Sam, in Calumet City, knew nothing of the turmoil.

Chapter 10 – Back to the Beginning

1.

The faint moon glow lightened the sky as Suzanne pulled the drapes back. Her face hurt, blood and mucus clogged her throat and aches tormented her body. In a trance of perplexity, time didn't matter. She pulled a housecoat over her nightgown, treated her mouth, brushed her teeth and felt for tenderness in her nose and head. Running her fingers over the discolored bruises on her chest, she winced, recoiled and let out an "ouch".

What's next? Find Harry, apologize and make up? That could never be a solution. He was the aggressor. He hit first. It was up to him to apologize. No! She hit first. No! He grabbed an arm first. What difference did it make? She looked in the open bedroom door at the end of the hall; no one there. His car wasn't in the garage nor parked in the driveway. Collapsing on the settee, she lit a cigarette. Emitting a screech at the sudden pain in her lacerated mouth, she stubbed it out, wiped the tears and shivered. Her chest and shoulders hurt. Wrapped in a blanket, she prayed somebody would share her misery, listen to her troubles, love her for herself and not care about money or business or real estate or church talk or—somebody like Daddy. Always when troubles came, she could go to him. A despairing sigh lingered on her lips. She reached for a cigarette, then remembered the discomfort of the last one. She lay back on the pillows and closed her eyes.

She gambols through tall grass heavy with purple and yellow wildflowers. He hides somewhere, waiting … waiting … waiting for her to find him. Daddy! Where are you, Daddy? Daddy, may we go back, all the way back to the beginning and start again? A raindrop moistens her cheek. I can't find you, Daddy. She turns to look behind her and sees the mess. Her life litters the fields; the grass and wildflowers gone. Look, Daddy! Look what I've done. A crowd of people stand in the distance; Harry and Sam, Nadia and Olga, Syd and Mr. Matheu—each holding a dove. She turns back. Daddy! I want a dove like everybody else. I wished for it. I tried to buy it. Help me, Daddy. Please help me find a beautiful white dove. He vanishes. She floats in an ethereal aura searching … searching … searching … and then she hears his voice … and she sees him standing a long way off. He speaks softly. She doesn't understand. She runs to him but when she looks, she is no closer; she doesn't understand. A shaft of light burns her face. Suddenly, she hears his voice through the ether of time from far, far away. It is clear and she understands at last.

"Go back, Suzanne. Go back to the beginning."

The sunlight struck her face as it crept above the sill. She stirred engulfed in a sense of realism. A bold presentiment filled her with determination, her mind crowded with memories pulling her back, back, back to the beginning before her life became corrupted, back to the inner city, back to Albert. She lay on the settee and closed her eyes. A distant voice penetrated her mind. *Go back, Suzanne. Go back to the beginning.*

She showered, dressed and went to the dining room for breakfast. Impatient to get away, she left her unfinished breakfast, hurried to her room, changed to her most unpretentious, utilitarian dress and casual loafers. She applied heavy make-up to her swollen face and rinsed her mouth again. With a white, wide-brimmed hat secured with long hatpins, she plucked a flower from the table arrangement and departed without a word, striving to rid her mind of her abhorrence of Harry. She felt wretched. She never loved him. What a fool she was. Her depression deepened, leaving only perplexing questions she should have asked herself long, long ago.

She hailed a taxi.

2.

Roosevelt Street was busy with traffic and anonymity. She gazed at the old warehouse, the site of her first job. The building was in need of repair. The sign that once hung above the door—

JOE AND ALBERT - JANITORIAL SERVICES

—hung no more. She remembered asking Daddy why Albert had his name on the sign. After all, he was just an employee.

> Because Albert and I are equals. Sure, I have money and he doesn't. Sure, I own the business and he owns nothing. But these things don't set me apart in some superior way. He's human same as me, even if our skin is different. I can bestow dignity and pride with a few dabs of paint. Some day Albert may own this business. That's why his name is on the sign.

How prophetic! She stood motionless telling herself she remembered everything he taught her. It wasn't true. She remembered only those things that served her purpose, that satisfied her own egotistical motivations. She forgot humility.

She tried the door. It opened easily, squeaking almost inaudibly. A young colored woman in her twenties sat at the desk behind the counter. She sat where Suzanne first processed invoices and recorded costs.

"Yes 'um."

"Well . . . um . . . ah . . . well, you see, I used to work here. I was just walking down the street when I saw the old building. I just wanted to look in."

"Com'on in. Look 'round. T'ain't bothering me none."

"Thank you. I worked right there at that desk you're at. I sat in that same chair."

"Musta been long ago. I been here maybe five, six years. I don't 'member no white folks 'round here."

"Albert? How's Albert?"

"Albert! Y'all know Albert?"

"Yes. Albert's name used to be on the sign over the door. Joe and Albert, it said, Janitorial Service."

"Hear now. Y'all come here."

She led the way down through the office into the back of the shop. The memories came back; not much had changed. The old storage racks for supplies stood along one side. The tool crib was gone. She remembered Albert made a special enclosure and kept the key on a ring with dozens of others.

"Anybody break in here, I'm gonna make it hard as I can for 'em to steal my stuff. Yes, sir. Anybody does that, they gonna have old Albert to deal with." She could hear his slow drawling voice followed by the deep-throated chuckle.

The swing doors on the loading dock at the rear were bolted shut. A heavy timber prevented access from either side. Covered in cobwebs, the doors had not opened for years. The decrepit ladder with the wide board rungs leading up to the mezzanine was still in place. They called the loft the *'Employees Lounge'*. Such good-humored, funny men they were, climbing up to set their lunches on the table. They sat in canvass backed chairs of unknown origin. In her first inventory, she listed them as company property, removing them later unable to find a purchase record. She smiled at her frustration. She wanted everything to be perfect and accounted for exactly as she learned in college.

The women came in at five o'clock in time for Albert to drive them to the jobs but the men often arrived at lunchtime and played cards in the afternoon. Albert's old lounge chair was the seat of honor. Somebody would plunk in it for the fun of hearing Albert cuss out the culprit. Daddy spoke again.

> Accept people the way they are, Suzanne. Because they use those four-letter words, you don't have to use them. It's not our role to teach.

"Up there." The girl pointed. "Y'able to climb that ladder."

"I did years ago. Lots of times. I guess I can still do it."

"Well, g'on up. Look 'round. I ain't gonna go. Careful now."

Suzanne removed her hat.

"Hold this for me, will you please."

She tested each rung as she made her way. Two vertical grab bars extended to the roof, each supporting a horizontal handrail from wall to wall across the mezzanine leaving a gap for access to the ladder. She paused in the opening. A timber barred the door to the outside stairs leading to the alley behind the shop. Cardboard secured with wooden slats replaced the broken-out glass. Mercifully, most of the panes in the clerestory windows remained unbroken. Evidently, no one had been in the loft for some time. She looked down; the young girl stood at the bottom of the ladder.

"When was the last time somebody came up here?"

"I dunno. Before the ark I suppose."

"Looks like it."

Two folding chairs leaned against the wall in the corner; one was open at the end of a crude table. The last person up here, whenever that was, sat there to eat. The tabletop, which was upside down, consisted of a wooden frame around the perimeter with cross members between them. Several boards lay across one end to form a flat surface. Circling the table, she searched the loft. Not much to see; nothing under the table; no sign of Albert's lounge chair; no glasses, cups, dishes, knives, forks, not even the little clean up sink and drinking spigot. Someone tore them out and capped the pipes. Even the space heater was gone. The girl yelled from below.

"Y'all see it?"

"No. There's nothing here. Only a table and some chairs."

"That's it"

"What?"

"The table."

Suzanne looked again. Of course! She removed the boards and turned the top over. Most of the letters had blistered and chipped leaving it illegible unless one knew beforehand what it said. Was the printing really that small and the letters so badly formed?

"What y'all doing' up there?"

"I found it. I'm coming down in a minute."

She looked at the sign as if saying goodbye. Or was she saying hello to a memory? She clambered down the ladder.

"It's not what I expected. It's so small. I remember it being much bigger. Are you sure that was the sign over the door?"

"I dunno. Weren't over no door since I been here."

"May I use the washroom to clean up?"

"Sure. Light's on the right."

"I know. Thank you."

Flicking the switch, Suzanne drew in her breath. The cracked washbowl and filthy toilet disgusted her. The trash basket overflowed and debris littered the floor. She shuddered, turned on the water, rinsed her hands in the cold stream squirting sideways and left as quickly as possible.

"Do you ever clean that place?"

"What for? Tain't nobody ever come in here."

"For yourself, for your own use. How can you use a filthy place like that?"

"Don't bother me none," the girl said, walking around Suzanne to close the door.

"Well it should! Aren't you in the cleaning business?"

"Not much we ain't." She shrugged as if she didn't care one way or the other. "Couple places. That's all."

"I'm not surprised."

Suzanne started for the door, then turned back.

"You didn't answer my question."

"What question?"

"Albert. How's Albert?"

"Just fine far's I know."

"Where could I find him? Does he still live in the same place?"

"Got a smaller house now. G'on down Roosevelt couple blocks. Turn right. Two blocks. Turn left. Y'all gonna see a little white house on your left. This time of day, Albert be setting on the porch. If he ain't just bang on the door. He'll be there sure."

"Thank you."

Again, Suzanne started for the door.

"Hear now, y'all forgot your hat."

Accepting the hat, she set off at a brisk pace to meet Albert, annoyed and angry. Daddy's efforts, the endless hours devoted to customer satisfaction, her careful administrative structure, every blessed thing gone. It wasn't right. She put the blame on—who was that? The owner? The manager? She shifted the responsibility for the desecration. It was Albert's fault. After everything she'd done for him, Albert let this happen. She should have known he wasn't to be trusted.

3.

She walked fast, consumed by her determination. At the corner, she stepped off the curb to a loud screech of tires.

"Chrisake ya dumb bitch! You're in Chicago."

The truck pulled away. Her cross light was red. She waited, her face hot midst the mumbling crowd. The light changed, the crowd crossed. Her pace slowed, hearing the voice ringing in her ears again.

Poor idea to get into a discussion when you're emotionally upset. You can't think clearly so you say something stupid. Don't do it. Wait 'til you calm done.

She stopped. Looking at herself in the store window, she realized she still carried her hat. Flouncing her hair back, she placed it on her head, inserted the long hatpin and turned to confront the few people who watched her.

"Would you like lessons?" she asked.

An increasing crowd funneled along in the same direction she walked. Lunch time, she supposed. She wasn't hungry but something to eat would allow her emotions to settle down. Besides, she didn't want to arrive at Albert's at mealtime.

The purse snatching!

She walked along to where it started. Maybe Danny's Place was open. Her tongue roamed her injured mouth. She couldn't imagine forcing down a bowl of his horrid chili; maybe he'd have some decent soup.

Retracing her steps, she returned to the traffic light and headed down the side street toward the restaurant. The throng moved in the same direction, ambling along the sidewalk. Where was Danny's place? Funny how memory plays tricks. In the next block, she recognized the dilapidated house where Mama Baker lived. The boy snatched her purse right here; or was it on the other side of the street? Yes. He ran down the street through the light from Danny's Place. Now she remembered the dreadful experience. Retreating along her path, she saw the line shuffling through an open door; a soup kitchen. That's where they were going; free meals for the destitute. That's Danny's Place! She dared herself to enter.

"Excuse me. Who's in charge here."

"That's Missus Grant. She's in charge here now."

"Thank you."

Suzanne worked her way towards the designated Mrs. Grant who appeared to have six arms and four legs all going every which way at the same time. She slopped the most revolting mixture on to plates at an incredible rate.

"Keep it moving," she ordered. "Keep it moving. Here you, only one. Put that other plate back. PUT IT BACK I said. Guard! Guard! Get that son-of-a-bitch. Kick his ass on out of here."

Wherever Danny was, he wasn't there. She could not recall such a depressing scene. Her wrath changed to chagrin. These poor people, starving, hounded by guards, cursed at; what did they do to deserve this treatment? Ready to encounter Albert, she intended to question him logically without losing her composure. She would demand an explanation but do it politely. She slowed her pace, took a deep breath and marched onward to her encounter with the infamous Albert.

4.

Rounding the corner, she saw the small house nestled between two larger ones. Behind a white picket fence, shriveled wildflowers grappled for existence amid a host of weeds appropriating the neglected lawn. What a shame! The house so pretty, a jewel in a garden of thorns; how much prettier with cultivated garden and lush green grass; perhaps a lilac bush to conceal the neighbor's ugly window blinds shutting out the world.

He sat on the porch: So that's what happened to his chair. His head turned. She waved. He did not respond. She swung the gate open and heard the rusty hinges squeak.

"Who's that? Who's there?"

Her heart thrilled at the sound of the deep resonant voice she remembered so well. He spoke as if about to tell a joke or burst into laughter.

"Hello, Albert. Don't you recognize me?"

"Suzanne! I'd recognize that voice anywheres. My! My! Nice of you to visit. It's been a long time, ain't it? Now let's see. The last time we met was when we signed off on that last payment, weren't it? Come over here. Come over here and take my hand, honey. Oh my! It sure brings joy to my heart to hear your voice."

He lifted his hands from his lap holding them in mid air. She walked towards him, arms outstretched. He made no movement to meet her hands. She lowered hers to his. He wore dark glasses with side shields completely covering his eyes and shutting out the daylight. He was blind!

"Albert! Oh Albert!" Tears swelled in her eyes. "It is so good to see you. I'm sorry I've been away so long." She reached down encircling his broad shoulders, hugging him with her cheek against his face. "Tell me." She sniffled. "Tell me about yourself. Tell me all that's happened."

"No tears. No tears now."

"They're tears of joy, Albert. Not tears of sorrow. There's a difference you know."

"That's right. I know the difference. Last year Sarah died. I guess it was partly my fault. Makes me feel bad. She talked 'bout her pains, her hurt a few years back. 'Aw, tain't nothing but old age,' I said. Got her some pills and stuff. Maybe helped some. Every so often, she'd say she was hurting. I'd get more pills. Kind of stuff they advertise kills the pain. Then last year—I ain't sure where we is right now, August, I think. Anyway 'bout a year ago she started bleeding. She come to me. 'Albert, I's pissing blood, I am. We gotta do something,' she says. I got a taxi and took her down to the hospital. Too late; she was so full of sickness the docs couldn't do nothing; died less than a month later. Maybe if'n I took her to the doc when she first complained she'd been alive now . . .. You still there?"

Suzanne listened quietly. She nodded her head occasionally forgetting the necessity of confirming her presence from time to time.

"Yes. I'm still here. It's just so sad, I couldn't speak for a moment."

"Don't feel that way. You know we all makes mistakes. I think of my mistake as a good mistake. You see, she's gone but now I can't never die. I have to stay right here and live forever. If'n I die and meet my Sarah up there, she's gonna scold me so bad she's gonna send me plumb to hell."

His deep coarse belly laugh came from the depths of his being. Suzanne marveled at his ability to dismiss his personal tragedy.

"You haven't changed, Albert. Not one little bit."

"Well, that ain't true. I have changed. These old eyes have changed and now I can't do hardly nothing. But y'all gonna stay awhile ain't you. After we's talked a bit we can go in the house and I'll show you 'round. Inside, I take off these blinders and put on the damnedest pair glasses you ever seen. They let me see a little bit; enough to make by way 'round the house. Can't read none. Listen to the radio. Get the news that way. And listen to them funny shows; Lum n' Abner, Amos n' Andy. Takes my mind offa my troubles."

"So you still have some vision."

"Just knowing you is setting there, Suzanne, why it fills my mind with memories. I met a lot of fellows in my lifetime but I never met anyone like your daddy. I 'member our first meeting. He was looking for somebody to help on them houses he was always fixing up. This was long before we had the office building. Don't 'member how I heard about it. Don't matter anyway. I goes over to see him. Your daddy always considered both sides of everything."

"I remember that very well. He'd say, 'What's the other side of the question?'"

"The way I recall it was, 'What's the other side of the coin?' But I guess that's the same thing."

"I guess so."

"That very first day, before I'd done a stitch of work, he takes a coin out of his pocket. 'This here coin got two different sides,' he says. 'See that.' 'Yes, sir,' says I. 'This side here says if'n y'all work and y'all do your job good then you're gonna be a success and have a good life. The other side is just an old bent coin says if'n you is lazy and don't want to work then you gonna have nothing. Get to work now, he says, and let's see what kind of coin y'all got in your pocket."

"I never heard that story before."

"I guess nobody had no reason to tell it. Don't know as I ever told it before neither. Can't 'member when that was. Long before the turn of the century, I know that. I worked for your daddy near fifty years, I did. Wonderful years they was too. I never met a man so tough and so honest. He built lots of houses down here in this neighborhood where everybody curses and swears at their landlord who don't do nothing for 'em. Only one they never cursed was Joe Haldimann. If'n they had a complaint they'd come to me. Did you know that? Did you know I was Joe's caretaker?"

"No. No I didn't"

"One time he come to me with one of his 'this side - that side' stories. 'Y'all can learn to read and speak better than you do or you can stay the way you are.' We talked 'bout it and he convinced me to study some and to practice my reading, which I done. As a reward, he put me in charge of the rental units down here in my neighborhood. People had a complaint they'd come to me. I'd fix their problem and if'n I had trouble I'd let Joe know and he'd get right on down here and do something 'bout it. Yes 'm. There wasn't a complaint that wasn't handled in a day or two."

"That was Wilbur's job when I came to work for the company."

"That's right. Wilbur took over from me. He could read and write much better than me but I learned some like your daddy told me. There was no secrets from your daddy. He explained 'bout the leases and how they worked and all. Then when my reading improved to the point Joe was satisfied that I was willing to improve then he let me do all the leasing, arranging prices and all. I'd bring him the lease when it was ready to sign. I'd collect the rent and take it to the bank. I never seen such a trusting man as your father."

Suzanne's heart ached as she listened to his stories. So much existed between the two men, she wanted to hear more.

"Your stories bring tears to my eyes. But tell me more. I want to learn more about him. I loved my father so much."

"We all did, missy. We all did."

They sat in silence each in a reverie about Joe Haldimann. She thought she should say something then changed her mind. She knew he groped in the dimly lit passages of his memory. Better to let him drift slowly through the dusty corridors than to illuminate his way with blinding interruptions. She waited. In a few moments, he started again.

"You know there come a time when I never seen your daddy so low. Everything he worked for he thought was gone. Here was a man who made me what I was, who taught me to go out and make myself something, who told me over and over there was two sides to every coin, here was a man who was destroyed. We sat together that night. We sat in silence. Finally I said, 'Joe,' I said, 'why don't y'all tell me what it is that's happened? Tell me what it is that's gone wrong.' He told me how Mister Charles Arlene called him; told him how impressed he was; how they wasn't gonna charge no interest or nothing like that. He told me he walked out of that man's office like the president of the United States had just said, 'Joe you is the greatest.' Few years later—I guess during the depression of ninety-three—they was about to take it away from him. You know, in all the years I worked for your daddy, I didn't do much for him and he done so much for me. He provided me with work. He set goals for me I never could have set for myself. He made me a better person than I was. And suddenly it was destroyed. I 'member how discouraged I was. I went home and said to my old lady, 'Sarah,' I said, 'we done gone lost everything.' She asked me why and I tried to explain. She said, 'Y'all don't have no problem. I don't understand,' she said. 'There just ain't no problem.' 'Why?' I asked. She said, 'You work for as honest and true a white man as exists. Just tell him to sign the lease. Tell him to lease it to himself. Then the problem ain't no problem.' And that's what I done. I said 'Joe, there ain't no problem. You sign the lease. You make this here place your headquarters. You make it the place where your business is gonna be run from.' And that's what he done. It was so simple; the other side of the coin and for some reason he couldn't see it. I've wondered 'bout that. I've wondered 'bout that all my life. There's something I don't understand. And I tell you I still don't understand how a man so smart as your daddy couldn't see something so simple as my Sarah. The contracting business, cleaning business, them companies mister Syd made, every one of them operated out of that building 'til the day he died at a cost what was less than anything he could have got anywheres else in Chicago. And at that very moment he couldn't see the other side of the coin. Maybe it was the time he was marrying your mamma. Maybe he was in love. Maybe that was it."

Suzanne laughed. "You did that for him?"

"No, I didn't do nothing. It was my Sarah done something."

"I stopped by the old office today. I was upset. The place is a mess. It broke my heart walking down the street to see the sign gone. Joe and Albert. No sign. I went in. A young girl sat at my desk. Maybe twenty-five, twenty-seven, something like that. I asked about the sign. She told me where it was. I climbed up the ladder to the *'Employees Lounge'*. I found it."

"Y'all went up to the *'Employees Lounge'*. To-day you done that?"

"Yes. Today."

"Ain't that something. 'Member them fellows going up there setting in my chair. This very chair I'm setting in right here today. 'Member that? You son-of-a-bitch! Get out of here! Get out of my chair. Why you young fu—excuse me I forgot for a minute who I was talking to—why you young nigger I'd say, you think you got some kind of privilege here to sit in my chair. Then we'd laugh together. Excuse me I forgot. But that's the way it was."

"I remembered. I thought about Daddy saying because you used four letter words, it didn't mean I had to use them. 'It wasn't our job to teach,' is what he said."

"Maybe that's what he said but it wasn't true. It was his job to teach. He was always teaching, always making life better for everybody. And you know because he made life better for everybody else he made life better for himself."

She paused, not knowing what to say. That simple sentence told the story of her marriage. An old uneducated black man she lived with for a year when she was four told her the lesson of love she'd allowed to escape.

"And for you too," he added.

"I guess that's true," she whispered.

"That business. It's a shame 'bout that business. You was good to me Suzanne. You made it possible for me to own a business. Me, an old nigger without no schooling. And you gave it to me."

"You paid for it."

"That's right. But you gave me something to work for and you gave me an opportunity to make something to pay for it with. And now . . .."

He didn't finish, pushing himself up from his chair.

"Come on in and see them funny glasses."

She rose, reaching for his hand.

"Lead the way," she said.

The bright, cheery atmosphere attracted her. The house was finished in light colors; white curtains, light gray carpets and painted white ceilings.

"It's beautiful," she gasped.

"You see, it's all white or nearly white. That's so I can see easier when I'm inside."

He removed his shaded glasses and donned a pair of heavy magnifying spectacles. They stared at each other. His pupils filled the whole spectrum of the glass. He squinted through the thickest lenses she ever saw.

"Come a little closer. I can see you now but I can't make out the features." She took a step towards him. "My, you surely look like your daddy," he mused. Before she answered he said, "Now if'n that ain't so, don't tell me. That's the way I want to 'member you and that's the way I see you now."

She smiled. "Yes," she lied, "I do look like Daddy."

She examined the surroundings. There were cobwebs in the corners at the ceiling. There was dirt on the floor. Everywhere she looked there were signs of poor housekeeping.

"You do your own house cleaning?"

She waited for the reply. There was a pause.

"Ah . . .."

Another pause.

Silently, she sucked in her breath. How thoughtless!

"I'm sorry. I didn't mean to embarrass you."

He moved towards the corner of the parlor reaching out until his hand found the back of a chair. Slowly he sank into it. The movements were slow, deliberate and cautious. Had she upset him? Or were these the movements of a blind man being careful to avoid a fall? She wanted to go to him, ask forgiveness, put her arms around him and comfort him. She didn't mean it the way it sounded. But she froze, horrified at her own callousness. The silence seemed interminable. What had she done? At last he spoke, his voice like like a prelate reciting a dirge.

"For all what's been given to me, for everything your daddy done for me, for this house, for having enough money to live out my years, for forty-three years with my Sarah, I wanted to say thank you. I chose my son, our only son. I wanted him to understand. I wanted him to have those things like was given to me. I did what you did. I took our contract, the agreement you made for me. I took it to a lawyer. I said make an agreement like this between me and my son; make it possible he should have this business, that his life get as much as mine from all what's been given to me. My son signed the agreement. Then he found excuses. He found there were hard times. He found it hard to keep customers. He found it hard to get new customers . . . but . . . but . . .."

Tears dripped from his chin. She went to him, dried his face with her hankie and held his hands.

"Albert," she said, "you don't need to explain. You don't need to tell me. Before I came here, I went there. I went to the old office, to your office, to Daddy's office. You don't need to explain. I saw for myself. I saw the old sign that used to hang over the door. Joe and Albert - Janitorial Service. That's what it said. Albert, I want to have a new sign painted. I want to see a new sign above the door. One that will tell the whole world this is the business of Joe and Albert."

"Won't do no good. No. Don't do that, Suzanne. It would be a mistake. Joe is dead. I will be soon. Joe and Albert are gone. No. He has to paint his own sign just the same as you. You young ones has to do it yourself. But he doesn't want to. Suzanne! My dear Suzanne! Please understand. You can't do it for him. He has to do it for himself and if he don't want to, then there ain't nothing you and I can do. That's just the way it is. Don't go back, Suzanne. Don't go back 'til there's a bright new sign hanging over the door. A sign what's been painted by him for himself."

She thought of her own life, how it, too, needed a new sign. She sought to change the subject.

"Is there anything I can do for you Albert?"

"Yes," he answered, "yes there is."

He paused; a smile lifted the corners of his mouth.

"Come to see me. Come down here and talk to me. Come so we can talk together 'bout a fellow I once knew, fellow by the name of Joe Haldimann. So I can hear 'bout his daughter. So I can tell that girl all the stories I know 'bout that fellow so's she can write a history of Joe Haldimann."

She promised.

Chapter 11 – Ice Cream Man

1.

On Tuesday, Suzanne cast aside her self-induced recriminations and found rejuvenation in Albert's words; Rocco struggled with self-doubt. He awoke seized with a foreboding of disaster. Did dumb-ass Matheu pull a fast one? The bugger didn't give him a damn copy of the papers he signed. How was he going to explain all the legal crap with his signature on a goddamn piece of paper? Who was the Secretary of State and what did he do fercrisake? In the restaurant for his morning meal at eleven, he barked at everybody and yelled at the chef where he'd eaten countless breakfasts.

"This is the worst goddamn joint I ever been in and I'm not coming back."

The word spread.

"Rocco's madder 'n hell; better step aside."

Nobody knew why.

His irrepressible worry intensified hour-by-hour and his temper matched it, step-by-step. He tried to reach Harry.

"Yes, he was at the bank early this morning but we have not seen him since."

"No, he wasn't in his office and we don't expect him."

Despite an agreement that he was never to call Harry at home, he called anyway.

"I'm sorry, Mr. Matheu is not in today."

In the evening, Harry didn't show at the bar. In itself, this was normal because it wasn't Friday, but Rocco, having worried himself to a state near insanity, didn't connect Harry with the day of the week. His self-assurance reached an all-time low that Harry, had he known, would have relished. Having tormented himself into an uncontrolled state of apprehension, Rocco drank too much, growled at everybody, visited a whorehouse with ineffective results and went home to bed at three in the morning.

The telephone rang at nine o'clock Wednesday morning. After the eighth ring, Rocco blinked his eyes. The daylight hurt. He reached from under the covers and clutched the instrument.

"Huh," he groaned.

"Mr. Rossetti?"

"Huh."

"May I speak to Mr. Rossetti please."

"Yeah."

"Congratulations, sir. I wonder—"

"Go away fercrisake."

He slammed the receiver on the hook.

An hour later a vague recollection of talking to somebody surfaced in his mind. Jesus! Was that Harry?

Forgetting his threat never to come back, he entered the usual restaurant for breakfast at eleven. The place was a bedlam. A flashbulb popped in his face; then another; and a third. The boys crowded around all babbling at once. Rocco stood in the middle of the dining room, hands on his hips shouting at everybody to shut up.

"What the hell's going on?"

He heard the word congratulations or variations of it in a dozen different voices. Then somebody delivered the message he didn't want to hear.

"The Don wants to see you right away."

A newspaper lay open on the counter. He shuddered at the confirmation of his worst fears.

"ROCCO ROSSETTI BUYS MABEL-CONES BUSINESS"

2.

Before the newspaper published the story, Rocco enjoyed the senior position of the non-blood relations, the most reliable, trusted and loyal captain in the family. He did as ordered and he didn't ask questions; the Don's favorite and everybody knew it.

"My son," said the Don in his raspy voice, "why do you want to be in the ice cream business?"

"Padrone, the son-of-a-bitch conned me."

He did not have a choice because he could not lie to the Don. He made a mistake and he admitted it. He told the story exactly as it happened. The Don, with his expressionless voice and detached arrogance, dismissed him telling him to get rid of it.

Rocco's troubles had just begun. He received written notice calling for immediate payment of forty-two thousand five hundred dollars from the Blankenship Bank. Then came warnings from suppliers threatening to stop deliveries and demanding immediate payment of outstanding balances. After he refused to talk to a lawyer who called about a breach of contract, he received a formal notice filed by thirteen Mabel-Cones franchisees. Two days later another attorney representing thirteen property leases asked the new owner to confirm the existence of the contracts and his intent to honor them. Rocco was liable for more than a hundred thousand although nobody knew exactly how much. The final figure depended on the decision to stay in business or to negotiate the wind-up with the operators and cancel the leases.

The Don was incredulous as the claims flowed in. Worse, the calls from other families embarrassed him.

"It was a mistake; just a little mistake. A shyster conned one of my boys who made a mistake. Nothing to worry about. There's a contract on the bum what set him up. No problem; no problem at all; be gone in a couple of days."

Around the country amusement replaced worry as the media uncovered details of the hoax. The orders to Rocco were simple; get it settled.

Rocco failed. Inexperienced with the machinations of the media, he said Mabel-Cones was out of business. The resulting headline suggesting bankruptcy produced a bevy of legal documents with creditors hurrying to get in line. One pundit wrote an article with a questioning headline.

WHO IS ROSSETTI AND WHAT'S HIS GAME

It questioned the integrity of the new owner and posed humorous possibilities about the forays of the Mafia. Rocco followed by denying bankruptcy, which produced another round of articles that pulled no punches alluding to Rossetti's shady reputation. The shops closed and sales stopped. Lawyers appeared in court with liens and lawsuits. The family became the butt of jokes circulating the underworld. The Don's temper ran short.

"This is the third time, Rocco, I told you. Settle it, keep your mouth shut and forget all the crap about getting even."

It was beyond Rocco's ability.

Exasperated, the Don ordered him to take the problem to Sergio Cellini.

"Rocco, what I do depends on what you do," Cellini said. "Simple question; are you running the ice cream business or are you getting out?"

"I'm gonna ice that son-of-a-bitch."

"I know that, Rocco, but that's not what I asked you. Are you in or out?"

"Out."

"Okay. Get out of here and keep your mouth shut. If anybody asks you a question, and I mean anybody—your pals, your enemies, your whores, reporters, anybody except the Don—you say no comment and that's all you say. You don't make any threats, you don't mention Harry, you don't tell them I'm working on it; you don't say anything. Got it?"

"Got it."

"Then get out of here."

Except that his clients didn't see the humor, Cellini would have laughed. His assessment of Harry was accurate. As the investigation unearthed details, he came to admire Harry's ingenuity. He met first with Jim Blankenship and his lawyer.

"Gentlemen, I am an investigator, not a lawyer," Cellini said. "Mr. Rossetti elected to settle your claim out of court. With that in mind, may I have the details."

"Certainly. This is a copy of the August 28 sales contract signed by Rocco, Harry and witnessed by a notary. Accompanying that, you will see a short paper initialed by Mr. Rossetti that allows Matheu to withdraw thirty-five thousand dollars as settlement for accrued wages and goodwill. Lastly, here is a copy of the canceled check. Our claim is fully, properly and legally documented and we do not intend to negotiate for less than the full amount, which includes attorney's fees."

Every claimant was the same; each had factual, authentic documents leaving Rocco not a leg to stand on. The only people left out were the operators and the storeowners but their claims were indisputable beyond agreeing on a final amount. Rocco paid out of his own pocket, which was not nearly as degrading as the loss of respect in the family. The final tally came to one hundred thirty-eight thousand dollars.

The negotiations with the operators revealed that forty thousand dollars from July and August sales were missing. The difference between the operator's weekly checks cashed by Harry and the bank deposits clearly proved that Harry stole it.

"How did the newspapers find out?" Rocco asked.

"Harry wrote the story and mailed it to them."

"I'll kill—"

"Don't tell me what you're going to do," Cellini said. "You better take a lesson from your friend Harry."

"From that—"

"Shut up!" Cellini waved his hands cutting off Rocco's blasts of hatred and threats of revenge. "Let me tell you how Harry pulled this off. It's simple. He didn't tell anybody what he was doing."

"What do you mean?"

"No one has appeared in this investigation whose testimony is worth a damn against Harry. The fellow who did the forgery denies it and we have no proof. The notary who witnessed the documents says he has a hundred customers a day. He doesn't remember you but your signature happens to be in his visitor's log."

"I didn't sign nothing in any visitor's log."

"So it's a forgery but the judge won't care. He'd sooner lock you up than minor players like Matheu and his pals. I suppose your attorney could make a case but I wouldn't recommend it. You open the door and invite the DA in and who knows where the investigation will lead."

"I'm going to get him," Rocco snarled. "I'm going to squeeze Fishbein till he sings."

Cellini smiled across the desk. "I've already done that. He mailed the certificates to Harry Matheu, General Delivery, Las Vegas. Have a nice trip, Rocco."

Chapter 12 – Clarence Burroughs

1.

Suzanne believed her father relayed her problem to the Lord, and the Lord heard him. To travel the emotional minefield from the anguish of a crumbling marriage to peace of mind could only occur at the hands of the Lord.

"Nadia, I've had a bizarre day and no lunch. Would you bring some tea, please? Perhaps some bread-and-butter. Don't go to any trouble. A little of whatever you have so it won't spoil my supper."

She skimmed the newspaper, half expecting her mental distress from the day before to return, surprised that it didn't. Nadia brought the tea tray and placed it on the coffee table.

"Will that be all, Miss Haldimann?"

"Thank you."

A covered serving dish nestled beside the tea service. Suzanne lifted the silver top and smiled. Nadia and Josef could not serve bread and butter any more than Sam could give up baseball. Cinnamon toast with the crusts trimmed, open face lobster tidbits, two dainty quiche tarts and half an apple, peeled and sliced circled a lace doily decorated with parsley and celery. Sampling this and tasting that, the dish was suddenly empty, undoubtedly spoiling her supper. She lit a cigarette and rang the bell for Nadia to remove the tea tray. Alone in the living room, she reflected on her marriage. She would close the door on Harry Matheu and get on with her life.

"You have a telephone call from downtown, Miss Haldimann."

Suzanne took the call in her private office.

"Miss Haldimann, I've arranged our meeting for Friday after Labor Day at nine o'clock. Is that satisfactory?"

"Perfectly. How long do you think we'll be?"

"Not more than two hours. It's the formal contract signing and shaking hands. Their major investor will attend but I imagine it's for the publicity; more a social event than anything else."

What would she have done if he had asked to meet immediately? Not to worry; in ten days the bruises would vanish and the swelling subside. Attending to her other business at the same time would be a good idea since she'd be downtown anyway. She called Clarence Burroughs, arranging to meet in his office at four o'clock the same afternoon. Then she called Silverstein.

"Why are we meeting?"

"Harry and I had a fight. I'm afraid we're at the end of the road."

"Where is Harry now?"

His voice took on a serious tone

"I don't know." She sighed not wanting to talk about the details. "He left after the fight and hasn't come home. Can't this wait until next week?"

"That depends. Did he hit you?"

"Yes."

Cross-examination over the telephone was not what she intended.

"I'll tell you about it next week."

"Are you swollen? Black and blue?"

"Yes, but—"

"A photographer will be at your house at nine tomorrow morning." His voice signaled urgency as he assumed his command post. "Have him take pictures of every blemish on your body. I mean everywhere even if it is embarrassing for you. Have you changed the locks?"

"For heaven's sake, Phillip, he's not a thief."

He paid no attention while he bellowed at somebody. She could hear him issuing orders like the captain of a ship engaged in a sea battle. "Yes, today. Now," he roared, then came back on the line to Suzanne.

"A couple of men will be there in a few minutes. They will identify themselves as Dominic Lock Service. They will change all the locks and leave new keys."

"Phillip, is this necessary?"

"I don't know. Probably not, but we'll do it anyway."

"What do I say to Harry?"

"If those men get there soon enough you won't have to say anything because he won't be able to get in. Otherwise, should Harry call have the servants say you're not home, no matter if it's three o'clock in the morning. Now what's your idea of how to settle this?"

"Phillip, I haven't had a chance to think about it. I don't want to hurt him. I only want him to leave Sam and me alone. No visiting privileges. I'm willing to make a reasonable monetary settlement, at least enough for him to pay his debts."

Silverstein signaled his disagreement with an audible moan.

"Suzanne you are too generous but I won't argue. I suggest we set the amount not to exceed your guarantee at the bank less all expenses incurred by you including attorney fees. You've all ready given that much anyway."

She shook her head. There were times when his efficiency irked her.

"Even changing the locks?"

"Of course. Why not? We could always concede that as a gesture of goodwill. What's his financial status right now?"

"Broke, I think."

"What a shame. After all you did for him. Does he owe the bank?"

"I'm sure he does."

"I suppose his collateral is your note. I imagine he lied to Blankenship but we can't do anything about that."

"Phillip you're unmerciful."

"That's what you pay me for; mercy's too expensive. We'll try for a settlement out of court."

He asked a few more questions. The home was solely hers? Yes. Had Harry ever contributed anything to the upkeep, maintenance, municipal taxes or anything else related to the property? Not a cent. Had Harry ever contributed to the ordinary cost of living, like food, light, heat and so on? Never.

"Like shooting fish in a barrel," Phillip mumbled. "See you next Friday at eleven."

Silverstein called early the next morning with the news of Harry's exploits.

"He's tricked Rocco and it won't cost you anything. Blankenship is returning your guarantee."

"Then we don't need the photographs?"

"We certainly do."

"Why?"

"Harry has disappeared."

2.

On Friday of the next week, Suzanne arrived for the contract signing to find a message from Phillip that he rescheduled their discussion of the divorce to one-o'clock. It didn't matter since she intended to spend the day downtown anyway. She joined the men in the conference room.

"Miss Haldimann, this is Mr. Jenkins."

Jenkins, smiling broadly, accepted her outstretched hand in both of his.

"Jerome," he said.

Suzanne expected formality with strangers.

"Suzanne," she said, ill at ease.

He did not release her hand. She struggled to pull it from his grasp.

"You wouldn't remember."

He was a good-looking man, middle-seventies, tall with a pleasant face and a full head of gray hair. He resembled her father, especially the eyes.

"Remember what?"

Unable to fathom his greeting, she could not hide the anger in her tone.

"It's been a long time."

His smile bordered on laughter. Suzanne gazed around the room to discover everybody watched the exchange. It was as if they joined in a conspiracy, their smiles about to break into laughter.

"You've changed a lot," he added, "and I must say you are beautiful."

"Mr. Jenkins! Please; I don't know what you're talking about."

"I suppose not. It's been many years."

More perplexed than ever, she relaxed realizing they perpetrated a joke prepared before her arrival.

"All right," she said looking into his eyes, "when did we meet?"

"When you were four."

"Four!"

"I don't blame you for not remembering."

"Four," Suzanne repeated. "And what was the occasion?"

"Your mother's funeral."

Suzanne's mouth dropped open.

"Gracious! You're one of Jane's children."

"Yes."

"So you're my . . . what? Cousin?"

"I don't think so. I'm your father's cousin, which I think makes me your great-uncle, or something like that. I don't know."

After the contract signing, Jerome and Suzanne talked in Harry's office.

"I remember your father when I was a boy in Tupper's Corners. I was the youngest in our family, eight years younger than he was. He was strong and worked all the time but he always had time to play. I remember he'd take us for rides on the hay wagon and tell us stories. I think his secret was to make work into a game."

Suzanne smiled.

"It certainly was. I don't know about his early days, he never talked about his parents much. But when I was old enough to understand his work, I learned it was a game to him."

"Talking about the family embarrassed him, I imagine. I think even as a child, his father embarrassed him."

Suzanne's heart skipped a beat.

"Embarrassed about his father. Why, for heaven's sakes? What would embarrass him?"

"You don't know the story of your father's birth?"

Suzanne looked away to conceal her blushing.

"He told me a little about his mother."

"The story is a family chronicle. I suppose somebody more inhibited than my mother would have buried it but not her. She loved the story of the morning your father came into their world."

"Tell me, please."

"Your grandfather, Jack, was a drinker and womanizer. He hated his father; that would be your great-grandfather. They fought about everything until the old man ordered Jack to work for his room and board. Jack quit school and never learned to read or write. When he got a little older, he occasionally drank himself into a stupor on Saturday night. In 1854, on a Sunday morning in early September Jack lay sprawled on his bunk after a big night in the bar. The cattle, bellowing like foghorns in the morning mist, woke him. As he headed for the barn, his bleary eyes saw a crate on the front porch. An army blanket lay folded loosely on top with a note pinned to it. He took the note and stuffed it in his pocket when something moved. He fetched a stick and flipped the blanket fold back. Nothing. He caught the blanket again, pulled back the second fold. Down the steps he stumbled and ran to our house across the road.

"Jane, who could see humor in anything, doubled up with laughter. Her laughter brought her husband. 'Look here, Jim, look at this,' she said, 'Jack has a baby. A baby in a box.' They laughed till they cried. 'What the note says, Jack, is; this is yours.'

"Jack went home, carried the baby into the house. Whatever it was, it howled its head off. He used to say he figured it was female because it made more noise than the cows. Out in the barn he could still hear the howling. It suddenly dawned on him the baby needed feeding. He fetched the two-wheeled manure cart, loaded in the baby and took it to Jane. Her loving instincts responded. She took in the child. They decided his birthday was September first and they named him Joe."

"Did anyone ever know for sure who my grandmother was."

"No. Jack had a wide assortment of bed companions. Everybody agreed it was an oriental woman. They remembered her pregnant around town during the summer and then she disappeared."

"Then what happened?"

"Joe, like his Dad, didn't like schooling and didn't try. His pleasure was working. It was a pleasant time for Jack with Joe working the farm but he didn't change his ways spending many a Saturday night with his head swimming in whiskey. Joe didn't care for his father; found him embarrassing. On the other hand, I think he respected Jack's work ethic. Nothing, not the pains, the aches, the weather, the hangovers, not a single excuse ever kept Jack from his work. Joe had to accept the drinking but Jane said he always looked for a way out. Then came the famous fire and he was gone, returning to Tupper's Corner only twice after that. The first time was to get signatures when he mortgaged the farm. The second was for Jack's funeral."

"He often told me the story of Mr. Tolliver who took the mortgage on the farm. Until this moment, I thought Tolliver's funeral ended the story. Now, I find my grandfather sitting on the porch at Tupper's store"

"He didn't do anything after Joe left. To him it was somebody else's property. Joe paid Jane for his room and board but Jack just whittled on Tupper's porch. He died a while later. George Tupper performed the funeral rites in his little church on the corner. Afterwards everybody gathered at the old farmhouse. Seven families attended. Jane was sick and my father took her home. Most of us paid our respects and left. With no female member of the family to comfort, the women left the men to console the only remaining relative. They considered it fitting to remember Jack by drinking Kentucky bourbon provided by his son. The event finished in a dedication at the store where old Jack had expanded on the splendor of his son's achievements in Chicago. In the true spirit of the occasion, they renamed the intersection at the crossroads Jack's Corner. The next day the blurred recollections and George Tupper's contradiction of the events of the evening, resulted in the denial of your grandfather's only memorial."

Suzanne smiled. The story didn't offend her and she wanted to hear more.

"Will you come for supper tonight?"

"Thank you, I'd love to."

"About six, then."

3.

Suzanne left the office looking forward to the dinner hour. On the elevator, her thoughts turned to the complexities of the business world. She liked her partners; they shared a trust in one another, she as a source of clients and they as successful disciples of her theories. The doors of the elevator opened. With a mission to carry out before the meeting with Silverstein, she pushed her meditations aside and stepped into the clothing store.

"Is Mr. Matheu downstairs?"

"Yes he is. Would you like me to call him Miss Haldimann?"

"No, thank you. If I may, I'll go down and say hello."

It would be impossible for Harry not to blab to somebody. She wanted to insure his parents were not the target of his lies. As soon as she saw Mr. Matheu, she knew the answer.

"Hello, grandpa. How are you?"

She spoke softly, hoping not to alarm him. She failed. Mr. Matheu jumped as if she snuck up behind him and yelled boo. His face blanched and his nervousness belied his weak smile.

"Oh, Suzanne, Olga and I are so sorry. It is terrible. Terrible. We want to help so much. What can we do?"

"Have you seen him lately?"

He stammered, stuttered and coughed.

"Harry was here," he said at last.

"When?"

"A week last Tuesday. He told us . . .." He paused and it wasn't hard for Suzanne to guess why.

"He said I told him to get out." She looked at his pale face. "Is that what he said, grandpa?"

He nodded.

She glanced about; the employees looked away quickly. Obviously, Harry's exploits were the major topic of conversation. They strained their ears to hear the discussion. She took Mr. Matheu's hand, led him into the private cubicle and closed the door.

"Grandpa, I know you don't want to hear this but I'm going to tell you the truth. He beat me. I have photographs of the bruises on my body. I'm sure you don't want to see them. I'm sorry to tell you this but Harry lied to you."

He looked ghastly but said nothing.

"Would you like a drink of water?"

He shook his head. She continued.

"Do you know where he is now?"

"No, not now." He paused and gulped for air. "He left. He stayed in the apartment for two days and made us swear never to tell anyone. He said if you found out he'd —"

"Never mind. I don't want to know what he said. Then what happened?"

"On the third day, about six o'clock in the morning—it was just getting light—he woke us and said good-bye. He said we would never see him again. Then he left."

"You haven't seen him since?"

He hesitated. Obviously, there was more. She hated dragging it out of him but she had to know but he could not find the words.

"I understand," she said softly holding his hand, "but if you don't tell me then I can't do anything to help."

At last he spoke.

"We watched from our balcony; a big black car. We couldn't see anybody. He got in the back seat. The car drove away. That was all."

She knew where they took Harry but didn't have the courage to tell the old man. She put her arm on his shoulder and kissed his cheek.

“I’ll do what I can, grandpa. You go back to work now. I’ll let you know the minute I learn anything.”

She helped him to his cutting table hoping she would never have to tell him the truth.

4.

Suzanne sank into the visitor’s chair in Silverstein’s office. Despite her feelings toward Harry, Mr. Matheu’s revelations depressed her.

“Have you heard from Harry?” Phillip asked.

“Not a word. Did you expect I might?”

Phillip sat at his desk, faultlessly dressed as always. She wanted to know if Mr. Matheu made his suit but she thought it impolite to ask.

“Yes, I did. Con artists like to boast when they pull a neat one. They’re like the cat that brings the dead bird home to show its competence as a hunter.”

“I don’t think he would show off for my benefit.”

“Probably not. Anyway, he’s left.”

“Left?”

She sat back in her chair fully aware of what was coming next.

“Don’t you mean gone?”

He smiled.

“My dear, no one has seen Harry since your spat. If Cellini can’t find him, then he’s not in Chicago.”

“Cellini once told me if you crossed the Mafia you ended in the lake with your feet encased in concrete. My father-in-law told me an hour ago that last week he saw Harry drive off in a black limousine at six o’clock in the morning. I think that tells us he’s at the bottom of the lake.”

“I don’t think so. If such were the case, Cellini would tell me. He said he has some indication that Harry may be in Las Vegas.”

“I don’t believe it. May I smoke?”

Phillip reached across the table for the silver lighter and an ashtray.

"It doesn't matter. Alive or dead, we will file for divorce on the grounds of incompatibility, unethical, if not dishonest actions, plus his unconscionable attack on you. I should think an annulment would be no trouble. I doubt if the court will look on his hooking Rocco as a favorable relief for you."

Suzanne's reaction was one she seldom experienced; she was wordless. It never occurred to her that Harry performed his escape for her benefit. The fact he lied about his need for immediate cash—Harry lied about most everything—did not flabbergast her, nor did his deceitful cunning in extracting money from Rocco. The astounding fact was the sheer stupidity of alienating that beastly monster who would seek revenge until the day he killed Harry. She walked across the room and gazed out the window. Silverstein was on his feet and standing beside her.

"What is it?"

"It is so provoking."

"Why?"

"I would rather have given Harry the money he took from Rocco and stole from the business than be haunted for the rest of my life."

"Suzanne! What are you talking about?"

"You tell me Harry is still alive. It will only end when he is dead. Mark my words, Phillip, the end of this will be disaster. Harry, alive, is a covetous, grasping fiend and Rocco is an avenging brute and I fear my assets lie in the battleground between them."

"Don't be silly. You've no involvement in their affair."

She returned to the settee and sat, lighting another cigarette.

"Cellini said there will be no police investigations or any lawsuits and incidentally," he smiled as if about to tell a joke, "between you and me, he admires Harry's magnificent swindle."

The expression on his face was an open book; Phillip agreed with Cellini.

Suzanne stubbed out her cigarette, avoiding Phillip's eyes. He waited a moment then sat beside her.

"What's bothering you, my dear? I can tell there's more."

"Phillip, I don't want to talk about it."

She rose to leave but he restrained her.

"It would be inexcusable to allow you to leave without knowing your problem."

He smiled confidently and took her hand.

"Phillip," she hesitated not sure if she should continue. She freed her hand, walked to the door and turned to face him, her decision made. "The inference that you share Cellini's admiration annoys me. Harry is an ass, an incorrigible, stupid idiot to involve himself in such a swindle. Vindictive as it is, I'm sorry to say I hope he is at the bottom of the lake. I never want to see him again. Please do what you must as quickly as possible to dissolve my marriage. Good day."

She left the office with trembling hands, ignoring his protests.

5.

In the lobby, she hesitated beside the pay phone. It took a moment to make her decision.

"Mr. Cellini, I have an hour and half free and I would like to see you immediately. Would that be possible?"

"Ah! Yes. Miss Haldimann let me assure you it is always possible for you to see me without notice. How soon will you be here?"

"I'm down town. I suppose half an hour in a taxi."

"Very well."

"I must be back downtown by four so I do not have time to sit in your waiting room."

"I shall see that does not happen."

In the taxi, Suzanne determined that seven years had passed since she'd last seen Cellini. On that visit when he told her Harry was loan sharking with Rocco, should she have recognized the warning? Had she been more insistent with Harry—foolish rehashing of the past would not change the present. She stepped out of the taxi and opened the office door to the clickety-clack of the fastest typewriter in Chicago.

"Go right in," the peroxide blond said, "he's waiting for you."

Cellini sat behind his desk with his arms folded. He wheeled around to greet her, reaching out with his right hand.

"Ah! Yes. Miss Haldimann, what a pleasure."

"Thank you, Mr. Cellini."

The vivid recollection of her previous visits flooded her mind. As before, she melted in his presence. They faced each other holding hands longer than necessary.

"You said your time is short. What may I do for you?"

She withdrew her hand and sat at the conference table.

"Tell me about Harry, please."

"I suppose you know of his daring escapade with—"

"That's why I'm here. I've come from Silverstein's office and I don't understand why you men gloat over such stupidity."

The smile did not leave his face.

"Why Silverstein or anyone else—the public in general—would gloat is, I'm afraid, not my business. As for myself, I do not gloat. As you suggest, it is the ultimate act of stupidity for many reasons not the least of which is the very nature of his wife."

She looked away for a moment, swayed by the magic of his words.

"Thank you."

He gazed at her until her head came up and their eyes met.

"Shall I go on?"

"Please."

"I am not proud of what I do, Miss Haldimann. I do it because of the circumstances in which I find myself."

She looked at him more intently.

"Couldn't you not do it?"

"That is a different story that we do not have time for to-day."

"I'm sorry I interrupted. Please go on."

"The people who engage my services display a great deal of arrogance exercising their power without regard for the consequences of their acts. They do it for egotistical reasons that they do not admit, even to themselves. When the tables turn, I cannot deny my admiration for he who had the courage to face them. I know Harry's motivations were not honorable. They were, in fact, just as egotistical as my client's. That he succeeded in giving one of them a taste of his own, I confess, amuses me. If that offends you, I'm sorry."

Her eyes shifted and she did not appreciate his explanation.

"Let me continue. You are here because you believe you are in the battleground between the two of them."

Suzanne gasped and her eyebrows arched.

"How do you know that?"

He wheeled his chair away from the table.

"Is it not true?"

He poured two cups of coffee, placed them on a tray and wheeled back to the table with one hand, holding the tray in the other.

"Coffee?"

He smiled.

Her mind traveled back to the first time she wondered how he could read her mind. Nobody she ever met could read minds yet he did as if it were quite ordinary.

"Yes, that's how I feel."

"Ah! Yes. It is unfortunate you did not hear me the first time we met."

"What do you mean?"

"I believe my words were to the effect that Harry was smart but, unfortunately he did not always tell the truth."

"I don't remember you saying that but if you did I wish you had been more forceful."

"If I had shouted it and marched a brass band through the office, you would not have heard me. You were in love, Miss Haldimann and nothing I could do would change that fact. Milk or sugar?"

"No thank you."

"Ah! Yes, I'm afraid Harry has signed his death warrant. He is a bad penny and his loss will not be mourned by many."

Suzanne laughed.

"No, Sergio he is not a bad penny, he is a bent coin of worthless value."

He, too, laughed.

"Well put. I believe if you have a four o'clock appointment, it is time for you to go."

She rose and took his hand.

"Thank you."

He clasped her hand in both of his.

"The pleasure is all mine. My door is always open to you. Please, do not hesitate to enter any time."

6.

In March of 1925, when Clarence Burroughs welcomed Suzanne to his client list, he do so based on her expected annual receipts in excess of half a million dollars. By the fall of 1929 when the pseudo-rich financiers jumped from skyscrapers, Suzanne's investments were near the top of his client list. He estimated she would become his wealthiest client in two years. By 1936, she had surpassed all of them mainly because she didn't flaunt her wealth buying yachts and castles in Spain.

For twelve years, their association had been friendly and comfortable. More than once Suzanne regretted her failure to be more assertive during their brief college romance. Love and fun had been missing from her life and he was both lovable and humorous. As she rode the taxi to his office, she recalled the telephone conversation the week before. She had dialed his number at seven thirty, knowing he always started early in the morning.

"Burroughs."

"Clarence. It's Suzanne. I got your note. Why don't you have Mildred type your letters properly?"

"Nonsense. Think of the overhead expense. If I remember right, there were five or six words in my note. If Mildred had done it, it would have been two-and-a-half pages and said exactly the same thing. What's up?"

"That's my line. Not yours. You asked me to call."

"That's right. I did, didn't I. Could you come by the office after four? Today? Tomorrow? Soon?"

"Next Friday be all right?"

"Great. See you then. Bye."

He hung up before she had a chance to say good-bye.

At two minutes to four, Mildred greeted her.

"Hello, Suzanne. It's nice to see you again. Could I get you some coffee? A soft drink perhaps?"

"I think not, thank you. I'll just sit here contemplating my misery. In a few minutes the oracle of prosperity will open the gates and dispense his words of wisdom to us lesser mortals."

"Perhaps not that long. The market hasn't been exciting today; he's probably only made a few million. No fun at all."

Clarence appeared at the door.

"I heard your insulting remark Miss Haldimann and I want you to know that I am charging your account two thousand dollars for gross insults. Mildred is witness to those remarks and will testify against you in court. Deduct it from her account, will you please, Mildred."

"What a shame," replied Suzanne, "Mildred has just liquidated my entire account with this organization."

"Do come into my private chambers while I tie you to a chair and seize your funds. After which you may go out and hunt for that revolting husband of yours." He closed the door behind her and paused. "I've said something I shouldn't have said, haven't I?"

"You are a sensitive man. Yes you have. Your timing's off. You've never made any secret of your dislike of Harry but you're not up-to-date on the latest possibility." She sank into the easy chair in the corner and related her conversation with Mr. Matheu in the store. Sitting opposite her, he listened intently.

"I shouldn't laugh but your description is priceless. I can just see the old man quivering while you tell him his son loves his new life five hundred fathoms down."

"I didn't tell him that. I only guessed it. I don't know where he is."

"Anyway, you won't have trouble with the divorce; inhumane and savage treatment, something like that. Maybe you could charge overindulgence in alcohol during prohibition. That's pretty good these days. The temperance gals would love it."

"Oh! Do shut up Clarence. For your ears only, I have just come from an appointment with my attorney who admires Harry's bravado. His spy tells him Harry isn't at the bottom of the lake and nobody knows where he is. That's the end of the story. Now what is it you wanted to see me about?"

"Jolly good show. I hope he did escape; it was a daring escapade. Would you like a drink?"

"You men are all the same. Thank you, no it's too early in the day."

"Nonsense. The markets closed five minutes ago, which means the bars are open."

"I have a guest for dinner. Is that better?"

"Very well, I, too, shall be a martyr. May I begin my story?"

"Please do, I can hardly wait."

"I have many clients," he said, rising to fetch his cigarettes from his desk, "among them the richest people in Chicago and therefore I conclude, also among the smartest people in Chicago."

"I question your reasoning," she interrupted. "It might be better to conclude they are among the most crooked in Chicago. Go on."

"You have a scathing tongue, my dear. I take it the meeting with your lawyer was not to your satisfaction. Smoke?"

"Thank you. Go on."

"Some of my clients allow me to buy and sell on their behalf without prior approval. I have never lost money on these speculative ventures. As you well know, I take minimal risks. My objective is to preserve capital with modest but reasonable growth."

"Oh! God, Clary, I don't need your sales pitch. I know the sound of your own voice praising your genius is music to your ears but really Clary, I'm not in the mood. The answer is no. I will not allow you to spend my funds on your whims, no matter how damn brilliant you are. Get to the point or I'll miss my dinner engagement."

He sat again, leaning forward as if revealing a secret.

"Have you ever heard of a man named Babbage?"

"No. One of your undercover agents, I presume. Or perhaps one of your underworld clients."

"Not at all. He was an Englishman who fooled around with some sort of super calculating device about a hundred years ago. Incidentally, a lady by the name of Augusta Ada, a women I picture much like yourself, fiendishly clever—"

"Oh! Do stop it, Clary, sometimes you make me sick."

He smiled at her remark and was silent. Their eyes met. Neither looked away for an instant. She saw something deeper than amusement. For a moment, the normal flippancy disappeared like a little boy about to confess. Suzanne reached for the ashtray.

"Yes, well, it may interest you to know she was the only daughter of Lord Byron, the poet."

He paused for her reaction but when she said nothing, he went on.

"This brilliant lady allegedly succeeded in storing, on Mr. Babbage's machine, something called Bernoulli's numbers. Don't ask," he held up his hand to arrest her question. "I don't know what they are beyond the fact that she actually did it. Even if it was merely adding two and two, it was, I'm sure you will agree, a remarkable feat. In 1896, a man named Hollerith formed a company called The Tabulating Machine Company, which improved on the idea of calculating machines. Enter Mr. Thomas Watson who became president. In 1924, he changed the name to International Business Machines. Then he bought an outfit called Northeast Electric Company. Presto, he's selling electromagnetic typewriters. Now I believe somewhere there's a bunch of guys fooling around with something called analog machines. I have also learned that something called binary numbers has crept into their vocabulary, although, I confess, I don't know what that means."

Suzanne laughed.

"It puts me in mind of Harry pleading with me to invest in his misbegotten ice cream business."

"No. No. I'm serious. This is something big, Suzanne, believe me."

"So what do you want from me?"

"You are a widely known and respected personality with your light shining like a beacon on the horizon of knowledge, whatever that is. I want that little old professional service of yours to start making inquires about these developments. I'm a broker and that, my dear lady, is almost as nefarious as being a lawyer. The insider information is simply not available to me. It's hard to get in the door. You have a successful business and an impressive list of clients. You are a consumer known to prefer to buy your services rather than employ them. You've tons of money for investment. It all fits together so nicely. When somebody builds a better mousetrap to put into the market, they look for two things; the people who catch mice and those who have the money to buy the cheese. Suzanne, my dear, you're perfect for this job. I am asking you to start making inquiries into this stuff. I'll give you the names of the people to contact."

His proposition amused her. He was deadly serious, an unusual circumstance for him, and she was past the point in the day where she would consider any such atrocious scheme.

"I am looking forward to the end of this incredible day," she mused. "I learned my husband disappeared from the face of the earth after pulling a fast one on his archenemy who is undoubtedly scheming his revenge against my assets. I am sitting with my broker who, by his own admission, is almost as bad as a lawyer, and who has put forth a sneaky little scheme to recruit me as an industrial spy. And I am going home to dinner with a man who claims to be my great-uncle and who will surely try to persuade me to invest millions in a diabolical scheme to sell weapons of destruction to Hitler."

She rose to say good-bye with her hand outstretched. He bypassed her intended handshake and took her into his arms. He kissed her lightly on the cheek.

"Think about it," he said.

Chapter 13 – Mother and Son

1.

Sam arrived home Labor Day evening after the championship game in Calumet City.

"Mother! What happened?"

Sitting in the living room, he listened while she told the story of the fight.

"He hit me before he left. He was mad and ungrateful."

"Where did he go?"

"I don't know, dear. Nobody knows where he is."

"Oh."

He sat motionless letting his eyes roam the room as if to insure his father did not hide somewhere. She waited for his next question.

"Is he coming back?"

"Mr. Silverstein had all the locks changed so your father can't get in. I told Nadia and Josef to keep the doors locked. Nadia will show you where she put the keys."

"Does it hurt a lot?"

For an instant, she didn't know what he meant.

"It's getting better."

"Oh. I guess I'll go to bed now."

"Before you go there's more. I'm afraid it would be unfair to let you to go to school without knowing what he did."

She told him everything she knew about Harry's swindle.

"How much money did he steal?"

"In round figures; forty thousand from the ice cream business, thirty five thousand by deception at the bank and twenty-five thousand from Mr. Rossetti."

"Does he have to pay it back?"

"He'll probably go to jail, if they catch him."

"No. I mean Mr. Rossetti."

"Not the forty thousand your father stole, but the rest, probably."

"Gee."

Sam went to his room. School began the next day. A week later she asked what he thought about his father.

"Nothing. I don't care what he did."

2.

On Wednesday in the second week of September, Suzanne sank into a living room chair to read the mail. She shuffled through the pile. The top letter, addressed to Mr. & Mrs. Harry Matheu, came from a church. The writer not knowing her name irritated her. Probably another of the endless pleas for funds. She sighed, set the letters on the floor and opened the newspaper. Nadia carried in the afternoon tea service.

"Thank you, Nadia."

"Your welcome, Miss Haldimann. Oh! The mail's fallen on the floor. Let me pick it up for you."

"It didn't fall. I put it there."

"Oh! I'm sorry."

As Nadia sorted it, she recognized a letter from the church in Calumet City.

"There's a letter from our church," she said.

"I know. Put it in the office, would you please."

"Yes, Miss Haldimann."

As often happened, her mind shifted to Harry. Where was he? What devilish trick was he planning next? She heard the side door slam. Her heart skipped a beat. Had somebody left the door unlocked? She couldn't face him. She could hear muffled voices in the kitchen. The door burst open.

"What did it say, mother? What did it say?"

"Sam! You frightened me. What did what say?"

"The letter. Where is it?"

"Sam! Calm down." She laughed. "Whatever are you talking about?"

"The letter from the church. Are you hiding it, mother?"

"Oh! That letter. I didn't pay any attention. Nadia took it to the office."

He dashed off and came back with the letter.

"Can I open it?"

"May I open it, please," she corrected.

"Please."

"I suppose so. Wait! Perhaps I should look at it first. It might be a surprise."

She watched Sam rip the envelope open, confident it would be seeking a donation, likely in support for the baseball program. All the parents probably got one.

"Wait a minute, Sam. How did you know I received a letter from the church?"

"Nadia told me."

"She did, did she? I'll have to speak to Nadia about that," she said as sternly as she could. "You better let me read it first."

Sam passed the unfolded letter and sat on the settee.

Dear Mr. and Mrs. Matheu,

This year the Church of St. Stephen the Martyr introduced a baseball program for the 10 to 12-year old boys of our parish. Your son Stefan, as a temporary resident of our community, shared in this activity. In his participation, he displayed extraordinary knowledge of the game.

At the end of the season, the men in the parish who contributed their time to this venture selected the players they judged to have excelled in various categories. Your son won the Most Knowledgeable Player award.

The Men's Club will announce the names of the winners at a banquet in the Parish Hall on October 11 at 5:30. We invite your attendance.

Yours faithfully,

Fr. Keith Henderson

"Sam, it's a lovely letter; not what I expected at all."

What should she do?

"Let me sit beside you," she said moving to the settee. "It's an invitation to a parish dinner at the church on October 11. It's a baseball dinner."

He looked into her face.

"Can we go, please mother?"

"May we go, please."

How many thousand times had she made the same correction?

"Okay. May we?"

"You don't need to ask. Of course we'll go." She had the letter folded in her lap. "There's something else. I don't think I'm supposed to tell you, at least that's what the inference is, but I'm going to let you read it. Then I'm going to ask you to tell me about it; tell me what you haven't yet told me about your summer."

She handed him the letter and watched him read it. She could see he read it twice. He looked up from the letter. His face glowed.

"Gee, that's neat. I like Tom a whole lot."

"Who's Tom. The letter doesn't say anything about Tom."

"He's my coach."

She could not remember seeing his eyes sparkle so brightly.

"Tell me more."

He launched into the game of August 6 starting with his plea to coach at third base. He told her about the game in detail; every move, every play, every out. It was the first time he told the story to somebody who wasn't there to witness it. He displayed the signals explaining the meaning.

"When the game ended, mother, Tom said, 'Nice going, Sadsack, nice going. Great game.' And he shook my hand."

"What did he call you?"

"Sadsack. Everybody calls me Sadsack."

"What does it mean? Why?"

"Mother, I'm not a good player. I can't throw far. I miss catches. I can hardly hit the ball out of the infield. So," he shrugged, "they call me Sadsack. I guess it means I'm no good at baseball."

The insult hurt her.

"Oh, Sam, I'm sorry."

"No, no, mother you don't understand. It's great. I love it. I love having a nickname. It's like the players in my books. Everybody has a nickname. I want to be Sadsack. I don't want to be Sam any more."

She gaped in amazement at the astonishing change.

"Why don't you wash for dinner now." She squeezed his hand, then held him back. "Would you like to go to a baseball game on Saturday?"

It was his turn; he stared at her open-eyed. Without warning, he whirled to face her putting his arms around her neck. She clasped him to her bosom.

"The Cubs game this Saturday?"

She nodded affirmatively. "Yes."

"It's the last Saturday of the season." She could not see his face as they clung to each other. Suddenly, he released his grip and crossed the living room with his back to her. "I'd like that."

She was glad he didn't look back.

At the supper table, Sam continued relating his summer experiences. They talked of the children, the church and baseball.

"Sam, tomorrow I'll ask Josef to get the tickets for the Cubs. Where should we sit?"

"On the third base side."

"Is it best to sit up high in the stands or down close to the field?"

"Close."

"Why?"

"So we can hear what they say when they yell at one another."

She guessed.

"You want to be as close as you can to the third base coach?"

"Yeah. That'd be swell."

"What time should we be there?"

"Eleven."

"Eleven o'clock? The game doesn't start until one."

"I know, but we need to be there early."

"I don't understand."

"That's when the gates open. At eleven."

"What do we do from eleven to one?"

"Watch warm up and batting practice."

"Oh! I guess I'll learn. Will you teach me?"

"Sure."

Nadia removed the dinner plates. Sam gobbled his dessert.

"Got to go now. Thanks mum."

It did not occur to her that he wanted to be out of the room before she lit a cigarette.

3.

Sam glowed as he watched the baseball players. He had never seen batting practice and warm-up before. He jabbered away explaining what the players were doing. When the game began, he subsided into a study in concentration.

"Wow! They make it look so easy."

He watched the motions of the third base coaches trying to guess which movements were significant, which were decoys. His obvious knowledge and recognition of what was happening on the field thrilled his mother. She, too, had a wonderful afternoon. Before he went to bed, he came to her office.

"Thanks mum. That was swell."

No single incident, majestic moment or sudden revelation brought the changes Suzanne noticed in Sam's life. In the past, he gobbled his evening meal in the kitchen with Nadia and Josef, seldom taking fifteen minutes from start to finish. Now, he ate in the formal dining room with unaccustomed ritual. His mother taught him table manners, etiquette and social graces. Sometimes they sat at the supper table for over an hour. She made it enjoyable. They held animated conversations and sometimes Sam would forget to eat.

"Why, I'm almost finished and you've hardly begun. Eat or Josef and Nadia will have gone to bed."

In the past, Sam seldom saw his parents in the morning before leaving for school. In the new orchestration, Suzanne was at the breakfast table each morning waiting for him. When he came in from school, she was there to greet him. He accepted her presence, darting into her office to talk about the events at school, his assignments, whatever might be on his mind. She enjoyed his conversations and helped with his tasks.

Not only did Sam thrive in the changed environment but Suzanne did also. One evening, before he hurried away from the table, he told her how much he disliked the smell of cigarettes.

Chapter 14 - Escape

1.

Harry huddled in the back seat of the limo with the shades drawn. He directed the driver north on Lakeshore Road, peeking under the blinds to observe the traffic. His anxiety subsided as his confidence increased; nobody tailed them. They drove through Rockford and followed the Illinois River stopping for long rest periods along the way waiting for darkness to overtake them before they arrived at the Peoria City limits. Harry paid the rental fee and a bonus for a convenient memory loss. As the lights of the car disappeared, he walked into town toting his duffel bag, suitcase and briefcase. He introduced himself as Stefan Matuszewski at the rooming house two blocks off Main Street on the edge of town.

"Isn't that an awful name?" He laughed at the proprietor in a gracious high-society manner. "Just call me Matt. And what is your name, my dear lady."

"Thelma Broadmore."

"May I call you Thelma, Mrs. Broadmore."

"Please do. Would you complete the guest register, Mr. . . . ah—"

"See what I mean?"

"Yes. Mr. Matt is easier, isn't it?"

"Matt will be fine." He smiled. "You don't need the mister."

She watched over his shoulder as he scribbled his name.

"And your address, please, Matt."

"Thelma, I'm sorry. It's a little embarrassing but, well, I don't have a permanent address. I lost my job in Rockford and I'm here looking for work. But don't you worry." He opened his wallet. "Here's two weeks room rent in advance and a twenty-five-dollar deposit for board. You let me know when that's used up and I'll give you some more."

His manners, his deportment, his clothes—Thelma recognized her new boarder as a gentleman of means. He held her hand in both of his for a moment longer than necessary as he handed her the money; European aristocracy, she thought.

"Thank you, Matt."

Her dreamy eyes suggested she was divorced or had lost her husband. Harry smiled in the knowledge he overplayed his part. As he settled into his room, he wondered if the quality of his meals might be a shade above that of the other boarders.

Every morning he left the rooming house after breakfast and returned for supper at six. He continued his role as the model boarder, neither drinking nor congregating in the parlor with the other roomers. When Thelma tried to lure him into her private quarters, he played the role of the perfect houseguest for a few minutes and then excused himself.

He checked the main post office every day. Three weeks and two days after his arrival in Peoria, the certificates arrived in the name of Harry Matheu together with a small check and a note from Abie that congratulated him and wished him luck. At the bottom Abie wrote, "Harry Matheu? Who's he? I've never heard the name before I read about him in the newspaper."

"That's my kind of guy," Harry said as he burned the letter down by the railroad tracks.

2.

Twenty-four hours later Harry left, sneaking out after supper without telling Thelma, hoping she wouldn't notice his departure until morning. He wore dirty overalls, a soiled flannel shirt, scuffed boots half laced and an old peak cap pulled down over his eyes as he walked into the truck stop diner. His baggage consisted of a lone duffel bag; his other trappings were gone including his expensive suit and fancy shoes. He plunked onto the counter-stool near the door where he could listen to the drivers talk. Truckers slouched over their coffee and doughnuts bemoaning their miseries. A big fellow squeezed onto the stool beside him. He ordered dinner and looked at Harry.

"What you hauling, Buddy?"

Harry glanced at his companion, sneered and sipped his coffee.

"Shit."

"Bad, huh!"

Harry chomped his doughnut, rocked slightly on his stool, turned as if to spit on the floor but thought better of it.

"This joint stinks. I ain't had a worse doughnut in fifteen years."

The big man looked at him out of the corner of his eye but said nothing as he watched the waitress deliver his dinner.

"Thank you, honey. How about you fill my buddy's coffee cup? But don't give him no doughnut, he don't like them." His laugh came from his belly, deep and loud.

"Thanks," Harry muttered, eyeing the dinner plate while the girl filled his coffee mug. "Which way you headed, mister?"

"Souff," the fellow gargled between huge mouthfuls.

"Could you take a passenger?"

"I suppose." He gulped, then belched.

"Where you headed?"

"Looking for work."

Doing his best imitation of a hungry tramp, Harry moaned as he watched the plateful of food disappear.

"Can't get no work in Peoria. I heard tell them outfits down south is hiring. Maybe get on there; leastways that's what the fellow said on the telephone."

"Yeah. Who's that?"

"Can't remember the name."

The big fellow snorted, wiped his mouth on his sleeve and emitted a loud guffaw.

"On the lam, huh! Don't make no never mind to me. Come on. Climb aboard and we'll head down the road apiece."

They drove until midnight when the driver announced he had enough. Harry was hungry.

"How about I buy you a sandwich or something?"

"Sure," the driver said. "Truck stop here's got real donuts."

After eating, they walked to the truck. Harry reached out to shake his hand, anxious to find another lift.

"Say what's your name, Buddy?"

"I thought I told you. You've been calling me Buddy all along. That's my name; Buddy." Harry looked across the yard towards a line of trucks. "Buddy Leyland," he said, "same as that truck. My old man always said I'd be a trucker with a name like Leyland. Yes, sir. That's why he dubbed me Buddy, you know, from them Buddy-L toy trucks when we was kids."

"Yeah. Yeah, I understand. Just like my name's Jungle Jim."

The deep belly laugh boomed into the night. Harry shook hands and picked up his duffel bag.

"Yeah. Thanks for the lift, Jungle."

He wanted to get away from this guy and find a place to sleep. He'd seen a 'ROOMS' sign not far back. Too late; they'd remember anybody calling at this hour. He could sleep outside if he must but a run-in with the police would ruin his escape. He sat in an all-night diner talking to a cop goofing off. He said his name was Buddy and when the cop asked his last name, he said, "Buddy-L."

Lift by lift, trucker by trucker, Harry moved south, resting in small towns, avoiding cities. Rocco, with Mafia pals a telephone call away, would have the word out in the big places. Town after town, Harry thumbed the yellow pages looking for small truckers. Eventually he'd find a trucker in Arkansas or Mississippi needing a driver. Buddy Leyland would move into town, find a place on the outskirts and keep quiet.

"Read about that fellow up in Chicago, can't remember his name—"

"Harry Matheu."

The first topic of conversation with each new driver was the Chicago swindle. Throwing the name into the conversation gave Harry a lift and inflated his ego to the extent that everybody seemed to know what he'd done.

Buddy Leyland lost Harry Matheu. Harry never had a mustache. Buddy had one. Harry wore wire-frame specs; Buddy's were black, horn-rimmed shaded glasses. Harry's hair was brown and thinning; Buddy sported a full head of grayish-black hair custom-made in a shop in Peoria. Each morning, he shaved his face and head. Soon Buddy Leyland couldn't remember the name of that fellow in Chicago who pulled the stunt on the Mafia.

In Springdale, Arkansas, he found what he wanted.

"I ain't got no family," he told the supervisor. "Nobody to come home to so I find what I need on the road. You know what I mean?"

He winked but didn't say his greatest fear was finding somebody at home he didn't want to meet.

"I like to drive at night; pick a lay over spot a couple hours out of the next big town. That way I miss most of the traffic and after dark there's only a few cars on the road."

Buddy was there and back faster than anybody else with the result he got most of the long hauls.

In Peoria, Harry had sold the telephone stock for a discount of two-thousand dollars. His last expense before leaving town was a whopper. The cop charged him fifteen thousand for the police report, funeral records and cremation certificate. Nineteen thousand in expenses closed the book on "Operation Golden Swindle". To cast the success in a positive light, he had over eighty thousand dollars in his duffel bag that was never out of sight.

The last step was to register for social security. He told lie after lie; born in the Utah desert; father a transient railroad worker; mother a prostitute who died and he didn't have a birth certificate. Whatever they asked, he had a tale to tell. Not only did they not find any criminal record in the State of Utah, they didn't find any record at all. His fingerprints weren't in the FBI files. Eight months after he applied, they accepted him. At last, he could move his money. He opened several bank accounts and made conservative investments. Buddy Leyland planned to move on in a year or two. He remembered his tools in Gary and sent a payment for another year. He hoped to work his way north and dreamed of his own mechanic shop. Gary would be a good place to work.

3.

Thelma waited until ten in the morning before summoning the courage to knock on Matt's door. She tried again at noon. Terrified, she called the police. When they opened the door, the room was empty. A hundred-dollar bill lay on the dresser.

"Mrs. Broadmore, the man is dead. It's in the paper this morning."

After routine questioning, they dismissed her. She hurried to read the article about the gunfight in the rail yard. The next day she read the obituary and trembled at the thought of boarding a criminal.

"I couldn't believe he left without saying good-bye but I did appreciate the parting gift."

In Chicago, several people took notice of the obituary published in the Tribune.

> Died: Harry Matheu, alias Stefan Matuszewski, suddenly in Peoria, Illinois. The cause of death was indeterminate due to mutilation of the body. Cremation took place in the Peoria City Cemetery on September 29, 1936.

4.

Rocco took the telephone call sitting on the edge of the bed in his Vegas hotel room.

"How you doing, Rocco?"

"Sergio! I ain't doing a damn. We're staked everywhere. Ain't a sign of him."

"Do you have anybody in Peoria?"

"No family. Some friends."

"Somebody in Peoria shot him. You know anything about it?"

"You're shitting me."

"No I'm not; reported in the newspaper. You know about it?"

"Ain't heard a word."

"Well, you're wasting your time in Vegas. Soon as you get back call me."

"Take two three days."

"You be in my office three days from today at five. Got it?"

"Got it."

"Don't do anything or talk to anybody until you talk to me."

Cellini hung up and wheeled himself around his desk. He looked at the man lounging on the chair and burst out laughing.

"Ah! Yes. It's a shame to see such talent go to waste."

"Rocco got no line on it?"

The visitor pulled a cigarette package from the pocket of his blue pin stripe suit. He struck a match when he caught Cellini staring at him.

"I forgot, boss."

He blew out the match and threw the cigarette in the basket.

"What you thinking, boss?"

"I'm thinking Matheu is ten percent guts and ninety percent fool. There's no way anybody shot him in Peoria or any other place." He pushed his way over to the coffee urn. "Let me think for a minute." He filled his coffee mug, dumped in some sugar and wheeled back to his desk. He picked up the telephone.

"Leona, call Peoria and get the name of the funeral home that did the Matheu cremation."

He hung up and smiled.

"Take the undertaker for a ride. We don't want him, the name of the cop or anyone else who's in on the deal. And we don't care how much money changed hands. We only want to confirm that it's fake." His guest rose to go. "One more thing. I want a copy of the death certificate and any other certificates they cooked up. Be back here in twenty-four hours."

The door closed behind his visitor. He lifted the telephone and dialed. He sipped his coffee while he listened to the ring.

"Cellini speaking. That you, Phillip?"

"One moment, please."

She must have been in his office for he answered immediately.

"Silverstein here."

"Don't do anything about Matheu. I'll be in touch in a day or two."

He hung up without waiting for a reply.

5.

The telephone rang in Miss Haldimann's office at home.

"I presume you read about Harry in the paper today," Silverstein said.

"No." Suzanne tensed wondering what Harry had done this time.

"He's dead. Death notice in the Tribune."

A shudder assaulted her body, exploding everywhere at once like a thunderclap. She quivered and her breath came in bursts. Knowing she must say something, she reached for banalities.

"How dreadful! I'm sorry."

"I don't have details beyond the newspaper report. I'm expecting more information in a day or two."

The reverberations rang in her ears and she wasn't sure what Phillip said. She reached again.

"I'm always sorry when somebody dies."

"There's not much to tell. Apparently—"

"Phillip, I'm sorry. May we talk about this later? Tomorrow perhaps."

"Certainly. I'll call as soon as I have word."

"Thank you."

Suzanne believed she had conquered her emotional reaction to death when Roberta died. This unexpected invasion threw her back into emotional turmoil. Why did Death choose to expose her to such sudden violence? She was past caring about Harry; she thought him a fool. It was Death. She hated Death bursting in on her when she was unprepared. Death brought loneliness like none other. She loved the serenity of being alone and hated it when Death drove Peace away. Suddenly, she was infuriated with Harry. She reached for the telephone.

"Mildred, it's an emergency. I need to speak to Clarence right now."

"Please, Suzanne, may I take the message? You know he doesn't—"

"Harry's dead!" She hung up.

Almost immediately, Clarence called. She welcomed his voice.

"I'm sorry, Clarence. I shouldn't have spoken to Mildred that way."

"I'll apologize for you. What happened?"

"I don't know yet."

"I don't care about Harry, I mean to you."

He cared. He didn't joke or spout a stupid wise crack. He cared. She didn't know what to say. Before she recovered, he continued.

"Why don't I pick you up about five. We'll have a drink and dinner and you can tell me about it."

"You're sweet. Thank you. I'd like that."

In the morning, confusion filled her mind. She and Clarence enjoyed a pleasant evening, the kind that warmed one's heart without overtures or innuendoes. She enjoyed confiding in him, revealing thoughts she never would have told Harry. He said nothing romantic, nothing about another date but somehow he conveyed an interest in her. Maybe wishful thinking on her part; she'd known Clarence for twenty years. He'd never taken a serious interest but last night she sensed it. The telephone rang. Like a schoolgirl, her heart beat faster. Would that special something still be there? A second ring. What would he say? She smiled, waiting for one more ring. She picked it up.

"Silverstein here."

"Oh!"

"Something wrong?"

How astute he was.

"No."

"I wanted you to know I have the death certificate on my desk. Did Harry have a will?"

"Not as far as I know."

"It doesn't matter. It won't take long to settle everything and you'll be rid of him."

He paused as if in doubt; an unusual circumstance for him.

"Is there something else, Phillip?"

"Well, I was going to say it's strange how I received the documents."

"Did Mr. Cellini get them for you?"

The question came so quickly it surprised her. She hung up before she had to offer an explanation.

6.

About three the next afternoon, a swarthy man with black hair combed straight back walked into Abie Fishbein's office. Without a word, he laid the Tribune on the desk open at the obituaries. A second man, larger than the first, closed the office door and plopped into one of the two upholstered visitor's chairs.

"Yes," Abie stammered, "I . . . I . . . I saw that in the paper."

"Did you know this Matheu fellow?"

"Who? Me?"

"Yeah. I'm talking to you."

"No. Oh, might have met him somewhere, but no."

"That so?"

Abie managed a smile.

"Yes. Can I do something for you?"

His interrogator wore a blue suit with heavy pin stripes, broad lapels, a ridiculous tie covered in blue apples and orange tennis balls, a white flower in his lapel and he bulged all over.

"Yeah. I want to look at your books."

Abie looked at his fingernails.

"No! You'll have to get a court order first."

The man in the chair spoke.

"What did you say, Abie?"

The speaker had not removed his fedora. The brim was low shielding his eyes, his nose was flattened into his face and gold-rimmed teeth showed when he spoke. He wore a loose-fitting gabardine jacket that was open half way down. A hand reached inside the jacket and withdrew a pistol. He rolled the cylinder letting the ammunition fall into his hand. One by one, he put the bullets back and closed the cylinder with a snap. The weapon disappeared inside his jacket. Abie's mouth hung open, his head twisting and turning as if seeking an escape.

"I didn't hear you, Abie"

The broker wiped his brow with a quivering hand. He stood, then reached for the telephone. Pinstripes blocked his movement.

"No Abie. Your books."

"What books?"

Pinstripes' laugh was devoid of humor.

"What business you in, Abie?"

"None of your goddamn affair."

The perspiration was visible on his forehead. His body shivered as he clutched the edge of the desk with both hands.

"I'll call the police."

"Aw, shut up."

A flat palm struck him across the face and he fell backward into his chair.

"Your books, Abie. We don't want none of the company crap. We want your books, the ones what says what Abie owns and how much dough Abie's got in the bank." Abie sat, wide-eyed and terrified. "If them books ain't here in this office, then you tell us where they're at and we'll go get them. See, Abie, no problem."

Fishbein did not answer. His face was white, all except his lips that assumed a purplish hue. He clenched his teeth and the jaw muscles jutted out.

"Abie, I can be a mean son-of-a-bitch if I lose my temper. Speak, Abie, or we're taking you out of here and there ain't nobody going to stop us."

Abie opened and closed his mouth several times. Fedora put his hand inside his jacket. Finally, Abie formulated the words.

"My personal business is at home."

"Smart, Abie, smart. Let's go."

They rode to Abie's house in a chauffeur-driven limo with dark glass windows and parked in the driveway of a modestly expensive home with well-kept grounds and a two-car garage. The chauffeur, wearing black pants, leather jacket and peaked cap opened the doors. The three men walked up the rear stairs; Abie unlocked the door. A shrill voice greeted them.

"That you, Abie?"

"I have some guests."

"Oh my! I'm not dressed."

"We're going to talk in the office. You stay upstairs."

Abie led the way to the den. He pointed to the chairs.

"Sit down."

"Abie, we ain't here for no fucking tea party. Get the books and we'll get the hell out of here."

"I don't know what you want."

"Abie, one more stupid remark from you and I'm going to plow you. I'm going to plow you so goddamn hard it'll be two years from next Tuesday before you stop hurting. Now get the books."

Abie got the books. They turned to go when Mrs. Fishbein came hurtling into the room.

"Oh my goodness—" were the only words that escaped her throat before Pinstripes put his hand on her chest and pushed. She tumbled backwards, hit a chair and fell to the floor. When Abie turned to help her, Fedora grabbed his arm and dragged him out to the car. As they made the turn out of the driveway, they saw Mrs. Fishbein yelling after them from the back porch.

Twenty minutes later they arrived outside a dingy office building in Cicero. They escorted Abie Fishbein into the waiting room of Sergio Cellini. All of them sat, including the chauffeur. Nobody spoke. Pinstripes took the ledgers and gave them to a tough blonde behind the reception desk. She left the room and returned in a few minutes.

"It'll be about half an hour, maybe longer," she said.

Pinstripes stood.

"It's been a pleasure to meet you, Mr. Fishbein. Georgie's going to stay here to keep you company. Don't you worry about nothing, Mr. Fishbein, everything's going to be fine."

The next hour was the longest Abie ever experienced. Nobody talked or moved. The blond read; the chauffeur smoked and Abie worried. When he was about to collapse, the receptionist spoke.

"He'll see you now." She pointed at a closed door and returned to her book.

"Who?"

"Mr. Cellini."

Abie knocked.

"Go in, don't knock," she yelled.

Abie went in and stared in disbelief at the biggest man he had ever seen.

"Ah! Yes. Mr. Fishbein. Please have a seat, sir."

Abie looked around to see where the voice came from; surely not this huge man. There was no one else in the room. Abie, consumed by fear with his willpower exhausted, sat. The giant propelled himself around the desk and parked his wheel chair. Abie stared where the giant should have had legs.

"My name is Sergio Cellini, Mr. Fishbein. I believe there's been a little misunderstanding and I hope we'll be able to straighten it out without any problem. I believe my associate, Mr. Smith, spoke to you a few weeks ago concerning a Mr. Harry Matheu. Perhaps you remember."

Abie nodded.

"Ah! Yes. Good. I think you may recall that you assured my associate that the certificates that you bought on Mr. Matheu's account were mailed to Las Vegas."

"I don't remember."

"Ah! Mr. Fishbein, only four weeks ago and you don't remember. Please try to recollect the circumstances. To refresh your memory, the meeting took place downtown on September eleventh. Would you like me to tell what you ate for dinner?"

"No." Abie's hands trembled. An annoying tick developed in his left eye and he shook his head. "No, I think I remember."

Cellini smiled.

"Ah! Yes. Would you care for coffee? Or a cigarette? A shot of whiskey, perhaps?"

"No. I mean yes. I'll take the whiskey."

"Delighted."

Cellini wheeled to a bar at the far end of the office. He returned with a tray in one hand propelling with the other. Two six-ounce glasses were two-thirds full.

"Care for water with that?"

"No."

Abie clutched the glass with two hands. His face contorted as he gulped the whiskey in three swallows. Cellini watched without touching his.

"Another?"

"No."

Cellini smiled. "Ah! Yes. A little whiskey at the end of a trying day is pleasant. Don't you think so, Mr. Fishbein?" He sipped his drink.

"Look. What the hell is this about?"

Cellini smiled once more and sipped again. He wheeled around behind his desk.

"Draw up a chair, Mr. Fishbein, and let me show you something."

One by one, Cellini itemized the expenses incurred in the settlement of the Matheu fraud. Halfway through, Fishbein asked if he could have another drink.

"By all means, but would you help yourself, please. It's so much easier for you to move than me."

Abie returned and gulped at his drink while Cellini finished his itemization.

"And that, Mr. Fishbein, totals one-hundred and thirty-eight thousand dollars. Now, I see here in your books that you hold some very valuable securities. You have a nice home in the northwest corner of the city and a substantial bank account. Without doing the calculations, I would estimate your worth about a million and half. Would you agree it's a conservative estimate, Mr. Fishbein?"

Fishbein nodded.

"Now my client feels that you were instrumental in misleading him. At this point it does not matter why you lied."

Cellini paused and stared into Abie's eyes. Abie shifted, scratched his head and twisted in his chair. He glanced at Cellini, who held his penetrating stare. Abie put both hands on the arms of his chair, wiped his brow with a handkerchief he took from his coat pocket, stood and immediately sat. Still Cellini stared. Finally, Abie spoke.

"What do you want?"

"In a word, Mr. Fishbein, reimbursement."

"What? You mean . . .?"

"Yes, Mr. Fishbein, I mean one-hundred and thirty-eight thousand dollars."

"You go to hell."

Cellini turned his chair sideways, put his elbow on the desk, stroked his chin and ignored his guest. Abie stood.

"You can't get away with this," he yelled. "I'm getting out of here."

He strode to the door, yanked it open and froze. There stood Pinstripes with Fedora behind him holding a gun while the chauffeur smoked in the corner. Standing in the main entrance door, he recognized Rocco Rossetti. Nobody moved and nobody spoke.

"Have another drink, Mr. Fishbein," Cellini said. "Serve me one too, please, while you're pouring." Abie walked back to his chair, empty-handed.

A melodic voice so soft Abie could scarcely hear reached his ears.

"Would you care to know the name of my client?"

"I think I know."

"There are moments when he is quite irresponsible and I can do nothing to control him."

Abie sighed.

"Could we settle for something less?"

"I'm afraid it's too late for negotiating. Perhaps had you been more truthful . . .."

Cellini shrugged and spread his hands in the manner of a priest dismissing the congregation after Mass. The room was silent. Cellini smiled pleasantly.

"Ah! Yes. Well, Mr. Fishbein, I believe you understand the situation. Do you have any questions?"

Abie did not respond.

"No? Then you understand it is not my business to act as a collection agency. As you may have noticed, Mr. Rossetti is in the other room. I think he will be glad to accept your payment or make suitable arrangements although you may find his interests rates exorbitant. I'm sure he will explain the consequences of . . .. Well, there's no need for me to go into details other than to caution you not to take him too lightly. Good day, Mr. Fishbein, I do hope it has not been a trying experience for you."

The next day Mr. Fishbein's lawyer recommended that he swallow the pill and perish the thought of revenge.

"Let's see if we can't find a way to write it off as a business loss," he suggested.

Chapter 15 - Unmasking

1.

Suzanne's life changed as if Harry's death released her from bondage. The lighthearted exuberance proffered by Clarence replaced the nervous tension Harry spawned. She and Clarence continued to live in their separate homes, he in a downtown apartment, she in the house in Evanston, but they often slept in each other's beds. Not only did they have money to spare, they had time to share. She accepted his challenge to research the business innovations.

"Sometimes I think these people are dreamers, Clary. They expect huge increases in office efficiency by automating everything without regard to the millions of people they'll put out of work. They talk of the enormous market in one breath; how small the world is in the next."

"I wouldn't pretend to understand." He shrugged. "More than that, I don't want to understand. Some are good, some bad and I only want to know which is which and where I invest?"

"Yes, I recall your infatuation with the almighty buck."

He smiled.

"Show me the shooting star where I hitch my wagon."

They reviewed her findings. Her analytical mind evaluated each organization. She selected. He accepted.

"It can't be that easy, Clary. You're investing millions and just like that you accept my recommendation."

"My dear Suzanne, I couldn't get better information anywhere."

"You exasperate me."

Exasperated or not, he bought according to her recommendations. Disposing of the slow movers, increasing his position in the active ones, he amassed major holdings in the developing field of business machines.

2.

Discovery of the private pursuits Sam did on his own initiative surprised Suzanne. She recalled the loose-leaf book with baseball statistics. Once she came across a scrapbook of newspaper clippings; another time a photo album with school pictures. She didn't spy; he left them on his desk or the night table beside his bed without any attempt to hide them. His scope of interests did not amaze her so much as his diligence, so unlike Harry. She didn't associate Sam's prolonged interest in his projects with her father either, who was quick to teach and delegate. She attributed his perseverance to Grandfather Matheu.

"Sam, I was in your room," she began one evening at the dinner table, "just before your father left. I noticed a book where you keep baseball statistics. Do you still do that?"

"Oh, that! One of my books showed how to do it. When I tried, I always got it wrong. Sometimes I was close but I stopped because it's in the paper everyday anyway."

"What did you do then?"

"I rated the players different ways like how many hits and walks and stuff like that."

"How long did you do it?"

"I don't know. About half the summer, I guess."

"Do you do anything like that now?"

His head came up with a frown. He looked at her as if he objected or wanted to know why she asked but he shrugged and answered in the same casual tone.

"Sort of. Well, no, not really, it's different."

She waited, hoping he would explain without prompting. After a moment, she continued.

"Do you mind telling me about it? You don't have to, I'm just interested, that's all."

Nadia cleared away the dishes and brought dessert.

"I don't mind. Thank you, Nadia. It's stuff I like to do. You know, keep track of names and addresses."

"Names and addresses! Whose, for heaven's sake?"

"Everybody's"

"Why?"

"Just so I'll have them. You told me lots of times you didn't have friends when you were young. I'm not sure I believe you. I think you forgot. You went to school and you went to college. There must have been people in your class. You couldn't have gone alone so you forgot."

"Well, I . . .."

Sam finished his meal and rose to leave.

"May I be excused, please?"

"Stay for a minute more, I'm fascinated. Tell me more about what you were saying."

Sam stood at the end of the table, standing on first one foot, then the other. A silence fell each expecting the other to start. At last, Suzanne spoke.

"I send Christmas cards. What do you do?"

"Sometimes I send a card or something."

"Do you. To whom?"

"I don't know. Tom. Granny Magda. Somebody at school, maybe. Kids on the ball team. You know."

"You mean a postcard?"

"Yeah. Sometimes a letter."

"What do you say?"

"I don't know. Depends. Great game. Happy birthday. Stuff like that."

Suzanne didn't confess neither her father nor Harry sent cards. She realized, except for Christmas, she was equally guilty.

"Do you mind me asking?"

"No." He shrugged. "It's okay."

"When did you start? Where did you learn?"

"Father Henderson said it was a good idea. He told me you forget people. It was funny when we talked about it. He said he wished he'd done it when he was young. I said he was just like you. I said all you old people pretend you don't have any friends. He laughed and said he guessed I was right."

"Sam! You didn't say that!"

"Sure I did. You can say anything to Father Henderson. If you want to know about anything—girls or babies or anything—just ask him."

Suzanne didn't realize her mouth hung open. Her coffee cup stalled in midair. She gulped and continued.

"Sam, my dear, I guess you're a lap ahead of me. I thought my job was to teach you. I think it's the other way around."

Sam started for the door.

"Tom's the same way," he said over his shoulder. "You can ask him anything too. They're like big brothers."

Clarence tried to fulfill the father image. Where Harry had chastised, punished, reprimanded, scolded and spanked, sometimes severely, bordering on abusive, Clarence was equally offensive with indulgence to the opposite extreme. From childhood, Sam gave his love to the women in his life and Clarence could not break the barrier. At the age of ten when Sam met paternal love for the first time at the Magdelaine house, it was too late. Magda became the beneficiary of his devotion. Her insistence on religious instruction pushed Sam to Father Henderson. When he returned in the fall of 1936, Father Henderson's compassionate teaching and Harry's departure opened the door to a genial year between Sam and his mother. Clarence's interference closed the door and caused the affinity to dissolve. Sam refused father-and-son overtures and Suzanne, blinded by her love, accepted the rejection as normal teenage behavior. He became a troglodyte in his room once more. Maternal discussions ended and his wish to be in Calumet City magnified.

3.

"I'll be leaving next month," Buddy told his supervisor.

"Yeah. What's the matter? Not satisfied?"

"I ain't complaining; just tired of driving."

His wages were good, his investments profitable. After two years in Arkansas, his fortune exceeded a hundred thousand; not bad considering the first eight months he had to keep his cash hidden in the duffel bag. Dreams filled the monotony of long hours behind the wheel. He looked back on his life; conceding a mistake or two, he'd done all right. He was forty-two years old. Given all the pluses and minuses, he rated fixing trucks in the army his most pleasurable occupation. He'd buy a garage in Gary, maybe a service station, peddle gas and fix cars. The dream blossomed into determination. He moved on in September 1938.

Buddy found a run-down service station for sale on Fifth Street near Broadway, the busiest corner in Gary. It had two gas pumps, two service bays with pits, an office, storage room, air compressor and two washrooms. Buddy raised his cash offer three times ending at sixty thousand dollars before the owner agreed to sell. After a week of cleaning, he recovered his tools from the storage depot and arranged them along the rear wall in the service bays. When his new sign arrived, he held a one-day opening event offering five gallons of free gasoline to the first twenty-five customers and free drinks to everybody else. He sold cigarettes, chewing gum, soft drinks and candy. Business poured in.

Leyland's Service Station opened at six in the morning and closed at six in the evening. Buddy lived in a basement apartment on Jefferson between Fourth and Fifth, only a half-block from the station. Working twelve-hour days seven days a week left no time for other interests.

A swarthy man sauntered into the garage one day in the middle of November.

"My car's broke down," he said. "I need a mechanic."

"Oh yeah! Where is it?"

Buddy had seen this kind before; tough guy who drove for the mob.

"Around the corner on Broadway."

Buddy sized him up; snap-brim fedora, belted trench coat, collar turned up, dark eyeglasses—typical Chicago tough guy; the low-life who liked to play big shot throwing money around when the boss wasn't looking.

"I'd help except I'm alone here."

"You go look and I'll mind the station."

Buddy laughed.

"Sure. I'll go around the corner and ain't that the damnedest thing, there ain't no car there. I come back and you're gone, my cash with you."

The customer drew a wad from his pocket and peeled off a couple of c-notes.

"Take this and your cash and go fix my car." It was an order that Buddy was glad to accept. "I'll mind the station while you're gone."

"Well," Buddy said, "you don't fool around, huh. Give me your keys."

He opened the till, stuffed the cash in his pocket, grabbed a toolbox and hustled around the corner. The engine turned over but didn't start. It didn't take Buddy long to find a cracked distributor cap.

"The points are wet," he said when he returned.

"Can you fix it?"

"If I got the parts. If not, I'll get you going and you'll have to go to a dealer. Only take a few minutes."

Harry rummaged through his parts bin.

"Hey, you're in luck, mister."

Stepping out of the storeroom, he noticed the customer glaring at him with a curious look. He put his hand on Buddy's arm.

"Where'd you get them tools?"

"None of your business. They're mine and get your hands off me."

"That so?"

"Yeah, that's so. I've had them for a long time."

The man backed away, a smile flickering at the corners of his mouth.

"You sure they ain't never belonged to nobody else?"

"No. They're mine, I told you. I've owned them for years. What's the hell's the big idea?"

"Nothing. Just wondered." He fumbled around in his pockets. "Cigarette?"

"Not now. I'll do your car first."

"Got a light?"

"Jesus, you want me to shine your shoes, too."

Buddy struck a match with his thumbnail and held it out.

"Thanks."

As usual, Buddy ate his supper in the restaurant across the street. He pulled out his roll with two hundred-dollar bills on top.

"What a day," he said to the manager at the cash register. "Best pay I ever had for a fifteen-minute job."

He strolled east along Fifth, paying no attention to a man leaning against the brick wall across from the garage. He waited for the traffic light at Broadway, crossed and strolled back west to Jefferson, smoking and enjoying the air. He let himself in to his apartment, sank into his chair. Exhausted as usual, he opened a beer, lit another cigarette and picked up the newspaper. Why did that guy ask about the tools? Funny question; damn nosy bugger. He remembered buying those tools after his army discharge when Rocco hired him to—

"Jesus Christ!"

He hurried back to the garage, unlocked the door and looked at his toolboxes. Every one of them bore a label clearly marked, "Property of Harry Matheu". Even the small box he carried over to Broadway had the label on it. He switched off the lights, locked the doors and sat in the dark wondering what to do next. He pulled the wad from his pocket and counted it—six hundred forty-two dollars. Damn good day; best day he ever had. As he shoved the money back in his pocket, he noticed a man across the street in a dark suit leaning against the brick wall. Buddy stamped out his cigarette. He sat still, his face strained, mind whirring. He looked at his watch. Quarter to eight. That guy left about four. A telephone call; plenty of time to drive to Gary from Chicago.

Buddy watched a man hurry along the other side of the street. He stopped to talk to the fellow leaning against the brick wall. They both left. They crossed at Broadway. He lost sight of one, the other walked towards the service station. Buddy edged into the dark storage room leaving the door open. He heard somebody trying the overhead door in the first bay, then the second; both locked. Buddy peeked out from the storage room to look through the window in the opposite direction. A shadow moved. What the hell is going on? A third man approached and knocked on the door. Buddy slunk back into the darkness of the storage room. Another knock. He heard the glass shatter and the shards cascade across the concrete floor. He grabbed a tire iron and slid further back into the darkness hiding in the corner behind the bins. A foot crunched on the floor; another and another. The lights came on in the storage room. Buddy saw the glint of metal.

"Mr. Leyland, would you step outside, please."

Buddy didn't move. The voice spoke again.

"You got two choices, Buddy. You can walk out on your own or we drag you out. Don't make no difference to us."

Buddy stepped out.

"Come with us, please."

The man lead the way around the building, Buddy followed, the other two walking behind him. They paraded down the dark alley about fifteen feet past the garage. Buddy's eyes had not adjusted to the darkness.

"Stop right there," a voice said.

"Well, if ain't the late Mr. Matheu."

Only one person in the world spoke with a gravel voice like that. He heard a shuffle behind him. Two men pinned his arms behind his back. Rocco growled at him.

"Whoever you are, you're a dumb son-of-a-bitch."

The fist connected and his head flew back.

Buddy had no recollection of the beating he took. A firefighter found him lying in the alley when they arrived to put out the blaze in Leyland's Service Station.

The hospital reported the patient should recover in four to six months, probably another six months in rehabilitation; at least a year before he would work again, if he were able to work at all. He had a fractured skull, a broken jaw, four broken ribs, a punctured lung, a cracked pelvis, both legs broken, one of them in two places, a ruptured spleen and bruises all over his body.

A week passed before Buddy regained consciousness. Another week floated by before the police arrived to interview him. The first question was his name.

"Are you Buddy Leyland or somebody else?"

"Yeah. That's my name."

"You sure?"

"What happened to my tools?"

"Your friends torched the place. Nothing left worth a damn after the fire."

"So why do you think I'm not Buddy Leyland?"

"Somebody wanted you bad. We thought for a minute you might be that fellow Matheu who pulled the swindle a couple years back."

Buddy laughed. "Who me? You think I'd be hanging around here if I pulled a stunt like that?" He began to recite the nonsense he fed to the social security people in Arkansas. They stopped him.

"Why did somebody try to kill you?"

"I don't know. Robbery, I guess."

"Robbery?"

"I had about six hundred and forty-two dollars. Did you find it?"

"No. We didn't find nothing."

"Then the thieves took it."

"Come on, Buddy. Six-hundred-dollar thieves didn't mangle their targets and torch buildings."

Three weeks later the detective's report read, "Victim failed to cooperate." The investigation closed.

4.

Suzanne and Clarence sat in the kitchen of his luxurious apartment. He turned the pages of the Sunday paper.

"Here's a guy mugged in Gary a couple of weeks ago. He's all smashed up. Listen." Clarence read the inscription under the photograph. "Hospital authorities report Buddy Leyland, pictured above, received multiple injuries in the fire that destroyed Leyland's Service Station at Fifth and Broadway in Gary two weeks ago." He shook his head. "Can you believe this? Look at this guy."

Suzanne glanced over his shoulder, then leaned down to look closer. The blood drained from her face.

"What's the matter?"

"Clarence. That's Harry!"

"What!"

She collapsed at the table studying the photograph.

"Can't be," Clarence said. "Says his name is Buddy Leyland."

"I don't care if they say its Santa Claus. God, Clary, I was married to the guy for fourteen years. It's too incredible."

A shiver ran through her body.

"Toast is burning."

"You look after it."

"Are you all right?"

She rose to her feet.

"No, Clarence, I'm not all right. I want you to take me home."

"When? What do you mean?"

"Now. I want to go right now. Please. I never want to see that man again."

She pounded her fist on the picture screaming, " No! No! No!"

He tried to take her into his arms.

"No. I want to go now. Now, Clarence! Now!"

In the car she held a hankie to her face and said nothing. At home without a word to Clarence, she ran to the house calling for Sam.

Chapter 16 - Inheritance

1.

Sam was indifferent. His father was out of his life, whether alive or dead didn't matter.

"Mother, if he's coming back I'm leaving."

The conviction buried in his words astonished her although she knew no possibility existed that Harry would return.

"Where would you go?"

"Calumet City."

She took him into her arms.

"You love it there, don't you?"

"Yes, Mother, I do."

The discussion ended and she sat alone in the office pondering if Buddy Leyland could possibly be Harry. Perhaps a look alike; Phillip said he had Harry's death certificate. Strange how she knew Cellini provided it. She disdained supernatural mysticism and its transcendental derivatives but she had experienced sensory perception as a spontaneous verbalization without forethought. Could Cellini see into her soul even when they were miles apart? She looked out at the bare trees. The first snow would come soon. Her hand hesitated on the telephone. Phillip would never question the authenticity; it would defeat his purpose. No, there was only one choice. She called Sergio Cellini for an appointment.

She alighted from the taxi at ten the next morning. The waiting room was empty. The blonde receptionist typed furiously and nodded towards the door.

"Shall I go in?" Suzanne asked

"He's waiting for you, honey."

She knocked and opened the door. He wheeled around his desk and greeted her with an open hand.

"Ah! Yes. Miss Haldimann."

She shook his hand and felt relief, as if a friend had lifted a heavy cloak from her shoulders.

"Please sit down. Coffee?"

"No, thank you."

"Very well. What may I do for you?"

His eyes bored into her as if reading her mind and she sensed a mental nakedness. Lightheadedness freed her inhibitions. She realized how much she adored him, not sensually, as one adores a lover but divinely, as one adores a prelate. She hesitated for a moment.

"Is it about Buddy Leyland?"

She laughed.

"Mr. Cellini, are you a mind-reader?" Thoughts of the fireside on Daddy's knee flashed in her mind. "I've never met anyone like you. You know what I am going to say before I say it."

"Ah! Yes." His eyebrows arched, his shoulders hunched and his hands lifted as if there were no explanation. He motioned to the bar. "You sure you won't change your mind about coffee?"

"All right. Could I get some for you?"

"Kind of you."

She carried two cups to the conference table.

"Cream or sugar?"

He shook his head and she sat. Opening her purse, she withdrew a newspaper, laying the picture of Buddy Leyland face up: "Is this Harry Matheu?"

This bizarre cripple, the antithesis of the private investigator, exhilarated her. Confined to his office, he nonetheless knew the answer to her questions, sometimes before she asked them.

"You inspire my confidence," she said. "Somehow I'm more comfortable talking with you than any person I know."

He answered her admission with a simple nod of his head conveying his wish for her to continue.

"Why is it that death devastates me?"

"There's no answer to that for it's not something you control. Tell me why you ask."

"I have had two bitter experiences this year. That picture of the man in Gary sent a shock wave through me. I needed to talk and there was no one I could think to answer my question except you."

"I'm honored. I hope I may help. Please continue."

She sighed, took a deep breath and began her story.

"When I sold the cleaning business to Albert, Daddy's partner, I neglected him for a long time. During the night after Harry beat me, I awoke about three, went downstairs and fell asleep on the living room settee. I dreamed of a voice telling me to go back. When I awoke with the sunshine pouring in the window, I could hear Daddy's voice ever so clearly telling me to go back. Go back where? Suddenly, I decided it meant go back to the office. It was terrible; everything I remembered was gone. I was afraid to look in Daddy's private office. I left. As I walked, a truck almost hit me and I thought the message was to go back to Danny's Place, the restaurant near the office where I first met Harry. It was worse than anything I could imagine; a soup kitchen with an awful woman who cursed at everybody. I went to Albert's home, annoyed and angry with him for all my problems. I found him unchanged, laughing at life despite incredible problems; his wife died of cancer; his son failed in business and he was blind. I had come back to an old uneducated black man I lived with for a year when I was four to rehear the lessons of love I allowed to escape. Without reprimand or rebuke, Albert restored me by showing me love. After that, I visited every week or two.

"One day last spring, he wasn't sitting on the porch as usual. I hurried into the house. He lay sprawled on the floor. I called the police who said he had a heart attack and died while struggling to reach the phone. They were callous, rude and vulgar, kicking his body, shoving it into a body bag and taking it to the morgue.

"I called a funeral home and arranged a burial beside his wife. Nobody came; not even his son. The preacher asked me to say something. I stood beside the casket, faced the empty seats and tried to speak. I couldn't. The tears flowed down my face. The preacher held my hand. 'Albert,' he said, 'those tears express our love. There are no words to say how much we care. That you gave us so much kindness, love and happiness is the greatest eulogy we can offer. We shall always remember you.'

"The two of us went to the cemetery together for the burial. I went home and cried myself to sleep."

Suzanne rose and turned her back, dabbing at her eyes.

"Shall I go on?"

"Of course. Please finish."

She resumed her seat controlling her emotions.

"I suppose you knew Syd Sidorowitz?"

"Yes."

A faint smile crossed her lips.

"Then you know how he protected my interests."

He shrugged and flared his hands again.

"Not in detail but it doesn't matter."

"Three weeks ago, a doctor called to say Syd experienced a heart attack that would likely be fatal. He asked me to hurry to the hospital. When I arrived, Syd lay motionless, his eyes closed. The doctor shook him gently. He smiled and took my hand. I didn't know what to say. Then he spoke in a soft voice, gasping between each word or two. He thanked me for coming. I felt terrible. He asked me to listen and say nothing while he made his confession. When he was young, he embezzled ten thousand dollars. My father bailed him out and bonded him."

Suzanne's voice trailed off to a whisper.

"He died, Sergio. Right there before my eyes."

She walked to the corner by the bar and stood with her back to him weeping softly into her hankie.

"Don't be ashamed of your tears." He wheeled to the bar. "Would you like a little brandy?"

"No, thank you."

"Coffee?"

"Please."

He took her hand and led her back to the table.

"Cigarette?"

"Mr. Cellini! You know smoking isn't permitted in this office. Besides, you don't have an ashtray."

"Ah! Yes. I suppose I could find one."

"Don't bother."

"Thank you."

They sipped their coffee in silence; not an uncomfortable silence, but rather a soothing moment for reflection. He waited. She nodded her gratitude, taking another sip.

"I think that's the last," she said. "They're all dead now and I can't imagine more secrets hidden in my father's life. If there are, I don't want to know them. I can't stand any more."

Her voice rose.

"Can you imagine my father baling him out, letting him have the money so he could get out of trouble?"

Her voice grew shriller.

"Can you imagine me pressuring my father to get rid of him, telling him he could buy the same service cheaper from outside the organization?"

She was almost hysterical in her self-incrimination, her tears flowing freely.

"Can you imagine how Syd felt about my insinuations, my suspicions?"

Her voice came crashing down and she buried her face in her hands.

"I've been so blind. So stupid."

Cellini made no effort to console her, offered no platitudes to grief. When he spoke, it was his beautiful voice, soft and melodious like an opera tenor singing an aria that soothed her.

"You must realize there was a pact between them. A pact never to tell. But Syd was right. He couldn't die with the knowledge you didn't know. It wasn't that he broke the pact; it was his need to tell you he loved you and forgave you. You must realize Syd kept himself alive until he told you. He wanted you to know what Joe Haldimann did for him. Don't condemn yourself. I imagine your investigations pleased your father. Perhaps part of the challenge for him was to wonder if you'd ever find out."

She stared at him wide-eyed.

"Why would you think that?"

"What was it he always said? There's two ways to look at everything—a shiny side and a bent penny in everybody—some-thing like that. I'd say he looked at you and wondered if you would ever see the bent side of Syd's coin. Suppose you did figure it out, what then? Don't you think it would have been worse? Don't you believe had you known your father harbored a convicted felon you would have been putting double locks on every door? I'll bet that's what your father thought. What do you think? What's the other side of the question?"

She paced the floor, deep in thought while Sergio sat motionless. She returned to her seat opposite him.

"It never occurred to me to ask myself any question beyond my lack of trust." She paused for a moment. Her tears had stopped and a smile began to form. "You're right. It's a good question. What would he have said? It's funny isn't it? When you're young, you think you have all the answers. If you don't have the answers then you spend all your time trying to find the answer. You don't ever stop to ask yourself, what's the question?"

"I think that's a personal statement," Cellini responded, wheeling himself around his desk. "I don't think that's universally true. I think that's Suzanne Haldimann."

"You're right. That's Suzanne Haldimann!"

She prepared to leave. He watched her peering into her open compact, brushing her hankie across her eyes.

"Could I use your washroom to freshen up a little?"

He did not move or answer, but looked at her with his penetrating eyes. She froze with her compact in her face as if trying to hide behind it.

"What have I done?"

"Ah! Yes. So you don't want the answer to your question?"

A frown formed and no words came.

He laughed.

"You've forgotten the question."

Her face reddened.

"I'm afraid I have."

"Ah! Yes. Perhaps it would be a mistake for me to remind you but I fear you would remember later."

"Please?" Suddenly she laughed and reached across the desk to touch his hand. "Please tell me what I'm missing."

He pointed to the newspaper still open on the table.

"Oh," she said. "Is that Harry?"

"Yes."

"Will you tell me the story?"

An overwhelming happiness possessed her when she left Cellini's office. Sergio had worked his magic; more than magic, he had performed a miracle. She sent him a check for one thousand dollars.

He returned it uncashed with a note of gratitude.

2.

Several weeks later a letter arrived from the law firm of Shultz and Greenwald inviting Miss Haldimann and her son, Stefan, to discuss the will of the late Mr. Sydney Harold Sidorowitz. At the appointed hour, Suzanne and Sam entered the office of Mr. Herman Greenwald.

"It is a pleasure to meet you, Miss Haldimann. Your reputation, as well as that of your father, precedes you. And Stefan, I am pleased to meet you also."

A round of pleasantries followed, leading into the subject of the meeting.

"I infer from reading the will, Mr. Sidorowitz was a long-time associate of your father. My father prepared the will many years ago; the original date of execution is June 7, 1887, if you can imagine. That, I believe was about seven years before your birth, Miss Haldimann."

"Yes. I was born in 1894."

Suzanne quelled her anxiety for him to get on with it, whatever *it* was. She imagined he rehearsed dramatic presentations. The question on the tip of her tongue was to inquire if he performed professionally on the stage or only for private showings.

"There is a preamble to the will expressing a debt of gratitude to Joe Haldimann, obviously written by Mr. Sidorowitz himself. You may be aware Mr. Sidorowitz was criminally responsible for an embezzlement."

"Yes. Mr. Sidorowitz told me on his deathbed."

"I am sure that was a traumatic experience for you. In any event, the preamble explains his gratitude to your father who stood bond for him, as well as his sincere wish to make retribution. There is only one revision to the will. Before I go into that, however, I should like to explain that a clause in the original will provides for his wife if he should marry. Since he never married that codicil is obviously void."

Suzanne almost smiled thinking about Clarence's technique of communicating. The meeting had now consumed thirty-five minutes, Sam fidgeted and Mr. Greenwald had not got to the point. Clarence could have covered everything he had said so far in five words. She remembered him saying Mildred Jackson could take five words and turn them into a two-and-a-half-page letter. She wondered if Mr. Greenwald and Mildred had gone to the same school.

"Now," Greenwald continued, "to come to the revision. It notes your mother died in July 1898. The revision, dated January 22, 1908, states that he bequeaths his entire estate, share and share alike, between all of Joe Haldimann's surviving children and grandchildren existing as of the date of Mr. Sidorowitz's death. As far as we have been able to discover, having exhaustively searched throughout all of Mr. Sidorowitz's records and files, there is no further revision or updating of his will. Therefore, Miss Haldimann, the only two qualifying people are yourself and your son Stefan."

He paused, smiling generously at both of them with a grand theatrical gesture expecting gasps of astonishment with the unavoidable question about the size of the estate. Neither Suzanne nor Stefan gave him the least satisfaction. He frowned and continued like an actor whose soliloquy has failed to win applause.

"Mr. Sidorowitz's estate is about six-hundred thousand. After probate, taxes and fees each of you should receive about a quarter of a million dollars. I should imagine the processing could take as long as a year."

"Are there any stipulations about trusts for funds bequeathed to minors?"

"There are no checks whatever."

The meeting ended.

"We are most grateful for your time and courtesy. I am sure you are aware Phillip Silverstein is my attorney. I would appreciate all further matters go direct to him. Thank you, Mr. Greenwald."

"Suzanne," mused Clarence after she told him the story over a cup of tea, "you ought to be a writer. You wouldn't have to use your imagination. Don't make anything up; just tell your life story. Everybody will believe it's fiction."

"Sam and I talked it over. Does this happen to other people? Or are we the only ones?"

"Them what's got, gets, I suppose."

Chapter 17 - War, Love and Baseball

1.

Every year from 1936 through 1942, Sam lived at home in the winter and at Magdelaine's in the summer. His increasing baseball knowledge and organizational skill raised his fame in Calumet City to that of a celebrity. The community judged the rich kid from Chicago with the oriental face a prodigy destined to manage in the big leagues. They accepted his leadership and admired his enthusiasm. Sam had the good sense not to feud with those who held a different view. He asked Father Henderson for guidance and politely suggested his detractors do the same. His mentor, Tom Gordon, taught Sam baseball strategy, deluged him with books and hired him part-time as a clerk in the store. In 1942, Sam graduated from high school.

"No, Mother, I'm not going to university. High school was a big enough struggle for me. I never want to see the inside of another classroom."

"Are you going to move to Calumet City?"

"Ruth and Tom have an extra room at their house. I've agreed to rent it and pay for my meals. It's a neat set up."

Suzanne acquiesced knowing objections, if she had any, would be cast aside.

"I hope you'll visit once in a while."

"Sure, Mother."

Sam loved his job as a full-time employee of Gordon's Hardware Store but it soon ended. A few weeks after his eighteenth birthday in 1943 the army drafted him.

"I wouldn't tell my mother this," he said to Tom when home on furlough, "but the army makes me wish I'd tried university. It's the most miserable existence you can imagine."

His army friends teased him unmercifully about his constant letter writing. He took it like a man because writing kept his spirits up. He composed long letters to his mother, Father Henderson and Tom Gordon; cards and short notes to his winter school friends and his summer baseball pals. He chose light-hearted words, confessing his misery only to Father who responded with understanding and encouragement as opposed to sympathy, which Sam didn't want. The continual writing resulted in a steady stream of return mail.

Tom Gordon's letters were depressing tales of misery about his business. Seemed like everybody in Calumet City went to war.

"Hang in there, Tom," Sam wrote. "No matter how bad it is, it can't be worse than this. As soon as this mess is over, I'll be back and we'll talk about me buying the store, if you'll consider it."

Suzanne wrote newsy letters in short choppy phrases.

"Bought Grandfather Matheu's interest in the store. They retired to Florida. Sold Evanston house. Took apt't overlooking the lake. Clarence is teaching me to drive. What kind of car do you think I should buy? Josef joined the navy. Nadia gone to live with Magda."

News of the servants made him wonder if he would ever have another good meal in his life.

A letter just before D-Day surprised Sam.

"Free at last. Sold Mathard for cash. Excellent price. The last of my partners joined the military so I closed the consulting business. Studying creative writing at Northwestern."

Sam never knew how he got across the beach in Normandy. He followed his sergeant with no idea what was happening. Later, when he tried to describe his reaction, he could only recollect sitting in a shallow foxhole eating cold canned stew, watching the sunset with the incessant gunfire for dinner music.

"What day is it, Sarge?"

"Tenth of June."

"You're kidding."

"What's the matter?"

Sam removed his helmet to scratch his head.

"I don't know, Sarge."

He scratched again and took a mouthful of food. When he finished eating, he wiped the utensils with his fingers and rubbed them on his pants. He lay on his back shaking his head. Then he laughed.

"Sarge, I just can't hardly believe we've been fighting this lousy war for four whole days. God Lord, where'd they go? I don't remember sleeping, eating, pissing or shitting."

After the invasion, an eternity passed before the mail arrived. Its arrival swamped Sam. He replied to his mother, Father Henderson and Tom then read the others. Suzanne's letter in August, which he didn't receive until the end of September, brought a sad message; his grandfather died in Florida. He tried to express his sorry, carefully penning a condolence letter to his grandmother that he mailed the first week of October.

Suzanne's next letter was worse; Olga died six weeks after her husband. The letter described his grandparent's life and love for each other. In November, he learned his grandparents bequeathed their estate to him. The value did not concern him; he wrote to Clarence to invest it. He didn't tell his mother he believed the money should have gone to his father, if he was still alive.

Although he received copious correspondence, he led a lonely life in the army. In December 1944, at the Battle of the Bulge, shrapnel fractured his leg. After six months rehabilitation and a few months in the occupation, he returned home to the greatest thrill of his army career—his honorable discharge four days before his twenty-first birthday.

He walked out of the demobilization center with a slight limp and a duffel bag over his shoulder that he threw away at the first opportunity.

2.

"Mother, the only place I want to work is Tom's store. He didn't do well in the war, almost quit. He wants to sell and I'm going to buy it."

Never before had Suzanne heard Sam speak like his father. Delving into business without thorough investigation was so like Harry it frightened her. Her worst nightmare coming true made her glad she had taken precautions about his inheritances.

"Sam, I don't think that's a good idea. There are so many reasons not to buy it, especially in a failing community."

"He would have closed, I think, except for one reason. I wrote to him, told him as soon as I returned, I'd buy it."

Two weeks later he approached his mother.

"Tom and I have worked out a plan. The store is worth a hundred thousand plus inventory. My inheritance from Sidorowitz is better than half a million thanks to Clarence and his business people. I want to preserve my funds for a lumber warehouse geared to contractors. I think that's the coming business. So I'd like you to lend me the money to buy the store."

"Me?"

"Wait, now, before you say no. This is a stepping stone to the future lumber business. If I'd gone to university, we'd have spent lots on tuition and board and all that stuff. Think about buying the store as my college education. It's my introduction to selling. I couldn't have a better professor than Tom. Besides, it'll continue to be the retail outlet for the local people who don't have cars."

Suzanne put her skills to work for Sam, convinced the deal would never go through when he learned the futility of trading in a dying community. Although Tom and Sam had reached agreement, she controlled the purse strings.

"It's not that easy, Sam," she explained. "I understand there's no deception, no schemes and the books are open but that doesn't make it a good deal for you. We need a market analysis. What's happening in south Chicago? What's the market future? Is land development expected? We must have answers to these questions before setting a true value on the store."

"Hell, Mother, that's a load of crap. You've been fooling around with that stuff too long. Let's settle the price, give him the dough and get on with it."

Her refusal to commit to such a casual approach irritated Sam. She embarked on a detailed investigation knowing the results would most likely be unfavorable. In three weeks, her findings yielded the expected negative answer. Main Street, USA, was in decline and Calumet City did not justify a different conclusion. She called Sam and Tom to a meeting in her office, suggesting Tom's attorney and tax adviser attend. Tom came alone.

"I'm willing to listen to what you have to say Miss Haldimann, but I make my own decisions."

"Do you remember a baseball banquet a long time ago, Tom? It was the first time I met you. I called you Mister Gordon to which you took exception. Would you please drop the Miss Haldimann business? My name is Suzanne."

She smiled.

"No problem. Glad to, Suzanne."

"Thank you. Now there are certain facts we must face."

She presented a list of items devaluing the property while trying to put a bright face on the negotiations.

"I want to make certain we have an equitable agreement for the transfer of a business property that is past its useful life. My father always referred to the other side of the question. That's what we want to discuss to-day."

Tom could not refute her findings making the negotiations one-sided. He had two choices; close up or sell for half its value. Suzanne lent Sam the money on a ten-year note.

They met in Silverstein's office in January 1947, to sign the papers. No sooner did they lay their pens down than Sam stood to speak as if addressing a formal assembly.

"I wish to thank the board of directors, of which I am the only one, for appointing me president and general manager of Gordon's Hardware Store."

Three puzzled faces looked at him.

"In my twenty-one years of life, the famous business counselor, Miss Suzanne Haldimann has guided me."

Suzanne blushed.

"For heaven's sake, Sam, what are you doing?"

He looked at her with a disdaining glare.

"Miss Haldimann! I have the floor. Please be quiet."

"Sam, don't be silly."

"Quite right," chirped Silverstein. "Let the man speak."

"Thank you." Sam continued. "Miss Haldimann's theory is that small business should buy services outside the company."

Suzanne opened her mouth but Silverstein put a restraining hand on her arm and nodded towards Sam.

"Under this theory, I am immediately engaging a consultant."

Suzanne pulled her arm from under Silverstein's hand and looked up sharply.

"What are you talking about?"

"I'm hiring a consultant."

"Sam!" She walked around the table and stood beside him, ignoring Silverstein's furious gaze. "You must ask me first. Don't be like your father hurtling off in every direction."

"Mother, please sit down. This is no whim. I'm serious."

"No, Sam. Let's discuss it first."

"No! I am hiring Tom Gordon as a consultant. Period. End."

Suzanne sat. Tom gaped. Silverstein laughed.

"What's Tom going to consult about?"

"He's the new commissioner of the Chicago Professional Softball League."

Sam looked at Tom whose mouth dropped open.

"Kind of disappointing," Tom said to Father Henderson after Mass the following Sunday. "I mean the price she offered but she did her homework and I couldn't argue. Sam didn't say much; let her do the talking. Frankly, when I yielded, I thought they skinned me. Turned out Sam wasn't talking because he was dreaming. After Sam's speech when Silverstein got his mother calmed down, he said, 'I know you're disappointed, Tom. I know you wanted a better price.' Then he told the three of us about his dream. He wants teams from all over Chicago sponsored by commercial interests. The first to sign is Gordon's Hardware Store. He said he wasn't offering me a job, he was telling me I had one and he wasn't taking no for an answer. Father, that boy, I mean he's something else. Sitting there in astonishment, I could feel my eyes welling up. I had to turn away. He made the hurt disappear and made me feel good to boot. I've never seen a boy like him. But I know why he's like that. He took lessons from you, Father, that's why."

Good-natured banter between Sam and Tom filled their spare time.

"Listen, Tom, I'll bet I can have this store hustling before you get your baseball league going."

Tom laughed.

"You won't win that bet, Sam, you make it too easy for me. Why don't you give me a real challenge."

Tom embarked on a massive publicity program. He arranged for local community newspapers to write about the new league starting play in the spring of '48. He wrote articles about Sam and the store; Sam and his background; Sam and the game of August 6; Sam and the army; Sam and his letter writing . . . Sam Matheu . . . Sam Matheu . . . Sam Matheu. The idea spread through south Chicago among the communities on the lakeshore. It never made the city newspapers. By mid-autumn of '47 Tom had eight stores to sponsor teams the next year. The publicity didn't harm sales in Gordon's Hardware Store.

3.

To succeed drove Sam. It motivated him because he believed Suzanne anticipated his failure as she did Harry's. He had paid no attention to how she setup his inherited funds. It shocked him to learn everything was in trusts that he couldn't touch without her approval. His assets exceeded eight hundred thousand dollars and he couldn't even borrow against them. The final blow came with her authorization for Clarence to send him two thousand dollars a month. He would have thrown it back in her face except he needed the money. She wouldn't listen to his arguments and refused to change the arrangements. He felt suffocated under her wing. She demanded that she approve everything he did, leaving success as the only means to overcome her interference.

The fuel that drove him was sentiment. The memorable experiences of his life occurred in Calumet City. He shut out the memories of Evanston and his father, filling his mind instead with affection for the Magdelaine family, his admiration of Father Henderson and his companionship with Tom Gordon. He realized all of them were his seniors, some by many years. In November, he celebrated his twenty-second birthday. If he was to have a birthday present, he hoped it would be romance, somebody his own age to share his triumphs and disappointments. Attendance at a boy's private Catholic school, followed by three years in the army, resulted in few young women's addresses in his book.

Fate decreed his gift would be the challenge of the store. He threw himself at the challenge, tossing one idea after another at Tom.

"We have to change the atmosphere. That's the number one priority. I want a store people visit, not just to shop but for more than that, for companionship to pass the time of day. Tom, I hate entering a store to browse. I'm self-conscious and uncomfortable and end up buying junk I throw away when I get home. We have to make this place different."

He couldn't remember when the idea sprang into his mind. Forever after when people asked, he said it happened at three o'clock in the dead of night. The next morning he bolted down the stairs to the breakfast table.

"Tom, I got it. My mother wrote to me about my great-grandfather Haldimann; an illiterate guy who spent his time on the porch at some place called Tupper's Corner. I can see the old geezer sitting on a bench with a corncob pipe, spinning yarns about the Civil War and the old west."

Tom and Ruth thought he'd lost his mind. He called his friend, Auggie Donatelli, a classmate who was now an employee of Donatelli Construction Company. He explained the design criteria— the front porch at Tupper's Corner.

"You need an architect," Auggie advised, introducing him to a man named Scully who assigned Eleanor Lang to the project.

"Make it comfortable for people to visit," Sam specified. "I don't care if they buy anything or not. I want a sit around and talk place."

After Christmas, he approved the design. Auggie set to work clearing a space in the center of the store forty by twenty feet. The façade of Tupper's General Store rose along the back wall. A couple of steps, beside a hitching rail, led up to an open platform. Weathered wood columns supported a simulated canopy. Secondhand benches and chairs from the old railroad station substituted for benches and rockers. Brass spittoons and a red and white barber pole decorated the platform. Below the platform was a board sidewalk. A soft drink cooler stood in the corner; the old fashioned kind with a block of ice to cool the drinks that sat half immersed in cold water. A hamper of fresh apples occupied the opposite corner. Ten cents for drinks, a nickel for an apple; a tin box hung from the wall for customers to drop their payment, or make change, payment on the honor system. A large sign hung from the canopy.

Sam's Country Store at Tupper's Corner
Come in and set awhile

In the spring, Sam planned a week of celebrations; an open house with free hot dogs, popcorn, soft drinks, balloons and prizes. Martha Arlene's reaction was one of excitement. At ninety-four years of age, her great-grandson's enterprise delighted her. Nothing would satisfy her short of a visit. She attended a gala event on Friday night of celebration week. Sam treated her like royalty with red carpet on the sidewalk and door attendant in white overalls. Tom issued a press release and her picture appeared in the *Tribune* ensconced on the porch at Tupper's Corners, sipping ginger ale from the bottle and entertaining the crowd. She reminisced about old Chicago, talking about politicians and criminals as if she knew them personally. For Martha, it was slumming, an unforgettable evening.

Sam sought to celebrate the success of the store opening in some special way. He invited Eleanor Lang out for dinner and dancing, a night on the town.

Sam stressed the "come in and set awhile" phrase—if you want something ask for it, or else just wander around, sit down and spin a yarn. The folks trooped in to inspect, greeting the new installation with assorted lavish praises like "Wow!" and "Gee!" Word spread and more people came to see for themselves. Consultant Tom held court on the porch clad in overalls and a ten-gallon Stetson, the ghost of old Jack Haldimann himself. His job was to greet his friends, make new friends, talk about his softball league and ensure everybody helped themselves to a drink or an apple. The store was open seven days a week. On Sundays it opened at ten after Mass and closed at four.

"Just in case some folks have an emergency or need something special," Sam told everybody. The real reason was to allow the men who worked six days a week to stop by for a chat. He proudly announced Gordon's would be on Main Street, Calumet City, forever, or for at least as long as he owned the business. Tom arranged a publicity announcement inviting the newspapers to send their writers and photographers. Several articles appeared using Tom's headline:

NEW STORE OWNER PLEDGES TO MAINTAIN GORDON'S HARDWARE STORE ON MAIN STREET

"You can't do that, Sam," Suzanne protested. "Suppose sales are bad, and you have to close. It'll be terribly embarrassing."

They sat at the same table where he had eaten countless meals with her. His mind recalled his childhood apprehension on hearing his parents yelling and bickering. That his conversations with his mother degenerated to the same level disturbed him.

"You have no understanding of the people in Calumet," he said, trying to calm his voice. "They've been buying in that store for thirty years or more. They don't have cars and can't go running off to some remote place to get what they need. They appreciate a local store and they'll patronize it."

"Rubbish," she responded, her hand thumping the table. "People go where the prices are lowest."

"Back off, Mother," he yelled. "As far as I am concerned you're a lender. We have an agreement and as long as I meet my payments, you have no business in my store. The day I don't, you exercise whatever our agreement allows, foreclose or take over the goddamn place or do whatever you like. But until that day comes, mind your own business."

"Now you listen to me. This is the same argument I had with your father over the idiotic Mabel-Cones business. First, you paid too much—"

Sam didn't hear the rest. He left the dining room and slammed the door on his way out. Driving home, he wondered about her unfinished exclamation. Paid too much; for what? It couldn't be the store, she'd squeezed that dry. He guessed, had he waited, he would have heard "—to the contractor." He didn't care.

"Sam's right," Clarence declared later as he and Suzanne reviewed the spat. "Remember what your father always said about the other side of the coin. If Sam succeeds it will be a glorious accomplishment that you would not want to take from him. So you're better outside looking in. If he fails and your hand is on the tiller, guess who'll be the bent coin and get the blame. Same conclusion, my dear, back off and don't interfere unless asked."

Sam's apology cooled the tempers but through the spring and summer months Suzanne and Sam seldom talked with each other. He met his obligation to her and that was that. "Sales are great," was the beginning and end of the business conversation.

4.

Despite the busy days, thoughts of the lumber business lurked in the back of Sam's mind. The first step would be design, the second would be site selection and last would be prying his money loose from the trusts. He needed guidance and he didn't want it to come from his mother. He liked the work Eleanor Lang did on the store renovation. He gave her a call telling her he was ready to discuss the lumber business dream.

"You'll have to talk to Mr. Scully. He's the senior partner. I'm just a junior here."

"I don't want to talk to him, I want to talk to you."

"I'm sorry, Sam, but if it's about architectural services there is nothing I can do."

"Yes there is. You can have dinner with me."

"Oh! No! The last time we went out it took me three days to recover."

"That was a celebration. There will be no big night in downtown Chicago this time. We'll have a quiet evening here in Calumet. What do you say?"

Sam took her to the most unimaginative place he could think of; the well lit dining room of the Main Street Hotel. They had a cocktail in the bar before dinner.

"I feel like I'm going on a movie stage," Eleanor commented as they entered the dining room.

"A new client for you. Think of the possibilities of re-designing this place. Built about 1890 and all they've done since is install five-hundred-watt light bulbs in the ceiling."

Sam enjoyed the dinner even if uninspired; at least there was plenty of it. Eventually he steered the conversation to his dream.

"Why can't you design it? The guy you work for will have preconceived ideas about selling and will be absolutely rigid. No, I want you to do it."

"I can't do what ever I want. I'm an employee. I do what I'm told."

Sam smiled and looked at her, saying nothing. They ate in silence. At last, she spoke.

"What are you thinking?"

"Did you meet my mother when we were doing the store?"

"No. I didn't"

"I'd like you to meet her. Perhaps we could have dinner with her and Clarence."

"Who's Clarence? Your dad?"

"No. Clarence is her boy friend. I suppose I shouldn't say this but it's funny. My parents didn't get along, fought a lot, you know, arguments, yelling at each other, all that stuff. Finally he walked out, or maybe she kicked him out, I don't know. Anyway they got a divorce and her lawyer arranged an annulment so she wouldn't be in trouble with the church if she married again. She took a liking to Clarence about three weeks later. In the next twelve years, she never married the guy. She and Clarence went to college together and if either of them recognized their noses pointed the same way as their feet they would have married then."

"What does that expression mean?"

"What expression?"

"Nose pointing the same way as their feet."

"Same as knowing which way is up. We used to say it a lot in the army."

Suzanne insisted the dinner party be at her apartment.

"Clarence, I'm so excited. Do you realize this is the first time Sam has ever invited a girl home to meet me? I can hardly wait. I wonder what she's like. Isn't this wonderful."

"Holy smoke, Suzanne, what are you saying! If he was bringing home an aviator or high-wire circus performer or something extraordinary I could understand your excitement, but she's just a girl. Look out the window, there's lots of them walking up and down the street."

"Men! I might have known. There isn't one ounce of romance in your soul. Bed is all you think of."

"Why don't we wait until the young folks get here. Perhaps they'll join us."

"I'll thank you to mind your manners. And keep your naughty mind above your belt buckle."

When Eleanor walked in Suzanne stopped breathing. She gaped at the beautiful oriental girl; petite with a well-proportioned body, short black hair and the same deep, mystic black eyes as Sam; a beautiful couple, matched like a set of Dresden figurines. Suzanne was ecstatic.

Clarence performed admirably with his jovial chatting about trifles and nonsense, encouraging everyone to join in, and making an ordinary evening at home a memorable event. Sam bided his time.

"Do you smoke?" Suzanne asked.

"No, I don't," Eleanor replied. "I tried once but it made me sick."

Sam cringed inside as his mother played matchmaker.

"Eleanor knows tobacco makes me sick. It's a wonder I ever lived past my tenth birthday with all the smoking in this house." He turned to Eleanor. "I used to carry a knife so I could cut my way through it."

"Sam. You exaggerate."

"Speaking of exaggeration, could you tell Eleanor how you started the clothing business. As I recall you said it was an impetuous adventure. Didn't you go to Cincinnati and talk grandpa into coming to Chicago?"

"Oh, Sam, I don't want to talk about it."

"She's being modest," Clarence interjected. "I'm sure it would interest Eleanor. Go ahead, tell her, Suzanne." He paused for a moment, looked at Suzanne's shocked face and began to laugh. "Tell them about the train trip."

Suzanne controlled her temper. She explained Mr. Matheu's tailoring skills.

"Harry and I recognized his great ability and decided to create a business for him."

"As I remember the story," Sam interjected, "from start to finish the entire episode took four days. Is that right, mother?"

"I would rather not discuss it. How is Tom's baseball organization progressing?"

On the way home, Eleanor asked why he embarrassed his mother like that.

"You obviously upset her," she persisted. "I thought for a minute if she had a gun she would have shot both you and Clarence."

"I wanted you to know the third most successful adventure of her life was impetuous."

"I don't know what you're talking about. What did she do?"

Sam's voice was nonchalant masking the excitement within.

"Her most successful venture, of her own doing, was the consulting business. The next, by somebody else's doing, was her success at inheritance. She's excellent at that. The third was the clothing business which is still going strong although she sold her interests during the war."

"I still don't understand."

"I want you to realize I have my mother's impetuosity. I have decided to open my own architectural design firm."

"What!" Eleanor screamed. "You can't, you're not licensed."

"Then I'll have to hire somebody who is."

They drove in silence.

Does she realize what I'm saying?

Does he mean to finance my career?

Sam took her hand. He didn't look at her as he drove.

Dare I ask her to marry me?

I hope we get home soon.

Eleanor groped for words.

"Why do you think your mother and Clarence never married?"

"I haven't the faintest idea."

Dare I?

Will he?

"I could tell they get along well together."

Sam walked Eleanor up the steps to her home. They faced each other. Her head tilted back. She placed her hand on his shoulder.

"I enjoyed meeting your mother; and Clarence, too. He made it such fun. He's a humorous man." She inched towards him, looked into his eyes and whispered softly. "Thanks for a lovely evening."

"You're welcome. I'll call you again."

He dashed down the steps, leaped into his car and was gone while she stared after him.

Sam talked aloud driving home.

"You ass. She was pleading for a kiss. Why didn't you? What do you do now? Go to Father Henderson for lessons."

He called the next evening. She sounded cool and disinterested but agreed to go to a movie on Saturday night. At the show, he put his arm around her shoulders and touched her cheek with his lips. On the porch at her house, he held her firmly as they kissed goodnight.

"What's the matter, Sam?"

Tom and Sam stood outside the church before Mass the next morning. Sam grinned sheepishly.

"I'm in love, Tom. I've found a girl. The best part is I think she loves me too."

Eleanor and baseball consumed all of Sam's time and energy with the lumber business a forgotten dream and Tom managing the store. Sam wanted the wedding and honeymoon to take place before the baseball season started. They set the date while mothers, aunts and assorted relatives complained about rushing the prenuptial parties. Sam wanted to marry on a Monday because it was Eleanor's birthday. There was no way. The bride's parents, Suzanne and everyone else, whether involved or not, dictated Saturday was the day to exchange vows.

"All right," Sam declared, "if I can't change the wedding date, I'll change your birthday. From now on it's the twentieth of April. If our kids know what's good for them, they better be born on April twentieth. That way I'll only have one date to remember to buy gifts. I'm sure Mother could pay somebody to have Easter and Christmas moved to April twentieth"

Most of Calumet City attended the wedding with a multitude of Sam's acquaintances and a large contingent of the bride's relatives and friends. Gordon's Hardware Store closed for the day. Tom felt fortunate the store closed only for the wedding day. He thought at one point it might close for the entire summer. It wasn't as grand as the wedding of Joe and Elizabeth but Martha Arlene loved every minute of it. The newly-weds were so beautifully matched. She wished Charles could have been present to hear the vows of that dear sweet couple. She loved formal weddings beyond all other ceremonial events.

When the happy couple returned from their honeymoon Sam gradually came down to earth.

"There isn't the slightest reason you can't open your own architectural office," he explained to Eleanor. "You have a state license. I have a big project for you. You will have the opportunity to create money. It's perfect."

Eleanor agreed. Sam rented an empty shop in the same block as the hardware store. Auggie soon completed the renovations. A professional sign hung in the window.

ELEANOR MATHEU
ARCHITECT

At last, work began on Gordon's Building Materials, Inc. Tom appreciated the name selection. Sam worried about how to open the purse strings.

5.

Neither Sam nor Tom had the entrepreneurial skill or the political power to set up a citywide softball league. Tom integrated eight teams from South Chicago and northwest Indiana into a local organization. He hung hundreds of posters and persuaded radio personalities to interview sponsors, managers and players at every opportunity. Banquet and service clubs delighted in his after-dinner presentations. When spring arrived at the start of the second season of play, he enlisted local celebrities to throw out the first pitch, sing the national anthem and pose with the players. A popular sport energized by community spirit spread across the southern end of Lake Michigan attracting five or six hundred fans at every game. Local bookies lent their enthusiastic support encouraging the bettors to part with their money.

The top team was Gordon's Hardware because of two exceptional personalities. One was Sam with his knowledge of the game, his constant awareness of opposing weakness and his flamboyant managerial style. His strategy made the difference, squeezing extra runs and creating winning situations. Sometimes his bold tactics backfired resulting in a loss but his team led the league as the most disliked, except in Calumet City.

The star on Gordon's team was Henry, the taxi driver. Born and raised in Calumet City, he quit school at sixteen to drive a cab in his father's fleet. The army drafted him in 1942. After basic training, he entered a motor pool in Virginia where he chauffeured army brass and played softball in his idle time. The speed and accuracy of his underhand delivery became legendary. He returned home in 1946 with enough benefits to marry, buy a house and rent a cab. He stood first in line to sign up when Tom announced the new league.

Chapter 18 - Buddy and Sam

1.

The doctors cut and patched Buddy Leyland, wrapped him in plaster cocoons and smiled as they left. Gradually recovering consciousness, he became aware of his surroundings, striving to recollect how he arrived in his predicament. A barber shaved him in bed and held a mirror for the patient to examine the results. He didn't have his wig but he didn't need it with his head bandage like a turban.

"I don't look like me."

"Not in all that plaster, you don't. But you look okay for the press."

"What press?"

A reporter burst into the room followed by a photographer toting a large camera. Before Buddy knew what was happening, a flashbulb popped in his face.

"Hey! What are you doing?"

"Don't move," the photographer said, "I'll get the other side."

"What the hell do you mean, don't move? Nurse. Nurse."

"Hey, man," the reporter said, "you're going to be famous."

"Yeah," chimed the photographer, "gonna make all them Sunday papers."

"Christ! No."

"What's the matter with that?"

The nurse didn't respond and Buddy could do nothing about these hustling maniacs.

"You be sure to get my name right."

"It's Buddy Leyland, isn't it?"

"No. It's Harry . . . just joking. Yeah! Leyland like on trucks."

Despite Buddy's fretting, as far as he knew nobody connected him to Harry; the public defender, doctors, nurses, social workers and orderlies attending to his needs never mentioned Harry. Nor did the police or the courts.

Reports about his affairs depressed him. The public defender came to visit.

"Lost on every count. The court closed your bank account, sold your assets that weren't much and awarded the proceeds to the hospital. The city auctioned the service station land and took the money for back taxes and the court gave the rest to the doctors. How come you didn't have any insurance on the building?"

"What the hell difference does it make. If I had, the court would have give it to the hospital anyway."

Harry heard nothing further from the lawyer for three months. When he came back, Harry couldn't remember who he was or what he did.

"Hank Schmidt. I'm your court appointed lawyer."

"Oh! I suppose you brought another bag full of good news."

"Yep. The IRS won a judgment for income taxes."

In September 1939, penniless with debts he could not hope to pay, the hospital turned Buddy Leyland loose to wander the streets.

A welfare agency arranged a disability pension, found a job as a custodian in the hospital and negotiated a mouse-infested one-room basement apartment. He swept floors, removed trash and did menial tasks for minimum wage with one third garnisheed by the IRS. In the lax supervision, nobody cared if he worked or if he was there at all. He filled out his own time card and swiped food to take home. Mostly, he sat in the cafeteria chatting. Life was a humdrum routine, shuffling to the hospital, frittering away the hours and shuffling home.

Isolated and friendless, his mind played tricks. If this and not that, he'd have had plenty of money. If Rocco had and he hadn't or maybe the other way around but it wasn't his fault. No! It was hers. That wop in Cicero blabbed everything; told her about Peoria and she told Rocco. Each scene in his demented dreams followed a trail leading to Suzanne. Through the winter, his hatred and wish for revenge became maniacal demons dancing in his nightmares. In the dead of night, he developed retaliatory schemes of ferocious brutality only to discard them in the light of day.

A little before noon on a Sunday morning in the spring, he set out for his one decent meal of the week. He pulled his key from the lock and found himself looking into the face of a woman he'd never seen before. She was standing in the doorway of the apartment across the hall.

"Good morning."

He smiled at her, bowed and directed her to go first.

A smirk crossed her face as she mounted the four steps to the exit door.

"Where you going?"

He followed her up the stairs.

"Lunch."

On the landing, she turned back to look at him.

"I'll come with you."

He held the door and watched her exit. She wasn't pretty but she wasn't ugly; motherly would say it all. Her hair in a bun didn't suit her; short and curled would be better. Not fat; robust was the word that entered his mind as he viewed her large breasts. In his woeful financial condition, he could not afford to buy them but after his long period of celibacy, his arousal came easily and he wondered if they might be free.

"Dutch," he said leading the way down the alley to the street.

"Of course."

They turned south on Jefferson.

"You live alone?"

"Yes. You?"

They paused for a car to pass on Fifth Street, then crossed in mid-block.

"I live alone, too."

He held the door for her to enter the restaurant.

"Eat here often?"

He pulled a chair and held it for her.

"Pretty much except when I eat at the hospital."

They ordered the Sunday special.

"Where do you work?"

"Movie theater."

He unfolded his napkin and spread it across his knees.

"Doing what?"

"Tickets. Sometimes concessions."

The waiter brought their meal.

"See good shows?"

"No. Always working."

They ate in silence. She noted his graceful manners.

"Where'd you come from?"

"Arkansas."

"Don't eat like a southerner."

"Raised in Cincinnati."

"That where you learned beautiful manners?"

"Yes."

"Tell me about it."

He told his story.

She laughed.

"What about you?"

"I don't talk about me."

"Why not?"

"It's a lousy story."

They finished the meal, lit cigarettes and ordered coffee. Harry's head nodded in the manner of a man assessing a major decision. The corners of his mouth curled, more in admiration than amusement as his gaze surveyed her breasts and crept upward until he looked into her eyes. Her tongue circled her mouth. He suggested a stroll down Broadway. She told the story of a broken home and a sour marriage.

"Two kids gone bad; one in prison." She sighed, shrugged and smiled. Harry judged it resignation, not regret. "I left Boise without telling them. Heard of kids running away from home? In my family, mama did the running. Couldn't stand the lot of them."

"Hear from them once in awhile?"

"Never and don't want to."

Two loners at ease, unafraid of each other and finding therapy by telling their stories. They walked down the four steps to the basement apartments.

"Coffee?"

"Sure."

They sat in her one-room unit, drank two cups each and smoked.

Buddy stood.

She held his hands.

"Want to stay a little longer?"

She raised his hands and pulled them to her breasts. He caressed her and felt for the buttons on her blouse. Her hands found his belt buckle. They played the scene in slow motion, shedding their garments, caressing their bodies. At last, they stood naked and panting. The climax was fast, too fast for her. In half an hour, they did it again. Harry didn't return to his apartment that night. Before he left for the hospital, they made love once more.

"By the way," he said on his way out the door, "what's your name?"

"Moira Finch."

He took a long slow look at her, a smile crossing his face as he remembered Jungle Jim.

"Yeah," he said. "Mine's Buddy Leyland."

2.

Moira provided relief that brought comfort from loneliness. Once or twice a week, he'd camp at her place and wait for her arrival after midnight when the theater closed. They'd talk a while and bit by bit she learned Harry's tale of woe. In the morning, he rose early while she slept. On Sundays when they were both at home, she showed him how to rid his place of mice and helped him wash the walls and floor. They cleaned the furniture scrounged by the agency and bought deodorizer to kill the stink. She threw out his dime store utensils, bought better cutlery and plates at the pawnshop. After finding a good second-hand mattress and buying sheets, she slept in his bed occasionally.

Sundays they ate their mid-day meal at the restaurant across Broadway and strolled down to the lake afterwards. On a bright June afternoon, they sat on a bench by the waterfront watching the boats. Buddy feared what was happening to them.

"This is crazy," he said.

"What?"

He hesitated, afraid to talk about the subject on his mind. He remembered the day they met; easy talk and wonderful sex. Gradually, emotions interfered and it wasn't the same casual friendship any more. He wanted to tell her how he felt. He couldn't find the courage.

"Having two apartments when most of the time we're in the same one."

She sprang to her feet, hands on her hips.

"Don't you talk like that."

"Like what?"

"Like you're thinking love and marriage and all that shit."

Buddy laughed.

"Sit down," he said between guffaws.

She sat.

"What's so funny?"

"You just gave yourself away. I didn't say anything about love and marriage."

For the first time in their acquaintance, he saw a look of discomfort. She didn't blush—she wasn't capable of that—but a self-conscious sheepishness contorted her face.

"I won't talk about it," she said. "Besides, I'm not divorced and maybe my husband's still alive. And if we married, I wouldn't know if my husband was Buddy or Harry."

In September, he moved across the hall. For lease purposes and other ridiculous technicalities, she adopted the surname Leyland preceding it with Mrs. when needed by some silly agency rule. In her private affairs, her job, her banking, her social security and tax returns, she remained Moira Finch. She earned sixteen fifty a week; Buddy netted nine not including his small pension. They co-existed in the same room occasionally sharing their bodies for an hour or two after midnight, keeping their personal financial affairs undisclosed and splitting common expenses.

Buddy wondered about his friend Harry Matheu. Adorned in false mustache, wire frame spectacles and peak cap pushed well back to expose his wig, Harry approached the clerk at the social security office. He played the same game as Buddy Leyland; bad accident; couldn't remember much; totally disabled.

"No, sir. As far as I can remember, I've never paid social insurance taxes but I need to register."

They wanted to see his medical history. It took time to swipe appropriate records and return them after the forger finished. When everything was ready, the forger refused to let them out of his sight until he was paid. Harry had to steal money from the hospital.

A year after applying, Harry Matheu came alive again, registered in the social security program. He applied for a driver's license and received a permit to operate a taxi. Harry was two people, both legitimate. One of him was a substitute cab driver, the other him worked in a hospital. He revealed his success to Moira.

"Maybe they call this dual-citizenship." He laughed.

She groaned. "Are you sure them guys didn't bang your head?"

3.

Harry's life changed. He put in forty hours a week at the hospital that he performed in thirty-two or less, scrounged a free meal in the cafeteria every day and drove a taxi in the evenings. At midnight, he met Moira at the theater and they went home together. The notion that one of him could do one job and the other a different job captivated him. Neither made enough to pay income tax but each could live for half what it used to cost.

"You're crazy," Moira said. "That's a dumb way to think about money."

"That's not what I'm thinking about."

"Tell me."

"I'm thinking if one of me did something and disappeared, could the other go on living unaffected."

"Stupid."

She rolled over and went to sleep.

Harry stared at the ceiling, hands beneath his head, his vengeance reawakened. Six years living with Moira didn't get him anywhere. The big house in Evanston, two servants, new car every year, snappy clothes; that's what he wanted. He couldn't have it because Suzanne denied him. The thought of guns and knives was detestable. Poisons were a more attractive medium. He had no idea how to deliver them but that could wait. First, he had to learn about them. He asked casual questions at the hospital, infrequently so as not to raise suspicions, gradually amassing information, including how to pilfer a small quantity should an opportunity arise.

The old thoughts returned reinforcing his loathing, his desire to avenge the misery she caused. His hatred festered in his mind like a malignant cancer growing ever worse. His frustration fed on his inability to find a foolproof plan. He became annoyed with Moira when no retaliatory scheme developed. The repercussions of an act of violence did not concern him. He believed his safety lay in his existence as two people.

On a cold February day in 1948, Moira and Buddy returned from the usual Sunday meal. Buddy dropped into a chair to scan the newspaper. A picture caught his eye.

"Isn't that interesting," he mused. He read the article slowly devouring each word. "Look at this Moira, my kid owns a store. He must have bought it with his mother's money. Damn kid, if he doesn't do what she tells him she'll break him. I think I'll introduce myself."

Moira fell asleep.

Sam went to the private office to take a call.

"Sam Matheu speaking."

"My name is Buddy Leyland, Sam. I'd like to meet you."

"What is it you'd like to see me about, Mr. Leyland."

"Well, you see, it's a private matter. You see—"

"Mr. Leyland, please come to the point. What is it you want?"

"Well, I want to meet you."

"What for?"

"I can't say on the telephone."

"Mr. Leyland, unless you can be more specific I'm not interested."

"You see, I mean, it's hard to talk on the telephone like this."

"Why don't you practice a little. When it gets easier, call me back. Good-bye."

Moira and Buddy sat at the little table with the newspaper spread before them. He poured out yet another story about his ex-wife and only son. There had been no discussion about his former life for years but suddenly here it was, only it wasn't the same version she heard before. Twelve years of suffering and resentment cascaded out of him.

"My accident was no robbery. I couldn't tell the police the truth because if Rocco found out, he wouldn't make a mistake the next time. But never you mind, I know who pulled the strings to have me rubbed out. It had to be my ex only there'd been a mistake. They left me for dead but I wasn't dead. Now, at last, I can get even."

He ranted about blackmail, robbery, kidnapping and even murder. Moira shook her head in disbelief.

"For God's sake, Buddy, you're insane. Stop it. Let bygones go. It's over. Forget it." She hid her trembling hands beneath the table. "I'm going to bed."

Over the course of the following weeks, he persuaded her to go with him to see the store in Calumet City. She agreed provided that's all they were going to do.

"We're just going to case the joint."

They elected to go Easter week when Moira had two days off. She had to be back Good Friday for the weekend crowd. They left early Wednesday morning.

On the bus, they studied the newspaper article. The plan was for Moira to visit the store, talk with the folks and see what was what. If anybody asked her name, she was Moira Finch, not Mrs. Leyland. Buddy couldn't go himself because somebody might recognize him.

Moira fretted.

"How will I know your ex?"

"You'll know all right. She's high-class, wears fancy clothes. Don't worry about that."

Buddy sat in a booth in the cafe diagonally across from Gordon's Store drinking coffee.

"Waiting for my friend," he told the waitress.

"I've never seen any place like it," Moira reported. "I said I came from Gary. I'd read about the store in the Sunday paper and wanted to see it. The sales girl directed me to Tupper's Corner. If I hadn't seen the pictures, I'd never guessed what she meant. A man in white overalls with a big Stetson greeted me as if I were his sister. I sat on the platform with an apple and a coke talking to the men. All kinds of people were coming and going, both men and women, some with kids."

"I saw them. Looks like a popular place."

"More like a small department store than a hardware store. I could hear the cash register click every so often. Four men sat there chewing the fat. A woman come in with some kind of plumbing problem. The men talked about it but couldn't agree what the woman should do. Finally, one of them decided he'd go to her house and look at it. In a few minutes, him and the woman came back. He said it needed a new rubber washer. It cost five cents. Then he said he'd install it. When he came back, I asked how much he charged for a service like that. 'I didn't charge nothing,' he said. Imagine. All that talk and trouble and the store sold a five-cent washer. I put a quarter in the tin box to pay for my apple and drink when I left."

"Did you see anybody looked like my ex?"

"No way. Them's working folks, not society folks."

"How about the kid?"

"A young boy, Chinese like the picture in the paper, must have been him."

"We better go some other place to eat. Maybe the store employees eat here. Perhaps the kid too. Better not hang around. We'll come back in a couple of hours."

Buddy Leyland walked into the hardware store a few minutes after two the same afternoon.

"Like to talk to Sam Matheu," he said to the girl.

"He's in the back. Just a minute, I'll call him."

Sam led Mr. Leyland into the private office.

"Are you the same man who called a month or two ago?"

Sam watched him closely; hefty, four or five inches taller than Sam; clean shaven, his face scarred from some terrible accident. He wore dark horn-rimmed glasses although there was no glare in the office. A black toupee capped his head. He had large hands, like a farmer.

"Yes, I did call."

"As I remember you were having some difficulty telling me exactly what was on your mind. Are you ready now?"

Sam kept his voice casual, his tone polite.

"Well . . . uh . . . er . . . you see—"

"What I do see Mr. Leyland is whole lot of confusion. Please, sir, I don't have time to waste."

Mr. Leyland removed his glasses. He reached up and pulled the wig from his head. He stared at Sam for a moment.

"I'm your father."

Sam stared at Mr. Leyland for several seconds.

"Well," he said.

He blew the air from his lungs with a long audible sigh. He inhaled deeply.

"Well," he repeated. He took another breath. They stared at each other. Sam broke the silence.

"It's not exactly what I expected and I guess Bob's my uncle. I don't believe you."

"It's true, I'm Harry Matheu."

"All right, let's suppose you are. Tell me something about myself that only my parents would know."

Buddy rambled about Mathard, Matheu's Men's Furnishings, Mabel-Cones and Suzanne Haldimann. Sam interrupted.

"Everything you're saying is common knowledge. Tell me, Mr. Leyland, when is my birthday?"

"Uh . . . I've forgotten."

"Well, let's try another. How is your father? Is he well and still working at the clothing store?"

"Yes! I haven't seen him for awhile but I believe he is."

"I see. I think I'll call my mother and let her know you're here." He picked up the telephone.

"Don't do that, Sam." Panic showed on Leyland's face. "Won't do any good."

"Might," Sam muttered as he dialed.

> *"Hello. This is Sam. Is Mother home, please? . . . I see. Would you ask her to call when she comes in . . . at the store, yes, or at home this evening if she's late . . .. Thank you."*

During the call, the visitor take a cigarette from a cardboard pack. Sam watched the tapping on the box and the flourish as the thumbnail lit a match followed by deep inhaling of the first puff and the audible expulsion of smoke. The actions seemed strangely familiar as if seen in a dream.

"I'm sorry, Mr. Leyland I cannot stand tobacco smoke. It makes me sick. Would you put that cigarette out please."

Sam noted the slight yellow nicotine stains on the fingers of those big hands as they squelched the cigarette; stains he had loathed so much when his father touched him.

"Are you going to be in town for a day or two Mr. Leyland? Where will I be able to reach you?"

"I'm not sure. I don't know."

"Is there anything else you'd like to say?"

"Only that I don't blame you for not recognizing me. But it's the truth. I am your father. I'll come back tomorrow. We can talk about it some more."

Sam escorted his guest to the door. He watched Mr. Leyland walk across to the diagonal corner and enter the cafe. While Sam pondered what to do, Mr. Leyland came out with a woman; the same woman who spent the morning in the store talking with Tom.

"I've got to go on an errand," he told the girl at the register.

He followed the couple as they walked down Main Street. They entered the hotel. He could see them talking with Billy, the clerk, at the desk. The discussion ended. Sam darted around the corner, watching as they scanned the street in both directions. They were arguing about something. They went back into the hotel and he lost sight of them. He wondered if he should go in when he saw them crossing the lobby. Again, they talked with Billy. No sign of registering. Some waving of hands, more talk and Billy took a pencil and paper. They came out, studied the sketch and headed down the street. Sam had two choices; follow or talk to the clerk. Billy was easier.

"Hi Sam, what you doing here?"

"No time for questions and answers, Billy. Here's a five spot," he whispered, "tell me where those folks were going."

"That sleazy rooming house over on Hundred-fifty-eighth. You know the one?"

"Yeah. Thanks."

Sam jumped in the cab at the door.

"Hey, Henry, take me over to the boardinghouse on Hundred-fifty-eighth."

"Gee, Sam, you kidding? You'll get crabs in that place."

"You keep your damn mouth shut and drive."

"Now just who is it I'm not supposed to tell?"

"Nobody, you hear."

Sam slipped him a five.

"I get a lot deafer for ten. I lose my memory for twenty."

"You don't even use a gun to stick up a fellow." Sam laughed, passing over another fifteen dollars. "Just stop at the corner. Don't drive down the street. Thanks for the loss of memory, Henry. And don't forget to report that on your income tax. Put down highway robber where it asks for occupation."

Sam waited in the dark alley across from the rooming house. Mr. Leyland probably had difficulty walking long distances, crippled as he was. They might have stopped for food or rest. Sam peered in both directions when he saw them turn the corner. He dodged back into his hiding place. They located the address and went in. Soon a light came on in a second floor room. The woman looked out. That's where they were staying, no doubt about it.

Sam hurried to the corner, glad to be back on a brightly-lit street. He returned to his office where he found a note that his mother called. He decided not to reveal Mr. Leyland's claim that he was Harry Matheu. He dialed the number.

> *"This is Sam. Is mother home, please? . . . Thank you . . . Hi, Mum . . . Yeah, I'm fine. You? . . . that's just old age, don't worry about it. Listen, I have a question. A guy came into the store to-day. Said his name was Buddy Leyland. Gave me a cock-and-bull story about knowing you. Ever heard of him? . . . Leyland, Buddy Leyland . . . Gary, Indiana, I think, I'm not sure . . . I asked him questions . . . he didn't know the answers . . . He said he was coming back to-morrow . . . I don't know, he didn't say what he wanted . . . maybe he's trying to put the snatch on me or something . . . If you think of anything, let me know would you . . . Okay, thanks. Hope I didn't disturb your dinner . . . I did! Sorry about that. Is Clarence there? . . . Good. He'll help you calm done. Say hello for me . . . Yeah. 'Bye now."*

Sam wasn't his usual ball of energy Thursday. It was noticeable to everyone that something was wrong. Tom cornered him in the office.

"What's your trouble, to-day?"

"Remember that woman yesterday. You talked to her in the morning."

"I sure do. I thought that was great when Will went over and fixed her tap. Cost her a nickel. Plumber would have charged twenty-five bucks. We'll get miles of publicity from that. Terrific, eh?"

"That's not who I'm talking about."

"Oh! You mean the other one from Gary. She wanted to know all about everything. Will stunned her when he told her he didn't charge anything for fixing the plumbing."

"That was her man came in after lunch. Gave me a cock-and-bull story; said he was my father. My God, Tom, it upset me. I think I was ten when my parents separated. It was the first summer I played baseball for you. That was '36 wasn't it?" Tom nodded. "The spring, maybe June of '36, was the last time I saw him. Now he shows up, tells me his name is Buddy Leyland, and in the next breath says he's my father."

"What did you say?"

"Asked him if he knew my birth date. He didn't. Asked about his dad, if he was still working in the clothing store. He said he thought so. Tom, his dad died in Florida during the war. 1944 I think."

"Should we notify the cops?"

"What are we going to say? A man came into the store and told us a fairy tale. Please arrest him. Come on, Tom, be realistic."

"Sorry. You're right." Tom paced across the office to look out the window. "Isn't he obviously phony if he couldn't answer your questions?"

"Let me ask you a question. When's your daughter's birthday?"

"Gee. I think it's—no maybe that's Tom, junior—"

"Q.E.D." Sam laughed. "In spite of the questions, there was something familiar about him. I can't define it but I noticed it when he took a cigarette and lit it. It was like a replay of a dream, as if I'd seen it before."

"What are you going to do if he comes back? Maybe there's some way to trace a guy and find out his background."

"Must be; cops do it all the time."

"You could hire a private detective," Tom suggested.

"Not a bad idea. I might do that. Satisfy my curiosity, if nothing else."

Sam's unproductive day ended as he locked up at six o'clock. He asked Eleanor to go to a movie to free his mind from the turmoil. It didn't work. They left half way through the picture and tried to think through the problem walking home. A horn sounded; Henry beckoned to Sam.

"None of my business, Sam, just thought you'd like to know I got a call to pick up a fare at the boardinghouse. Took a woman to the bus depot. I asked where she was going. She said Gary. Thought you might like to know. Want a lift home, free?"

Sam lay in bed, tormented through the night. The idea that Leyland might be his father pained like a dagger plunged into him he couldn't extract. He had never liked his father and he didn't like Leyland. Gradually his agonizing yielded to fear. The childhood abuses flooded his mind. This horrible, terrible, abusive beast had come back with his poisonous venom. He came to destroy, to take away success. If Harry couldn't have money, he wouldn't let Sam have it either.

4.

On Good Friday, Sam went to church, then to the store. The riddle posed by Buddy Leyland was less bothersome, the first shock having worn off. He was able to rationalize, convinced his father had returned. The descriptions and accounts related by Buddy the day before did contain facts only a person intimately involved would have known. What incentive would Buddy have to claim to be his father if, in fact, he wasn't? Obviously, the guy lived in the poor house, or right next door to it. Therefore, his motivation for coming to Calumet could only be money. Buddy probably didn't know Sam had inherited wealth in his own right but he would know of his mother's wealth. That must be it: money. Again, he consulted Tom.

"I can only believe he's after money."

"How do you think he plans to get it."

"There's nothing in my life to blackmail. Kidnapping?"

"Can't be. He's made no secret of his presence in town, in the cafe, in the hotel lobby, in the store and at the rooming house. Lots of people have seen him around town."

"Doesn't seem like it could be unfinished business between my parents with Silverstein protecting her. If it's money, Tom, I can't imagine how he plans to extract it."

"Let me get some coffee. I'll be back in a minute."

Sam's mind soared. What other possible explanations could there be? Perhaps the guy was not his father, but a look-alike who shook down Harry somehow. The doubts lingered. Tom came back.

"I've decided I'm going to try another round of personal questions if he shows again. If not, I'll forget it."

Sam didn't get the opportunity to forget it. About eleven o'clock Buddy called.

"Let's have lunch," Sam suggested. "Where are you staying?"

"At the hotel on Main Street."

"I'll get my car. Pick you up in an hour. Twelve o'clock at the hotel entrance."

Sam pulled to the curb at the hotel in his red Triumph.

"Hi Buddy," he yelled, "climb in."

"Where we going?"

"Out in the country. Everybody knows me here. We need to go where we can talk. I'm not convinced you're my father. Most of the stuff you told me yesterday was more or less common knowledge. If you were my father, you'd know a lot more about me than you said yesterday. Mostly you just talked about my mother. Why don't you tell me something else."

"I'm not sure what I can tell you."

"That confirms my doubts."

"Wait a minute. Let me think."

Buddy wore a frown and rubbed his chin as they drove.

"Nice car you got, Sam. How come you bought a red one?"

"What do you mean?"

"Don't mean anything. Instead of black or green or some other color." Suddenly Buddy sat up straight. "Wait a minute; I remember something. The first summer you came to live in Calumet I bought you a bicycle. It was a red bicycle and it had a three-speed gear on it. I bought it because I thought you'd like red. I only guessed, don't remember you ever telling me you liked red. Anyway, I told Josef to hide it for about a week until the day you were leaving. I bought you a baseball glove, a bat and three baseballs too. The morning you left, I gave them to you. Josef had the stuff in the garage. We jammed the bicycle in the back seat with your clothes and junk. You sat in the front and he drove you down. Do you remember that?"

The story stunned Sam. It was exactly what he remembered but he wasn't about to admit it.

"I'm not sure I remember. Anything else come to mind?"

Again, they drove on, each deep in thought when Buddy burst into laughter.

"Here's one. Nobody knows this story except your mother, your father and maybe a teacher or two. Now if I'm not your father I'd have to be the best detective ever lived to track this down. I'll bet your teachers don't even remember."

"All right. What is it?"

"I'm not exactly sure of the year but I'll guess when you were in grade three, but it may have been grade four. No matter which, you suddenly decided you were going to change your name. You decided to spell it M A T H E W. A week later you added an S. Then when the talking was over, you told me your name was Sam A. Mathews and the A didn't stand for anything because you didn't like the name Arlene."

Sam knew this man was his father. They had long since passed the city limits. They pulled in at a roadside restaurant.

"Look Dad," Sam started, "I'm stunned. You wear that ridiculous black toupee on your head and dark glasses; you have obviously been in one horrendous accident or else someone beat the shit out of you; and you dress like a tramp. I haven't seen you for twelve or thirteen years—I'm not sure how long—and with no warning you burst into my life. I don't even know what to call you—Buddy? Mr. Leyland? Dad? What the hell, I think I'm entitled to an explanation. How about you talk for a while?"

"All right, I'll take this hairpiece off but I've worn it so long I feel naked without it."

"Why? I don't mean why do you feel naked, I mean why do you wear it?"

"I've had a lot of trouble," Harry began. He told a complicated story of his life from the time of the divorce to the present. As usual, he skirted the truth. He avoided an explanation of his relationship with Moira but simply identified her as his wife. He talked about the boardinghouse in Peoria never mentioning the faked death. His driving career for an Arkansas company ended with a terrible truck accident in Gary. Then somebody mugged him for six hundred forty two dollars. He tried hard to make a go of his life but everything went against him. He came back to Calumet as soon as he read about Sam because he wanted to atone for his errors. When his story ended, his words carried little truth.

"I think I'm going to call you Harry. That's your name. That okay?"

"Yes, that's okay."

"You said something yesterday that almost convinced me your were telling the truth."

"What's that?'

"You said your dad was still working in the clothing store. Your dad is dead. Retired in 1944. Moved to Florida. Died the same year I think, or maybe in '45. Your mother died about three months later. If you were trying to con me, you would have known that. It would be plain stupid for you to pretend they were still alive when you knew all about Mathard, the clothing business and all that stuff. I knew you hadn't talked to your parents in a long time. Grandma wrote during the war and told me they hadn't seen you for years. You may or may not realize it but you broke their hearts. That, and those little yellow tobacco stains on your fingers when you struck the match in my office. That's what convinced me."

As they drove home, Sam turned to his father.

"What the hell do I do now?"

"What do you mean?"

"What do I tell Mother? I've already told her about Buddy Leyland calling on me. I told her you claimed to know her. I also told her you said you would be coming back to the store. Soon as we get back, she's going to ask questions. Do I tell her who you are?"

"Probably better not if she doesn't know. I don't know what you tell her."

Arriving back in town, Sam drove down Main Street not stopping at the hotel.

"Hey, let me out here," Harry yelled. Sam kept going without saying anything. He pulled up in front of the boardinghouse on Hundred-fifty-eighth.

"When you leaving town?"

Harry didn't look at Sam; his lips moved but no words came out. He faked a cough that didn't fool Sam for a second. At last, he just answered the question.

"Probably tomorrow."

"Look! Give me your address. Have you got a telephone where you live?"

"No we don't have a telephone. Who's going to call us? If the hospital needs me, they leave a message with the landlord. Otherwise nobody ever calls." Harry wrote out his address on a slip of paper. "Here's where I live."

They sat outside the rooming house with the motor running.

"Harry, I don't want you to come to the store tomorrow. I think about half what you've told me is bullshit. I guess I think you are my father but I also think you are one hell of a liar. If you think you are ready to level with me come by our house and meet my wife. Here's my card with the address and the telephone number. But I'd rather you didn't. Right now, I want to think about this. I want you to go home and leave me be. This has been, I don't know what you call it, upsetting, I guess. I need some time to make sense of it."

"Well, I suppose," he stammered, "if that's what you want. But ... but ... but I told you the truth. I want to hear from you. It's been a long time. For everything I did wrong, I guess . . . I'm sorry. Maybe you'd let me try to make it up, if I can."

"Sure, Harry."

5.

Sam suffered through a week of anxiety and indecision before he told Suzanne the truth. The old man was in a mess. Maybe it wasn't his fault. There were twelve years of history missing. He asked himself to dinner at her place and said he didn't want Clarence to be there. He told her the story after dinner over coffee.

She refused to help.

"I settled with that man in 1936. That was the end of him in my life."

"I'm not sure you're right," Sam countered.

"What do you mean?"

"Only that he's back."

"He didn't come back to me, he came back to you. I don't want to see him, talk to him or even hear about him. If you do, that's your business, not mine. But I'll tell you this. If you have anything to do with him, you'll regret it. Somehow, he'll get you in trouble. I advise you against any association with him."

"Those are harsh words. The guy is destitute."

"Sam, have you forgotten the abuse you suffered? Have you forgotten how he handled you, how, through the grace of God, Father Henderson was able to help you recover? Sam he's a beast."

"You're right. I'll let it go."

Sam couldn't let it go. Eleanor suggested they walk together and talk.

"Do you mind if I go alone?"

"Yes. I think it's better to go together and talk it out."

They took long walks in the evening.

"Where is Mother's sense of compassion? She taught me about the duties of wealth. Are these selective? Did you only consider those who qualify in some arbitrary way, those you like? Isn't it my duty to help my father?"

"I believe it is. The bible says so."

"I set aside the inheritance from his parents for some vague purpose. Maybe this is it."

"Sam, no matter what else you may or may not do for your father in the future, why don't you send him a hundred dollars a week, at least for the summer months if not permanently."

The next day Sam bought a money order because he thought Harry wouldn't have a bank account and might have trouble cashing a check.

"Harry, something to help," he wrote on a small card.

Sam and Eleanor continued the conversation at supper that night.

"There are so many unanswered questions. I wonder if Harry beat her and she doesn't have the courage to tell anyone."

"Maybe he made threats that kept her from revealing the truth."

"I never recall Mother with bumps or bruises. They drank and smoked in the living room, sometimes laughing and joking, sometimes yelling and screaming, but never striking each other. It was a marital contest of wills, a battle of inflated egos perhaps, but not a physical war of blows. You know, Eleanor, I think their marriage was void of affection. Each blamed the other, neither facing the reality of failing to create a sincere relationship."

"Why not talk to Father Henderson?"

Father agreed compassion was in order.

"A well-to-do son should aid his impoverished parent. You have enormous wealth. At twenty-three, you have eight-hundred-thousand dollars invested, you are the sole owner of a successful store and you'll inherit a fortune from your mother. I believe it is right and reasonable that you should do something to ease your father's plight."

"I'm giving a hundred a week during the summer. Do you think that's right?"

"Certainly. I'm sure he will be grateful. There's no urgency to make any other decision. Summer is starting. We have time to think. Let's talk about it during the summer and see if we can do something else. We'll decide in September or October, before the cold weather sets in."

Discussion with Father always provided peace of mind and resolved problems. He never left a person alone to bear the burdens single-handed.

"What a comforting counselor he is," Sam said to Eleanor when he returned.

Chapter 19 - Operation QpeeQ

1.

Sam continued the gifts through the winter with an extra five hundred at Christmas and three hundred at Easter making the charity an even six thousand a year. He put no restrictions on the use of the money, asked no questions and sought no gratitude. Since his mother failed to teach his father how to handle money after fourteen years of marriage, Sam knew he couldn't do it either.

Buddy Leyland did not tell Moira about the weekly income. He stowed it in his duffel bag, tied in five-hundred-dollar bundles. The money whetted his eagerness for revenge while his fingers itched for more. He gave up the taxi but kept his hospital job where the wage had increased slightly. With the IRS off his back and the other debts forgotten or forgiven, his hospital pay provided for his needs.

The South Chicago Softball Association opened their second season in May. Buddy attended every game, placing hundred dollar bets, the maximum the bookie would cover.

"How come you're going to ball games?" Moira asked. "You never showed no interest in sports before."

"I've got nothing to do in the evenings and Saturdays. The games are good. You interested in going?"

"When?"

"They play Tuesdays and Saturdays. There's two teams representing Gary so there's nearly always a game here in town."

"Can't; have to be at the theater. Besides, I'm not into baseball.

Buddy won more than he lost. One week he bet against the point spread and won big on five to two odds. The bookie dubbed him "Lucky Leyland". At the halfway point of the season, he had a net gain of twelve hundred, a sum he considered as slow as the stock market in the twenties. The thrill of winning brought memories of Fishbein's tutelage but the dedication Abie demanded didn't work in baseball. Box scores, newspaper accounts and attendance at every game yielded few clues. He could surely uncover a better way to faster profits.

Moira awoke as he pulled his duffel bag from under the bed.

"What are you doing?"

"Going to Calumet City for a few days," he said stuffing his gear into the bag.

"What for?"

"Interested in this baseball stuff. Want to talk to Tom Gordon who runs it. See what I can learn."

Moira rolled over and shut her eyes.

"Going on the bus so I can catch the game at five. I'll stay for the Saturday game and come back Sunday morning."

After the Tuesday game, Buddy trudged towards town, thinking how to make his money grow faster. Gordon's Hardware didn't win because they were good; they won because the pitcher threw the ball so fast the batters could hardly see it, let alone hit it. Had Buddy taken the point spread and bet five, he'd have won a couple of thousand. He racked his brain for a new idea. Betting Gordon's Hardware to lose would likely offer the bets odds. If he bet the bundle, he could win as much as thirty-five thousand, if a bookie anywhere would cover him. But how to set it up to be sure there would be no downside risk?

Buddy felt as if struck by lightning. Of course! He kicked himself for not thinking of it sooner. Get Henry to throw the game. How do you do that? Sam would know instantly so Sam had to be in on the deal. No way; he'd tell Tom for sure and the entire scheme would blow up. Then it came; after all the years of vengeance and hatred, a plan sprang into his mind.

"Holy Jesus! It might work."

He looked around to see if anybody heard him.

The last bus left at ten. He hurried to the depot. At two in the morning, Moira heard somebody at the door.

"It's me," Harry shouted, as he yelled at her to let him in.

She peeped through the crack.

"I thought you were staying in Calumet till Sunday." She pushed the door closed and released the chain. "What happened?"

"Got an idea." He opened the refrigerator. "Anything to eat?"

"No. Put out the light."

She pulled the blanket up to cover her head.

"Want to talk about it now?"

"No, I told you. Not tonight. Put out the light."

Buddy, exhausted from the late night, dragged himself out of bed in the morning by force of habit. He had a week's vacation but with nothing else to do, he ambled off to the hospital. As he trudged along pondering details of his scheme, he realized how fortunate he hadn't told Moira his idea that would work only if he was alone in the apartment. He'd pick a fight; get her so mad she'd walk out or he could toss her out. At eight, he sauntered in to the corner bar to fortify his determination. Home at midnight, slightly drunk, he waited for her. The moment he started his complaining, she lost her temper. Then he lost his. They shouted and cursed at each other.

"Look, Moira. If you don't like it, go away. Get out of here!"

He yelled and raised his arm as if to strike her with the back of his hand.

"You and your stupid crazy work hours."

Moira looked bewildered.

"I ain't accepting any ejection notice from you no matter what crazy idea rattles your brain. There's the door. If you want to be alone, you leave, not me. I'm going to bed."

Buddy tried to keep the argument going but Moira wouldn't listen. She refused to let him under the covers. He slept in the sleazy wingback chair they bought at the junkyard. He left without talking to her in the morning.

Moira arose at her usual hour wondering if she dreamed the conversation. It gnawed at her through the afternoon and into the evening. At one o'clock, she arrived home in a fit of anger and shook Buddy awake.

"What were you talking about last night?"

Buddy blinked at the light.

"You talking to me?"

He couldn't have picked a worse response.

"Listen, you creep, I'm not leaving." She stood beside the bed with her hands on her hips. "You've got two choices, Buddy-boy. Either you apologize or you get out. Make up your mind. Either way I'm not talking to you until you decide which it is."

"You go to hell," he mumbled and covered up his head.

She tore the blankets from the bed.

"Get up!"

He grabbed the blankets from her.

"I told you once, go to hell. Now go."

She chose not to continue the fight. Instead, she put on her nightgown, put out the light and climbed under the covers. Putting both feet on his back, she pushed him out for one more night in the sleazy chair.

The next night Buddy waited up for her and when she arrived, he stared at her in silence.

"Well," she said.

"I want you to get out for your own good." He spoke in a soft, tender voice. "I won't tell you my plans but I'll tell you this. If I'm caught we'll both spend time in the cooler."

He had her attention.

"Why! What are you going to do?"

He smirked like a child with a secret.

"I won't tell you."

"Damn you."

His smirk changed to a patronizing sneer.

"If I tell it makes you an accessory, like it or not."

She gasped.

"You going to murder somebody?"

"Poison, I think."

She paced across the room, then turned violently to face him.

"You're crazy! You're a maniac and I'm supposed to sit here and let you drag me into jail?"

"You said you wanted to stay." He spread his hands in a not-my-fault gesture. "If it'll make you happy I'll apologize. I'm sorry I lost my temper. Now I'm going to bed and you can go about your business and do whatever the hell you like."

"I'll call the police. That's what I'll do."

He smiled at her as he sat on the bed unlacing his boots. He pulled his socks off, dropped his drawers and unbuttoned his shirt. Naked, he walked towards her rubbing his hands together, drooling saliva like a slobbering dog. He laughed like a maniac at her scream.

"You leave me be."

"Okay." He got into bed. "Don't say I didn't warn you. Put out the light."

The next morning as soon as he left for the hospital, she arose, packed her belongings, most of the cooking utensils, all the food and moved out. When he found her gone, he considered it an omen of success. The ease of evicting her pleased him and he wore a malicious smile.

Alone in his own apartment, he spent the last two weeks of August perfecting his plan. Not a raving maniac, as Moira said, not weird and wild, no, he was cool and calculating, a swashbuckling pirate with a map of the buried treasure. Harry Matheu, controlling each event that would satisfy the injustices. Before he quit his job at the hospital, he stole a little cyanide.

On the last Saturday in August, he set off to find a locale for his escapade. He drove west from Calumet City on route 30 passing through Frankfort searching for a lonely, deserted area. A dirt road marked "DEAD END" went off to the south. After a mile through empty fields with no houses along the way, it entered a heavily wooded area. The road died about five hundred yards into the forest.

He tied a red ribbon to a tree branch. He noted the landmarks on his way back, affixing ribbons as direction markers where a stranger might go wrong finding the place. He recorded every turn and the distances between them. The next road to the west, a mile further along route 30, paralleled the first one. One farmhouse stood near the highway, otherwise there were no inhabitants between the farmhouse and the forest. A dirt road, overgrown with weeds and tall grass continued south from the edge of the woods, provided the perfect escape route.

He returned to Gary, bought enough food for the next two weeks and holed up in the apartment. He wrote out the details of his plan, scripted the speeches, rehearsing them until he could recite them in his sleep. The suspense mounted like an actor anticipating opening night. He sought to satisfy his fascination with military code names. He ranged through retribution, vengeance, get-even, square-off, payback—nothing suited the brilliance of his scheme. His inability to find a suitable name dampened his enthusiasm. He sat sulking in the sleazy chair, his mind searching. Without a name, he would fail. A sudden flash flicked his memory; a discussion with Suzanne a long time ago.

"What did you say?"
"QpeeQ."
"What's that?"
"Teacher's nickname."
"Meaning what?"
"Quid pro quo."

"That's it." He jumped from his chair. "Operation QpeeQ." In his demented state, he roared and shortened it to Q-Day.

Q-Day was September 11, 1949. On the third of September, Q-Day minus eight, his completed plan lay on the table before him—clever, ingenious and exciting. He admired it; unquestionably, the best work he'd ever done. Euphoria inspired exultation, his aches and pains of the past ten years gone. He rose early, went for a walk, ate a good breakfast at his favorite restaurant and returned to spend the day reviewing the plan.

On September 4, the softball playoffs started in Calumet City, Gordon's Hardware versus Cunningham's Grocery; the first two games in Calumet on Saturday, Q-Day minus 7, and Tuesday, Q-Day minus 4. On Q-Day, the following Saturday, the game would be in Gary. After that, it didn't matter what happened, Buddy Leyland would be gone forever and Harry Matheu would control his own destiny in his private paradise.

Gordon's won the first two games. On Thursday, Q-Day minus 2, Buddy in wide snap-brim fedora, dark glasses, belted trench coat and pointed suede shoes arrived in Calumet City. With cigarette dangling from his mouth, he hailed a cab on Main Street.

"Hey! Saw ya pitch dat last game. Ya done good."

"Thanks. Where to?"

"Jus' agonna talk a minute. Drive 'round. We'll talk, huh."

"What you want to talk about?"

"Wanna maka some money?"

"Sure. How much?"

"Five g's."

Henry jammed on the brakes, pulled to the curb and twisted around to study his passenger.

"How much! What for?"

"I tol' ya, drive 'round." The gravelly voice was angry.

"Sorry, mister … ah, what'd you say your name was?"

"Don't matta 'bout my name."

"Okay. What do I have to do for the dough."

"Trow da game on Saturday."

"You crazy."

"Lissen, kid. Lemme offa the bus depot."

Henry wheeled into the taxi stand at the depot. He turned to see his passenger in the rear fingering a huge wad of bills.

"Okay, mister. What's your name and what gives?"

"Jus'a make sure your team loses. Me 'n the boys'll look ya up afta the game. Here's fifty for the ride."

Buddy stood in the depot watching the cab leave. He walked across the street to a car rental office.

"I won't be returning here, I'll drop it off in Gary," he told the desk clerk. He stopped at a pay 'phone on his way out of town, dialed the number, placed his handkerchief over the speaker, and prepared to talk with a deep southern accent.

> *"May I speak to Miz Matheu, please ... this is Detective Grossman from Springdale, Arkansas ... Miz Eleanor Matheu? ... there's nothing to worry about, it's nothin' serious, only a small matter concernin' a Mr. Harry Matheu who, I believe, was formerly married to a Miz Suzanne Haldimann, your husband's mother. We are havin' some trouble locatin' Miz Haldimann and we thought y'all might be able to give us her telephone number ... Thank you, Miz Matheu. Hope I didn't disturb y'all. Good-bye"*

As soon as he hung up, he dialed Suzanne's number. He wanted to be sure to reach her before her daughter-in-law called. He projected the same deep southern accent.

> *"May I speak to Miz Haldimann, please ... this is Detective Grossman from Springdale, Arkansas ... Miz Suzanne Haldimann? ... there's nothing to worry about, it's nothin' serious, only a small matter concernin' a Mr. Harry Matheu who, I believe, is your ex-husband. I expect to be in Chicago on Saturday an' I'd like to call y'all about noon or one o'clock to arrange an appointment ... just for identification purposes. It won't take but a minute to look at some photos ... Thank you Miz Haldimann ... we're not sure, we're havin' difficulty locatin' him ... no, there's nothin' further at this time. Thank you, Miz Haldimann, I'll call Saturday*

mornin' soon as I arrive in town. Hope I didn't disturb y'all. Good-bye"

Buddy returned in the rented car taking short detours, stopping and starting to make sure nobody tailed him. In Gary, he turned in the car and headed for the Western Union office. He sent a night letter.

SAM MATHEU GORDON'S HARDWARE
CALUMET CITY, ILLINOIS
OLD FRIENDS CALLED SAID THEY FIXED
SATURDAY GAME STOP TOLD POLICE NO WAY
DOUBLECROSS YOU STOP FRIENDS BEAT ME
PRETTY BAD STOP THINK LEG BROKEN MAYBE
RIBS STOP ALL BETS CALLED OFF STOP DO NOT
VISIT TOMORROW GETTING X RAYS STOP
PLEASE VISIT SATURDAY BEFORE GAME STOP IF
NOT HERE MESSAGE ON DOOR. SIGNED HARRY

Buddy made his way home on foot with an air of confidence he hadn't felt since he skinned Rocco. Every move worked and he eluded everybody. The only person who knew his address was Sam. He cased his building just the same before unlocking the door.

Q-Day minus one dawned bright and clear. Harry left early, bought a newspaper and entered the usual restaurant. His first concern was the weather forecast; partly cloudy, some wind and no rain until Monday—perfect. He relaxed, enjoyed his breakfast and sat for a time reading the paper. He spent the remainder of the morning leaning against a building reading the paper, walking to the next corner, sitting on the bench at the bus stop, always in a position where he could check his apartment for unexpected visitors. He feared Sam might come over a day early or do something dumb like call a doctor. Various cars came and went but not a suspicious one among them.

After lunch, he bought the last items he needed to put the plan in action. He returned and hung around outside until four; no sign of anybody. He inspected his apartment finding nothing disturbed. Dumping his supplies, he went out again looking forward to nightfall. No one ever came around after dark but he had to be vigilant. At eight, he went to a movie. He stopped off at the corner bar on the way home; nothing unusual; nothing exciting had happened. He started for home a little before twelve. His nerves were tense like a soldier's the night before a battle. He lay on his bed in the dark anticipating Q-Day.

2.

Eleanor hurried home at five o'clock, her mind cluttered and troubled. The material handling design for the new warehouse wasn't right. She stopped at the grocery to buy a couple of small steaks for supper. The telephone call worried her; what a mistake she had made! She wanted to talk to Sam about it but he wasn't home. She couldn't wait. She dialed Suzanne.

"This is Eleanor speaking. Is Miss Haldimann in, please? Thank you."

"Oh! Suzanne, I'm feeling terrible."

"What's the matter, dear, are you sick?"

"Sick at heart."

Eleanor told her about the telephone call from Arkansas and how she gave the man Suzanne's privatetelephone number without thinking what she did.

"I'm so sorry. I want to apologize for my forgetfulness."

"It's all right, darling," soothed Suzanne. "He called me. He wants me to identify some photographs of Harry. He set up an appointment for Saturday. He assured me there was nothing to worry about."

"I'm so relieved," Eleanor sighed. "I guess that means you won't be going to the game in Gary."

"Oh, heavens. I forgot about it. No, I won't be able to go now. That is unless he gets here early. I'll have to wait and see."

"You've made me feel so much better. Got to get Sam's supper. Thanks again. Love you. 'Bye."

3.

Sam slumped into a chair at the kitchen table. Eleanor noticed his preoccupation.

"What's the matter, Sam?"

"Crazy. You won't believe how crazy these Mafia guys are. Imagine the lunatics offering five thousand dollars to throw the game. Obviously, they're placing a big bet on the underdogs, probably thousands at four or five to one. Then they send some goofball to scare Henry who is so damned frightened he'll probably lose tomorrow anyway. Harry refuses to go along and rats to the cops. The Mafia guys beat him up and steal his money. He ends up with a busted leg and all his money gone. Crazy! Crazy! Crazy!"

After supper, they took coffee into the living room. They sat in silence. Eleanor knew when he was ready, he'd say whatever was on his mind. She also knew if she passed the time with idle talk he would never begin.

"I think I'll have another cup of coffee," he said. "You?"

She nodded. He filled the cups.

Sam stood and paced the floor.

"Well, I know you're waiting for me to say something. I don't want to be bitter but sometimes, in spite of myself, I think I never want to see or hear from either of my parents again. My whole life with them stinks. When I was a kid, Harry beat me. Afterwards Mother would come to my room and try to make up in some way I never understood. I didn't want to be home, and, to a degree, I guess I succeeded. I know Suzanne, Harry and Nadia thought I wanted to be away because I loved Granny Magda. Well, yes, I did love her but that was because there was no love at home. There were times when I wanted to run away but I didn't have the guts. I'm no hero. I found that out in the war. Long before that, I found out I was no athlete either, much as I wanted to be. When Harry left, everything changed. I don't think Mother realized the biggest gift she ever gave me was going to a baseball game at eleven o'clock in the morning. I knew if I'd gone with Harry we would have arrived twenty minutes after the game started, if we arrived at all. Then, when he was gone,

I found a parachute. My free fall was over. Granny Magda insisted I take religious instruction every day. For the first week or so, I hated it. I wanted to be at the ballpark but I didn't realize what was happening. I didn't even notice my attitude change but somehow beyond my control, I found I wanted to go for that instruction every morning. If, for some reason there was no baseball, rain, nobody showing up, whatever, it became less disappointing. It was okay, because I spent the first part of my day with Father Henderson. He regenerated everything my parents destroyed. It wasn't an obligation any more. It was fun and a joy. When Harry showed up at the beginning of last summer, I didn't know what to do. That terrible fear came back, the foreboding of something terrible about to happen. When we agreed I should send him money, I felt better as if I was doing something to conquer my fear. Father agreed, and so did Tom. Mother told me I was wrong. I didn't believe her. I didn't think she had a Christian attitude. I doubted her. Father and Tom were more considerate of Mother's position than I was, but still, they thought giving Harry money was right, especially because of the inheritance from his parents. I even considered finding him a job in Calumet, maybe in the hardware store. He was, and still is, my father. Despite Mother's warnings, I had to do something. Don't misunderstand, I'm not feeling sorry for myself. I learned a long time ago, feeling sorry for myself doesn't do any good. I kept the baseball statistics, made address lists, did those other dumb pastimes because I could do them without any help, even if I couldn't do them right. They were actions I could do without my parents, without my teachers, without friends, in summary, games I could play without love. I didn't think of them in those terms when I was a kid. It was only later, in the army, when I came to realize why. Perhaps I'm upset now, because my hero, Father Henderson, was just as wrong as I was, but I'll get over it the same way I've overcome everything else. The difference is I have love now and it makes my life complete. I love you so much Eleanor, and I can forget the other idiotic people who have crowded my life."

"I love you too, Sam, with all my heart."

She put her arms around his neck and he held her tight. After the kiss, she continued.

"I hate to see you so depressed when, together we have so much. And so many new opportunities on the horizon; maybe it's even time to think about a family."

She paused, then started again.

"May I say something else?"

He nodded.

"I think you're wrong when you feel betrayed by Father Henderson. Of course, it's Christian for a wealthy son to provide funds to his destitute father. What answer did you expect him to give? I think you have to be realistic in your evaluation of the answers you get from anybody who may not have all the facts. Your mother had the facts, Father Henderson didn't. In the end it turned out Suzanne's advice maybe was wiser than his. That's all. You were right to help Harry and even if Father had all the facts, I believe he would have advised you the same way. The difference is he has no hate in him whereas your mother, I'm sorry to say, is overflowing with vehemence."

"You're right. It's crazy. Tomorrow'll be a better day."

He held her in his arms and she responded with another kiss.

"What are your plans for the game?"

She told him about the detective's call, explaining his mother would probably not be attending.

"Let's you and I go down early in the morning to find out what's happened to the old man. We'll leave about eight, stop for breakfast on the way."

"Are you going to call your mother?"

He stepped back with a horrified look.

"No way! We've already talked about Harry enough. She's irrational in her hatred. I don't want to hear all that bitching again."

Had Harry known the consequences of his actions, he would have spent a more relaxed Q-Day minus one. Neither Suzanne, Sam or Eleanor had the slightest suspicion of what was about to happen.

Chapter 20 - Morning, Q-Day

1.

At twelve minutes after eight in the morning, Tom Gordon winced at the sound of screeching tires anticipating the crash that never came. He heard a double acceleration. Quietness fell. He knew the time because at that moment he happened to glance at the clock wondering how much longer he could lie in bed. Why did young men who drove Triumphs squeal to a stop and rev the motor? No time to philosophize; he struggled to his feet making a mental note to ask sometime.

Sam burst through the front door.

"Hey, Tom! You awake yet? "

"You've got a hell of a nerve, Sam, arousing the entire neighborhood then bellowing your head off without the slightest regard for my newspaper that is lying out there on the walk. You inconsiderate bum. Why didn't you pick it up for an old man."

"Oh, shush." Sam grinned. "You're not so damn old you can't get your own newspaper. Besides the neighbors should have been up long ago. Listen, Tom," his smile faded, "there's a change in plans. Eleanor and I are leaving now. My old man's in trouble again. We're going to see if we can help him."

"What'd he do now?"

"You won't believe it. Last night he sent a telegram about some kind of fight; thinks his leg is busted again. Maybe he's in the hospital. I'm not sure."

"Really? Sit down. Tell me about it. Breakfast?"

"No. We plan to eat on the road. See you at the park."

The motor revved. The tires screeched.

Tom picked up his paper and examined the sky.

2.

The sun shines brightly on a dingy apartment where apathy makes the impoverished residents blind to the eccentricities of their neighbors; oblivious to the unusual; uncaring and inattentive to peculiar activities. No one sees or hears a red Triumph squealing to a halt with one exception; Harry watches from the only window in his apartment. A young man leaps out and boasts to the girl sitting in the car.

"Told you we'd make it by ten. Won't be long."

No witness sees the young man enter the building. Harry hides behind the entrance door to his apartment, purposely left ajar. The footsteps halt at the bottom of the stairs. The visitor reads the handwritten note pinned to the door.

COME IN
IT'S OPEN.

The door swings open.

"Hi, Harry. It's—"

Harry swings the cast iron frying pan. He humps the unconscious form to the bed, applies a gag, ties the feet and arms to the four bedposts. He gloats; he has pulled it off, even if more viciously than he intended. He remembers the girl. His naive failure to anticipate the obvious enrages him; he should have expected Sam's wife. Irrational anger surges. He barges out to the Triumph. With feigned gentility he coaxes her out of the car, drags her into the apartment, crushing her hand, banging her knee against the doorjamb. Her scream freezes in her throat as he thumps her to insensibility with a blow from the cast iron frying pan. He lifts her into the only chair in the room, swings her around to face the corner and wraps a rope about her upper torso entrapping her arms. He passes the rope behind the chair back, pulls it taut, runs it under the seat enclosing her legs and forearms in a dual loop, brings the ends to the rear and ties a knot beyond her reach. He looks at his handiwork with relief. His confidence returns. He smiles with satisfaction, priding his spontaneous ingenuity. He crows over the mute form lying on the bed, picking at the ropes, making sure they're secure.

"Not my fault, Son. Blame your mother." He shrugs. "So long."

He twists the timer dial setting it to four, or a little after, near as he can see in the dark. He crouches, heart thumping, summoning courage for the escape.

Check the corridor . . .

. . . close the door . . .

. . . hear the night latch click . . .

. . . pull the notice off the door . . .

. . . start up the steps . . .

. . . out into the daylight.

He limps towards the car trying to whistle. No sound comes. He opens the door, glances both ways and slips into the driver's seat. The red Triumph moves away attracting no attention. No one reports two bodies bound in the darkness of a basement apartment in Gary, Indiana.

3.

At ten thirty Suzanne's telephone rang.

The maid answered. "Miss Haldimann's residence."

"Miss Haldimann, please. This is Phillip Silverstein."

"One moment, please."

Suzanne picked up the phone in her private office.

"Hello, Phillip. What an unexpected pleasure."

"Don't talk. Just listen. I've—"

"Harry!"

Every muscle in her body tensed. She couldn't breath as if Goliath compressed her chest until she could no longer draw air into her lungs. For one ghastly moment, she feared she would faint as Harry rambled on, unaware of her turmoil.

"Listen and listen good. I've got Sam and Eleanor. At four o'clock this afternoon an explosion's going to blow them both to hell and you, my dear Susie, won't ever see them again."

"Harry!"

"Shut up! Would it make you feel important to know that only you can save them?"

"Don't be an ass, Harry."

"You call me an ass one more time and I hang up. How would you like that?"

His voice dripped with bitter sarcasm. She breathed deeply to relieve the sudden pain in her chest.

"What do you want, Harry?"

"Two-hundred-fifty thousand dollars. That's what I want."

"All right. I'll give it to you. Tell me what to do."

His mirthless cackle riled her as she began to recover her senses. How could she trap him?

"Now listen good. You write ten checks to cash for twenty-five thousand each. Then you call your banker, or your lawyer or anybody you like and get them certified."

"Harry, I won't do any such thing."

"Oh yes you will. Remember at four o'clock there's no more Sam and no more Eleanor."

"You'll go to jail for the rest of your life, Harry."

"Hell, I will. If you don't bring me them checks by two o'clock I'll kill myself and you'll hang for murder. I got poison in my pocket; uhhun, a whole package; enough to kill twenty people. And I got a plan so they'll hang you for it. It don't take much, you know." The insane, triumphant cackle assailed her ears. "You've always blamed me. Well, it ain't my fault; you refused the abortion." Another cackle confirmed his insanity. "I don't give a shit any more. Too bad, Susie dear but you have to pay for it now."

Suzanne's mind raced, searching for alternatives. What could she do? No matter what, she would need to hear his entire proposition before she acted. She listened without comment.

"Got your pencil and paper? Write it down so you don't forget." He spelled out the directions to his secluded spot. "Now when you reach the edge of the woods, turn around and come back to the big tree. You won't see me but I'll be there, don't you worry. Open the doors, front and back, and the trunk too, so I can see nobody's hiding in the car. Go to the tree and put the checks in the box. Remember I'll be watching you. Go back to your car and stand in front of it for five minutes. If the checks are okay, I'll leave the directions to Sam and Eleanor. Then you can leave and go get Sam. If anything goes wrong, like the police show up or anything like that, I burn the note, take the poison and die. Two hours later Sam joins me. Any questions?"

"Harry, don't do it. I'll meet you anywhere you like—blindfolded if you want—and give you five hundred thousand, or a million it that's what you want."

"Susie dear, don't call the police."

"Did you hear me, Harry? A million dollars."

"No. I didn't hear you."

"What do you want? Tell me what you want and I'll give it to you."

"I want you to have an abortion like you promised."

"Harry! You're insane."

"You promised."

"Listen, Harry, I'll give you five million. I won't tell a soul."

"That's stupid, Susie. Your clown Burroughs would know and he'd tell the whole bloody world."

"No. Harry. He wouldn't know."

"You'd tell that Jewish lawyer of yours. No sir. Quarter of a million. Cheap, ain't it, Susie."

"Harry."

"Shut up! I've heard enough of your whining. Hurts don't it, when the shoe's on the other foot. You get anybody involved and you'll regret it. You've always hired somebody to do your dirty work. This time you do it yourself. See you at two."

4.

Tom glanced at his watch—a little after ten. He leaned in through the open door.

"You ready yet? I'll get the car."

"I'll be a few more minutes. Don't be impatient, it doesn't start till half past two."

"A few minutes! More like twenty, I'll bet."

"I didn't hear. What did you say?"

"Nothing. What are we doing about lunch?"

"We'll pick up a sandwich somewhere."

Tom missed his twenty-minute guess by about forty minutes. It was nearly eleven when he and Ruth set off for Gary.

"You know, Ruth, this summer's been better than a health tonic for me. I'm alive again and having a hell of a time to boot."

"Yes, I've noticed. I haven't forgotten how depressed you were during the war. I never believed Sam would buy the store."

"I did. When that kid gives you his word you can put it in the bank."

Tom ruminated on the good fortune brought to him by Ruth and Sam. Years ago, Ruth directed his focus from rebellious youth to serious entrepreneur. Only the two them, hand in hand leaving the wedding altar, embarking on the adventure of their life—he with apprehension, she with assurance—operating the store for thirty-three years. Their children prospered from love, life and labor learned in that dingy emporium. Curious how her magnetism defied definition. She attracted regular clients as easily as a flower attracts bees. In truth, she managed the enterprise with her scintillating personality that propelled the engine of his being. She was the type who evinced a query of *'who turned on the lights?'* the moment she entered a room. It wasn't her beauty; she wasn't a beautiful woman. It was her lack of pomposity; her disarming manner of hiding her intelligence behind a pretense of scatterbrained impetuosity; and her consideration, never denying anyone concern for their problems. Tom learned long ago to rely on Ruth's calm reasoning and pragmatic intelligence. Eliciting her guidance created no shame. Early in their marriage, a blanket in a child's bedroom accidentally caught fire from a heater placed too close. He skittered about in panic, accomplishing nothing, while she calmly pulled the blanket from the bed and stamped out the fire.

Ruth's thoughts roamed in a different direction. Presentiments pervading her mind upset her. They aroused anxiety. On the other hand, they were usually false alarms, her worries unfounded. She vacillated between fear and hope: fear of the unknown; hope for a false premonition. She said nothing.

5.

Suzanne collected her thoughts. Clarence was in New York. Next on the list was Philip Silverstein. Semi-retired, she doubted if he could handle the situation. She called the bank.

"This is Suzanne Haldimann speaking. I need to talk to Mr. Samuel Watson right away. I'm in dreadful trouble."

"I's sorry, ma'am, we is the cleaners. We's cleanin' up here, tha's all."

"Do you have the emergency telephone number. Please. Tell me how to reach Mr. Watson. Please. I need help right away. Please."

The voice on the other end paused.

"Don't have no numbers 'cept the police. If something happens, I'm supposed to call the police. You want me to call the police?"

"Hurry please. No! No! Don't call the police."

"You got to make up you' mind. Yes or no."

"No. Goodbye."

Suzanne searched her business cards; surely, the bank officers would have home telephone numbers on their cards. They didn't.

Three Samuel Watsons plus sixteen others with the first initial S appeared in the directory. Where should she start? She looked at her watch. Ten minutes since Harry called. She put her head down and shut her eyes tightly to calm her pulsating heart. A bomb to kill Sam and Eleanor! If she could find Harry, killing would be too good for him. She gripped the arms of the chair, then relaxed, gripped and relaxed. How do you find somebody in Chicago when you don't know where they live? She started out of the office as tears welled in her eyes. Who to call? What to do? She turned back to her desk, buried her head in her hands, brushed the tears away and threw back her shoulders. Don't panic. Get control and think. Who would be in the office on Saturday? The church would be open. What could they do? No, she needed somebody to act, find Sam and Eleanor, arrange the money, defeat Harry . . . she knew who to call. She looked for the number and dialed.

"Miss Haldimann speaking. This is very urgent. May I speak to Mr. Cellini, please?"

"Ah! Yes. Miss Haldimann."

The pleasant voice encouraged her resolve. He would know she was in trouble. She wouldn't have to tell him.

"How nice to hear your voice. What trouble brings you to my doorstep."

She almost broke down.

"Mr. Cellini, I've a dreadful problem." She blurted out the story. It took several minutes for him to sort out the details.

"Have you notified anyone?"

"No. I tried but—"

"The police are not aware of this?"

"No."

"Very well. You will need to come to my office immediately if I am to help you. Is that what you want?"

"Yes." Her willpower holding back the tears faded. "Yes, please, please, please help me."

"Miss Haldimann, take a few minutes to compose yourself. I know it is difficult but you must do it. In your present emotional state, it would probably be better to take a taxi but you will need your own car to make the rendezvous. Do you think you are capable of driving?"

His voice, serene and confident, calmed her.

"I don't know. Tell me what to do."

"I can't. I can only tell you that driving yourself is better but it will be a grave error if you are involved in an accident."

"Oh."

"It's five minutes to eleven. Be here no later than quarter to twelve. Wear comfortable clothes that permit you to move quickly and no hat. "

She took a deep breath.

"I'll be there."

In her room, she looked at herself in the mirror; eyes swollen and red. She splashed water on her face and applied a touch of make-up. She changed her clothes, donning slacks, blouse, sweater and low-heel shoes, all the while gasping for air. She couldn't recall having such difficulty breathing. She selected a small handbag for money, license and cigarettes.

At ten minutes past eleven, she examined herself in the mirror, speaking to her image. "How did I get in this mess?" Motionless, the answer echoed in the chambers of her mind. Overalls—simple, plain, unpretentious denim cloth; her father's honored costume, her husband's deceitful guise. Overalls—a suit of honor worn by one, a cloak of evil worn by the other. Overalls—the patrimony bestowed upon Joe Haldimann by an illiterate father, passed on in a way she couldn't comprehend.

"Clarence! Oh God! How I wish you were here. How I wish you were going with me on this awful mission. Thank God you don't wear overalls."

She looked at her watch; time to go. She froze with her hand on the front door knob, summoning courage, preparing for an ordeal she could not rehearse. Overalls! She hated them; that horrible, dirty, blue cotton fabric she knew Harry would be wearing. She wanted to hit him, strike out, do something to protect her child.

What if he attacks?

Entering the kitchen, the cutting knives in the rack above the preparation table caught her eye. Taking the meat cleaver, she spoke aloud, her words resounding in the empty kitchen.

"Just in case I get the chance."

She rushed to the bedroom, transferred her belongings to a large tote bag placing the cleaver in an upright position. She fled to the car, raced out of the drive and turned into the street with a screech.

She heard a voice. Daddy sat beside her in his overalls. Think about the other side of the coin. She drove to her meeting, praying for courage.

6.

Suzanne's previous visits to Sergio Cellini had always been by taxi and she paid no attention to the route. Unfamiliar with the side streets, she followed the main arteries impatiently urging the traffic lights to change. Cars were parked on Cicero Boulevard bumper to bumper. She drove slowly glancing quickly at the street numbers. A large man in shirtsleeves with a fedora down over his eyes—ugly with a flattened nose—stepped out from behind a car signaling her to stop. She lowered the window.

"Miss Haldimann?"

She nodded.

He waved his hand and a car pulled out from the curb.

"Park there," he growled, pointing at the empty space. She maneuvered into position directly outside Cellini's office.

The number of people assembled inside astonished her. They lounged in the waiting room apparently unengaged in any particular activity except smoking. Her escort marched her across the room and through the door into the private office. As always, when she walked into this man's presence a change came over her. It was the wondrous feeling of total confidence that exuded from him that buoyed her.

"Ah! Yes. Miss Haldimann. The circumstances are most unpleasant but it is a pleasure to see you nonetheless."

His appearance shocked her. He was older, grayer, his faced ribbed with tiny blood vessels although his voice remained as melodious as ever.

"It's good to see you, Sergio."

A tear dropped from her eye.

"Enough sentimentality. We must get down to business. First, I need all the information you can give me concerning your son and his wife."

"I can't tell you anything beyond his intention to visit his father this morning."

"Where?"

"In Gary, I think."

"Do you have an address?"

"No."

"That is unfortunate. No clues where we might find Harry?"

"None."

He smiled at her, unperturbed.

"Very well, we'll work with what we have. It is enough."

She looked at him wide-eyed.

"Enough for what?"

"To find them. Will you excuse me, please."

He wheeled through the door and into the waiting room. She followed, watching him through the open door. He spoke Italian in an authoritative tone quite different from the voice she loved so much. Several of the men stood. One of them, a man in a pinstripe blue suit spoke. Cellini answered. Pinstripes addressed the men. Six of them left. Cellini spoke to a man in black pants and leather jacket. She thought she heard the name Rocco but couldn't be sure. Black-pants left. Cellini returned and shut the door.

"It's a wonder they're not all dead," he said, his voice calm and sweet, "the way they chew those cigarettes. Ah! well, it is their funeral, not mine." He smiled. "Now Miss Haldimann, please sit down and tell me the story. We have plenty of time. Let's start with the instructions."

She read to him from her telephone notes.

"Ah! Yes. I am not familiar with that area. Perhaps we should send somebody out to have a look. One moment, please."

He called in two of his subordinates who listened intently to the directions.

"Get out there in the old truck. Drive down the road. Don't stop or give any sign that you're looking for anything. Take a dog with you. When you reach the turnaround in the woods, park the truck, get out with the dog and search around in the woods, look for mushrooms. At exactly two o'clock walk back up the road towards Miss Haldimann's car. Do whatever is necessary to stop Harry."

He waved them on their way.

"Now then, Miss Haldimann, we are not rushed. We have plenty of time to handle this situation. Please tell me the entire sequence of events again from the beginning. Take your time and try to leave nothing out."

Suzanne repeated the experience while he interjected questions.

"You had no warning of this, no previous suspicions, no prior telephone calls?"

"Yes there was a call. The day before yesterday from a detective in Arkansas who asked for an appointment today—Oh! My God, it was him, Harry, making sure I was going to be home today, that I wouldn't go to the baseball game in Gary."

Cellini asked about Harry; his mental condition; his physical condition; did he re-marry; did he have any other children? She didn't know except what Sam told her.

"Well," Cellini concluded, "he doesn't have much to live for, does he? Please help yourself to coffee while I think for a moment. Perhaps you might pour one for me also."

He wheeled behind his desk and closed his eyes. As if in a trance, he did not notice her place the cup in front of him. His left hand came slowly to his chin. He rubbed his jaw like a man testing if his shave was satisfactory. At last he spoke.

"Ah! Yes. With the lives of Sam and Eleanor at stake, we must assume that Harry is not bluffing. Therefore, you will have to do exactly as he instructed and you will have to do it alone. Do you think you will be able to?"

"Yes. For Sam, I would do anything. Please tell me precisely what I am to do."

He paused and stroked his chin.

"Before we review your routine, we must make one more decision. I believe it better to avoid the police. Therefore, we cannot ask your bank to guarantee the checks. We probably don't have time for that in any event. You could take false checks to lure him from his hiding place but cash would be better. The sight of dollars would, I believe, lead him to a false move. Hence, I recommend that you take two hundred fifty thousand in cash and put it before him."

In wide-eyed disbelief, she shrieked, "Where could I possibly get that much cash?"

"Do you have a problem with my reasoning?"

"Well, no. I don't understand."

"Meaning you agree that presenting cash would be better?"

Harry loved to flash a roll of bills. Cellini was right.

"I don't know how you recognize traits in people but you always seem to know. You're right, cash would be more attractive to Harry. He probably didn't ask for cash because he didn't think I could get it on such short notice."

"Precisely."

He lifted the telephone and spoke in Italian. He replaced the receiver and wheeled around to the conference table.

"Please sit down over here, Miss Haldimann."

He took pencil and paper and drew a map as he reviewed Harry's directions with her.

"You are to do exactly as I say. You must not show any indication of distress. Calmly get out of the car, open the doors and the trunk. Take the briefcase—it will be here in a few moments—from the car and walk towards the tree. As you do so, talk in a very loud voice so you may be heard at considerable distance. We do not know how far distant Harry will be and it is essential that he hear you."

Her face was pale and she squeezed her hands with her elbows on the table. He paused and looked into her eyes. Placing his hand on hers, he said, "If you would like to smoke, I would understand."

Her heart overflowed as her tenseness vanished. She couldn't help but smile, even as tears trickled from her eyes.

"Mr. Cellini, smoking is prohibited in this sanctuary."

He laughed.

"It has been called many names before, but never a sanctuary."

"That's what it is for me. Please go on."

"Ah! Yes. Well, as you approach the tree, you will say in a very loud voice that you could not obtain checks and you have brought cash instead, all of it in unmarked bills. Open the briefcase and place it at the base of the tree. Return to your car, wait five minutes, pick up the instructions and leave. Drive down the road. You will meet a man in a blue pinstripe suit at the intersection of the main highway. Give him the directions to locate Sam and Eleanor and return to my office. That is all. Do you understand?"

"What about Harry?"

"There is no way this lunatic will escape this time. I am confident by four o'clock the problem will be resolved and Harry—well, let us say he will no longer bother you."

"You mean—"

"Miss Haldimann, don't ask, just accept."

The telephone rang. Cellini grunted something into the receiver and a moment later a man entered. He placed a large brown briefcase on the table and left.

"Please open it, Miss Haldimann."

She drew in her breath at the bundles of cash.

"You will notice the bundles are of various denominations. You will also notice they are not marked."

"I wouldn't recognize a marked bill if I saw it."

"Very well, take my word for it." He reached across and snapped the case shut. "That's it. You're on your way. I shall await your return. Be careful of the case, it's heavy."

She did not move. When his eyes met hers, she lowered her head.

"Ah! Yes. You have a problem?"

"No, " she replied keeping her head down. "Well . . . "

"Well what?" he asked gently. "Out with it."

"Well, I guess I'm confused, not by your instructions, I understand. I know what I am to do. I thank you so much, Sergio. I can't thank you enough. But, well, it's my feeling inside, my loathing, absolute hatred for this man. Perhaps it's self-incrimination that I have allowed him to use my money, my father's money. I have allowed him to malign his own parents. Yes, I have even allowed him to use my body, my very soul for his personal gratification and he does this. That he could do such a thing to me, to our son, is devastating Sergio. It's tearing me apart inside. I want to destroy him so I'll never hear his name or see his face again. I know it's not Christian. I know I'm supposed to forgive but I can't, I just can't."

"In that case Miss Haldimann, I have two suggestions. The first is to put those thoughts out of your mind. This is not the time for you to see wrongs corrected, to seek retribution or to demand justice; there is too much at stake. You are a strong and willful woman. Exercise that strength now. Will yourself, control your emotions, force yourself to do just as I have said. My second suggestion is to give me whatever implement you are carrying in your handbag."

How did he always know what was on her mind? She could keep no secrets from him. She handed him the meat cleaver.

"You will not need it," he said. "For your own sake and that of Sam and Eleanor, please do exactly as I said and nothing more."

"I will. Thank you for everything"

Chapter 21 - Afternoon, Q-Day

1.

Buddy Leyland, in black toupee and horned-rimmed shaded glasses, turned up his jacket collar and walked back to the Triumph after Harry's phone call to Suzanne. An hour later, he drove into Sam's garage, parked, put the keys under the seat. He glanced over his left shoulder, then his right. Exhilaration mixed with pride. Harry planned Buddy's arrival at mid-morning expecting the garage would be empty. Selecting the black Ford parked in the darkest corner, Buddy removed the tags and left on foot. Twelve minutes later he showed his driver's permit and signed for the rental car reserved the day before; a black Ford, undistinguishable from thousands of others on the road. At forty minutes past twelve, he drove through Frankfort and continued west to the dead end road, turned south at the next side road, passed the farmer's house and stopped behind a ridge in a gravel gully under a tree. Leaving the driver-side door open, he listened for several minutes; birds chirped and squirrels skittered about but he heard no human noise.

Harry stepped out of the car. He changed the tags and buried the old ones in the gravel. He put on his old peak cap at a jaunty angle; looked rakish in the car mirror; the wire spectacles suited him. Harry Matheu stomped on Buddy Leyland's heavy glasses, crushing them into unrecognizable pieces. He shredded Buddy's toupee and scattered the pieces. He looked around and smiled; Buddy Leyland had vanished from this world forever.

Harry Matheu walked through the woods and across the field to his chosen tree imagining the scene as the rental clerk tried to explain the curious disappearance of the car and driver. He could not help but smile with victory within his grasp. The only tactical flaw was the arrival of Eleanor and he handled that brilliantly. He measured thirty spaces to the northwest and found the hollow he dug on his last visit. He lay down and looked at his watch; forty minutes to wealth and independence.

A farm truck crept slowly over the ridge inching towards the woods. Two men rode in the cab; another was on the bed with his feet dangling off the end, restraining a large dog on a leash. He watched them craning their necks, looking everywhere as if selecting a spot to exercise their animal. A glint of light caught his eye; maybe bird-watchers with binoculars. They disappeared into the trees. Harry crept forward, keeping low and hid behind a shrub, parting the branches for a good view. The man in the back jumped down yelling instructions, his voice audible but not clear enough to distinguish the words. The dog ran and yelped while the man untied the red ribbon marker. The dog sniffed and began a zigzag hunt through the trees. It worked its way up the hill coming ever closer to Harry who froze in terror. With no place to hide, the beast would surely find him and he could do nothing about it. A whistle blew. The dog halted and faced its master. Another whistle blast and the animal charged back to the truck. The trainer put him on a leash and the three men disappeared into the woods. Harry crawled back to his sentry post wiping his shirtsleeve across his brow.

Twenty-three minutes to go.

Gasping for air and trying to relax, he heard an engine on the other side of the rise by the gully where he left the car. He could not determine the direction of travel but it sounded so close it would soon top the rise. Keeping on the low side of the crest, he raced to the safety of the shadows among the trees. A farm tractor mounted the grade hugging the tree line, then turned away, traversing the hill. A hatless driver clad in a business suit steered with one hand and smoked with the other. The engine noise subsided and Harry breathed again. Once more, he crept to his hiding place wiping his wet palms on his overalls as perspiration rolled from his brow. His breath came in short gasps as he watched the second hand of his watch and counted.

Twelve minutes to go.

He watched the second hand, then averted his gaze because it moved too slowly. When he looked the next time, only thirty seconds had passed. He stared at it, counting the minutes, one by one. With three minutes to go, a car came into view. He crunched down into his hole with his head just high enough to see through the tips of the grass. He'd forgotten to ask the make of car she drove. A blue Buick passed and disappeared. He raised up higher, moved forward where he could see the car maneuvering to avoid the truck. He did not see the men or the dog. The driver opened the door and peered out. It was Susie. Harry hurried back to his post looking both ways for the tractor and the dog. He saw neither. The Buick came over the crest and stopped beside the tree.

Suzanne emerged from the car at one fifty-nine. Leaving the door open, she moved to the rear and opened the trunk. With slow, deliberate paces, she opened both doors on the right side, stepped around the open driver's door and retrieved the briefcase from the rear seat. She carried the case to the hood, looked skyward as if praying. At last, she opened the case The tree stood twelve feet off the road; the ground firm, the grass low. She walked towards it in shortened steps.

"Harry," she yelled, carrying the open case on her forearms like a pagan offering a sacrifice to the gods, "I have cash; two hundred fifty thousand in cash, Harry. I couldn't get checks. I have two hundred fifty thousand in unmarked bills in the case, Harry."

She glimpsed the tin box at the base of the tree with the lid open. Placing the briefcase beside the box, she returned to her car, took her position in front of it and closed her eyes, her head facing down the road.

2.

The word cash delivered a tremor of alarm; some kind of a trick; maybe an explosive that would detonate the minute he touched it. He examined it; looked real enough from ten feet away. He crept closer eyeing the case with the occasional glance towards Suzanne. She wasn't afraid of any explosion. By God, maybe she did bring cash. He crawled through the grass holding the yellow scrap of paper with the directions to Sam and Eleanor in his mouth. He ran his hand around the outside of the case and felt the edges. By God! Cash! He glanced towards the road. She had not moved. He fingered the money, pushed his hand down between the bundles. Cash. All cash right to the bottom. He put the directions in the tin box, put the lid on and closed the briefcase. He pushed the brass clips into the slots and stood.

Suzanne turned her head at the sound of the clips. Dirty blue overalls, half-laced boots flared at the top, black jacket and peak cap—she saw him outside Danny's Place standing in the slush smirking at her. Harry heard the running feet, glimpsed the wide-eyed, maniacal face, saw the flailing fists. He swung and hit her a violent blow with his open palm.

"You bitch," he hissed.

She tumbled to the ground. In his blind fury, he picked up the tin box and flung it across the field. She lay moaning on the ground as he disappeared over the hill.

The tractor operator, watching from the other side of the rise, automatically ducked his head as he glimpsed a glint of something flying across the field. He turned as Harry careened over the brow, down the hill towards his car. The tractor man waved. Harry was ten feet from the car when the bullets hit. Three men appeared, picked up the briefcase and waved back to the tractor operator.

At eight minutes past two, Suzanne heard an engine. She couldn't understand a tractor bouncing into view with three passengers clinging to the rear. A dog smelled her, wagging its tail and tried to lick her face. She fended him off.

"Take him away," she shrieked.

She blinked to clear her eyes and shook her head. The taste of blood filled her mouth and she spat it out. Four men gazed down at her. She didn't recognize them.

"Where's the box?"

A deep gravel voice answered.

"What box?"

"The directions to find Sam."

"Whatcha talking about?"

"The directions to find Sam. He put them in a metal box."

"Ha! Ha! Too bad, he threw it away."

"Where?"

"Dunno. Over there some place."

"Oh God! No! We've got to find it."

They laughed at some uncouth remark she didn't hear as she stumbled across the field.

"Where did he throw it? Help me!"

Another wisecrack followed by a laugh; they corralled the dog but didn't move to help her.

At eighteen minutes after two, a black car with shaded windows drove down the road. It stopped. A man in a blue pinstripe suit got out.

"What's going on?"

"The son-of-a-bitch threw the box away," said gravel-voice. "She's looking for it."

Pinstripes nodded to the car and three men got out.

"Get up there and find that goddamn box," he ordered. "And you guys get off your asses and start looking."

They scattered across the hill.

"Around here somewhere," gravel-voice said.

"I've got it," Suzanne yelled. She raced back to pinstripes. "Here, take it. Please hurry."

Three of them raced to the car while the others straggled back from the hunt. Suzanne collapsed.

"I can't go on. I hurt. I can't drive." She began to weep. "Will somebody please drive me to Mr. Cellini's office?"

3.

Nothing moves in the basement apartment. There is no sound. Light leaks past the edges of the drawn roller blind covering the window. Eleanor's head slumps down, her upper torso restrained by a rope across her breast, her body limp. Consciousness begins to seep through her veil of insensibility. She squeezes her eyes shut and sees the colors of the rainbow. A shiver runs through her body and she looks through water-filled eyes at her trapped arms and legs. Unable to recall where she is or how she got there, she raises her head, which hits the back of the chair; pain explodes in her brain but her cry of pain never escapes. Her tongue pokes at something in her mouth. The taste is terrible. In wide-eyed disbelief, she focuses on the rope wrapped twice over her legs and under the chair and once around her upper arms and remembers Mr. Matheu dragging her into the room. Sam came in first. She wonders where he went.

She studies the chair. It is old and decrepit and reeks of tobacco smoke. The darkness shields the dirty, smelly room from view and she cannot read her wristwatch.

4.

Tom found a parking space a couple of blocks from the field. It was two forty-two when they walked through the gate to the ballpark. Henry stood at home plate in an argument with the umpire and Cunningham's manager. The fans jeered and yelled. The game had not started. Tom walked into the center of the argument.

"What's going on?"

Henry looked relieved.

"I'm trying to tell this guy we can't start without Sam."

Tom turned to the umpire.

"Get this game underway right now. Henry, you take charge if your manager's not here. There's no excuse for delaying the start of a game."

"But—"

"Don't but me. Get your team organized and get this game started. There'll be no postponement and no forfeiture. You manage the team or get somebody else to do it."

"Yes, sir,"

"Play ball," the umpire bellowed.

Tom took Ruth's arm and guided her behind the stands.

"How could Sam allow this to happen? He's a bear for punctuality."

"Oh! Tom."

She clung to his arm.

Absorbed in his own thinking, he didn't notice Ruth's blanched face. "Sam left this morning. He and Eleanor were going to visit his dad. Lord, I hope there hasn't been an accident. What do you—what's the matter?"

For a moment, she looked as if she would faint.

"I knew it. I knew something was wrong."

"What are you talking about?"

"It doesn't matter."

As always, she amazed Tom at her resilience. She reached up and kissed his cheek.

"It was a shock for moment. I'm all right, let's go. Give me his father's phone number. I'll call him while you check the police."

"I don't think his father has a phone."

"We'll look it up. Where's the nearest phone." She ran down the street, crossed over and burst into a restaurant. "What's his name?"

"Matheu or Leyland."

"Tom!" She put her hands on her hips. "For heaven's sake, pull yourself together. He doesn't have two names."

"Yes he does. Sometimes he's Harry Matheu and sometimes he uses the alias, Buddy Leyland."

"All right. I'll check them both."

She smiled at the cashier.

"We have a bit of a crisis, may I borrow your phone book, please."

It took five minutes to reach a dead end; no accident report; no Harry Matheu; no Buddy Leyland.

"Tom, I think we should go to the police. Let's get the car."

5.

Eleanor cannot understand how her uncontrolled fascination with the chair has eased her panic. She is calm, thinking clearly. She pushes up on the rope across her knees with her left forearm. Her left thumb hooks over the lower strand. She pushes down towards her knees, sucks in her stomach, presses her legs down into the leather padding and her right hand slips under the first rope. She repeats the procedure, energized by her first success. Her right forearm escapes the second strand but the rope around her chest binds her upper arm. She cannot reach the gag to loosen it. The struggle with the lap bindings has pulled the torso rope tight hurting her breast. She pushes it up to ease the pressure and it suddenly slips over her left shoulder. She wiggles her left forearm from under the lap ropes. Easily she frees her right arm. The encircling rope lies loosely round her neck. She removes the gag. Exhausted, she pauses to rest.

6.

Ruth and Tom approached the desk officer at seven minutes after three.

"Look, lady, this ain't no family problem bureau. You're talking about a twenty-three year old kid. Might have done anything; maybe something ordinary like a flat tire; out of gas, maybe. Who knows? Maybe he done something dumb but he ain't been in no accident. We ain't got no accident report; nothing from the hospitals so there ain't been no accident."

"I understand, Officer, but this is extraordinary. You must understand, something is wrong. Is there some way we could trace a man named Harry Matheu, sometimes known as Buddy Leyland?"

"I thought you was looking for a kid. Now you're lookin' for somebody else. You sure you know what you're doin', lady?"

Ruth turned away and Tom saw the anger in her eyes. He clinched his fist and gave a little punch in the air to urge her on. She grimaced and turned back to the desk.

"You don't understand, officer—"

"That's right, I don't understand."

"That's his father. If I could just—"

"Who's his father? Madues or Laylen?"

Ruth raised her voice.

"Officer, listen to me. The boy we are trying to locate is Sam Matheu. That's M A T H E U." Tom stepped forward putting his hand on her forearm. She continued in the same high-pitched voice. "He is visiting here, or is supposed to be visiting here, from Calumet City, to play baseball."

"Easy," Tom whispered.

"His father lives here in Gary. His name is Harry Matheu but sometimes he uses the alias Buddy Leyland—L E Y L A N D." She sighed and her voice came down. "If we could contact his father perhaps we could locate the boy."

The officer stroked his chin and peered at her.

"Well, now, That's interestin' What's the a-k-a for? Some kinda crook?"

"That doesn't matter."

"Oh! It don't matter, huh? Well let me tell you something lady—it matters." The sarcasm left his voice and he shouted at her. "You come in here askin' me to go find some crook holed up some place in Gary? Maybe you don't know it, lady, but hoods don't register their home addresses in this precinct."

Ruth shook her head.

"Please, officer," her voice was calm. "He's not a crook. We just need to find out where he lives."

"Here's a directory. Look it up."

"He is not listed in the directory. We already looked. We need his address."

"Now what do you expect me to do about that?"

"What about the license bureau? How do you check on somebody's record if there's an accident?"

The officer stared at her with a you've-reached-the-end-of-the-road look and I'm not doing anything to help you. Tom took her arm and steered her to the entrance foyer. Before he could say anything, she whispered into his ear.

"Listen, Tom, it's going to take a disoriented act from a neurotic female to convince this lout to act. It'll work better if I do it alone. You jump in the car and check at the field. Come back quick as you can. I'll work on this idiot. I'll stay right here and wait for you."

She walked to the desk, her head down. Drawing a hankie from her purse, her visage contorted, her modulated tone soft and pleading, eating at this hard-hearted guy.

"Help me, officer, please." She wiped at her eyes. Suddenly, an unexpected stroke of luck; her whining reached another pair of ears. A stern voice emanated from the inner office.

"What the hell is going on out there?"

"Nothing, sir. This here lady—"

Ruth flung herself at a large redheaded man as he came through the door.

"Please. Oh! Please, help me."

He pushed her aside.

"Stan, call the damn license office. Get her what she wants and get her the hell out of here."

"Yes, sir."

The desk officer grabbed the telephone. He flung a paper and pencil at Ruth.

"Write them names for me."

He bellowed into the telephone as if it were the most urgent matter in the entire city.

"And make it snappy. Lieutenant Adams wants to know right now. Do you hear?" He slammed down the receiver. "It'll take a while," he said. "There's some chairs in the hall round there. I'll call you soon as they call back."

"Thank you," she cooed. She wanted to spit in his face.

7.

Suzanne stumbled into Cellini's office at twenty past three. She stood at the door to his private office looking at him, afraid to speak. The briefcase with the money was on the conference table. He smiled.

"Ah! Yes, Miss Haldimann. Your face is swollen. Did he hit you?"

She nodded, unable to smile in response.

"It was my fault," she said, her voice barely audible. She sank into the chair by the conference table. "We lost thirty-five minutes looking for the box." Her arms folded across the table and she put her head down. "I gave it to your man. I don't even know what it said."

He pushed his chair around the table and stroked her hair.

"Ah! Yes. We'll find out soon enough."

They did not talk as he continued to caress her. His touch was gentle, so soft and soothing. She closed her eyes. Her face hurt a little less. Five minutes passed before he spoke.

"Ah! Yes. I know what pain is like."

She did not raise her head.

"Tell me about it, please."

He was silent for a moment.

"No. It is a story I do not tell. I have never told it."

She raised her head. His confidence was gone. His shoulders slumped and he looked terrible, the veins like rivulets of blood draining his brain.

"Then it's time you did."

She forced a smile and took his hand.

"It's not a pretty story."

"Mine is not a pretty story either."

She sighed and fell silent holding his hand. When at last she spoke again, their eyes met.

"Is yours worse than mine?"

He pushed his chair close to her. She carried his right hand in both of hers, held it to her lips and listened to his story with her eyes shut.

"My father was a hit man for the Mafia. An unconscionable drunkard with a heart of stone, he hid his shame in whiskey. One night when I was fourteen, he came home drunk and found my mother in bed with another man. He asked no questions. He sprayed them with machine gun fire. I ran to stop him and he turned the gun on me. The doctors could not save my legs."

Suzanne squeezed her eyes at the horror of the scene and held his hand tight to her chest. She raised her head and saw him blinking before he turned away. Never had she imagined anything so heartless. Her father, Albert, Syd—their deaths were as nothing compared with this man's lifetime of suffering. He held her gaze. A smile tweaked his lips.

"Ah! Yes." His head nodded from side to side with almost imperceptible motion. "I never sang again."

She could not stop the tears. He drew a clean white handkerchief from his sleeve and dabbed her eyes.

"Do not cry, please. It makes me sorry for having told my story."

"I can't help it."

"Yes you can. Perhaps it made a better life for me."

She looked at him with a puzzled frown.

"How can you say that?"

"I might have followed in my father's footsteps."

"No. I'll never believe that."

"The Don was good. He paid for my education. Coached me in what I should know, sent business to me until I gained my knowledge of the underworld. That is how I knew about Harry Matheu when you came to see me."

"Oh."

Again, they fell silent. He withdrew his hand and pushed towards the bar. He propelled himself back with a bottle and two glasses. He poured two ounces in each, handed her one and raised the other. She raised her glass. They nodded at each other and drank their whiskey without a word.

8.

Eleanor hurts everywhere but she thinks only of Sam. She calls to him; no answer. She prays and calls again. Still no response. She listens; hears nothing. She calls a third time.

"Sam! Are you there, Sam?" There is no response.

She cannot see around the wings of the chair. The smell is nauseating; more intense than before. It is sickening. She convulses; only gas. She rests; another smell; not the gaseous expulsion of her belch, but something else she cannot identify. She returns to her ordeal. The binding ropes are slack. She pulls on one, the other tightens. She pulls on the chest rope. It tightens against the chair and pulls on her thigh. She pulls on one thigh rope. Holding it tight, she pulls hard. All the slack is gone, pinching her legs. The other piece is loose. She pulls both strands tightly across her legs and creates enough slack in the torso rope to reach the knot. Inch by inch she works the rope up. Oh! The pain! One more push and her head slips under the loop. Quickly, she pulls the rope around her legs, pushes it to her knees; steps out of the chair. She is free. She raises the window blind. Sam is immobile on the bed, arms and legs tied to the corner posts. She removes his gag. He breathes. Thank God!

"Sam! Sam! Can you hear me? Ouch! I can't, Sam. I can't undo the knots. Ouch! My hand! I think it's broken. Hang on, Sam, I'm going for help."

She races towards the entrance stumbling on the frayed floor mat. She struggles to regain her balance. Out of control, she slams against the front entrance doorjamb. Her agonizing scream goes unheard. She slumps to the floor, feels the dampness on her face and wipes at her forehead. Blood covers her hand. She gropes for the door handle. Her hand finds the knob of the night latch. Staggering up the concrete stairs to the street, blinded by the blood streaming from her forehead, she misses the last step and tumbles to the sidewalk. She is unconscious. A bright sun shines down from a cloudless sky.

9.

At fifty-two minutes past three Ruth came down the precinct steps.

"I've got the address," she bristled. "Thank the Lord for Lieutenant Adams. But that desk officer, really. Anyway, at least he gave me the directions. Let's go. What's the score?"

Tom laughed as he pulled the car away.

"Who else but you, in the middle of a crisis, would ask a question like that? It's three nothing for Cunningham."

"What are you saying? If it's such a big crisis how come you took the time to find out the score?"

"That's different. I'm—"

Ruth's screamed.

"Look! Over there! A woman lying on the sidewalk. Good Lord! It's Eleanor!"

She leaped from the car.

"She's hurt, Tom. She's badly hurt. Have you got a towel or anything in the car?"

He pulled two handkerchiefs from his pocket. Cautiously they raised Eleanor to a sitting position. She was in a deplorable state. The blood, oozing from the head wound, dripped from her chin. Her eyes blinked. She stared uncomprehendingly at Ruth.

"Speak to me, Eleanor. It's Ruth Gordon, dear. Can you hear me?"

The bloodied head nodded. The lips moved. The voice was a whisper.

"Sam. Sam. Get Sam."

"Where is he?"

"There in the . . . in the basement."

"Tom! Lift her up. Put her in the backseat of the car. I'll look for Sam."

Ruth hurried down the steps and paused at the open apartment door. Cautiously she peered inside. Instantly a mixture of odd smells assailed her—tobacco smoke and something else. Could it be gasoline? She inhaled strongly; yes, gasoline. She saw Sam tied to the bed. She called to him. He did respond; no movement of his head or body. She looked about, then sensed danger.

"Gasoline!"

The impending catastrophe electrified her. For no reason she could later explain, she looked at her watch. It was twelve minutes past four. Without rational thought, she understood the scheme she had uncovered. She intuitively grasped the urgency. She fled from the apartment yelling.

"Tom! Tom! Sam's in there tied to the bed. There's a terrible smell of gasoline. Take your knife and cut him loose. Get him out of there."

"I'll call an ambulance."

"No, Tom! There's no time. Get him out of there. Quick. Get him out. Hurry!"

Tom disappeared down the stairs. Ruth eyed the exit, moving slowly backwards towards the open car door. She counted the seconds . . . thirty . . . forty. Still Tom had not come out.

Without warning the glass in the basement window burst from its frame, cascading across the grass in a thousand shards. The building shook in a deafening detonation. Ruth gaped in horror. Tom and Sam had not come out. The heat wave struck her face as the black smoke curled from the shattered window. She could see the flames. She ran towards the apartment. Tom staggered through the open door holding the inert body of Sam Matheu, the back of his shirt aflame.

"Lie down, Tom! Lie down."

He rolled on the ground as she pounded and ripped at his burning garment. She glance at his back.

"Thank God you're all right. Can you get Sam to the car?"

"Yes, I think so."

Three strangers rushed from the building. Ruth was in command. She ordered one to help Tom carry Sam, another to call the fire department and the third to warn the apartment residents. She glanced at her watch. Only two and a half minutes had elapsed since she last looked. She closed her eyes to thank the Lord Tom suffered only a minor burn.

As she took her seat in the car, a large black sedan with shaded windows stopped in the middle of the street blocking their exit. A ridiculous looking man in a blue pinstripe suit stepped out. The stranger looked at Tom.

"Are they both alive?"

"Yes," Tom answered.

Pinstripes stepped into the black car as it pulled away. An ambulance screamed down the street with fire engines behind.

At the hospital, Ruth asked Tom who that man was.

"I have no idea," he answered.

10.

Cellini answered the telephone. He listened without a word. He closed the call and looked at Suzanne across the conference table.

"Ah! Yes. Sam and Eleanor are in the hospital in Gary."

She screamed.

"Do not be alarmed. They are alive. We do not have a report on their injuries."

Suzanne was on her feet.

"I must go."

"Miss Haldimann, if I may be so bold, do not go to Gary this evening. You have had a trying day. Go home, take a sleeping pill if you are so inclined and go tomorrow. Surely if you go tonight it will do no good. They will be under sedation and your presence will achieve nothing. Wait till tomorrow, I implore you."

She nodded.

"Yes," she said. "Yes, that's what I'll do."

She chose not to tell him she was in too much pain to drive to Gary. It was all she could manage to drive home.

Chapter 22 - The Final Sting

1.

On Sunday, Suzanne exchanged stories with Sam and Eleanor in the hospital in Gary. Ruth and Tom arrived in mid-afternoon and brushed aside the praise. Suzanne wanted to publicize their heroics but Tom persuaded her otherwise. She offered money. Tom refused. After tea at four, Suzanne announced her departure. Ruth drew Tom aside.

"She looks terrible. Let's go, too, Tom and drive behind her in case something happens."

"I've a better idea. You drive her car and I'll follow along."

Suzanne scoffed at such an arrangement but when Ruth slid into the driver's side, Suzanne handed her the keys without a word. At home, Ruth and Tom accompanied her on the elevator. She went to bed immediately.

On Monday morning, Clarence hurried from the train station to Suzanne's apartment. He listened to the horror tale. Her face was pale and her movements lethargic. She kept twisting her left shoulder and rubbing her upper arm.

"Do you have much pain?"

"I'm very tired, Clary dear. I have never been through such a debilitating experience. Then that drive yesterday. Thank God, Ruth drove home. I don't think I could have made it."

His face was grave.

"What about your shoulder?"

"I must have hurt it when he knocked me down."

"Come on, get your coat. I'm taking you to the hospital."

"Please Clary, don't push me. I'm all right."

"I wish I believed that."

She forced a smile.

"Don't be silly. I just need a few days rest."

"Here's your newspaper, " he said as he kissed her cheek. "See you tonight."

With the paper spread on the dining room table, she scanned the pages. Nothing of interest on pages two and three . . . four and five . . . six and seven . . . her eyes fell on page eight. She stared in horror. Gasping for air, she lurched to the door emitting muted screams.

"Clarence! Clarence! Clarence!"

Lacking the strength to open the door, she leaned against it sobbing.

Clarence stepped off the elevator on the ground floor, whistling as he strode through the entrance foyer to his car.

2.

Immediately after lunch, Mr. Antonio Serrento opened the front door of his establishment. A large man in trench coat, bareheaded with horn-rimmed glasses and heavy black mustache showed his identification.

"Frank Beckman, Chicago Homicide."

"Come in, please. This way, sir."

Beckman followed down the hall and stopped at the side entrance to the chapel. The funeral director pointed.

"What happened?"

"Well, sir, I had just prepared the casket and flowers for visitation this afternoon at three when she came to the door. I told her not yet. She insisted and . . .. " He spread his hands acknowledging his inability to decline such a distraught mourner. "I watched her kneeling on the prie-dieu, handkerchief to her eyes. She rose reaching out to the departed as if answering his call and leaned over—I thought to kiss him—when she straightened up and clutched her throat. She made a queer noise I didn't understand, then tumbled to the floor. I ran for water. She didn't move. I took her pulse. Even as I held her hand, she died there on the floor."

Beckman shook his head.

"Too bad. Let's find out who the hell she is." He picked up her purse. "May I use your office?"

"Certainly."

He dumped the contents, spreading the usual assortment of paraphernalia around the desktop and picked up the driving license. Two uniformed men passed the door pushing a gurney.

"Take her away, boys," he said, "we'll have to do an autopsy."

He sat in the visitor's chair staring at the license.

"Damn," he said, "sometimes it's hard to figure. Why the hell do you suppose a high-class dame like Suzanne Haldimann, with more money than the goddamn Bank of America, cared about a half-assed crook named Sergio Cellini?"

THE END